VIRGINIA MCCLAIN

SAIRŌ'S CLAW

A GENSOKAI NOVEL

Works by Virginia McClain

Chronicles of Gensokai

Blade's Edge
Traitor's Hope

Gensokai Kaigai

Sairō's Claw
Eredi's Gambit

Victoria Marmot

Victoria Marmot and the Meddling Goddess
Victoria Marmot and the Inconvenient Prophecy
Victoria Marmot and the Shadow of Death
Victoria Marmot and the Dragon's Rage
Victoria Marmot and the Road to Hell

Short Story Collections

Rain on a Summer's Afternoon

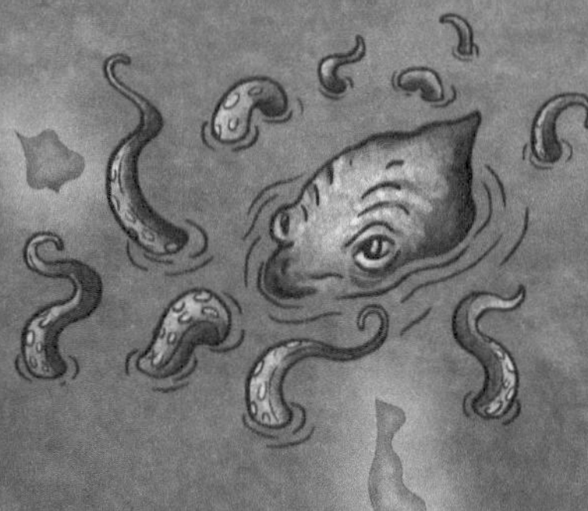

ZŌKAME ESTATE
SŌRYŪ VA
ATSUMI
SCHOOL
OF MEDICINE

KAI
SAKATA
NEW COUNCIL
CITY
AMI'S SCHOOL
FOR KISOSHI

To all the warrior moms,
may you embrace love as well as fury,
ferocity as well as calm,
and joy in all the little things.

Glossary of Terms

**Note - You don't have to read this glossary in order to understand the book, I just like to put it at the front so folks know it's here if they want it. Feel free to skip ahead, and only flip back here as needed.*

Gensokai is a fictional land. No part of these books is actually set in Japan. Nor is the world Gensokai inhabits meant to be earth at all. Nonetheless, much of the vocabulary for the books set in Gensokai borrow from Japanese to help give it the feel of the feudal Japanese culture that Gensokai was inspired by.

Some of the following terms are actual Japanese words, however, most of them are fabricated words made strictly for the purpose of this fictional work. Some are based in Japanese roots, while others are simply English terms made to apply to things in the book.

Please note that Japanese plurals are not denoted with an s, so you will see things such as: "three kimono" or "a hundred sanzoku" throughout the book.

cycle - *See seasoncycle
chawan - Bowl or cup used to serve tea (an actual Japanese term)
eihei - The elite guard of the Rōjū (an actual Japanese term meaning elite guard)
fuchi - The well of one's ki (taken from the actual Japanese word for abyss)
Gensokai - The name of the island realm in which our adventure takes place (taken from the Japanese words for element and world)
ha - The actual Japanese word for the sharp edge of a blade
hakama - The pants worn by Kisōshi (actual Japanese term for divided skirts that men wear on formal occasions or for certain martial arts)

hanko - A small slender length of stone or wood with an individual's personal seal/signature engraved on one end; often topped with a decorative figurine on the other end (actual Japanese word)

hebi-dan - This is a made up term containing the actual Japanese word for snake (hebi) and the actual Japanese word for level or rank (dan). In the context of the book, Hebi-dan is the lowest rank for a Kisōshi (it is the first rank they achieve through testing) whereas the highest is Ryū-dan.

hishi - The elite assassins used by the Rōjū (taken from the Japanese word for secret history)

izakaya - A tavern-like place where people go for drinks and food, most often consisting of private rooms for friends to meet and talk (taken from the actual Japanese word)

jima - (Also shima) suffix meaning island (actual Japanese word/suffix)

Josankō - The school where all josanpu are trained (taken from the Japanese words for midwifery and school)

josanpu - A woman trained in the arts of birthing and care for women's health (the actual Japanese word for midwife)

Kaa-san - Mom - affectionate shortening of Okaa-san which means Mother

Kaigun - navy (taken from the actual Japanese for navy)

Kami/kami - This word is taken from the actual Japanese for spirit or deity. For the purposes of this book the capitalized Kami means deity and the lowercase kami means spirit.

katana - The long curved blade used by all Kisōshi (the actual Japanese word for a single edged sword)

ki - A person's spirit or energy (actual Japanese word for spirit/essence)

kimono - Traditional clothing worn by men and women throughout Gensokai (the Japanese word for clothing —especially traditional Japanese clothing)

kisaki - The point of a blade (actual Japanese word for the point of a blade)

kisō - Energy manipulation (taken from the Japanese words for energy and manipulation —note that the actual Japanese definition differs from this made up usage)

kisōseki - A rare person who, due to an overlap in elemental powers, is able to track using kisō (word fabricated from a combination of energy manipulation and tracking)

Kisōshi - Elite warriors trained in fighting who possess an innate ability to manipulate one element (word taken from Japanese for "energy manipulation person")

mooncycle (moon) - Three tendays in Gensokai. Most common usage is "moon"

mune - The blunt back edge of a blade (actual Japanese word)

obi - The wide decorative belt worn with kimono (actual Japanese word)

oden - a popular Japanese street food, consisting of various boiled vegetables and fish products

Okaa-san - Mother, taken from the actual Japanese

oni - Demons or bad spirits

raiko - A rare kisōshi who can call on both water and wind (taken from Japanese roots for storm and caller)

rikuka - land people/lander, a slang term used by members of the Kaigun to refer to people from the mainland (taken from the actual Japanese for land, riku)

Rōjū - The ruling council of elder Kisōshi in charge of making all decisions for Gensokai (using the actual Japanese word for the Shogun's council of Elders) deposed in Rōjū 1119

ryokan - A traditional inn (actual Japanese word)

ryū-dan - See "hebi-dan"

sanzoku - A mountain bandit (actual Japanese word for mountain bandit)

saya - A scabbard (actual Japanese word)

seiza - A folded seating position (actual Japanese word)

senkisō - A Kisōshi with elemental ties to fire or air and thus to battle (taken from the Japanese words for energy manipulation and war/battle)

seasoncycle (cycle) - The term for a year in Gensokai, most commonly referred to as a "cycle"

Shiken - the Japanese word for trial or test, in the context of this book, it is the name given to Torako's walking staff katana

shoji - sliding screen door or window (actual Japanese word)

shinogi - The widest part of a katana, the part between the mune and the hasami (actual Japanese word)

shuriken - A small sharpened disk used as a weapon by the hishi, often coated in poison (actual Japanese word for "throwing star")

tatami - A mat made of dried woven grass and straw typically used as flooring, also a standard measure of length: approximately one meter by two meters in size (actual Japanese word)

tenday - A period of ten days (taking the place of weeks in this world)

tsuka - The hilt of a katana

uwagi - The jacket worn by all Kisōshi (taken from the Japanese word for a traditional jacket)

wa - Harmony (taken from the actual Japanese)

wakizashi - The short sword worn by kisōshi to accompany a katana.

yukisō - A Kisōshi with elemental ties to earth or water and thus to healing (taken from the Japanese words for energy manipulation and healing/medicine)

Yūwaku - The all female ruling power in Gensokai before the Rōjū took power

zantō - An ally of the Rōjū after they were deposed (taken from the actual Japanese)

10日 5月, 新議 8年

10th Day, 5th Moon, Cycle 8 of the New Council

⇒ Raku ⇐

"THIS REPORT IS most enlightening, Raku-san."

Raku bowed, her head touching the tatami that still smelled of whatever citrus mix had been used to clean it recently. She expected nothing less from the New Council receiving room, but it still made her nose wrinkle slightly.

"You must inform me the moment you learn anything more along these lines," Tsuku insisted. Raku frowned, even as she brought her head up.

"You wish to hear from me in less than a moon?" she asked. Of course, she enjoyed feeling like her work was appreciated, but delivering paperwork to New Council City more than once every three tendays seemed excessive, even to her.

"If you learn anything else about these agreements, then yes."

Raku said nothing for a moment and the grey-haired woman on the dais in front of her, composed and graceful as always, smiled and added, "If it is more convenient, you may send your next missive by hawk."

Now Raku raised an eyebrow. Of course it would be more convenient. It would also, under normal circumstances, be considered a waste of the hawk's time, regardless of the days of travel it would save her.

"I was not expecting these reports to incite so much curiosity, Tsuku-sama," she said, choosing her words carefully.

Tsuku smiled again, never glancing at the guards who stood beside the doors in the otherwise empty chamber, but somehow Raku understood that the missing gesture was intentional. She had been working with Tsuku for a long time, after all.

"The people have gone a very long time without a proper account of their own history. I consider it of primary importance that we share as much of the truth as we can confirm without delay."

Raku said nothing. She knew that Tsuku was indeed interested in the history that the Rōjū had hidden for so long—she wouldn't have a job still, otherwise. After all, the work she had done to help depose the Rōjū was no longer needed, and if the New Council had been more interested in burying the truth than uncovering it, she would not have found herself so gainfully employed in the secret archives that had been uncovered seven cycles ago.

But Tsuku's urgency suggested something else was afoot, and her reluctance to speak of it openly meant there was someone who disapproved, someone high enough up for Tsuku to be concerned about spies in the receiving room.

Raku bowed again.

"I'll be sure to send word as soon as I find anything else on the subject."

And then she stood and turned to leave the room.

She walked out of the enormous complex that housed the New Council and all of their offices, through the expansive gardens that surrounded the compound, over the bridges that connected the gardens to the main roads in the city, and resisted the urge to check her pockets or her satchel before reaching her horse. In fact, it was only when she was all the way home in her woodland cave, the one that Taka and Kusuko had gifted to her and Torako five cycles prior, that she finally reassured herself that all nine of the scrolls she had taken from the archives the morning of her interview were present.

She was almost unsurprised to find that the one she'd been reporting to Tsuku-san about, the only one that had been in her satchel overnight in New Council City, was missing.

1日 6月, 新議 8年

1st Day, 6th Moon, Cycle 8 of the New Council

⇒ Kaiyo ⇐

KAIYO LOOKED INTO the rolling mists and ran the small, owl-topped seal through her fingers, tipping it absently over one knuckle at a time. The combination of sea air and cloud cover left a tangy moisture on her tongue that she might normally have savored, but today she ignored it. Instead, she focused the entirety of her attention on listening—beyond the creaking of the deck beneath her feet, beyond the bare whisper of her crew relaying hand signals up and down the afterdeck—straining to hear the enemy before they heard her. Hoping that in doing so, she might live long enough to regret having volunteered herself and her crew for close patrol that morning.

The near-silence across the water stretched on, the fog muffling the soft sound of sails bending to the wind, gentling the already quiet slap of waves reprimanding the hull of the Wind Serpent. And well they might, for their scouts hadn't reported enemies within sight of the close patrol circuit in cycles. The most exciting part of this patrol should have been redirecting wayward fishermen from the mainland. *Of course* it would be on her watch that they'd sight another sail through the fog. Far too large to be a fishing vessel, and not the faded blue of a Kaigun ship either, as she'd known the moment her lookout had called the word sail—all of her ships were accounted for.

The stillness drew out like the tide and her whole crew held ready, the only motion the silent tip of her stone owl between her fingers, a motion she could not suppress, the only thing keeping her from screaming.

Kaiyo's hand stilled as she caught the faint sound of... something... muffled by the wind, the fog, and the waves lapping against the hull. She strained to hear, wondering if it had only been her imagination, and then the silence was shattered utterly by the unmistakable, terror-inducing crack of cannon fire.

"DOWN!" she cried, silently cursing whatever ill luck had put her ship in the path of an enemy armed with cannons.

A great splash of seawater coated everyone on the Wind Serpent's deck, but the shot was low, falling far short of the ship's hull. Kaiyo and her crew were in motion the moment they realized they were not dead.

"STORMCALLERS!" she cried, pulling herself to her feet and tucking the small, owl-topped hanko into her pocket even as she reached for the dagger on her belt. She hoped they were a long way off from daggers and close combat, but her crew approved of a bit of dramatic flair, and she would do whatever she could to focus them on the thrill of battle rather than the terror of cannon fire.

"Ready!" she called out, thrusting her dagger into the air for emphasis. She listened closely for the sound of the hatches sliding open on their spring-loaded tracks, transforming her ship from a seemingly toothless sloop to its true thirty-gunned glory.

"Aim!" she called next, wishing she could see the look of surprise on the approaching captain's face as the guns were run out of their hatches faster than should have been possible.

"Fire!" she screamed, releasing the brunt of a full broadside on the massive ship that loomed above the Wind Serpent in the swiftly shifting fog.

The guns cracked out as her crew timed their shots to the roll of the surf, and Kaiyo cursed whichever gaijin had invented the blasted things. They were as loud as they were devastating, and she wished they had never come into existence. But when the ships their patrols encountered had started carrying them, the Kaigun had had no choice but to adopt them too. Raiko could devastate any ship, cannon or no, but if one hoped to convince the enemy to surrender rather than merely die, one had to outgun them.

Which was precisely what Kaiyo planned to do.

"Run us home, raikotachi!" she called, brandishing her dagger in the air and pointing it towards Kaigunjima. "Let's see how well these gaijin like the answers they're looking for."

≈Raku≈

RAKU PUSHED HER hair from her face and then frowned as the scent of ink grew sharper and her skin tightened ever so slightly in a line just above her nose.

"Kami curse it," she muttered, reaching for the damp rag she kept on her lap desk. She wiped at her face and had to hope that she got it all. She didn't have time to go searching through their trunk to find the sole looking glass that Itachi hadn't managed to find and shatter in her toddler days.

She wiped her fingers thoroughly, in hopes of preventing any more smudges on her face, and then she took up her brush again and refocused on the characters in the ancient text that she'd been puzzling over for half the morning. She hadn't added any new strokes to the crisp parchment pinned under her right wrist recently, but she was poised to do so anyway as she glared at the faded, crumbling parchment to her left and willed it to make some kind of sense to her.

"Out… outer… outside?"

The characters in the scroll, which she was doing her best not to touch, for fear she would destroy it, were archaic at best. It had been almost a thousand cycles since they'd been handled by a human, let alone since the time they were written, and Gensokan had changed quite a bit in that time. But the word she was stuck on wasn't just an archaic version of a word she knew, as most of these characters wound up being, it was something else altogether.

"Outside sea? What does that even mean? On land? But that doesn't make sense with the rest of this sentence, 'We agree to open trade with the following outside sea lands,' no… 'on land lands' no, that's stupid, why would they use land twice? Ugh… Kami take this forsaken scroll! Why did ancient people talk in circles?"

"Raku-san? Are you there?"

Raku's head shot up at the sound of a familiar voice on the far side of the leather blanket that served as a door.

"Coming!" she called, as she carefully returned the lid to her inkpot and wiped her hands on the rag once more. She didn't think anyone would be surprised to see her covered in ink, but she liked to at least attempt to look presentable. She'd used to be able to work with ink all day and still keep her clothes unblemished and her face clear of even the slightest smudge, but somehow that had changed since having a child, and she wasn't even certain how. Itachi wasn't even here. How her mere existence led to Raku being an ink-covered mess was something she'd never understand. Perhaps it had to do with the tiny ball of energy always occupying some portion of her mind. Perhaps it was the same part of her mind that usually kept track of whether or not her fingertips were stained.

Ignoring that largely useless train of thought, she stood and headed to the door, such as it was, and pulled the flap aside to allow the bright summer sun into her small cave. Why had she not opened the flap as soon as the sun was up in full? She frowned, wondering when she'd become as distractible as Torako, but then her eyes focused on the faces of the two people standing outside her door and the edges of the frown reversed direction.

Of course, "people" was perhaps not the most accurate term for the pair that stood before her. Certainly, the elder woman with the white streak in her lightly greying hair fit most people's definition, but the large tree standing just behind her, whose trunk split in two about halfway to the ground, and whose upper bark housed a crinkled face comprised of lichen, amber, and moss, was not what most humans would include in the term. Raku, of course, was not most humans, and she could not think of Yanagi-sama as anything other than people.

"Yanagi-sama! Tenshi-san! How lovely to see you both! Would you like to come in?" She hoped she hadn't been staring at them too long before she spoke, but her brain was still stuck on the strange characters she'd been trying to modernize in her transcription only moments before.

"We can't stay long," Tenshi-san said, her bright green eyes reminding Raku warmly of two of her favorite people, "but we wanted to let someone know where we were going."

Raku nodded and gestured into the cave.

"Of course," she replied. "I'm sorry that Torako-san and Itachi-chan aren't here right now. They're out on a patrol and won't be home for a few more days. They'll be sad to have missed you. Especially if you're going to be away."

Tenshi smiled, and the gesture made Raku unaccountably sad. Yanagi tutted from outside the doorway.

"You may bid me farewell once you are done with Tenshi-san," he rumbled, in a breath of wind through leaves and branches.

Raku belatedly realized it might be rude to meet with Tenshi inside her cave when Yanagi would not be able to fit unless he changed his shape.

"I'm sorry, Yanagi-sama. If you—"

But the tree Kami had already wandered away from the door and seemed to be ignoring her.

"He had planned to give us some time alone anyway, Raku-san. Don't worry," Tenshi said, patting her arm.

"Is everything alright?" Raku asked, unable to ignore the feeling that something was off, despite how distracted she'd been a moment ago.

"I hope so," Tenshi replied.

"That's not entirely reassuring."

"I'm afraid I didn't come here to reassure you," Tenshi replied.

"Ah. Well, is this warning for me, or for Tora-chan?" Raku asked, feeling her stomach drop even as she did her best to sound flippant.

"Either. Both." Tenshi heaved a sigh that did nothing to reassure Raku. "I wish Tora-chan could hear this from me instead of anyone else, but… if anyone knows the importance of conveying information fully, it's you, Raku-san. So… if you would listen with the ears of a storyteller and repeat it with the accuracy of a scribe, I would be in your debt."

Raku did not like how formal Tenshi was being, not even a little bit. The woman had been cuddling Itachi and sneaking her mochi the last time she'd visited, chuckling every time Raku pretended to be stern about the girl having too many sweets. Tenshi hadn't spoken this formally to her since the wedding. Formality had all but disappeared the moment Itachi had been born.

"You have my word, Tenshi-san," Raku said, reaching out to hold the older woman's hand, unable to resist the need to offer comfort to the woman who had done the same for her countless times in the past four cycles.

Tenshi's smile seemed genuine but did not quite reach her eyes, as she allowed Raku to take her hands and drew a deep breath.

"I can't tell you much about what Yanagi-sama and I must do, because I'm not even that clear on what he needs me to accomplish, but… we're going to help my father."

Raku felt her eyebrows raise towards her hairline.

"Your father? You've never spoken of him before."

Raku didn't add that Tenshi had never spoken of either of her parents before, besides a few offhand comments about things she had done with her own mother as she was teaching Itachi how to fish, or how to hold a carving knife, or how to hide candies in her sleeves so her parents wouldn't notice… instead, Raku waited to see what else Tenshi would add.

"I never do. In fact, until recently, I wasn't entirely certain who he was. But over the past few cycles he has made himself known to me, and… well, he's the reason Yanagi-sama and I will be traveling to… well, he's the reason we'll be away."

Raku held her tongue for a moment, hoping that Tenshi wasn't planning to leave things that vague. What in the Kamis' names did she expect her to relay to Torako after this?

When Tenshi didn't continue, Raku blew out a breath and said, "Tenshi-san, you asked me to speak with the words of a scribe, but… you haven't given me much to pass on to your daughter. Do you wish me to tell her who her grandfather is? Or, at the very least, tell her where you've actually gone?"

Tenshi sighed.

"I hope to be back to tell her the details myself in a few tendays, a moon at most. In the meantime… well, I suppose I wanted to be sure that you knew I was gone in case you need someone to look after Itachi-chan. Yanagi-sama and I will both be out of reach, and I know he's the person you look to for Itachi-chan's lessons and… I thought it was best to tell you in person that neither of us would be here."

Raku took a deep breath and turned to look out of her door at the tree spirit who seemed to be holding court with a crowd of forest animals. Perhaps he was delivering a similarly vague note of farewell.

"This concerns him, too?" she asked, hoping to drag a few more details from Tenshi.

"It does," Tenshi sighed. "If you need to speak to us… well, it won't be easy, Itach—no, that won't do… Tatsu-sama will be able to get a message to me, or to Yanagi-sama, if there's an emergency."

That had Raku frowning. It was a full two tendays' travel to Tatsu-sama's mountain, and one could go almost anywhere in Gensokai in that amount of time. How on earth could it be faster to talk to Tatsu-sama than to simply find Tenshi and Yanagi wherever they were headed?

"Tenshi-san, are you…" Raku shook her head then, because the notion she was about to suggest was impossible. "What aren't you telling me?" she asked instead.

"My father is… not the normal kind of father…" the older woman stumbled to a halt.

"Tenshi-san, forgive me, but you sounded like you wished to issue some kind of warning when you first arrived, and now… well, I'll struggle to tell Torako-san anything at all after this."

Tenshi sighed again, and Raku could feel her jaw tense as she wondered if the woman had any intention of answering her with more than the barest vagaries.

"My father is a Kami," Tenshi huffed at last.

"So he's no longer with us," Raku spoke softly. "I'm sorry for your loss Ten—"

"No, he never was with us. He's not deceased. He was born in the spirit realm."

"Born in the… what are you saying, Tenshi-san?"

"My father is the moon Kami, Tsukuyomi."

Raku simply let her mouth fall open. She wasn't certain what else to do. There were many problems with that statement, and she hadn't the slightest idea where to begin. Unfortunately, the base statement was the least problematic. It explained all too much.

"Are you saying the reason that your granddaughter is abnormally powerful is that she is actually one-eighth moon Kami?" Raku hissed.

Tenshi looked a bit sheepish, even as she nodded.

"And in the past four cycles, it never occurred to you to tell her parents this bit of information?"

"I didn't want you to worry," Tenshi began, but Raku cut her off before she could get any further.

"Does Tora-chan have any idea?"

"I may have hinted at it when I told her about her own… condition, but no, I've never told her the entire truth."

"Lovely," Raku huffed, unable to contain her frustration. "No wonder she didn't speak with you until Itachi-chan was born."

The look of pain that crossed Tenshi's face when Raku said that made her wish the words unsaid.

"I'm sorry, Tenshi-san, that was cruel of me."

Tenshi waved a hand at her, as if to brush the apology away.

"You're not wrong. Torako-san had good reason not to speak with me until Itachi-chan was born. I won't pretend that I don't understand her anger, even if it hurts. I am grateful she was willing to reconcile for the sake of my grandchild."

Raku knew the issue of Torako's 'power' was complicated, and that Torako was so loath to speak of it that in their eight cycles together her wife had barely mentioned it more than once. Raku had been surprised and delighted when Torako had chosen to include her mother in their lives after Itachi was born. Tenshi had been one of the best parts of Itachi's childhood, and Raku couldn't imagine her daughter's life without the older healer. She'd been a calm, thoughtful presence in the girl's life, even when Raku and Torako had been at a total loss what to do with her—their daughter whose powers so greatly outstripped their own.

"It didn't occur to you that it might be useful for us to know why she was so powerful?" she asked, when she could finally speak without anger choking her voice.

"It did, of course it did, but… oh, Raku-san, can you imagine, even for a moment, how terrified I've been to lose Torako-san's goodwill again? What would you do, if you had a truth you knew Itachi-chan should know, but feared she would never speak to you again if you told her?"

Then Tenshi sighed and let out a humorless laugh.

"What a silly question. Of course you would tell her the truth anyway."

It was Raku's turn to laugh now.

"Regardless of what you think I would do, I understand your fear, Tenshi-san. I do. So… fine. You never told Torako about her grandfather. Why now, then?"

Tenshi finally looked up at Raku, her green eyes meeting Raku's head-on.

"We're about to go see him. To help him, and… it could be dangerous."

"You're…" and now Raku had to believe the impossible idea she'd had earlier, because it was the only thing that fit. "You're going into the spirit realm?"

Tenshi looked away, even as she admitted the truth with a dip of her chin.

"Yes. Yanagi-sama is taking me there. My father has asked me to help him, and… I'm not entirely clear on how I'm meant to do that, but it's important that I try."

"Why?" Raku asked. "Why help someone who never even showed up in your life until…" she let her voice trail off, unsure of why the moon Kami had revealed himself, and almost afraid to ask.

"I wouldn't go at all, but he said it's to protect Itachi-chan."

Raku gasped, feeling her muscles tense in response to a threat she could not see.

"Tenshi-san, it is time for us to go."

The loud, rustling voice of Yanagi-sama made Raku jump. She'd been so focused on Tenshi's news that she hadn't even noticed the walking tree's approach. His amber eyes blinked slowly at them, as if adjusting to the light of the cave.

"Yes, Yanagi-sama," Tenshi said, giving Raku's hand another squeeze. Raku had forgotten that the woman was still touching her until that moment.

"You'll tell Torako-san everything?" she asked, as she stepped towards the door of the cave, dropping Raku's hand as she went.

Raku followed mutely after, unsure how to respond.

"You'll let her know that I love her, and the reason I didn't tell her was only because I feared…" she didn't finish, but Raku knew well enough what she meant.

"I'll tell her," she promised. "But, Tenshi-san, Yanagi-sama, please, can't I help in some way? Can't I come with you? Or Tora-san? A warrior. Ryūko-san is a friend of yours, isn't she? If there's danger, shouldn't you—"

"Ryūko-san has done enough for Gensokai, and besides, she can't go into the spirit world. Neither can you. Torako-san might be able to with her heritage, but she might not after… everything, and we don't have time to find out what it would do to her, or to the realms. The best thing you can do to help is to stay here and tell Tora-chan what I've told you. This isn't her battle, or yours, not yet."

Raku had no response to that, so she swallowed the emotions that were hot in her throat and looked at Yanagi-sama instead.

"Itachi-chan will miss your lessons," she said, glossing over how she would miss the tree spirit's easy presence, and how Torako would miss his gentle teasing. She couldn't say the words. They would catch in her throat next to all the things she wanted to tell Tenshi.

"We'll be back before the season's change, youngling, don't you worry," Yanagi-sama boomed cheerily. "Tsukuyomi-san is prone to exaggeration. The threat is likely not as great as he supposes. Please tell Itachi-chan to work on her dreaming while I'm gone, and to keep an eye on the weasels."

Raku could do nothing but chuckle at those instructions, and then she wrapped her arms around Tenshi's retreating form.

"Itachi-chan will miss you, Tenshi-san, so will Tora-chan, and so will I. Come back soon, ne?"

This time Raku could feel Tenshi's smile against her cheek, all the way to her bones.

"See you soon, Raku-chan."

The odd pair, giant walking tree and smallish human woman, hadn't gone more than a few paces when Yanagi rumbled.

"Oh, I almost forgot. Raku-san, 'outside sea,' it's 'foreign.' The word you seek, is 'foreign.'" And then he turned again, waved, and before Raku could even remember what outside sea he'd been referring to, they had faded from sight.

⟨Kaiyo⟩

IT WOULDN'T BE long before the hundred-gunner had their answers, whether they liked them or not.

The Wind Serpent flew through the waves like the legend it was named for, its sails so full it felt as though it was barely touching the swelling ocean beneath it. Kaiyo had learned long ago that standing at the bow and laughing as the wind whipped her hair and the sea soaked her uniform would garner nothing but odd looks from her crew. Besides, she was a captain now, and such displays were considered unprofessional. But that didn't mean she couldn't stand on the stern deck, with the wind in her hair, the tang of the sea on her tongue, and a lightness in her chest.

Then she turned to look over her shoulder and the lightness in her chest vanished.

The hundred-gunner was practically on top of them. If she'd been fluent in whatever foreign script had been used to name the vessel, she would have been able to read it from here.

Kaiyo turned and shouted to all her kisōshi, calling for more speed, giving the signal for the raiko to manipulate the air around them and move the water along the hull, a tactic she rarely used this close to an enemy, but one which could not be avoided if she were to have any hope of outpacing them.

She was relieved to see the distance between the Wind Serpent and the other vessel growing, as her kisōshi bent themselves to their task, but the distance did not grow as steadily as she would like, as though the hundred-gunner had its own secret reserves that it called on now to propel it even faster.

It was unnaturally swift for a ship of its size.

Kaiyo frowned, calling again for more speed.

In less than a candle-burn, both ships had reached the much thicker fog that Kaiyo had been racing them towards, and she called for a final burst of speed that would tuck them neatly out of sight.

Her entire crew gasped as the hundred-gunner shot forward with its own surge of speed, just as the Wind Serpent was consumed by fog.

Kaiyo smiled anyway. The hundred-gunner might be closer than she had expected, or even thought possible, but her crew had kept them ahead of its guns, and now the massive vessel was well and truly caught.

She almost laughed.

Instead, she cried out for a sharp tack to starboard and she and her crew cut between a narrowing gap of giant sea pillars that were nearly invisible in the thick fog, but which Kaiyo would likely be able to find with a blindfold over her eyes. It was a maneuver that was only possible because of the high number of kisōshi on her crew. Even the most powerful of raiko wouldn't have been able to complete the movement alone.

Just as her bow threaded the needle of disastrous rock pillars, her signal-callers cried out like angry pelicans, their calls amplified by wind kisō, and the returning calls from the pillars brought a small, bitter smile to the corners of her mouth.

The hundred-gunner sailed on, either because they hadn't seen the Wind Serpent tack, or because they'd realized that following would be suicide. It was only a few heartbeats before the thunderous sounds of long guns and great guns rattled through the fog, splitting it with enough light and sound to wake the spirits and rattle the dead.

Kaiyo wanted to cover her ears but did not.

The fog cleared, even as the terrifying crunch of metal shredding wood assailed her ears, along with the screams of the dying. Kaiyo shivered, and it had nothing to do with the wind that now pushed the thick rolls of fog into little more than a low-lying mist.

When the Kaigunjima raiko had cleared the fog away completely, the foreign ship was already suffering another round of cannon fire. Kaiyo didn't take time to appreciate the crystalline waters or dramatic rocky pillars that lined her home harbor, she was too keen to watch the hundred-gunner and see how they chose their fate.

The much larger ship had already managed to angle themselves slightly away from the line of fire, but Kaiyo knew it would not be enough. The clearing fog had not only revealed the hundred-gunner itself, it had also revealed the entire purpose of Kaiyo's carefully managed retreat. Beneath a sparkling sun, across the tantalizingly clear waters of Kaigunjima harbor, sat row after row of ships, cliffs, sea pillars, and small atolls, all covered in cannon of every size, and all brought to bear on the foreign ship that had dared to breach their waters.

⇒ *Raku* ⇐

RAKU STARED AT the papers before her, the nearly crumbling scroll, the fine new washi, her brushes, and Yanagi-sama's parting words, which she had hastily scrawled on a scrap of washi before she could forget it. She'd made tea after Tenshi and Yanagi had departed, and the scent of the boiled green leaves still permeated the small cave, along with the warmth and smoke of the small cooking fire she'd used to boil the water. She'd made the beverage in a half-hearted attempt to distract herself from the emotions piling up inside her. Something about Tenshi's parting had felt wrong. The fact that Torako and Itachi hadn't been there to say goodbye chafed at her in a way that made her skin itch.

The whole thing was strange. Stranger than it should have been, even with Tenshi admitting that she was half moon Kami and was off to help with something in the spirit world. Why had Tenshi and Yanagi come to her? Torako and Itachi weren't home, true, but they were still in Yanagi's valley, and that walking tree spirit had always been able to track down any living thing that moved in his valley. If Tenshi had truly wanted to warn Torako, shouldn't she have found her, instead? Perhaps there hadn't been time. Perhaps, as quickly as Yanagi could find Torako and Itachi on their wide loop around the valley's perimeter, it would not be quick enough for whatever it was they hoped to accomplish in the spirit world.

Raku sighed, then sipped her tea, unable to shake the feeling of subtle wrongness that had accompanied her ever since Tenshi had appeared at her door. She looked at the scroll in front of her instead, hoping that her brain might at least latch onto the problem of making a thousand-cycle-old text legible to a modern Gensokan.

"Outside sea means foreign," she mumbled to herself. "Does that make this any more intelligible?"

She stared at the passage once more. "'We agree to open trade with the following foreign lands. Eh? Foreign lands. Foreign...'" she skimmed ahead in the document and looked over the list of what had seemed an odd jumble of sounds to her before, written only in Gensokan's syllabary without any characters to attach meaning to them. "Not just lands. Nations. As Gensokai is a nation. Outside sea... across the ocean. Other nations."

Raku's forehead dipped all the way down to the table as her eyes closed. Little wonder Tsuku-san had wanted to know more about the scrolls that had accompanied her. The one she'd made her last report on, that one had made statements about distant friends, and a glowing future for Gensokai, but it hadn't elaborated, save to reference the agreements laid out in a series of documents—most of which no longer existed. This one, however, was one of those listed in the text, and Raku now thanked her earlier self for having decided to recover the listed scrolls—those that remained, at any rate—from the "Hidden Library" before she'd even made her report to Tsuku-san.

"But why would anyone wish to keep this information secret?"

Then she shook her head. That was the wrong question entirely. She could think of a hundred reasons anyone might wish to keep knowledge like this to themselves. No, the question wasn't why—knowledge was power, after all—the question was who.

Raku ran through the likely candidates in her mind, even as she wrestled with whether or not to make her next report in person. She shouldn't leave without warning when Torako had been taking care of Itachi by herself for a tenday already. She'd gotten as far as packing her bag, though, when she realized that she absolutely could not leave without telling Torako about her mother's visit.

She sighed then and searched through her writing satchel for the tiny papers that fit in the tubes the hawks transported for those who couldn't communicate with them directly.

"This will have to do for now," she mumbled, as she carefully scrawled a brief, coded message to Tsuku, and then stepped outside to call a hawk.

Kaiyo

KAIYO WATCHED THE scene unfold before her with one hand gripping the railing tight enough to hurt, and her other hand absently tipping the small owl hanko between her fingers. She hadn't even noticed her hand removing it from her belt pouch.

The foreign captain's choices were limited. Even if the hundred-gunner could get off a full broadside without taking a single hit (and it had already taken more than one hit, so that was an impossibility) it would never be able to overwhelm the firepower now directed at it. There were too many cannon, aimed from too many directions and elevations, for any single ship to overcome them. That had, after all, been the carefully planned intent behind the harbor's selection and design. After the initial volley and the clearing of the fog, the guns around the harbor had paused, briefly, to let the enemy take proper stock of exactly what their choices were.

The hundred-gunner could flee (though again, fully half the guns leveled at it were attached to ships only slightly smaller than itself, which would happily give chase), or it could fight—and lose.

"Come on," Kaiyo muttered, her fingers tipping her owl end over end in a blur, praying for yet a third option. "Surrender."

But someone on that foreign ship was either incredibly dumb or incredibly stubborn, and before Kaiyo had even taken a full breath after her whispered wish, the first guns of its broadside began to ring out against the quiet that had settled as the fog had lifted.

"Damn them," Kaiyo muttered, as the cannon all around her rang out long before the three-master had fired more than a handful of its guns. Of course, it was the ship's captain who had damned them, not Kaiyo, but she didn't have the heart to watch her people destroy the larger vessel.

"That's a hundred guns wasted," Tanaka sighed, from behind her shoulder.

Kaiyo also sighed, forcing herself to watch the destruction, much though it hurt her. She had led them here. If she couldn't stomach watching the results of her own ploy, then she didn't deserve her command.

"Why would they…" but her voice faded away as she noticed movement in the cloud of gunpowder and destruction that now covered the water.

"Raiko!" she called, before Tanaka could even ask what she had seen. "Clear that smoke. Pull us around the pillars!" The latter was addressed to the rest of her crew.

Tanaka looked at her and raised a single eyebrow.

"Dare I ask?"

"Keep an eye on that fog, Tanaka-san."

Ever dutiful, Tanaka complied, and soon enough, as they cleared the far end of the pillar that had kept them out of the line of fire, it was clear to everyone what Kaiyo had seen.

The hundred-gunner had only been bluffing when it started its broadside. They'd been using their cannon—the smoke, noise, and confusion—as cover for raising a series of jibs and foresails and then… Kaiyo couldn't see what they'd done after that, but they must have had their own kisōshi, quite a few of them at that, because the massive ship sped forward at a speed Kaiyo could scarcely believe, all while making a tack that should have been impossible.

Kaiyo gripped her owl so tightly that it would certainly leave a mark on her palm.

Then she smiled, despite the tightness in her chest, despite the danger that lay ahead.

The hundred-gunner was running.

Kaiyo had never seen a vessel that wasn't Kaigun maneuver that quickly, that agilely, and indeed, if she hadn't witnessed it with her own eyes, she would never have believed the tale.

The fleet fired futilely at the stern of the quickly vanishing ship, the gunners doing their best to rake its stern even as the fastest Kaigun vessels began bringing themselves about to give chase. They hadn't been ready for it, because it shouldn't have been possible. And for all the damage the harbor guns had done to the hundred-gunner's decks and rails, the dead who no doubt strewed the deck of the fleeing enemy, they had purposefully spared the masts and hull below the waterline. Kaigunjima had standing orders to try to preserve ships for recovery whenever possible, especially a ship with so many cannon.

None of the dozen ships that lined the harbor managed to move in time to catch the fleeing vessel.

None save the Wind Serpent.

Kaiyo had never turned to train her meager guns on the enemy—that hadn't been her job. Instead, she had come around the pillars, hiding between them while the first volleys of cannon fire had been exchanged, in order to bear witness to the destruction she had brought upon the five hundred souls whose captain had made them enter Gensokan waters, thus threatening everything that Kaiyo cherished.

Even before the smoke had fully cleared, Kaiyo had called to her kisōshi for speed, directing two of her raiko to keep an eye out for friendly fire, aware that moving so quickly might put them in the path of attempts to rake the enemy's stern.

The Wind Serpent leapt forward with the force of kisō-filled sails, and they gained on the hundred-gunner, even as the rest of the fleet was still coming to terms with what the enemy ship had just done.

The stern chasers from the foreign vessel called out as Kaiyo's ship gained on it, but two more of her raiko sent the shots back easily, aimed with precision to disable the guns that had sent them. Unlike the hundred-gunner's cannons, her stormcallers never missed. It wasn't long before the stern chasers were silenced.

"I'm impressed that a ship with a hundred guns can move so quickly," Tanaka said, beside her once more.

Kaiyo nodded at the extreme understatement.

"It seems I owe an apology to their captain; she has made an able escape. I judged her too quickly, thinking she would sacrifice her crew for her own ego, as so many do."

Tanaka nodded, but did not smile or laugh. Kaiyo and her crew were deservedly proud of their small ship's speed, but they did not relish the death and destruction they were about to bring upon the other ship's crew.

"We could try to pull alongside and speak with them," Tanaka suggested, after a long silence in which they had almost halved the initial distance between the Wind Serpent and the foreign ship.

Kaiyo considered it seriously for a long moment.

"That has never gone well in the past, Tanaka-san, and I don't plan to let them kill any of my crew just to save their necks. They had their chance to surrender. Despite their agility and speed, it would have been the sensible choice when they were so vastly outgunned. I understand why they chose to run instead, but they've seen us fly. If they don't strike colors before we reach them, then that will be the end of it."

Tanaka nodded, his mouth a grim, silent line, his eyes still trained on the other ship.

Kaiyo's chest ached. She had half-hoped he would argue with her, even though she knew her reasoning was sound. She should not risk her people, no matter how clever this captain had been. She could not hope that they would not fire on her, or try to board her, even under a flag of parlay. More than one gaijin vessel had done so in the past, and she was long past trusting any sense of honor her enemies laid claim to.

She sighed, gesturing for one of her raiko to join her and Tanaka on the stern deck, as the distance between the Wind Serpent and the hundred-gunner diminished further.

"Hiroshi-san," she said, as the tall young man approached her. "Can you swamp that vessel at this range?"

The younger man looked at the distance, then slowly shook his head.

"Suzuki-san would be the best choice for that distance, I think," he replied. "I am not confident I could do it without also endangering the Wind Serpent."

Kaiyo nodded briefly.

"Thank you for your honesty, Hiroshi-san. Please take Suzuki-san's place at the sails and send her to me," she replied.

"You are too easy on our kisōshi, Captain," Tanaka said, as Hiroshi made his way across the deck to where Suzuki was pushing the winds alongside Eda.

"You want me to push him to try a technique he is less than confident in, when it might risk not only our entire crew, but our people as well?"

"He can do it," Tanaka replied. "I've seen him do as much in training."

"Accomplishing something in ideal conditions and with little consequence of failure is not the same as being able to do something under pressure in a situation with many factors at play that may not have been so in training. You know that as well as anyone else. He may well be able to do it, and if this were an emergency, I might insist that he try. But we have time, and I will not risk any of our crew just to make sure the boy knows how far he can push himself."

Tanaka merely nodded and continued staring out to sea.

Kaiyo smiled as Suzuki-san approached across the deck. She could see the woman in her peripheral vision, but it was Tanaka she kept her eye on.

"Why are you smirking, Captain?"

Kaiyo chuckled.

"You know why," she replied.

The faintest curl took over one side of Tanaka's mouth, and she wanted to cackle.

"You want to remind me that this is why none of the other captains will have me on their ships, don't you?"

Kaiyo said nothing, but her smile grew wider.

"Perhaps you wish to tell me that I'm here only because you took pity on me, and decided to give the most contrary second in the entire Kaigun a chance?"

At that, her smile fell away.

"Never pity, Tanaka-san. I saw potential where others saw a nuisance, that's all."

"Captain? You asked for me?" Suzuki's tone was polite, but Kaiyo was fairly certain the petite woman had heard everything that Kaiyo and Tanaka had been saying. Wind kisōshi were perfectly capable of bidding the air to carry the words of others to them whenever they pleased. That was a large part of why Kaiyo found Tanaka's tendency to second-guess her on deck a boon rather than a nuisance. When a large portion of your crew could hear you speak, no matter how much privacy you attempted to keep, there was an advantage to having someone second-guess you often in the hearing of others. It gave Kaiyo a chance to voice her reasoning where her entire crew could hear it (or hear of it later) and that meant her crew generally knew the "why" of her orders, instead of merely guessing at her motives.

It kept her honest, and it kept her crew loyal without the blind fanaticism that some captains seemed to expect, but which had always seemed senseless to Kaiyo.

"Yes, Suzuki-san. Hiroshi-san says that you would be the best choice for sinking the hundred-gunner from here," she said, nodding in the general direction of the enemy vessel that they were overtaking by the moment.

Suzuki took a long look at the ship, the clouds, and their own sails, then she nodded.

"Now, Captain?"

Kaiyo took a deep breath and then nodded, her face now devoid of any of the laughter she and Tanaka had shared a moment before.

Suzuki took a wide stance, her knees bent deeply as though sitting an invisible horse, and closed her eyes. Her breath instantly slowed and deepened. Kaiyo had seen hundreds of kisōshi work since joining the Kaigun, and it never ceased to impress her how different all of their techniques were. She knew that it wasn't necessary for kisōshi to close their eyes in order to bend elements to their will, but she also knew that Suzuki-san always closed her eyes before she called on the ocean.

Kaiyo watched the petite woman's body still as she focused inwards, and Kaiyo felt her own breath hitch as she sensed a change in the air all around them. Many of the crew stopped in their work to look at the doomed ship one last time and to touch, rub, or kiss the talismans they kept on everything from bracelets, to lanyards, to pins on belts, obi, or sleeves. Kaiyo wasn't sure how many different Kami were represented between the trinkets her crew kept amongst themselves, but she was fairly certain it was more than the ocean could hold. Which was only fair, she supposed, as many of them were wind Kami as well.

Kaiyo refocused her attention on the water around them, and on the ship they were now only a dozen lengths away from.

Which may have saved her life.

For, just as she felt the sudden drop in pressure that accompanied a raiko attack, the ship they chased did something impossible. Without slowing, with some sort of magic that Kaiyo could not comprehend, the hundred gun ship turned in place—as if it were no more than a horse pivoting in a ring and not a five-hundred-ton ship—and in doing so, released a full broadside on the Wind Serpent.

"DOWN!"

Kaiyo was screaming for her crew to drop even before the first crack of cannon fire finished sounding. As soon as the ship had turned, she had started calling out, knowing what was coming, even as her eyes told her the entire thing was impossible. No ship could move like that. Not her ship crewed half by kisōshi, not any ship in the Kaigun, and not this enormous ship before her. But even as one part of her brain objected to the reality she now faced, the rest of her brain took to shouting the orders that would save her people's lives.

Then the world became little more than the scent of gunpowder and the feel of splintered wood and sea water coating her back. She saw no more than darkness because she had thrown herself to the deck, bearing Tanaka with her, pinning him beneath her—some small part of her calculating that his life was more valuable than hers in the aftermath of an enemy broadside—ignoring his protests as she covered both her head and his with her arms.

As soon as the crash of shredding wood and exploding artillery had ceased, she leapt from atop her second and shouted at him to tend to the injured.

She needn't have bothered. He was on his feet and rushing to the nearest patch of blood before she'd even gotten her eyes to focus on the hundred-gunner once more.

Kaiyo desperately wanted to assess the damage to her own people. To see the faces of those who would never be setting foot on shore again, and to lend her strength to those who would spend the next few minutes fighting for their lives, but she didn't dare. This enemy was far more dangerous than she had suspected, and her lapse in judgment had already led to the deaths of some of her crew. She ignored the sick feeling that thought brought to her stomach and focused on saving those who remained.

The hundred-gunner had released its full broadside against her, but not in the traditional slow roll of guns from bow to stern. No, it had released a full barrage at once, a desperate move, and one that left them now unarmed as they scrambled to reload.

Kaiyo wasted no time.

"Suzuki-san!" she shouted, barely able to hear her own voice over the deadening sensation that a cannon attack typically brought.

No reply came, and she turned to see that the patch of blood she had noticed earlier was Suzuki-san, or rather, what was left of her. Tanaka was still bent over her, so she must still be alive, but Kaiyo flinched at what had become of the woman's legs. There wasn't much left.

She forced herself to focus. There would be time to mourn later.

"Hiroshi-san!" she screamed, instead.

In seconds the young man was by her side. His face was a mess of dust, blood, tears, and sweat, all of which she ignored. He was upright, and not so pale as to suggest he was bleeding to death.

"Hiroshi-san, I'll need you to sink that vessel right now," she said, her voice as even as she could make it. "I'm afraid Suzuki-san is otherwise engaged."

If the younger raiko hadn't seen his crewmate's legs torn from her body, she was not about to point it out to him. Instead, she directed her gaze at the other ship.

"Quickly, Hiroshi-san, before they have time to reload."

Hiroshi-san, who had been all too willing to pass off the job of sinking this ship moments earlier, made not a single argument or sound of doubt before raising his arms.

It was only because Kaiyo knew what to expect that the sudden tilt of the deck didn't send her sliding across the planks on her rear. Instead, she clung tightly to the rail and let her feet swing out from underneath her. She looked down and was impressed with Hiroshi's control, for all that he'd second-guessed himself earlier.

The Wind Serpent rose just at the top of a giant crest, the sea in front of them plummeting steeply down to the hundred-gunner and the sea behind them sloping more gradually to the open sea. What happened next should not have been possible, though it was an impossibility she had already witnessed a dozen times in her life. What took place before her was not a phenomenon that the sea ever created on its own, at least so far as Kaiyo was aware. The hole that Hiroshi had created—for what else did one call a circular pit in the sea that was big enough to consume a small island?—dropped down and down, so steeply and quickly that nothing could have escaped its ferocity, before the sides of it collapsed inwards, leaving the Wind Serpent bobbing in its awful wake and swallowing the hundred-gunner in a single, terrifying instant.

Kaiyo made herself watch, just as she had forced herself to watch the cannons firing on the enemy ship in Kaigunjima harbor.

She took no pleasure in the destruction of another ship, let alone its entire crew. And her heart ached with the loss of all that her people could have made of such a crew and such a ship if given half a chance, but she kept her eyes on the water that rushed to close over the enemy vessel. She watched as its decks, masts, and hull cracked horribly, completely, the wood rendered to little more than wet kindling under the sudden pressure of the ocean atop it, and she kept watching even after the ship's remains were out of sight.

It was only because she was watching so intently that she saw the boats in the distance.

"Kuso," she muttered, reaching for her glass.

"What is it, Captain?" Tanaka's voice asked beside her.

He was covered in blood, she noted, his hands, shirt, and leggings drenched with it, and she wondered how many of her people he had saved as she'd been so intent on destroying the enemy. He must have already treated the worst injuries among the crew, else he wouldn't have returned to her side. She tried not to wonder if that was a good sign or a terrible one.

"Full sail towards the wreckage, Tanaka-san," she ordered, without explanation.

Either Tanaka saw what she did, or else he could hear the note of urgency in her voice that begged him not to question her. He relayed the orders quickly, and in moments they surged into the frothing waters where the sea had just swallowed a ship with a hundred cannon.

It wasn't Tanaka who questioned her then, it was Hiroshi.

"Captain, I feel obligated to point out that these waters are not safe. The other ship's wreckage could be floating just beneath the surface and we—"

Kaiyo did not turn or acknowledge Hiroshi's words, but she handed the young raiko the glass and pointed.

Hiroshi pressed the glass to his eye and gasped as soon as he had it trained in the direction Kaiyo had indicated.

"How did they…" his voice trailed away.

Kaiyo shrugged.

"I don't know, and I don't have time to speculate. We must catch them before they reach waters beyond our patrols."

"Captain?" Tanaka asked.

Still not explaining, she passed the glass to Tanaka.

"Kuso," Tanaka muttered, and Kaiyo struggled to keep her face neutral. That might have been the first time she'd heard Tanaka curse.

She couldn't blame him, though. How else were you meant to react when you saw the crew of the ship you'd just destroyed, a crew whose mere existence was now a threat to everything you held dear, rowing themselves away in a half a dozen longboats?

Before Kaiyo could even issue the order, Hiroshi scurried from the stern deck and began organizing his fellow kisōshi at the sails, leaving her alone with Tanaka once more.

"How many dead?" she asked, without taking her eyes from the spot where she knew the boats to be, even though she could barely see them.

"Three, and Suzuki-san will never walk again without aid, but she is doing much better than I feared."

Kaiyo let out a breath and, for just one moment, closed her eyes.

"It would have been much worse if you hadn't cried out before the shot reached us. You saved many. Including me."

Kaiyo glanced at Tanaka briefly, wondering if he was seriously suggesting that she'd saved lives instead of getting more people killed by underestimating their opponent, then lost track of whatever question she'd planned to ask him when she saw his cheeks pink with blush. Was Tanaka embarrassed that she'd saved his life? It wasn't the first time she'd done so, but he had saved her life just as often. Yet the act had never brought color to his cheeks before.

"Tanaka-san?" she asked, unable to form a coherent question, but wondering what had come over him.

"If you hadn't jumped on me... that is, the ball that hit Suzuki-san was... Captain, I am in your debt."

Kaiyo swallowed. The thought of what had happened to Suzuki-san occurring to anyone in her crew made her mouth go dry, but if it had happened to Tanaka?

"Tanaka-san, in addition to being my second, you are the best healer in the fleet. Your life will always be the first life I save. Saving your life saves a hundred others."

She did not add that he was also the closest thing she had to a friend in this world. She didn't think it would do anything to help the man's blushing, so instead she turned to look at the longboats ahead of them.

"They are moving damnably fast for longboats," she murmured.

"There look to be six of them," Tanaka said, his voice back to its usual even tone. "Far fewer than a ship that size might carry, but even still, she must have known what we were doing well before you gave the order to sink her. She must have gotten half her crew off that ship."

Kaiyo smiled again, and this time it was genuine.

"Indeed," she replied. "I underestimated her again. She fights like Kaigun."

Tanaka nodded, but was silent for a moment.

"You look decidedly happy and I can't figure out why. If they escape us now, we——"

"They are in BOATS, Tanaka-san. Boats. Boats with no guns, boats with no sails. We will catch them yet, for all that they are faster than they have any right to be. We're still gaining on them quickly, and when we do, they will not be able to fire on us before we've had a chance to speak. They'll barely have a chance to——"

"They may still have guns, Captain."

Kaiyo frowned.

"But not cannon."

"No, not cannon. But they may have those small handheld devices we found on the last crew Ichiro-san brought in."

"Yes, but those 'guns' cannot put a hole in our hull. We can hail them from a safe distance, and if they attempt to fire at us, we can sink their boats with a turn of Suzuki-san's smallest finger, or Hiroshi-san's."

She frowned at the thought of Suzuki-san being unable to help them at the moment, but the point stood.

Tanaka was still frowning.

"We can rescue them, Tanaka-san. We don't have to kill them. There's a chance we can end this without taking their lives."

Tanaka said nothing, staring out at sea.

"Do you want them dead because they killed some of our crew?" Kaiyo asked, after a long pause.

"Yes, but you know I would never condemn them for it. They were defending themselves."

"Then why do you look so dour?"

"I don't like the idea of risking you in parlay."

"You never do."

"I believe that is part of my job description."

"Yes, well, it's part of mine to negotiate terms with the enemy." Tanaka sighed.

"Fine. Rescue them. But don't—"

Tanaka's voice cut off sharply and his face paled.

"Captain," he said, reaching for the glass in her hand without even asking her permission, and raising it to his eye. "We need to hurry."

The tone of Tanaka's voice was all Kaiyo needed to sharpen her focus.

She signaled for the kisōshi to add more wind to the sails without even asking what Tanaka could see.

"Why are we hurrying, Tanaka-san?" she asked, waiting for him to return the small telescope to her outstretched hand.

"Because over half of the enemy's crew is in the water, and I think I see sharks in there with them."

Kaiyo grabbed the glass from Tanaka's hand while it was still pressed to his eye, but he made no objection. Then she felt her jaw drop slightly as she took in the scene in the distance. Tanaka had not exaggerated. If there were a hundred people in the longboats themselves, there were another hundred in the water. There was splashing and struggling, and people in boats pulling people out of the sea, but there were also fins. More fins than Kaiyo cared to think about, enough fins to distract her from the other odd thing her eyes registered but her mind did not.

Instead of getting caught up in details, she called for more speed, and for the Wind Serpent's own longboats.

It was only when she and the crew she'd selected for the rescue mission pulled up within hailing distance of the hundred-gunner's struggling crew that she realized what her brain had snagged on earlier.

The sailors were all the color of southern island parrots.

Kaiyo gave herself one moment, the space of a single breath really, to appreciate how different it was from anything she'd ever seen before. How had she not seen it, even from afar, as the hundred-gunner chased them? She couldn't imagine not noticing, now that she saw it, because the skin, hair, and eyes of every member of the foreign crew were bright colors generally reserved for birds, flowers, and poisonous frogs. And from what she could tell, no two of them were the same.

The space of the breath passed, though, and she refocused on why they were here—to deny the sharks their feast. She could wonder at their differences later.

"We're here to help!" she shouted, waving the white cloth she'd attached to an oar. She hoped that these decorative people shared enough with the more boring foreigners she'd met over the cycles to understand that the white flag was meant to be a sign of truce.

Of course, she couldn't blame them for not believing she was trying to help. After all, she'd lured them into a harbor filled with cannon, and then done her best to sink their entire ship. White flag or no, she wouldn't have gone quietly with anyone who'd done the same to her crew, either.

Still, she had thought that maybe when the worst that any of those removed from the water received was a bit of rope around the wrists, or one of the ship's medics rendering them unconscious, they might have started to get the idea.

Instead, Kaiyo got a rather ferocious fist to the face as she pulled one fuchsia-haired, teal-skinned, yellow-eyed woman from the sea, and if she hadn't had so much practice fighting with a broken nose, she would have dropped the woman right back into the ocean, sharks or no sharks.

She managed to wrestle the tall woman over the gunwales though, and held her tightly until someone could tie her hands. Or she would have, had the woman not head-butted her and then sunk her teeth into her arm.

"Agh!" Kaiyo cried, feeling blood drip down her arm. The teal-skinned woman smiled then, though the action seemed only like a threat of more violence, especially with her blood on the woman's teeth.

"We aren't trying to kill you," Kaiyo said, staring the other woman in the eyes and hoping that some of her meaning might penetrate. "We don't kill unarmed swimmers."

Even as she said the words, she realized that the woman in front of her was far from unarmed. She had an exquisite katana strapped across her back. Kaiyo tensed as the woman raised her hand, ready to draw her own dagger if she had to, but the woman didn't reach for the blade on her back. Instead, she did the strangest thing. She licked her own knuckles.

Kaiyo heard shouts and looked over to see the six longboats that had come from the hundred-gunner—which were horribly low in the water due to being filled to capacity twice over— pulling alongside six of her own longboats, and clearly attempting to pull her crew into the sea.

"Don't hurt them!" Kaiyo shouted at her own crew. "Disengage and render them unconscious if you have to, but don't hurt them!"

The woman in front of her, with her hand still hovering near her own mouth, frowned then, and—faster than Kaiyo could track—the woman reached out and grabbed Kaiyo's wrist.

Before Kaiyo could turn the other woman's grab against her, she was shouting across the water in a language Kaiyo had never heard before, in a voice that carried like thunder across the waves.

Immediately, and without question, the hundred-gunner crew ceased fighting.

Then the teal and fuchsia woman bowed slightly and released Kaiyo's wrist.

Kaiyo watched her crew move through the hundred-gunner's survivors, removing their weapons and offering them water, and frowned.

"What's troubling you, Captain?" Tanaka asked, from his usual place at her shoulder. They were almost back to Kaigunjima, and she had been letting the afternoon sun warm her skin on the stern deck while she kept an eye on their brightly colored prisoners.

"Just wondering what made their captain order them to comply," she admitted. The teal-skinned, fuchsia-haired woman who had head-butted Kaiyo had continued to shout things to the rest of the hundred-gunner's crew periodically, and that—along with the crew's synchronized behavior changes after each shout— made it clear to Kaiyo she was indeed the captain of the sunken vessel. "It was a very sudden shift."

"I'm more curious about what happened to the sharks, personally," Tanaka said.

"What?" Kaiyo asked, finally turning to him.

"The sharks." Tanaka's face was its normal neutral, though his gaze was somewhat distant. "We saw multiple shark fins in the water before we launched our boats, but when we arrived at the hundred-gunner's boats I didn't see a single trace of them. What made a few dozen sharks disappear, with that much free food still in the water?"

Kaiyo frowned. She hadn't noticed the lack of sharks. She'd been too busy focusing on the bright colors adorning the people they were rescuing, and then on not getting punched in the face too often as she'd been pulling them from the water. She was still considering the question, wondering if perhaps some of the hundred-gunner's crew had water kisō, or some trick she wasn't familiar with for repelling sharks, when a shout from the main deck had her eyes flashing up and seeking out the source immediately.

"Damn," she muttered, and before Tanaka could even ask, she was down the ladder to the main deck and moving through the crowd to break up the fight that had just broken out between her crew and the hundred-gunner's captain.

Kaiyo made it all the way to the far side of the main deck before Tanaka caught up to her. By then, Hiroshi was in the teal-skinned captain's arms, with his own wakizashi held to his throat.

The rest of Kaiyo's crew stood a few strides away from the tableau, while the hundred-gunner's captain was surrounded by her own crew, who had adopted varying stances of readiness despite their bound ankles and wrists.

"What's going on here?" Kaiyo demanded, joining the ring of her crew surrounding their captives.

"Hiroshi-san was taking the sword from this one, and she pulled his own blade on him when he wouldn't give it back."

Kaiyo could see that the katana she'd noticed earlier on the other woman's back was now on the deck beneath her feet. Kaiyo sighed. She didn't want to kill any of these people, but she wasn't about to let them harm her crew.

"Your weapons will be registered with our armory," she said, turning to the woman who was holding a blade to the Wind Serpent's youngest stormcaller. "It will all be explained when we reach the housing center, but surely you can understand why we don't want to leave you armed?"

To be honest, it had taken her crew much longer to disarm the hundred-gunner's crew than usual, which was largely down to the way they had been captured. An enemy that surrendered in battle generally understood the requirement to lay down arms, and it was done quickly. This enemy... well, they'd been pulled from the sea and they'd stopped fighting without an official surrender, and... it was complicated. Kaiyo had, of course, had them all bound before she brought them aboard, and many had laid down their weapons in the boats. But the captain had never pulled the sword she carried from its scabbard, so Kaiyo had felt that letting her keep it for the duration of the trip to Kaigunjima would foster a feeling of goodwill, but now...

Well, now, she wasn't about to let anyone harm her crew, goodwill be damned.

She felt her fingers already tipping the stone owl seal from knuckle to knuckle, and wondered when she had reached for the item.

She kept her gaze locked with the fuchsia-haired woman's, taking a moment to appreciate the bright yellow of her eyes as she attempted to convey without words how much she would hurt the woman if she injured the raiko in her arms.

Much to her surprise, the captain of the hundred-gunner, with her eyes still locked on Kaiyo's, slowly began to release Hiroshi's throat.

And Kaiyo had just started to relax when the lookout cried out, "Skiff from the island, Captain! Waving the red flag!"

The hundred-gunner's captain tensed, even as Kaiyo felt her own hands ball into fists, and she was certain that even breathing wrong in the next moment would lead to disaster. For Hiroshi anyway. And she wasn't willing to have his blood on her conscience.

She took a deep breath and, without breaking eye contact with the other captain, she said, "Tanaka-san, how stable is Suzuki-san?"

"She's resting in the healing berth, Captain. I do not recommend that she move until she can be transferred to the hospital on Kaigunjima."

Kaiyo nodded. That was the reply she had expected.

"Tanaka-san, I'm going to need you and Hiroshi-san to work together for a moment. Do you think you can do that?"

She felt Tanaka step up beside her, and knew he understood her because she could sense him taking the stance he often used while gathering himself for a healing.

"Hiroshi-san, I have to go meet the skiff. Do you know what I want you to do?"

Hiroshi's eyes widened, but she couldn't tell if that indicated panic or understanding, so for good measure she added, "I think our guests are exhausted after their long day. They could all do with a bit of rest."

And then she turned on her heel and walked away from a wreck she was not qualified to salvage.

Kaiyo heard over two hundred bodies fall to the deck at the same time, but didn't turn to look. That sound meant that Hiroshi was still alive and had done as she'd asked. Which meant that it was no longer her problem.

Her problem was the small oared boat that had just pulled up alongside her ship, even though they were less than a league out from Kaigunjima harbor.

Her problem was the young woman in the green and blue uniform of the Kaigun's land forces climbing up the starboard rail and striding toward her with the gait of someone who has been scolded by the admiralty before and has no wish to repeat the event.

Kaiyo watched her, taking a moment to savor the even feel of the marble owl tipping through her fingers, as doing so took away some of the tightening in her chest that accompanied seeing that marine.

"Message for you, Captain," the young woman said, handing her a small scroll.

Kaiyo kept her face blank as she tucked her hanko into her belt pouch with one hand, taking the scroll with the other.

She even kept it blank as she read the missive quickly in the late afternoon light.

"You're dismissed," she said to the young officer when she had read the scroll once.

"Your reply, Captain?"

"I'll deliver my reply in person, Sansa. Dismissed."

The Sansa didn't question her a second time, thankfully. Kaiyo's patience was always rather low, but the message she'd just gotten from Admiral Saito hadn't done anything to make her feel more generous towards marines who didn't know their place.

Kaiyo gave credit where it was due though—the young woman didn't even spare a glance for the two hundred unconscious bodies that now littered Kaiyo's deck.

"Tanaka-san!" she called.

In a few heartbeats, Tanaka was by her side once more, and she finally allowed herself to look at the mess behind her.

"Report," she said, quietly, as her eyes took in the still forms of the two hundred or more brightly colored humans they'd recently pulled from the sea, and the small number of her own crew that had been standing a bit too close when Hiroshi had followed her orders.

"The newcomers don't seem to be any more adversely affected than any of our people by the sleeping shift. I haven't been able to check all of them, but those I have checked were breathing normally and had regular pulses."

"Good," she nodded, exhaling for the first time in more heartbeats than was comfortable. "Hopefully they'll stay that way long enough for us to deposit them in the brig. Someone else will have to finish disarming them, I'm afraid. We're needed elsewhere."

She sighed, then reluctantly handed Tanaka the scroll.

"What is it?" he asked.

"Read it," she replied, keeping her face and voice carefully neutral.

Tanaka, whose default expression was that of water that hadn't felt a breath of wind in an age, was unable to keep his eyes from widening ever so slightly. Kaiyo was probably the only one who would have noticed, especially since a heartbeat later his features were once more perfectly schooled.

"I'll get the prisoners ready for transfer," he said, dismissing himself.

Kaiyo wanted to object. She wanted to keep him by her side, ask him what he thought of the admiral's orders, and see if his guesses matched her own. Instead, she nodded and let him go.

She could see the outline of Kaigunjima port coming into focus in the hazy afternoon light, the hint of gunpowder still on the breeze from their action that morning, and she knew there was no time. Much as she wanted to be the one to take the prisoners to their new quarters, to ask them where they'd come from, why they looked as they did, and why they'd bothered to enter Gensokai's waters, she knew there would be no chance of that now.

The Admiral had called her to the mainland, and she had only enough time to grab the fifteen men he'd requested and make sail again before the evening tide.

Why he had requested fifteen men from the irredeemables section of the dungeon, she would simply have to ask him in person.

Awash in the myriad noises and smells of Kaigunjima's main port, Kaiyo watched carefully as her people unloaded the still unconscious crew of the hundred-gunner, hoping that Tanaka's assessment had been right. She didn't want to kill any more of the strangers than she already had. The fact that only two hundred remained, of what must have been a crew of nearly 800, made her shiver. She'd been responsible for the death of entire ships before, but that didn't make it any easier. Besides, she rather liked their captain. She'd proven a worthy adversary, in the end.

In that moment, Kaiyo wanted nothing more than to follow the last of the prisoners being carried off by the dock workers to the holding complex on the far side of the city, and wait for them to wake up, an event Tanaka promised was no more than a half watch away. Then, when her next breath brought the scent of deep-fried squid to her nostrils from one of the dockside vendors, her stomach joined the clamor of those wishing they could go ashore with their captives.

As much as she loved the sea, there were times she missed land. Most of those times were determined by her stomach. Endless rations of rice, salted seaweed, and dried squid made the prospect of freshly cooked food difficult to resist sometimes. She turned to look at the setting sun for a moment, wondering if she could somehow squeeze a quick trip to the wharves and their various food vendors into her preparations for their immediate departure to the mainland, and sighed heavily when she realized it would be impossible. She had to be here for the arrival of her father's "cargo."

Something steamy popped into her peripheral vision. She turned sharply and saw Tanaka holding up a small bamboo tray covered in takoyaki, slathered with sauces, and sprinkled with dancing bonito flakes. Not quite the squid she had scented on the breeze, but another of her favorites, regardless.

"I had to deliver the requisition to the irredeemables department and realized neither of us were going to get a meal in if I didn't make good use of my return trip," he explained, with a hesitant smile.

Returning that smile without hesitation, Kaiyo took the proffered tray of takoyaki. Tanaka had a matching tray in his other hand, and they both picked up the bamboo hashi that came with the plate in the same instant.

"Itadakimasu," they muttered in unison, before cramming the steaming balls of dough and octopus into their mouths.

For a few moments they ate in silence, and Kaiyo contemplated which Kami she must have pleased to earn a second like Tanaka.

Just as she was putting the final bite in her mouth, a commotion broke out at the bottom of the gangplank.

Kaiyo carefully masked her expression before looking up.

Fifteen men stood on the docks beside the ship, easily visible from where she stood at the starboard rail of the stern deck. The first three of the newcomers were all tousling over something. In a few heartbeats, the guards that surrounded the men had quelled the outburst, whatever it was.

"I don't like this," Tanaka whispered beside her.

She kept her gaze locked on the men now climbing onto her ship, but she didn't disagree.

"The admiral's orders are not for us to like or dislike," she said. "But I'll ask you to keep a close eye on our newest 'guests,' all the same."

Tanaka nodded and disappeared without a word, taking the two empty bamboo trays with him.

After she'd signed for the irredeemables, set a guard from her own crew on them, and wondered why, of all things, the Admiral had insisted they be allowed to arm themselves in the same missive that instructed that they not be allowed the freedom of the ship, she was finally ready to give the command to push off.

Instead, the sound of boots clacking quickly against the docks and a few shouts from below stopped her.

"Captain! Wait!"

To her surprise, it was the same Sansa who had delivered the message from Admiral Saito.

"Yes, Sansa," she replied, her tone cool. "We're just off to see to the admiral's orders. What do you want?"

"The new recruits," the Sansa said, breath heaving from her run down the pier, even as she yelled to Kaiyo, "the one you deemed their captain, she…"

And here the Sansa hesitated for a moment, as if the words escaped her.

"She wishes to speak with you," the young woman finished.

"She speaks Genoskan?" Kaiyo asked, interest piqued.

The other woman frowned.

"No. She… she made it clear she wishes to speak with whoever is in charge."

"The Admiral is in charge, Sansa," Kaiyo chided.

"But she…" the other woman's voice faded away for a moment, and Kaiyo wanted to let out a roar of frustration. She had to go, they were losing the tide, and she didn't want to keep her raiko awake through the night just because she'd been unable to get out of port in time.

"Inform her I will speak with her as soon as I return," she supplied.

The Sansa nodded, absently, and then frowned at her own feet.

Kaiyo restrained herself from yelling at the young woman. Then she gave the order to push off and head to the open sea.

Whatever the foreign captain had to say could wait. The Admiral had summoned her, and she dared not refuse him.

Kaiyo flicked her owl between her fingers and considered bringing the blade out to stab into the thick stack of papers under her hands.

"I still don't understand why Admiral Saito would order you to bring fifteen doshigatai to the mainland."

Tanaka sat across from her at the low table that folded down from the bulkhead of her cabin. They had been examining the same stack of parchment for the past watch and a half, attempting to determine that very thing. Kaiyo was already sick of the dusty scent of the washi that had clearly been buried in the prison filing system for ages, and even sicker of reading about the crimes of the doshigatai she was carrying in her hold.

"I don't know, but if I have to read about one more assault against a woman, I am going to go below decks and slit a few throats," she snarled. How could the Admiral have requested that these men be released, let alone armed? She was certain Admiral Saito would have a reason, but she was becoming less and less convinced that she would like it.

"I won't give you this one, then," Tanaka said, his mouth a grim line. His hands were clenched, perhaps overly tightly, on the paper he held in his hand.

Without thinking, Kaiyo flicked out the small blade embedded in her owl hanko and flung it at the far bulkhead. Tanaka, whose ear the blade has sailed right past, didn't flinch, but lifted his eyes from the paper in front of him to hers.

"Was it something I said?" he asked.

Kaiyo couldn't help it, she laughed. She folded over, face to the lacquered tabletop, arms splayed across stacks of paper, and cackled.

It was that or kill something.

After a few moments of uninterrupted laughter, she finally got up to retrieve the small blade, and just to make sure she didn't take off Tanaka's ear in a fit of rage, she placed the marble statuette in the small pouch at the front of her belt.

"Are you sure that's wise? I'd rather have your owl thrown at me than any of your other knives."

Kaiyo rolled her eyes as she resumed her place on the other side of the low table, legs folded beneath her atop the thin zabuton that cushioned her from the wooden deck beneath.

Tanaka, for his part, must have picked up a different stack of papers while she'd been retrieving her hanko, because he was looking at this one with his head tilted to one side, then handing it to her before she'd finished folding herself to the floor. Presumably not because he wished her to kill the men in her hold.

"This one is a bit different," was all that he said.

Kaiyo's eyes scanned the page, looking for what stood out from the rest of the files. Every other scroll, paper, and folder had been filled with descriptions of at least one, and generally more than one, heinous crime.

Two things caught Kaiyo's attention right away. The first was a lack.

No assault, no rape, no murder, not even theft. Most of the men described in the papers strewn across her table had committed more than one of those crimes. That was, after all, the way that one ended up in the doshigatai prison. The Kaigun gave people second chances, even third chances. They worked to rehabilitate rather than punish, and hardly anyone ever stayed in the Kaigun holding cells for more than a few months at a time. The doshigatai was reserved for those who had no interest in rehabilitation, or those whose crimes were too heinous to be absolved in the first place.

But the only crimes listed on this man's docket were escapes, which were far from the kind of offenses that would land one in the doshigatai prison and…

Kaiyo blinked to be sure she was reading this right—escape and blood magic.

"Kuso," she breathed.

Tanaka said nothing in response to Kaiyo's profanity, but kept his carefully blank gaze on her instead.

"Is Admiral Saito trying to get us all killed?" she asked.

"You think the blood mage is a threat simply by being here?" Tanaka asked, his voice neutral.

"Of course I do! Why else is the practice banned half the world over?"

Tanaka shrugged.

"Many things that are not understood are abhorred."

"So you're defending the blood mage, now?"

Tanaka said nothing for a moment, and then, "I just think it's interesting that with fourteen files, full of some of the vilest crimes we have laws against, the thing that makes you question the admiral's intentions is the presence of a person whose only crime seems to have been attempting to return home."

"Using blood magic," Kaiyo spat.

Tanaka said nothing, but returned his gaze to the papers on the table in front of him. For a moment, Kaiyo felt her stomach drop, as if she had just failed some kind of test. She was about to ask Tanaka what he'd meant by any of that when a shout on deck was followed by a rush of steps clambering toward her cabin and she was up and opening the door before her deck officer had finished raising her fist to knock.

"Captain, please come quickly! There's a brawl."

As soon as Kaiyo stood on deck it was clear where the trouble was.

Despite the cloudless sky and the sun that greeted her and Tanaka as they stepped out of her cabin and onto the main deck, something felt off, like the coming of a bad storm. She wasn't the least bit surprised to see that all the shouting and commotion came from the knot of fifteen men that weren't part of her crew.

She would ask later why the men were unbound. She'd left their guards with specific instructions, and freeing the men's wrists had not formed a part of them. For now, she would simply remind the doshigatai that they shouldn't risk her ire. She could only assume that her crew wasn't interfering because the men were only attacking each other.

She strode swiftly across the deck, not bothering to reach for any of her blades just yet, but taking in the details of the brawl. Two men at the center appeared to be attempting to rip each other's throats out with their bare hands, despite the fact that she caught the glint of steel on more than one man's belt. Around the central pair, a ring of five attempted to pull the other two apart. Around them, another ring of seven jeered or cheered, as if they had placed bets on the outcome. Perhaps they had. One man stood back from the others, and in fact, if their clothes hadn't been so drab, so unlike Kaiyo's crew's typical outfits, she would have assumed the man wasn't one of the doshigatai at all.

She focused on the men at the center. Her long strides carried her across the deck in a handful of heartbeats and then she wove through the two outer circles, easily occupying the shifting vacancies left by the men who were focused on the fight, ducking under the telegraphed punch of the larger of the two men, stepping between him and the smaller man, putting her hands on both men's windpipes, and squeezing before either of them realized they were no longer alone in their squabble.

"Good day, gentlemen," Kaiyo said, as everyone involved stopped what they were doing. The two men whose windpipes she currently held, with enough pressure to make it clear she could crush them before they could do anything to stop her, glared sullenly in her direction and she did her best not to smile.

"There seems to be a misunderstanding," she said, now that she had their attention.

"Chito-san took my—"

"Ah, ah," Kaiyo interrupted, keeping her voice light. "You mistake my meaning. I don't give a rat's shit about what you think the misunderstanding between you is. The misunderstanding that you should concern yourself with is the one that made you think it was acceptable to brawl in the middle of my deck. You are here by my invitation. If I decide you are no longer worthy of the invitation, I will feed you to the sea. Is that understood?"

The man whose life she held in her right hand nodded.

The man on the left said, "Little bitch, what makes you think you can—"

Whatever else the man planned to say was cut off with the crushing of his windpipe. He collapsed at Kaiyo's feet, making the horrible noise of someone who can no longer pull air into their lungs.

"Is that understood?" she asked the remaining men.

Murmurs of "Yes, Captain," and vigorous nodding surrounded her.

"Ichida-san!" she yelled, to her nearest marine. The woman came running and stood at attention.

"Get these men restrained again and placed below decks. Send whoever decided they could walk the deck unbound to my cabin. And—"

Then Kaiyo's own voice dropped away, as she noticed a deep blue streak on the deck, poking out from under the still-writhing man at her feet. She knelt to retrieve it and then held it away from herself, half-tempted to drop it.

It was a katana, sheathed in a deep blue scabbard engraved with a beautiful mountain landscape, with a pair of bright amber stones looking out from an inlaid silver wolf face.

It felt like a coming storm.

"Captain?" the marine asked.

"That's all, Ichida-san," she said. When she raised her eyes and turned towards her cabin she caught Tanaka's gaze.

"Save him if you can," she said, before he could ask her any questions she didn't wish to answer.

Then she took the sword that felt like a day gone terribly wrong and locked it into her sea chest as soon as she stepped through the door to her cabin.

2日 6月, 新議 8年

2nd Day, 6th Moon, Cycle 8 of the New Council

⚊ Kaiyo ⚊

KAIYO WOKE EARLY the next morning, the sun not yet breaching the galley windows, her hammock swaying slightly with the ship, and her mind still unsettled by the events of the day before.

Tanaka hadn't been able to save the man whose windpipe she'd crushed. She didn't regret the man's death. Though she generally required more provocation than insults to her person in order to kill someone, she had read through the dead man's file and she knew he had committed more than enough atrocities to warrant his demise. There was no death penalty in the Kaigun, but she was certain that there were a few souls in Kaigunjima who would sleep better knowing the man she'd killed wouldn't be returning, even to the prisons. In truth, she would be lying if she pretended she wouldn't have killed him anyway. No, the death of that man wasn't what was unsettling her. She was fairly sure *that* honor lay with the strange katana she'd hidden in her sea chest the night before.

Judging by the way her cabin felt too close and the air felt wrong, she was almost certain the strange blade was right where she'd left it, but she made herself check again, as soon as she was dressed. As expected, the blue scabbard still glittered at her, with the unsettling amber gaze of the silver wolf fixed on her the moment she lifted the lid of her battered chest.

She quickly dropped it and replaced the lock, tucking the small key back into one of the more secretive pockets on her wide leather belt.

Then, after a quick check to be sure all seven of her daggers were in place, she opened the door to her cabin and stepped out into the cold morning breeze that accompanied the rising sun.

She turned and quickly made her way up the stairs to the stern deck, pleased to see Tanaka was already present.

"Finished your rounds early this morning?" she asked, as she stepped to the middle of the small raised deck that topped her own quarters and then started a series of quick punches and kicks that would help to warm her up before she began her deeper stretching routine.

"Well, seeing as half the patients in the healing bay are dead, my rounds weren't particularly demanding. Suzuki-san continues to do well, despite her stubborn refusal to stay in port."

Kaiyo chose to ignore the hint of judgment in Tanaka's voice.

"I'm surprised the criminals didn't kill half the crew in their sleep," she countered, as she moved from basic punches and kicks into the more complicated stretching routine that was the precursor to her usual morning workout. "Or each other."

"If they've tried to kill each other, or anyone else, no one has reported it to me," Tanaka replied, standing by the rail as Kaiyo's stretching morphed into a series of kicks, flips, and spins that took up most of the available deck.

"Well, I suppose I should be reassured," she said, her breathing a bit fast as she continued her routine, "but I'm not."

She finished with a two-handed flourish that launched two of her daggers into the forward rail of the stern deck.

"I wish you wouldn't do that," Tanaka muttered.

Kaiyo smiled now, as she walked to the rail to retrieve her knives.

"You're right. It'll dull the blades," she said, returning them to the small sheaths on her belt. "And they're not balanced properly for throwing, anyway."

Tanaka frowned.

"I meant risking the life of whoever happens to be wandering in front of the stern castle, Captain."

Kaiyo's smiled widened.

"But you're right here to heal anyone who might get cut, and besides," she added as she saw Tanaka's mouth opening once more to protest. "I never miss."

Tanaka could not, in fact, argue that point, and he knew it.

"Be sure the crew are in their Lander clothes by the time we reach port," she said, descending the stairs to the main deck.

"And you, Captain?" Tanaka asked, eyeing the wide-legged pants that tucked into her leather jika tabi with their rubber soles, the flowing open-necked shirt she wore tucked into the wide belt laden with daggers.

"If the Admiral insists on requesting my presence 'as soon as humanly possible,' then he will have to receive me dressed as I am."

And with that she turned and pushed open her cabin door.

It took less than a heartbeat to know that everything was wrong. The papers on her low table, which she'd left in neat stacks topped with decorative rocks and shells the night before, were now strewn all over the room. Her sea chest hung open, the lock lying sprung on the ground, and most of her clothes were spread across the wooden floor.

She turned around, having not even stepped past the threshold, and scoured the main deck with her eyes.

Yet she saw nothing out of the ordinary. The first watch had taken its place while she'd been going through her morning workout and Tanaka's report, and while she'd occasionally turned an eye to her crew, she hadn't seen anything unusual on the main deck. Not that she would, if an experienced thief were trying to blend in with the crowd and use the watch change as cover for a hasty theft.

She sighed and looked back at her room.

Walking over to her chest it was instantly obvious what was missing. In fact, she was surprised she hadn't noticed the moment she opened the door. After all, her room no longer felt like a coming storm. Whatever else the thief had taken, she would bet the Wind Serpent that they'd truly come for the sword.

Kaiyo held her long glass to her eye and watched the horizon that was slowly solidifying into the unmistakable hard line of land. She sighed, enjoying the sunlight and tang of sea air for a moment before collapsing the glass and stowing it on her belt with a shake of her head.

She could already feel her stomach twisting. She hadn't spent much time on the mainland since the age of about 12, but her memories of it tainted the view every time she returned, and the mainlanders never did anything to rid her of the feeling.

"Landfall!" shouted a voice from above. She glanced up to the nest just above where she hung in the rigging, gave the lookout a nod, and then climbed down to the deck with the effortless grace granted by a lifetime of practice.

Her crew bustled around her as she made her way to her cabin, and she ignored the calls, shouts, and activity of a ship preparing to enter port, even though the sun had a few hand's-breadths of sky to traverse before they reached their destination. She trusted all would be in place long before Atsumi's lookouts would even mark the Wind Serpent. She crossed the main deck to the red sliding hatch that marked her quarters and slipped inside before anyone could ask her for orders.

She hesitated after sliding the hatch closed behind her and latching it, her hand automatically going to the hanko in her pocket and bringing it out to flip idly between her fingers as she stared at nothing in particular.

She ought to change, despite what she'd told Tanaka earlier, but as she flipped the small stone seal from knuckle to knuckle she couldn't help but move to the low table that held her charts, pinned in place by weights and her compass, along with the letter from Admiral Saito. She'd been surprised to find that none of her papers were missing, even with the disappearance of the katana. She'd half expected the thief to remove some of the records of the doshigatai, if not all of them. Of course, it wasn't as though the records she had were the only copies. Perhaps the thief knew that. Perhaps they simply hadn't had time to go through her papers properly. They certainly had made a mess of them, but perhaps that had only been a tactic to mislead her? As if anything could have made it less obvious that the katana had been stolen.

The thief had also left the missive from Admiral Saito. The note was coded, so it was possible they hadn't known what it said or who it was from, but it wasn't a particularly difficult code to crack. She had mastered it as a child, when her father had been in the habit of leaving her coded messages with directions to her favorite snacks hidden about their home.

Her gaze slid over the small, urgently scribbled missive and then snagged on the words that had been bothering her since she received it the night before.

...urgent mission that I cannot trust to anyone but you.

She didn't like the sound of that at all. She wouldn't have liked it even if she *hadn't* been ordered to bring fifteen doshigatai to the mainland, and to require her crew to remain aboard even as she was summoned to the admiral's office.

She sighed, sliding the blade from her hanko and stabbing it into the missive, pinning it to her table with a sigh of frustration. After a long moment, she retracted the blade into its concealed position in her hanko, folding the missive and stuffing it into the small, locking sea chest that housed her important documents.

Then she turned to the larger sea chest that housed her wardrobe. It hadn't taken her long to restow the damned thing after the thief was done with it. Kaiyo wasn't sure why the thief had decided to toss her clothing around her cabin after stealing the sword (which had been on top of the carefully rolled and folded items within the chest) but she had taken all of her clothes (the entire pile fit into her arms easily) to one of the raiko who had a talent for removing unwanted substances from clothes. When the woman's inspection had turned up nothing, Kaiyo had decided her wardrobe was probably safe.

She frowned now as she considered her chest and the clothes within. She had planned on ignoring the Admiral's request that she dress to blend in. She truly detested most Lander clothing. She found it as restrictive as it was dull. But if she didn't change, all the Landers would look at her as though she were some kind of theatrical attraction. And, while she sometimes took great pleasure in making the rikuka talk behind their hands when she passed, something was wrong enough that Admiral Saito had sent for her with great urgency and a request to blend in. She would comply, if only this once.

Wincing at the thought of what came next, she removed her wide-legged pants, her leather tabi, and her open-collared shirt, then changed into a simple earth-toned kimono, cloth tabi, and geta. There was nothing to be done about the shortness of her hair, so she let it be.

She tucked her hanko into the pocket she'd had sewn into the obi and then, after careful consideration, grabbed two of her smaller daggers and tied them between the layers of her outer and inner obi as well.

As Kaiyo made her way across the crowded pier of Atsumi she cursed three things. She cursed her kimono for shortening her stride, she cursed her geta for clacking so loudly against the wood planking (she thought a herd of goats would be stealthier), and she cursed herself for failing to eat before she left the ship. The scents wafting towards her from the food stalls that lined the outer edges of the wharf district triggered a painful reminder from her stomach that she had once again been too distracted by her duties to eat.

She glanced quickly at the sun and did some mental calculations. If she grabbed something on a stick, she could eat it on the way. People would stare once she cleared the wharf district, but she was so hungry, she doubted whatever she purchased would last that long.

She picked a vendor selling grilled mochi wrapped in pork with a sweet shoyu glaze because it didn't have a line, and because it was one of her favorite foods.

A few moments later she was walking towards the Saito estate, absorbed in the challenge of eating without getting any of the delicious brown sauce on her sleeves.

Which is why she practically slammed into a diminutive woman with grey hair and calculating eyes who she would have recognized anywhere.

"Fubuki-sensei?" she asked, as she waved her mochi stick wildly to one side to avoid stabbing the older woman.

"Ah, Kaiyo-san, how lovely to see you. Your mother will be pleased that you're not dressed like a ruffian. Aren't you a bit late to see the admiral?"

Kaiyo swallowed the first three replies that snapped to mind about none of those things being any of Fubuki's business, settling instead on a reply that was less likely to get her stabbed.

"What are you doing in Atsumi, Sensei? Last I heard you had retired to the woods on the island."

"And what business is it of yours, child? I'm here because it pleases me."

Kaiyo swallowed a smile this time, knowing that the gesture, however pleasantly meant, would likely earn her a painful wrist lock at the very least, and she didn't want to drop her mochi.

"I suppose I shall just learn to live with the mystery then," she replied, bowing slightly.

"Hmph. You used to have more backbone," Fubuki chided. "I suppose I will see you later this evening. You'd best get to the Admiral, he won't count chatting with an old lady as a worthwhile excuse for your absence, and besides, I have business of my own to attend to."

Kaiyo coughed to cover her laughter and bowed deeply so that Fubuki wouldn't see the smile on her face.

When she was certain that the older woman had shuffled off, Kaiyo rose from her bow, still smiling, and then frowned at the stick in her hand. All but one mochi had been removed. Of course, when she turned to look for the woman responsible, she had already disappeared into the crowd.

"Kuso," Kaiyo muttered, eating the lone mochi that remained before tipping the stick back through her fingers. Her old fighting tutor had always been nimble on her toes and quick with her hands, but the woman hadn't stolen the food off of Kaiyo's plate since she was a girl.

There would probably be food waiting for her at the Saito estate, she consoled herself. Probably.

It wasn't long before the wharf district gave way to the merchant district, the large clapboarded, thatch-roofed warehouses giving way to narrow wooden shops stacked beside each other. The merchant district was busy enough that Kaiyo decided it was probably in her best interest to hire a horse. The sun was lower in the sky than she liked, and Admiral Saito wasn't particularly patient even when he hadn't ordered a shipload of criminals and his most trusted captain to his side "as fast as the winds can bring you."

Luckily, she knew of a hostler on the next block and she had remembered to slip some mainland coins into her hidden pockets.

Once she was mounted, sidesaddle of all things because she was wearing the damnable kimono, her hands and body took over the process of directing the horse through the small, winding streets that eventually opened into roads lined with progressively larger homes, and eventually to the Saito estate. Consequently, her brain was free to mull over the question of whether or not she had handled the stolen katana properly.

She was almost entirely certain that one of the doshigatai had stolen the damnable blade, and yet she hadn't had them or their berth searched. She trusted her own crew above anyone. Even the gaijin among them, rescued from defeated enemy ships, were people that Kaiyo would trust with her life. Theft was frowned upon in the Kaigun, and it certainly warranted some sort of disciplinary action, but the doshigatai weren't her crew, she was merely transporting them at the Admiral's request. It would be obvious as soon as the men were unloaded from the ship that one of them carried the sword, and she would deal with it then. For now, she had other things to worry about, such as why she was the only person who could be entrusted with this mission, or why she'd been forced to bring 15 criminals of the worst kind to the mainland.

But her reverie was cut short as she noticed that her muscle memory had brought her and the horse to the Saito estate as flawlessly as ever. She nodded to the guards as they opened the gate for her then slid (only slightly awkwardly, thanks to the restrictiveness of the kimono) to the ground and handed the reins to a waiting hostler.

"Ah, Kaiyo-san, it is a pleasure to see you again. How was your recent delivery run?"

The voice of Saito-san's clerk refocused her attention, and she forced her hands to cease fidgeting with the layers of fabric that trapped her legs. She looked up into the wide, friendly face of the primary office clerk, a man she had known since childhood.

"Oh, boring, as usual, Atemi-san," she replied, following the man across the stone courtyard that formed the center of the southern half of the Saito estate. A tall wooden wall with a sloping roof of its own blocked the view of the neighboring homes, and the courtyard provided direct access to the gate, the main office, and the eastern family wing. Kaiyo was pleased to find that Atemi-san was heading to the main office, just as she was. "Port to port with wine, food, and textiles and not even a storm to keep us entertained."

She smiled conspiratorially, though if such were actually her day-to-day, she would probably have put her own dagger through her eye by now.

"Well, you see more of Gensokai than most!"

"Indeed, albeit mostly from the sea. Still, I won't complain. I am grateful to be so trusted by my father."

"Ah yes, few women are so lucky," the minister of records agreed with a genial laugh. "The world has changed much since the fall of the Rōjū, ne?"

Kaiyo smiled but made no reply beyond vague sounds of agreement. Atemi would patter on happily about the changes in the world and she would let him, because while he knew very little about how far behind Gensokai was from where it needed to be, that was not his fault, and he was one of the few men in her father's employ who truly seemed pleased by the progress that had been made in recent cycles.

Eventually, not long after they had both finished removing their geta and stowing them nicely in the cubbies on one side of the genkan, he noticed her not-so-subtle glances at the stairs that led to the second floor.

"Ah yes, you must be anxious to see him after all this time. I believe he is in his office. Go on up, if you like, and I will prepare some tea."

The smile she gave Atemi then was much warmer. He was perhaps the only man in this office beside Saito-san who wouldn't have suggested that she make the tea herself.

"If you have any onigiri, Atemi-san, I would be eternally grateful if they made their way onto the tray."

Kaiyo winked as she said the words, drawing a great laugh from Atemi-san even as she swiftly made her way across the tatami-covered floor, dodging nimbly between clerks carrying files from the small writing tables where accounting books lay sprawled beneath harried hands to the series of cubbies that lined the far wall from floor to ceiling, and made her way up the stairs.

"Come in," came the gruff response when Kaiyo tapped lightly against the sliding door that marked Saito-san's office. It never ceased to surprise her how well he played the part of slightly overtaxed but very wealthy merchant. The room was fairly sparse, the low table in the center covered with scrolls and sheets of parchment as well as bound folios full of accounting pages. The neat shelves full of scrolls that lined one wall were juxtaposed with a rather serene mural depicting a hazy mountain village with a gilded phoenix rising behind it through a summer storm. The other wall had a window that opened out onto the inner courtyard and allowed the sound of drilling guards to waft in through the warm spring air.

"Hello, Admir—"

"Kaiyo-san."

The tone of Admiral Saito's voice made it clear she was being reprimanded, even though the man hadn't even raised his head from his work yet.

"Hello, father," she amended.

Kuzuri Saito looked much as he had the last time she'd seen him about half a cycle ago, or at least, the top of his head did. His hair was greying at the temples, but his skin was still relatively smooth, for a man who had spent most of his life at sea. As he still hadn't even looked up from his papers, Kaiyo said nothing more, instead reaching for the hanko in her obi as she watched him tally columns of inventory.

"You took longer than I expected," Kuzuri-san said, still not looking up from the papers laid out before him on the low table.

Kaiyo had arrived before sunset, which meant it had taken her less than a day to sail a distance that a ship without raiko would have taken three days to cover. It wasn't a record, but it wasn't far off.

"I had... business to attend to. Not everyone is as pleased to see me as you are."

Kuzuri-san frowned, she thought, judging by the side of his face, but did not look up from his papers.

"And is your business concluded?" he asked, his finger pausing over a line of numbers.

"Locked away like a troublesome prisoner," she replied. "But it's probably something I should check in on before too long. There were some rather interesting developments just as I was leaving."

And with a jolt, Kaiyo realized she hadn't thought of the strange captain and her strange crew since she'd left Kaigunjima. Of course, she had been rather distracted by the doshigatai and the various problems they presented. She was looking forward to them no longer being *her* problem. Whatever her father wanted with them, he was welcome to them.

Kuzuri-san huffed out a grunt after her last comment, but she didn't take that as assent.

"I'm sure that whoever you left in charge can manage things. I'm afraid I'll be in need of your services for the foreseeable future."

"Oh?"

"I have an assignment that can only be entrusted to you."

"You did mention something like that in your missive," Kaiyo mumbled, running her left hand along the top of the scroll shelves on the far wall. She'd wandered across the room while they were talking, since Kuzuri-san seemed disinclined to look up from his accounting anyway. "Why exactly did you request I bring fifteen doshigatai along?"

She was almost amused by the low growl her father emitted at the mention of the doshigatai. Of course, to someone outside of the Kaigun, it was just a word, not necessarily a group of people condemned to the lowest dungeons of the navy they didn't know existed, but that didn't mean it wouldn't sound odd used in this particular context.

"I have another letter that you must read. Here." His voice was emphatic as he handed Kaiyo a folded parchment from underneath the accounting folio he was currently reading, and *still* did not look up. She unfolded the document and stared at the words for a moment, applying the simple cipher her father usually used for their communications. Even so, it was another few moments before the words truly began to sink in.

A scholar has discovered documents that could potentially ruin us. She must be brought in for questioning. It is utterly imperative that no one else learn of or suspect what she has uncovered. Once we know the extent of the damage she could cause, we will act accordingly. In the meantime, you are to function with an expendable crew, so as not to risk any of your own people. An exception will be made for Tanaka-san, as you will need someone you can trust in this venture. The scribe is well guarded.

Kaiyo felt her jaw tighten as the meaning of the words settled in. She didn't know what document existed that could possibly ruin them, but she trusted that Kuzuri-san would know such things. Her father had done all he could to ingratiate himself with the New Council after the fall of the Rōjū so that he would have access to precisely that kind of information. If the Kaigun were to do their duty and still protect what they held dear, they needed to know the ruling body's every move as it was decided. He had spies, of course, but spies brought information that was often too old to be useful. Being a sitting member of the New Council was far more efficient, and it had hardly taken any effort at all. He'd been an enthusiastic supporter of the dismantling of the Rōjū, and no one had second-guessed his change in allegiance, as the Rōjū had notoriously treated the merchant class as lesser citizens. The New Council claimed it would work to support all of its citizens equally, whether they were Kisōshi or not, and so far they had kept their word well enough that Kuzuri-san was mostly inclined to believe them. Or so he said. Kaiyo didn't know his true thoughts on the matter, only what he chose to reveal, and what she could guess from the very little his reactions let slip. One might expect that knowing him her entire life would broker her some advantage in knowing his mind.

One would be wrong.

"Are we going to kill her?" Kaiyo asked, perhaps letting Tanaka-san influence her speech more than she should. She considered it a small revenge for having worn a kimono on horseback at her father's behest. If she couldn't be comfortable, then she would ask uncomfortable questions.

Kuzuri-san's eyes snapped up to her.

"We will not be discussing this now," he replied, before returning to his accounting folios.

Kaiyo took a deep breath and a moment to appreciate the gentle weight of the seal tipping between her fingers, seeking a calm she did not otherwise feel.

"I was under the impression that killing people to keep secrets was a thing the Rōjū did."

Kuzuri-san's eyes did not lift from his accounting books.

"This is not a mere secret, Kaiyo-san, and you know it."

"Then what is it?"

"A way of life. Everything we've ever loved. The entirety of the Kaigun, and Kaigunjima. You know much that the Landers do not, but even you lack a complete picture. You've known battle, but you have never known war… Is it worth one life, a dozen lives, to save thousands?"

Kuzuri-san whispered the last few words, and Kaiyo wondered if he was overcome with emotion, or if he thought someone might be listening in his upstairs office. A few heartbeats later, before Kaiyo had even had a chance to fully process her father's question, the office shoji slid open and Atemi-san entered bearing a lacquered tray covered in all the accoutrements necessary for a tea ceremony.

Atemi-san placed the tray on the lone uncluttered corner of Kuzuri-san's low table and then turned and bowed himself from the room, his broad, genial smile in place as he did so. He winked at Kaiyo, but she couldn't help but frown at the lack of onigiri.

"Does he not bother to announce himself anymore?" she asked, once the cheerful man was gone.

"Atemi-san has never stood much on ceremony. Besides, when one is a mere *merchant*, one does not warrant quite as much bowing and scraping as one might... otherwise."

Kaiyo snorted, knowing full well that "otherwise" meant "when one is an admiral."

"Shall I make you some matcha?" she asked, finally folding herself to the floor on the opposite side of the table from Kuzuri-san.

It was Kuzuri-san's turn to snort, as he folded up the folio he had been reading and set it, and the other papers on the table, aside in order to make room for the tea tray.

"I would rather we be able to drink it, so no. Allow me."

And then he made the formal bow of a master of tea ceremonies.

Kaiyo smiled, warmed by the gesture. It was rare that Kuzuri-san ever went through the trouble of performing a tea ceremony these days.

Rarer still that he did for Kaiyo.

Of course, it wasn't often that they were in the same place of late.

"I'm honored, father," she said, returning his bow. A grunt was the only acknowledgment she received, but she was fairly certain that Kuzuri-san was feeling sentimental.

Kaiyo lifted her head and watched with interest as her father went through the intricate ceremony that always seemed to ground him in a way that nothing else could. She still believed his greatest disappointment in her had come when she had finally admitted that she had no interest in tea ceremony. That had been sometime around her twelfth birthday. It wasn't that she didn't respect the art. It would have been near-impossible to grow up with Kuzuri-san as a father and not learn to appreciate the beauty, concentration, and artistry behind the ceremony. It was just that Kaiyo was terrible at it, and she had other interests.

They did not speak while Kuzuri-san performed the simple yet elegant motions of mixing hot water and powdered tea leaves together. When described that way, it sounded simple enough, but anyone who has seen a true master at work knows that it is so much more than the turns of the chawan, the pouring of hot water, and the stirring of powder.

Kaiyo found watching the process almost as meditative as her father found performing it, and by the time he served her they were both well into their own contemplations. She took a sip of the tea and savored it. There were better drinks in the world, certainly, but none of them brought a sense of peace-tinged-with-nostalgia to her the way matcha did.

It was a long while later when Kuzuri-san finally spoke.

"I hope that no one will have to die for this, Kaiyo-san, truly, but there are many factors we must consider. There will be many risks, but the one risk I refuse to take is putting too many of our own people in harm's way. You will lead the fifteen… mercenaries, and use them to acquire the… goods that we must collect."

Kaiyo tried desperately to hold onto the calm she had gathered during her father's tea ceremony.

"You're asking *me* to lead the doshigatai against some Lander scribe?"

It wasn't just the fact that she was being asked to attempt to lead a band of the worst criminals in the Kaigun, it was also the idea that she needed fifteen men to abduct a scribe.

"They have skills that will be useful for this particular endeavor, and they won't be missed should things go wrong."

Kaiyo tried not to flinch at those words.

"There are only fourteen of them now," she said.

"Oh? And which one made the mistake of challenging you on the journey here?"

Kaiyo wasn't sure if she should take her father's assumption as an insult or a compliment, but he was accurate either way.

"I didn't bother to learn his name. The one who set an enemy ship alight with half the crew locked below decks."

Kaiyo watched her father's—her *admiral's*—face carefully for any sign that he might be surprised at the list of crimes these men had committed. Had he truly known who they were before he'd insisted she bring them to the mainland?

"Ah, yes, Dateki-san, I believe. He was mainly along for his muscle; he won't be much of a loss. But try not to kill too many of them before you reach your goal. The goods really are well protected."

Kuzuri-san then pulled a compact scroll from his sleeve and passed it to her. She took it and began to unroll it.

"You should probably read it later—you have a two-day sail to Sakata ahead of you. From there another two days or more by horse. There is a map included in the scroll. Don't show that to anyone else."

"I do not keep secrets from my crew."

"Nonsense, all captains keep secrets from their crew. And your crew will remain aboard your ship in Sakata. You will only take the mercenaries with you from there… and Tanaka-san, if you insist on endangering his life."

Kaiyo took a long sip of her tea as she considered her father's words.

"You would have me endanger his life without telling him why?"

"Your orders are that none of your crew are to know what is contained in that scroll, or anything else of your mission. Of course, they will know what your cargo is when you return, but I trust you to keep the cargo's identity hidden from them."

"If my entire crew will wind up seeing 'the cargo' as you put it, why not simply allow me to bring them along for the entire mission?"

Kaiyo's skin crawled at the idea of trusting the fourteen doshigatai with anything, let alone her life. She still hadn't mentioned the stolen katana to her father, or how she had handled it. The fact that she would now have to deal with the men who had stolen it for more than the time it took her to escort them somewhere in chains made her sick.

"You seem to ignore the number of times I have told you that the scribe is well guarded."

Kaiyo raised a lone eyebrow.

"You're telling me this scribe poses a major threat to a fully trained Kaigun crew?"

"I am."

Kaiyo reassessed her father's insistence upon secrecy and subterfuge. In the end, knowing that she could not refuse the order, that it was her duty as the future leader of the Kaigun to take on missions such as this one, even when she did not much like the means, she bowed and slid the scroll into her own kimono.

"Thank you, Kaiyo-san. You do your family honor."

Kaiyo swallowed the emotions that clogged her throat at her father's words. He rarely said such things, and she knew all too well that the family he referred to was more than just their blood relatives and the Saito name.

For a few peaceful moments, they both savored their tea in silence. Then Kuzuri-san broke both the silence and any shred of calm she had left.

"It has been too long since you have visited your mother."

Kaiyo almost dropped her chawan to the floor.

"My mother does not wish to see me," she replied, attempting to keep her voice even.

"Nonsense. She asks after you often, and begs me to request your presence at the estate."

"Sorry, I should have been more specific. My mother wishes to see a young woman she created, whom she can marry off to some son of a merchant who will bring our family great prosperity. However, she does not wish to see *me*."

Her father's mouth went through a paroxysm as he attempted to smile and frown at the same time.

"You should at least say hello. She would be very..."

His voice trailed off as he realized that whatever he was going to say was probably a lie. At least, that was what Kaiyo assumed.

"Happy? No, I'm not married yet. Grateful? No, she plans to berate me for not having visited earlier. Excited? Perhaps, but only at the prospect of shoving me in front of some potential suitor while I'm stuck on land."

"You know I wish for you to inherit our legacy, Kaiyo-san. She cannot take that away from you, no matter who she forces you to meet."

"She should know better than to try to marry me off in the

first place. I'm your heir. What can she possibly think I would gain from a husband?"

"She is... concerned about your reputation. You are away at sea for very long periods of time, and people are prone to gossip."

"Believe me, I know all about the rikuka tendency to gossip. But what does it matter? I don't need anyone else's approval to inherit your legacy. Only yours."

"Oh?" Kuzuri-san's mouth flattened out to a hard line. "Do you know what your mother does for our family? She may not know the true reason you spend moons at a time at sea, but she knows that you are protecting our interests, and she knows that you cannot succeed me if you do not have at least one foot on land."

Kaiyo frowned. Kuzuri-san did not often take her mother's side in these arguments. He knew where Kaiyo's talents lay, and he supported them. She was the only person besides him who kept a presence in both of their worlds, and so far she'd managed well enough. Something must have changed.

"What do you mean?" she asked.

"I am only successful in my position because of the contacts I have here on land, Kaiyo-san. Being an excellent sailor and a good captain is not enough to keep our worlds safe and separate. You cannot succeed me if your reputation is tarnished beyond salvage, and your mother has started to hear rumors that may be more than our family name can bear."

"What rumors?" she asked, suddenly curious. She hadn't thought she'd spent enough time on land in the past few cycles to even leave fodder for the rumor mill. But one should never underestimate the imagination of the rikuka. Especially among those wealthy enough to be bored.

"That is for you and your mother to discuss. I only know that she is concerned you will have difficulty, even with the rather accepting New Council, if things get much worse."

Ah. That would certainly explain why Kuzuri-san suddenly found himself on her mother's side of things. He would never do anything to tarnish their reputation with the New Council. Too much relied on it.

Her own feelings on the matter, a mixture of disgust and reluctance, must have shown on her face.

"You will go and consult your mother on this matter before nightfall. After dark, I need you to begin work on this latest matter."

She sighed, but did not argue. She might have little enough interest in her mother's antics, but an order from Kuzuri-san was not something she could ignore. Considering herself dismissed, she placed her empty chawan on the low table and stood to leave.

"Kaiyo-san," her father's voice said gently, before she turned away. "I know that you do not see eye-to-eye with your mother, but she does more for this family than you seem to appreciate. Without her, I would not have managed the change in regime even half as well. She has saved us all more than once, and without even knowing the truth of our mission."

His words gave Kaiyo pause. Her father rarely spoke so highly of her mother. Not that he wasn't always respectful of her when he spoke, but he was rarely this effusive in his praise. Kaiyo had always gotten the impression that her mother and father merely tolerated each other for the sake of running the family estate, managing the family legacy, and making children. This sounded like something more.... not quite affection, but a deep appreciation that she'd never heard before.

Kaiyo nodded, moved by how respectfully he spoke, if nothing else. Suggesting that she and her mother didn't see eye-to-eye was the understatement of the century. Suffice it to say that Kaiyo and her mother had very different ideas about what made a woman "good."

Giving her father one more shallow bow, Kaiyo turned to leave the room. If she was supposed to settle matters with her mother before dark... well, she should have started moons ago, if that was the goal, but at the very least she needed to start talking with her immediately.

By the time she reached the main residence of her childhood home, she could feel her shoulders hovering near her ears. She made herself take a deep breath and then rolled her shoulders back and down. Slouching only made her mother more antagonistic, and besides, Kaiyo wasn't here to be scolded like a child, she was here to deal with the political necessities of preserving her family's legacy.

"Kaiyo-chan!" came a high-pitched keen from a nearby doorway, as she entered the family residence across the main courtyard from her father's offices. She smiled, even though the noise was piercing. She had forgotten that Eri-chan would be home from school for the season. Kaiyo turned to smile at her little sister. The bright-eyed girl raced at Kaiyo with her arms held wide, and Kaiyo knelt as far as the restrictive kimono would allow, letting her sister's arms wrap around her neck as she ruffled her hair.

"You're taller," Kaiyo said, kissing the top of Eri's head as she stood.

Eri stared up at her and frowned.

"You haven't grown at all."

"Not for many cycles," Kaiyo chuckled, ignoring the evident disappointment on the girl's face.

"Come on, show me where Okaa-san is hiding," Kaiyo said, reaching out her hand. Eri took it quickly, and immediately began dragging Kaiyo down the wide hall that led to her mother's receiving rooms, talking as fast as a sparrow at suppertime. Kaiyo let the cadence of the young girl's voice wash over her for a moment before she finally started parsing out what the words meant.

"And Fubuki-sensei was here all morning but she wouldn't teach me how to stab the mean boy who keeps taking my comb, so I told her she had to at least teach me how to hit him in the face and she—"

"Wait a moment," Kaiyo said, pulling the seven-cycle-old child to one side of the wide hallway for a moment. "Fubuki-sensei was here *all morning*?"

"Yes, she and Okaa-san were planning something ALL day and they wouldn't let me in, even when my history tutor caught me climbing trees when I was meant to be copying a scroll on the eleven articles of the New Council. But that was—"

"Eri-chan, do you have any idea what they were planning?" Kaiyo asked, working very hard not to smile at the way her little sister evaded her lessons so deftly.

"No, they wouldn't tell me, and I couldn't even get the maids to tell me, they all just smiled and said I would know soon enough. Do you think it's a surprise for me? It's not my birthday for another two moons, do you think they're planning something early? Is it your birthday? I thought your birthday was near midwinter."

Kaiyo couldn't help but laugh.

"You're right, Eri-chan, my birthday is on the solstice. Good memory."

Eri beamed at the praise, then promptly resumed tugging Kaiyo down the wide hallway decorated with rolling landscapes in neutral watercolors.

Not sure what to make of the information Eri had just revealed, Kaiyo let her.

Before long, the rapid stream of narration extolling her own successes at evading her tutors with more interesting (and muddy) adventures faded, and they were standing before a gilded shoji with a daintily painted phoenix rising from a mountaintop as its centerpiece.

"No use pretending you're not there," came a voice from within. "I could hear Eri-chan from the moment she saw you."

Eri's cheeks reddened, and Kaiyo patted her shoulder and gave her a slight shove in the direction of the hall that led to the gardens. When she turned to look at her older sister, Kaiyo added a gesture with her chin in the same direction.

"Go on, no reason for us both to be in trouble," Kaiyo whispered. Eri flashed a small smile before dashing down the hallway.

Kaiyo took a deep, centering breath and opened the door to her mother's receiving room.

"Kaiyo-san, welcome home," her mother called from across the room, where she sat folded before a low table strewn with a variety of flowers, some of which she was artfully displaying in a decorative bowl. When Kaiyo failed to reply after a few moments, she finally looked up.

For just a moment, one that Kaiyo would later question the reality of, her mother beamed at her as though she were truly glad to see her.

The moment was shattered after a mere heartbeat, as a small frown replaced whatever else it was Kaiyo had imagined on her mother's face.

"Are you actually wearing proper clothes?" Nijiko took a moment to stare outlandishly past Kaiyo's shoulder and then look frantically around the room. "Who are you, and what have you done with my daughter?"

Kaiyo kept her own frown determinedly in place and shrugged.

"If you'd rather I change, I'd be more than happy to—"

"I never said that," her mother snapped, brandishing a pair of scissors at her. "I need you dressed properly. I'm merely surprised I won't have to send you to your rooms to change."

Nijiko took a second look at Kaiyo, as though scanning her for imperfections, which in all likelihood was exactly what she was doing. But her face remained impassive, until she reached her daughter's head. Then the frown Kaiyo was so familiar with returned.

"What have you done with your hair?"

Kaiyo sighed. She had rather hoped her mother wouldn't notice, but that had been an insane hope. Nijiko noticed everything about Kaiyo's physical appearance, and she would have to be particularly oblivious not to notice her hair.

"It's the latest fashion," Kaiyo lied, confidently. "I'm certain it will be all the rage here soon enough. The southern port towns are awash with women whose hair is too short to grab."

She was only half joking. There actually *was* a new trend in some of the southern port towns for women to cut their hair short enough that it couldn't be used against them by an attacker.

Sadly, there was nothing fashionable behind the trend at all. It had become rather popular amongst Kaiyo's crew, however, men and women alike. Especially as it suited a number of the more interesting fashion choices that Kaigunka made anyway. The advantage of not letting the enemy find a hold on one's head far outweighed whatever stigma her crew might run into on the mainland.

Her mother looked skeptical.

"It's not as though it matters, Okaa-san. Anyone you plan to parade me in front of today will only be interested in my purse. They should have little enough trouble overlooking my hair."

Skepticism deepened into a proper scowl on her mother's face, and Kaiyo hoped that she'd actually managed to provoke the woman into cutting to the truth of why she was here. She hated the way Nijiko talked around everything.

"The rumors that you need to overcome will take more than your purse, child. While you have been off playing sailor, the world has formed some very insulting opinions about you. Controlling the damage will take moons."

That was more honest than Nijiko often was with her, but since she'd heard as much from her father earlier, that was hardly surprising. If her mother had taken to explaining a problem outright to father, then it must have been serious indeed. Kaiyo was about to remind her that she wasn't going to be here for moons, that she was, in point of fact, leaving by the moon tide tonight, and was unlikely to return for a few tendays at least, but before she could even open her mouth, Nijiko was clapping her hands and calling for servants.

It really shouldn't have surprised Kaiyo that the first young woman to enter carried not only a tray full of delicate styling combs, but still another tray full of elaborate hair pieces that would make her shortened mane immaterial. Of course, mother probably had someone watching the Wind Serpent the moment it touched the dock. She would have known the state of her daughter's hair long before Kuzuri-san had told Kaiyo she would be required to visit.

Kaiyo sighed. Arguing would only draw the whole process out, and her father had made her promise to work with Nijiko instead of flouting her, just this once.

It wasn't that Kaiyo didn't enjoy clothing. Sometimes she even enjoyed putting on the face paints that had become popular amongst her crew members ever since they'd captured a ship full of powders and paints from a merchant vessel that either had thought smooth sailing somehow existed where there was in fact a rather large landmass or had been hoping to trade with Gensokai despite their centuries-long embargo. That ship's crew was still learning Gensokan and hadn't yet been able to properly explain why they'd arrived with that particular cargo.

But Kaiyo's version of dressing up and Nijiko's were vastly different. Nijiko wished to present a flower, just like the ones in her ikebana arrangements—beautiful, subtle, potentially meaningful, but always understated and calm. Kaiyo had never been any of those things. But it was no use telling her mother that, she would just insist that Kaiyo was whatever she chose to make herself.

Kaiyo sat down and let the young woman with the combs begin her work. Soon the comb girl was joined by a few other sets of hands, though Kaiyo was no longer in a position to see how many, as they were mostly behind her.

"You do realize I won't be here tomorrow," Kaiyo said to her mother, as the older woman knelt before her and began adjusting the collars on Kaiyo's inner kimono.

"Your father did mention that he had some assignment for you, but Kaiyo-san, I cannot advise that you take it. This is not a problem that will go away just because you sail off again."

Kaiyo took another deep breath and was jabbed with a decorative comb for her efforts.

"Okaa-san, I know that you think my social standing is more important than anything, but father has a mis—assignment for me that cannot be completed by anyone else. I cannot simply turn him down and run off with the nearest suitor because it suits your needs. Marrying someone may seem like the most important th—"

"The rumors are that you are currently bedding that horrible man who follows you around everywhere."

Kaiyo's mouth snapped shut as Nijiko interrupted her, not because she'd been cut off, but at the idea that she was bedding *anyone*, let alone...

"Do you mean Tanaka-san?" she asked.

Her mother's scowl deepened.

"The one who always speaks out of turn, and never leaves your side," Nijiko clarified, as though she couldn't possibly be expected to learn the man's name.

"I... you can't... have any of the people starting these rumors actually MET Tanaka-san?" she asked, unable to keep the sharp incredulity out of her voice.

"Of course not. None would ever deign to speak to such a person. But it does not matter. You are rarely seen out of his company. You sail with him for moons at a time, and no one sees you or any of your crew. He speaks to you with far too much familiarity and he looks at you with... fondness."

Kaiyo held up her hands to stave off any further descriptions of Tanaka.

Then she laughed.

"Tanaka-san? Really? I mean, out of everyone in my crew I just..."

She let her voice trail off, realizing that she had already said close to too much for the ears of the servants.

"I am NOT bedding Tanaka-san, mother," she said at last.

Nijiko sighed and resumed fidgeting with Kaiyo's collars

"I know that, Kaiyo-san. I am not at all convinced that you are interested in men, but... the rumor exists outside of what is true. As most rumors do. And now there is really only one way to fix it."

"Okaa-san," Kaiyo said, her mouth hardening to a straight line. "I am not marrying some stranger today, just because the society dimwits have gotten it into their heads that I am sleeping with my second in command."

She almost bit her tongue. It wasn't that it was a secret that she was the captain of her own ship in her father's merchant fleet, it was only that they tried not to go broadcasting it around if it could be avoided. Her mother didn't seem phased by the mention of Tanaka's rank.

"Indeed you are not. The rumors are far too insidious for that to work, anyway. Now, hold still."

Knowing that the price of fidgeting would be a sharp poke to the scalp, Kaiyo held still.

She did her best to keep her breathing calm and even as her mother and the two or more maids in attendance pushed, pulled, and prodded her newly attached hair into whatever they considered to be the height of fashion. Kaiyo only started to grow concerned when her mother pulled an elegantly wrapped bundle from behind her and then shooed the remaining servants out of the room.

"Stand up and hold out your arms. This will be easier if you let me do it."

Kaiyo started to open her mouth to object, but her mother's glare caught her and was as effective as a slap. She wasn't sure what new crime she had committed to incite Nijiko's ire, but she seemed as angry with Kaiyo as if she had shown up in her sailing attire riding on the back of a naked man. As she had, in fact, gone out of her way to arrive dressed as Nijiko preferred, and without even Tanaka in tow, Kaiyo couldn't fathom what she'd done to provoke her.

"I displease you," Kaiyo said, sighing. She wasn't being meek, simply honest. She looked her mother straight in the eyes when she said it.

"*You* don't displease me. But your actions do, child. You—"

"I am not a child mother. I haven't been a child for a decade or more. Can you not recognize that your twenty-eight-cycle-old daughter is as much an adult as anyone else in your acquaintance?"

"If you are such an adult, then why don't you *act* like one? Grown women do not go sailing off on ships full of men just to—"

"And children do not help their fathers run merchant fleets," Kaiyo retorted, before Nijiko could get going. What she *wanted* to say was that she'd stopped being a child the first time she'd had killed someone in self-defense. That a child didn't make decisions for a crew of three hundred sailors in order to keep them alive against unpredictable enemies and the dangers of the sea itself. But, of course, she could say none of those things because no one but her father and her crew was aware that they were true, and as much as she might wish to put Nijiko in her place, the Kaigunka way of life came first.

Her mother glared but said nothing as she tied on the elaborate kimono she had pulled from the cloth bundle. Nijiko had removed Kaiyo's drab brown outer kimono so quickly that Kaiyo hadn't even noticed the switch, and now she was halfway done putting on the vibrantly red and gold outer kimono in its place.

"Why are you dressing me for a wedding, Okaa-san?" Kaiyo asked, even as her stomach dropped.

"Because there is only one solution to these vicious rumors, child. As you would well understand if you had ever bothered to learn a thing about etiquette."

Kaiyo stuttered but couldn't think of any words for her defense. Her mother had finally lost it. But what hapless fool had Nijiko decided to force her on? Surely there weren't any sensible young men who were so desperate for a partner that they were willing to be married off to a woman who spent most of her time on a ship at sea and who had apparently tarnished her reputation beyond repair?

"I cannot." Her tongue felt heavy in her mouth. This couldn't be happening. Her father knew she was leaving tonight with the tide. How on earth did mother think she could marry her off this evening and send her off to sea a few hours later? Surely her would-be husband would object. "I have to leave tonight. You can't just—"

"Bring him in," her mother called over her shoulder, as she tied the final knot in the decorative obi that completed the wedding kimono. Kaiyo had to give her credit. She was exceptionally fast when it came to dressing someone in kimono.

The shoji behind Kaiyo slid open once more, and she heard a familiar gait behind her. She turned, confused but grateful, hoping that Tanaka was there to pull her away from this madness before her mother could condemn her to a life with someone she'd never met.

But when her eyes met Tanaka's, they found a strange trepidation that looked as out of place on him as the formal kimono that he was wearing.

"Tanaka-san?" she asked, her mouth running on while her brain put together the horrible truth that was standing before her.

"Since your second in command is the root cause of the rumors, the only non-scandalous solution is to marry *him*. Your reputation is almost beyond repair, but if all the scandal turns out merely to have been a prelude to a respectable match, society will forgive most of it, and forget the rest when it is no longer worth discussing. I'll be waiting in the courtyard to escort you to the shrine. Don't be long."

And with that, she turned and left through the shoji by which Tanaka had just entered.

Kaiyo simply stared after Nijiko for a moment, but before she could even move or think, Tanaka-san was prostrate on the tatami before her.

"I beg your forgiveness, Captain. I should have realized that my acquaintance with you was ruining yo—"

"Oh get up, Tanaka-san. This is embarrassing."

Tanaka stood. He still looked sheepish. She hated it.

"My favorite thing about you is that you don't do this kind of thing," she continued, gesturing at the spot on the tatami he had recently been pressing his head so hard against she'd thought he might be trying to tunnel out of the compound. Not that she would blame him if he were. A desperate escape might be the most sensible response to all of this. "Let's not start... whatever this is, off with self-abasement. This is no one's fault but my mother's. I can't believe she would do this to you."

Tanaka-san stared at her for a moment, but she could already see the steel glint in his eye returning.

"Surely, it is *you* she is vexing the most with this, Captain."

Kaiyo laughed. She couldn't help it. It was that or cry, and she didn't have the energy to cry just then.

"Kind of you to suggest, Tanaka-san, but I think we both know that I'm the one with the tarnished reputation who is married to her work and will have no time for a husband."

Tanaka smiled then, for just a moment, and replied, "Then I suppose it's a good thing that I am also part of your work."

"Ha! I suppose you are, at that."

She rubbed both hands over her face and blinked a few times. She still couldn't believe this was her mother's solution. Of course, she wouldn't let Nijiko force this on Tanaka.

"She can't make you do this, you know," she said, after a moment of staring at her hands and wondering how on earth she'd gotten to this point.

"She can, actually," Tanaka said, after a moment. "Your family is in charge of my livelihood and that of my family's. I cannot possibly risk that by turning your parents' offer down."

That made her stomach turn in a decidedly unpleasant manner.

"Tanaka-san, I won't let them. She can't force you. I'll talk to my father, or, I'll just give you everything I have in the bank and hide you for a few cycles until they forget about you. I won't let them force you to marry me. It's bad enough I have to do this to protect my family, but I refuse to let them pull you down with me."

Tanaka sighed and stared at the floor for a moment.

"Captain, I.... As someone who is also gone on a ship most of each cycle, and rather married to his work, my own prospects for marriage are... not excellent. I had not thought to marry at all, if I'm honest, but... I could think of a hundred worse prospects easily, without even spending much time on it."

Kaiyo chuckled again.

"Stop it, Tanaka-san, I'm blushing."

Tanaka's head shot up, but when he met her eyes the sarcasm must have registered because he smiled.

"At least this way we'll both actually see our spouse every day?" he suggested.

Kaiyo wanted to scream, but she wasn't really sure why. Tanaka was a good person, an excellent sailor, and probably the closest thing that she had to a friend. Honestly, if she were going to be forced to marry *someone*, he was an excellent choice. She even found him reasonably handsome, in an abstract sort of way. It was just that... she'd never planned to marry at all, and tying her fate to *anyone* else's seemed entirely too restricting.

"I had thought that even the mainland had moved past this kind of thing," she sighed, staring at Tanaka and suddenly wishing the poor man hadn't been assigned to her ship, for both of their sakes. "You don't hear anyone up in arms about Ryūko-san not being wed to that tracker she hangs around with. Mother hosted a dinner in their honor at the finest izakaya in town the last time she heard they were passing through. Why does no one insist that she marry that man everyone whispers she's bedding?"

Tanaka blinked for a moment and then replied, in a perfectly even tone, "I believe her ability to kill anyone who suggests she marry against her own wishes is a large part of it. And she's an orphan, so it can't be a matter of protecting her family's reputation. But beyond that, I assume it's that she's the Hero of the Realm, and our current government would not exist without her.

I would think that gives her an unfair advantage when it comes to damaging rumors about her respectability."

Kaiyo snorted and felt her hand move towards her hanko before remembering that it was tucked too far into her inner obi to reach, now that her mother had wrapped her up in a decorative obi so wide it covered nearly a third of her body. She'd have to unwind at least a ship's length of silk to get to her hanko, and her mother would probably drag her half-dressed through the square rather than allow her the time it would take to put everything back together after that.

For some reason, her aborted hand gesture had Tanaka reaching into the sleeve of the crisp black kimono he wore and pulling out a small package.

"Here," he said, and if she hadn't known better, Kaiyo would have thought his neck had reddened slightly when he handed it to her.

She took the small parcel silently, too surprised to find any polite words, and worked to undo the precise folding that held the silk wrapping in place. Within the silk was a small, delicately carved wooden box with a barely noticeable seam that she quickly pried open. The box folded on a neatly hidden hinge, and inside was a set of...

"Are these throwing knives?" she asked, holding up one of the small but hefty blades. Each one was a perfectly balanced and beautifully crafted work of art. The tiny hilts were inlaid with a very thin layer of jade. Not enough to throw off the balance, just enough to make them pretty as well as accurate.

Tanaka nodded.

"There are holsters under the little cushion," he added. "A few have pins on the back and can be attached to any fabric. Then there are two bracers that are thin enough to fit under most shirts, if you want to keep them hidden. There are only five of them, but I thought perhaps you'd like to have more than just your hanko in a pinch."

"Tanaka-san, why did you——"

"Before I was escorted to the estate today, I was told to buy you a special gift. A woman with greying hair—who seemed likely to stab me if I argued—dragged me from the ship and made me go shopping along the way. I wasn't told why, but it was made clear that it should be something beautiful and worthy of you. Luckily, she happened to stop and yell this at me near the city's best weaponsmith, and she did not stop me from getting you something I thought you might actually want. I'm sorry if I displeased you, it just seemed that—"

"Tanaka-san, please stop speaking. You never talk this much."

When he stopped, she finally took a deep breath and did her best to swallow the lump in her throat. "This is perhaps the best gift anyone has ever gotten for me, besides the hanko from father. I'm rather ashamed to say that no one informed me of this ploy in advance at all, and I have nothing to offer you in return."

Tanaka smiled then.

"Even if you had been told to buy me a gift that was beautiful and 'worthy of me' would you have been able to?" he asked.

She glared at him for a moment, the emotion she'd been overwhelmed with an instant before rather overrun with annoyance that he might be right.

"Can one buy a sense of when to keep one's mouth shut?" she asked.

Tanaka only laughed.

"If one could, I would have already purchased one, and a spare."

Her annoyance evaporated.

"Tanaka-san, I fear my mother is right, and I'll have to do this in order to fix my reputation and keep my inheritance, but... you shouldn't have to be dragged into this. I'm sure I can convince my parents that marrying someone else would work just as well. You don't have to throw away your future with mine."

The laughter left Tanaka's eyes then.

"Captain, if you are unwilling to marry me, I will cede my place to one whom you admire more."

She frowned.

"Tanaka-san, there's no one I want to marry. I don't wish to marry you, but not because you are in any way deficient, only because I don't wish to marry at all. I've no need of a husband, and I've never met a man or woman I've liked enough to want to tie my life to."

Tanaka raised one brow.

"Then, if there is no one you'd prefer, and you feel you must oblige your parents, please allow me to be the one. We are perhaps better suited to each other than even your mother suspects. Neither of us particularly wishes to be married. We both love our ship, and our crew, and our island. There will be no talk of starting a family, at least not from me, and I suspect not from you. And I'd never dream of suggesting you do anything with your time besides captain the Wind Serpent and run your father's... business."

The last he said while glancing around the room in which they stood. An excellent reminder that they were on land, in her parents' home, and in all likelihood being listened to by not only her father's spies, but also her mother's, and those of a few other merchant families and government agencies.

Kaiyo sighed.

"You're sure you don't want to back out of this? You could still find yourself someone who..." she was going to make a joke about babies and pining, but after how sincere Tanaka had just been it seemed wrong. "Someone who you actually love, at any rate."

Tanaka smiled again, and her stomach did something strange.

"Please do not trouble yourself on that count," he said, bowing slightly so she could not see his eyes. "Besides, if this doesn't go well, there's always divorce."

She chuckled briefly. It was true. Divorce was an option. At least on Kaigunjima. She thought it existed on the mainland as well, but she wasn't sure anyone had made use of it in centuries.

She tried to breathe her thoughts into some kind of order. She was furious with her mother, and with society, for putting her in this position, for thinking that a woman's value had to be attached in some way to a man's. For creating a world in which who she did or did not take her pleasure with was somehow more important than all the work that she did to protect her people, more important than the battles she fought. She was even furious with her father for needing her to do this in order to keep her the heir to their empire. Perhaps if he had not left so much of the Lander relations to their mother, he would know of some other way to salvage things, or to have prevented them from reaching this point. But, of course her rage couldn't change any of that. She wanted to be the leader of the Kaigun more than she wanted to be free of matrimony, and her mother understood the Landers and the New Council better than she did. That was the reality of things. She was angry, she would perhaps be angry for the rest of her life, but this was just a technicality. Some papers to sign, a show to perform, and then she could resume her normal life. And, she realized with a bit of surprise, with Tanaka, there was a chance it wouldn't even make her miserable.

So, after a moment of staring at the small knives in her hand, and then staring at Tanaka—who had chosen to carefully inspect his hands for a moment—Kaiyo shook her head to chase away any lingering doubts and then held the knives out to him.

"Come on then," she said, when he looked at her palm with mild puzzlement. "Help me put them on."

Which is how she went to her wedding armed with no less than six blades and a gently spreading sense that perhaps marrying the man she'd relied on daily for the past half-decade was not the end of her world.

Kaiyo tried to smile throughout the ceremony. She did. However, she was fairly certain the result was more of a grimace than anything. There was hardly anyone in attendance, which didn't surprise her at all. If *she* hadn't known she would be getting married that morning, she certainly hadn't expected anyone else to have known in advance. However, the few who were in attendance were surprising indeed. Fubuki-sensei, for one, was not only there, but grinning at her as if she was truly enjoying herself. Kaiyo wasn't certain that she'd ever seen the woman look like she was having a good time before, and she'd known her since she was Eri's age. Eri was also there of course, looking pleased if a bit confused, the latter part of which Kaiyo could certainly sympathize with.

The most baffling thing seemed to be Tanaka's family, two older people who seemed pleasant enough, but whom Tanaka didn't seem overly comfortable with, and a small girl around Eri's age, who hid behind Tanaka's legs and held his hand whenever possible.

Of course, her mother was there, looking quite pleased with herself, and her father was there looking slightly embarrassed. Not a look that anyone else was likely to identify on him, but one that Kaiyo could interpret from the way he failed to meet her eyes whenever she looked at him.

Beyond that, a few of the wealthiest merchant families had been invited, despite the fact that Kaiyo had never said more than two words to any of them and didn't even know their names.

And then there was the older gentleman, dressed in the finest kimono Kaiyo had ever seen, who remained quiet, watching from behind the crowd, interacting with no one, but never taking his eyes off of her father. He made Kaiyo's skin crawl.

When she tried to ask Tanaka if he knew who the man was, in the one brief moment she was able to speak with him before the ceremony, Tanaka was entirely dismissive of the man, as though he weren't wearing intricately embroidered black silk detailing every phase of the moon, or following Kuzuri-san with the gaze of someone who was assessing a prize horse. Kaiyo frowned and rubbed her fingers along the hilts of the new throwing knives that Tanaka had helped her secure to her wrists. The bracers that held them in place were designed to be scarcely noticeable, even when she was dressed in her wedding finery, and she took great comfort in the presence of the blades throughout the ceremony. Even when she couldn't run her fingers along the hilts, she could feel the slight weight of them against her wrists and know that she wasn't as vulnerable as she felt.

Kaiyo had never in her life imagined her own wedding. For all the time she'd spent contemplating the various ways to convince her mother to let go of the idea completely, she'd never once brought herself to imagine how things would be if Nijiko got her way in the end. Before today she had only attended two such events, at her mother's behest, for the daughters of her mother's friends. Generally speaking, she wasn't close enough to anyone to be invited to such affairs, at least not to the actual ceremonies, and she'd declined as many invitations to the parties held afterwards as she'd ever received. Why would she force herself to attempt conversation with people she didn't know and couldn't understand?

So she had very little basis for comparison, and absolutely no expectations of what the damned thing should be like, and still she felt wildly disappointed by the entire event.

It was short, at least she could give it that. From the time they appeared in the hallway outside the room where Kaiyo had learned her fate, to the time that they stood before the shrine and her father, acting in the role of priest—an honor she hadn't known he was able to claim, but which no one else seemed to object to—passed them the ceremonial cups of sake, had been less time than it had taken the sun to set.

Which is why they were all bathed in a pinkish golden light when Kuzuri-san invoked Tsukuyomi the moon spirit's blessing and brought an awkward silence down on the already strange affair.

Kaiyo blinked. Of course, she and Tanaka both understood the importance of Tsukuyomi to her father and the Kaigun. Their sailors prayed to the Kami who controlled the tides more than any other, but the Landers considered Tsukuyomi an ill omen, and certainly not a Kami one should call on to bless their favored child's wedding. Kaiyo scanned the crowd quickly, slightly horrified at her father's faux pas, since the entire point of this charade was to keep the Landers from spreading more rumors about their family, and she saw every face in the crowd making vain attempts to mask their shock and confusion. One face stood out for looking terribly pleased, eyes so alight with… something… that Kaiyo honestly thought they were glowing for a moment. The face, of course, belonged to the disturbing, finely dressed man at the back of the crowd.

Kuzuri-san cleared his throat and continued the ceremony, adding a few of the more traditional Kami to his blessing, and calling her attention back to the surreal task of marrying her second in command.

When it was all done, their offerings made, their sake consumed, their blessings toasted among the guests, and their rings exchanged—they'd recited the barest of vows they could reasonably memorize on short notice—Kaiyo and Tanaka walked slowly away from the shrine, arm in arm, with guests exuberantly escorting them back to the Saito estate. Kaiyo's mind had already turned toward the Wind Serpent and her crew, her feet wishing to turn her down the hill towards the harbor, but the crowd bore her and Tanaka unerringly toward her family's largest receiving room.

Kaiyo was so lost in thoughts of where she would rather be that she almost jumped when Tanaka squeezed her hand gently and whispered in her ear, "Which guest should I offend first, if we want your mother to send us on our way as quickly as possible?"

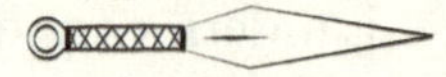

Kaiyo stood in her cabin, ignoring the soft sounds of harbor water against the hull of the Wind Serpent, staring with unfocused eyes at the distant ship lights visible through the galley windows, flipping her hanko between her knuckles and wondering if the unsettled feeling that she couldn't seem to shake—even after changing back into her ship's clothes, returning all her knives to their proper place, and washing away the powders and creams her mother had applied to her face—was from sake, the lingering sense of dread she always felt when she had to socialize with more than a single person at a time, or disappointment.

It shouldn't be the latter. There was nothing to be disappointed about.

She had never wanted to be married, so she didn't think it was possible to be disappointed about how it had happened. And disappointment was entirely the wrong word to encompass how she felt about being forced to marry for a duty she had not yet inherited. So, why did disappointment feel like the right word for what she was feeling?

It had nothing to do with Tanaka bidding her goodnight on the main deck so that she could retire to her cabin and him to his. It couldn't have anything to do with that, because she had no wish to engage in the usual activities that followed a wedding ceremony. She was fairly certain of that, and yet there was something that had felt wrong about letting Tanaka go to his cabin alone. Not wrong enough that she'd been willing to turn and follow him belowdecks, or invite him to the captain's quarters, but she suspected it was the cause of this discomfort all the same.

They were tied to each other now, after all. Was it wrong that she might at least want a few moments alone with him, if only to see how he was faring, after all of that?

Her thoughts were interrupted by a light knock on the door, and for a moment, Kaiyo's chest warmed with an emotion she was completely unwilling to name, before she took a deep breath and put one hand on her dagger. She crossed to the door just as it began to slide back on its own, and that fact was the first sign that made her certain it was not Tanaka who had knocked.

By the time the door had slid wide enough to grant a person entry, Kaiyo's dagger was fully drawn and pressed gently against the neck of the person who stood there.

Kaiyo's mind flashed through a series of memories until she placed the man before her, who smelled faintly of moss and autumn leaves, as a person she had seen before.

"Doshigatai," she spat, pressing the dagger more firmly against his throat.

"So your people have labeled me," replied a voice, higher and more musical than Kaiyo would have expected given the doshigatai's height. Kaiyo was of a height with most men in the Kaigun, but this one stood half a head taller than she. The man's face was narrow and long, with wide eyes of a glittering blue one rarely saw on the mainland. His hair was long and black, pulled into a slender tail behind his neck.

"But I would not call myself irredeemable by choice," the man continued, heedless of the blade at his throat.

"Why are you here? By rights I could kill you just for being out of your bonds."

She knew that her orders where the doshigatai were concerned had changed, but she didn't think that they had been made aware of that fact yet, and regardless, her father had made it clear that she was free to do whatever was needed to bring the criminals in line.

The doshigatai nodded, a careful move of the chin that managed not to open the skin pressed against the blade.

"Indeed, you could. I am here, believe it or not, because the other vermin I've been housed with have also broken their bonds, and I believe they mean you and your crew harm."

Kaiyo felt her eyes narrow and her mouth harden into a flat line.

"And what could you possibly stand to gain by warning me of this?"

"May I come in?"

"Give me a good reason not to kill you where you stand, first. Blood stains are easier to cover up on the main deck."

The man's next words all came out in a quick but steady stream of hushed whispers.

"I believe you have some use planned for us, or you would not have removed us from our dungeon. I assume the primary reason you've pulled a collection of doshigatai from their fates is because you expect most or all of us to die. I further suspect that the plan may require killing all of us in the end, even if we're offered our freedom in return for our services. I would like to bargain for my *actual* freedom in exchange for keeping the rest of these miscreants from killing you."

"And what makes you think I need any help from you in staying alive?"

"They are mere moments away from starting a fire in the belly of the ship in order to serve as a distraction that will lure you and your crew into an ambush."

Kaiyo swallowed, quickly calculating her options, and stepped back to let the man into her cabin.

3日 6月, 新議 8年

⇒ *Kaiyo* ⇐

KAIYO AND TANAKA pressed their backs to some of the larger barrels and took a moment to assess the smell of smoke that was quickly overtaking the scent of damp wood that usually pervaded the hold. Kaiyo took yet another moment to assess the angry whispers that reflected oddly around the full barrels of water and sake that lined the hold all around them.

She was tempted to pull the wet strip of cloth she had tied over her mouth and nose down far enough to berate Tanaka for making so much noise every time he moved, but she shook her head and reminded herself that it wasn't *his* fault he'd never been trained by Fubuki-san. Besides, she had much bigger problems to concern herself with.

Such as how close the smoke was to some of the sake barrels, despite her informant's insistence that the men were trying to create a diversion rather than kill everyone aboard, including themselves.

The doshigatai who had come to her had also insisted there wasn't much time, and on that front, he appeared to be correct. Either his comrades were all illiterate, unlikely since many of them had grown up in the Kaigun and the Kaigun made a point of educating all of its sailors, or else they were intentionally trying to burn the Wind Serpent to the waterline.

She ran her fingers over the hilts of the throwing knives in her bracers for a moment to help ease the growing tension in her shoulders. She had to time this just right, or they would all die.

Simple really. Succeed or perish. How many of her days came down to that very choice?

She wished that she didn't need to keep any of these men alive for the mission her father had given her. If she could just kill them all and be done with it, then…

Deep breath in, deep breath out.

She needed them alive whether she liked it or not, but first, she needed her crew alive. Thankfully, the raiko were bunked close enough to the stern galley that dropping from her windows down to theirs had been simple enough, since an early summer breeze in the harbor invited open hatches wherever they could safely be left. She had slipped in between her raikos' hammocks easily until she had found Hiroshi and gently shaken him awake. Tanaka had gone to rouse Suzuki, who had stubbornly insisted on remaining aboard the Wind Serpent despite the chance to remain on Kaigunjima when they'd offloaded the survivors from the hundred-gunner. When Kaiyo had asked her why, she had replied matter-of-factly, "Tanaka-san is the best healer in the Kaigun, and he'll be here with you. Besides, they'll take weeks to fit me up with prosthetics, and I can be useful to you now."

Kaiyo hadn't known just how truly the petite stormcaller had spoken until the doshigatai had laid out his companion's plans before her, but Tanaka had confirmed she was healed enough to assist with their plan, and Kaiyo was willing to use every advantage to keep her crew safe, and the doshigatai pliable.

There had been no time to try to evacuate the ship in case everything went wrong—there was no way to do it silently enough without alerting the doshigatai that they'd been found out—so they had simply moved as quickly as they could with the players they needed and now they would hope for the best. If the doshigatai who had come to her betrayed them…

Kaiyo shrugged the thought away. It was too late for that—she'd made a decision for her entire crew the moment she'd allowed the man to live and step past her cabin door. That was what captains did, much though she might hate it, and they would all be condemned or saved by little more than her intuition.

Kaiyo spat into the darkness between two barrels and stepped forward into the erratic light of the torches—*kuso! What kind of fools lit* torches *instead of weather lamps in a hold filled with sake and gunpowder?*—that the doshigatai held around the small fire they were attempting to corral near one of the barrels, a sake barrel, Kaiyo noted with a flush of panic.

"I wouldn't do that if I were you," she said, raising both of her hands to show they were empty as she stepped further into the light.

"Stay where you are!" one of the men screamed, brandishing a torch at her as if *she* were the highly flammable substance that would kill them all, instead of the barrel they were trying to set aflame as a "distraction."

"You do realize if the sake lights it will in turn light the gunpowder down the aisle there and kill us all, don't you?"

She gestured slowly with her chin in the direction of the barrels on the far end of the hold.

"There's water barrels between," said a short muscular man who stood directly behind the man absorbed with the small fire at his feet. "You'll have time to put it out," he sneered.

"You've clearly never seen wood and sake burning together, have you? The hold itself will catch, the water barrels won't be enough to stop it, and the entire ship will explode like midwinter fire flower. It's not too late. You can still put it out and return to your berth peacefully. I won't report it to the Admiral, and he may still grant you your freedom at the end of all this."

The man holding the torch and the man standing behind the fire lighter both spat, telling her how much they thought of her father's offer of freedom. She hated that they were right, but she knew she wouldn't choose any differently than her father had.

"Fine. Have it your way. Hiroshi-san?"

Hiroshi stepped into the light then, already raising his hands in the stance he normally took to call on wind and water, but there were a dozen men arranged around the fire starter and they had clearly anticipated a kisōshi attack. A man in the outer circle brought his own hands up before Hiroshi had even finished stepping forward, a gust of wind knocking Hiroshi back against the barrels that lined the far side of the hold. Kaiyo charged the man, hoping to distract him from a follow-up attack that might kill one of her strongest raiko, and she had one of her small daggers in her hand launching at his shoulder before she even noticed the drop in pressure that signaled what was coming. She saw the man who had attacked Hiroshi turn to her, his face a snarl of anger and pain, and then she felt her vision dim and dropped to the damp wooden floor as the world went black around her.

She awoke to Tanaka's hands pressed gently against her temples. The smell of smoke was weaker than it had been, but she did not like that she could still smell it at all. As her field of vision widened, she looked around and was relieved to see that most of the people before her were unconscious.

"You were only out a few moments, Captain," Tanaka explained. "But I thought it best if we put the fire out before we did anything else."

Kaiyo nodded, pleased that the motion didn't hurt. It was one of the benefits of being knocked out by a sudden pressure drop instead of drugs, or even a kisōshi's touch. Tanaka stood then, and offered her the five small blades he'd given her a few hours ago. She took them as she rolled to her feet, trying to determine why all five had left their sheaths. She didn't remember throwing all of them.

"I can't treat you if they're touching your skin," Tanaka whispered, as he made a show of checking her pulse once more.

Kaiyo didn't understand that statement, but as soon as she turned around, she realized now was not the time to ask about it.

Behind her, Suzuki was still held in the arms of the tall doshigatai who had come to warn her, and the rest of the doshigatai were slumbering on the wooden planks of the hold.

Then she turned back towards Tanaka and opened her mouth to ask about Hiroshi, but saw that her second was already by the young raiko's side, one hand on the man's forehead and the other on his wrist.

"Well, it looks like we wound up needing that double diversion after all," she said, to no one in particular.

She heard Suzuki laugh.

"Glad you were clever enough to think of it, Captain."

Kaiyo shook off the compliment.

"I'm very lucky that you are strong enough for this, Suzuki-san, and stubborn enough to stay with me when you should be looking after your own health."

Suzuki opened her mouth to argue, but Kaiyo raised a hand.

"Of course you are better aware of your abilities than I am, I only meant I hope you won't let me take advantage of them when you need to be healing."

Suzuki's frown did not lessen.

"Captain, I'm healed, thanks to Tanaka's ministrations. If I had enough of my legs to walk on it might be different, as he would have had to heal bone and tissues that had been destroyed, and even with his skills it would take time to get my strength back, but…. The legs are gone, and I know I'll get some very fine prosthetics once we're back on Kaigunjima. In the meantime, I AM healed. Tanaka made clean cuts at the knee and healed me right up. I can still use my kisō to help you, and I would much rather do that than lie around waiting to be fitted up with re-placement legs."

Kaiyo dipped her chin in acknowledgment, but couldn't let go of one last thought.

"You are clearly more than capable, and I won't relieve you of any duty you do not ask to be relieved of. But Suzuki-san, please keep in mind that not all healing is physical. You've lost something. You aren't any less for it, but it is a thing that may need mourning."

She turned then, after getting a curt nod from her strongest raiko, and took two strides towards Tanaka before turning back.

"Doshigatai, you did not betray us. You have my gratitude for your help. May I ask your name?"

Kaiyo had intentionally refused to ask for it before, half-convinced she would need to kill this man to save her crew and unwilling to know any more about him than she had to.

"My name is Lyt, Captain."

Kaiyo nodded.

"My thanks, Lyt."

She cleared her throat.

"Suzuki-san, see to it that he has a bunk assigned to him in the regular crew quarters. Perhaps near you and Hiroshi-san. I've a suspicion some of his fellows may try to exact revenge before we reach land."

"Not a he, Captain," Lyt said as she turned to go.

"What?" Kaiyo asked, unsure if she'd heard correctly.

"I'm not a he, as you keep referring to me. Xe and xir, if you please."

Kaiyo blinked, understanding coming slowly. Then her cheeks reddened with embarrassment.

"I'm sorry, Lyt. I'll get it right from now on."

Lyt nodded, a small smile on xir face, and Kaiyo turned and went to consult with Tanaka about Hiroshi's health, even though she could see from where she stood that the young man was beginning to blink himself awake and answer Tanaka's questions.

Once he was well enough to stand, she sent Hiroshi to fetch a crew that could be trusted to round up the doshigatai lying unconscious in the hold, bind their wrists and ankles, and carry them up to the newly reinforced cell that had been sectioned off from the main crew quarters.

It was only when she was once again standing alone in her cabin that she thought of Lyt, and xir strange height, and the fact that xe had honestly come to her aid. It was only when she was flipping idly through the doshigatai files with one hand and running her hanko through her fingers in the other that her eyes caught on the written form of Lyt's name. Right next to the crime that had gotten xir sentenced to the doshigatai prisons.

Blood mage.

"Kuso," Kaiyo muttered, jabbing the tiny blade through the page into the table.

Kaiyo woke with the sun that morning even though it meant only a single watch's sleep for the day. As soon as the doshigatai had been secured, she had woken a full watch to get the ship out of harbor and under sail long before first light.

She dressed quickly, hurrying out of her cabin intent on reaching the stern deck before Tanaka. She failed. He was already standing at the rail when she came up the ladder, so she gave him no greeting as she began the slower part of her morning routine. She needed to be alone with her thoughts, which was why she had hoped to beat him here. Just a few moments of moving her body without anyone else intruding on her space before she had to make any more decisions that affected the lives of everyone aboard.

She hadn't told anyone about Lyt. Kaiyo's gut turned at the mere thought of it. Xe had unquestionably saved them all from a horrible death. Xe had made a very compelling case for being allowed xir freedom when this was all over, and Kaiyo had allowed xir to mingle with her regular crew, the three hundred lives that depended on her good judgment. Yet her good judgment had allowed her to trust a blood mage. Could she be under some kind of compulsion? Is that why xe had seemed reasonable and trustworthy? Had the entire incident with the doshigatai been some kind of elaborate scheme by the blood mage to help xir escape? But that was ridiculous. Xe had been helping the watch on duty raise the sails just before Kaiyo had retired to her quarters. If xe had put some kind of compulsion on Kaiyo, xe would surely have used it for something more nefarious than being allowed to stretch xir legs and help her crew.

She was more than halfway through her entire routine when she realized Tanaka hadn't said a word to her since she'd arrived. In fact, he was so quiet that she had to turn towards the rail to be certain he hadn't left. She almost tripped over her own legs when she pulled a kick short to get a good look at him. He was leaned against the rail, half-turned to her so he could balance a small journal on the rail with one hand, making quick strokes with a charcoal stick in the other.

"Are you drawing, Tanaka-san?" she asked, trying to keep the surprise out of her voice.

Tanaka made a small grunt that she took for assent while making a few more quick strokes with the charcoal before snapping the journal shut and looking at her.

"You seemed like you needed some time with your thoughts," he replied, slipping the slim volume into his uwagi. She forgot, sometimes, that he was a kisōshi. Ridiculous, considering how powerful a healer he was, but he rarely dressed in the traditional hakama and uwagi that marked him as such, and almost never wore the swords that went with his rank. He wore them now. How had she not noticed when she'd first stepped onto the stern deck?

"You're looking formal," she said, gesturing with her chin in the general direction of his person. She decided not to thank him for recognizing her need to think, nor to comment on how easily he read her moods. She wasn't even sure what to say.

"I felt perhaps we should remind the doshigatai that they are outnumbered and overpowered. I've asked all our kisōshi to dress their rank today."

Kaiyo said nothing for a moment. She'd been asleep, and it was within Tanaka's purview as second to make such an order. After a moment she nodded. It couldn't hurt for them to see just how many members of her crew could call on kisō whenever needed. It was strange to think of needing to intimidate anyone who understood what the uwagi and hakama of a kisōhi represented. Their enemy had always been external, people who knew nothing of Gensokan culture, of kisōshi, of raiko. Perhaps the reminder would help. She shrugged the question away and decided to tell Tanaka the truth.

"Lyt is the blood mage," she said, as she stepped forward to face the sea next to Tanaka. The wind whipped the words away from her, away from the ship, fast enough that Tanaka would be the only one to hear them. She didn't wish to cause a panic.

"Ah, yes, I put that together when xe mentioned xe wasn't a man," Tanaka admitted.

Kaiyo turned to Tanaka and grabbed the collar of his uwagi before she even had time to think.

"You WHAT?!?"

"The blood mage was the only doshigatai with pronouns listed as xe/xir," Tanaka explained. "You would have known too if you'd had time to read the full file, but if you'll recall we had to stop a brawl not long after I handed xir papers to you."

"Why didn't you tell me this before I let xir loose on my unsuspecting crew?"

Now Tanaka's eyebrows rose to meet his hairline and he looked at her with an expression that suggested she had said something in a language he did not speak.

"Xe helped us. Xe could have let us die, or xe could have betrayed us to the doshigatai, or xe could have simply escaped last night when we were trying to save our people. Xe did not. I have no objection with xir bunking with our crew, and I'm not at all sure I understand why you seem to."

Kaiyo felt like she'd been slapped. This, this was the unfiltered commentary that had gotten Tanaka pushed out of every other crew he'd been placed on until he'd landed in hers. It was also the reason she'd wanted him to stay.

"What do you know of blood mages that I don't?" she asked, confusion quickly replacing her anger. Tanaka never contradicted her without good reason. *That* was why she'd promoted him to her second instead of shipping him off like an errant dog. He sometimes spoke before he thought of the consequences to himself, but he never spoke without *thinking.*

"Nothing, Captain. I *know* nothing of blood mages. I have heard many rumors. I have heard our gaijin friends curse their kind in low breaths, and touch talismans at their mere mention. But I've never met one, and I've never even read a reliable account of one. So far, the only blood mage I've ever encountered in real life is Lyt, and so far, xe has acted only as our most loyal crew members might."

Kaiyo felt her stomach turn. She'd heard ill-talk of blood mages since she was a small child. Any sailor in the Kaigun enjoyed a good tale, and the tales her father's crews had told her every time she had sailed with them had always been the wildest and most dramatic they could think of. They were like the stories of the kapas she heard on the mainland, or of the youkai, and the Kami themselves.

She sighed. She'd been thinking of blood mages like the monsters in fairytales her whole life, but this was no fairytale, and Lyt had so far done nothing to warrant her suspicion. She would keep an eye on xir. Xe was still a stranger, and xe had been condemned by Kaiyo's justice system for *some* reason. She couldn't imagine the Kaigun protectorate putting someone in the doshigatai dungeons for nothing. But the Kaigun had always believed in rehabilitation, and maybe the judges had made a mistake in Lyt's case.

She would watch xir closely and make her own judgments.

"Don't look so smug," she said, when she turned back to Tanaka and saw him grinning. "Just because you're right doesn't mean I can't kill you in your sleep."

Tanaka laughed.

"I can think of worse ways to die," he said, winking at her just as he turned and slid down the ladder to the main deck.

Kaiyo's feet would not carry her forward for a moment. She was rooted in place.

Had Tanaka just… flirted with her?

She swallowed.

Well, and why shouldn't he? They were married. Kami help her, she'd almost forgotten. They were married, and she half suspected she'd just been invited to Tanaka's bed.

She stayed on the stern deck under the guise of finishing her morning routine until she felt the heat leave her neck. Kami help her, what was she going to do?

5日 6月, 新議 8年

5th Day, 6th Moon, Cycle 8 of the New Council

⚞ *Kaiyo* ⚟

TWO DAYS LATER, Kaiyo had forgotten entirely about Tanaka's flirtation. First, her attention had been consumed with getting the Wind Serpent and its crew to Sakata as quickly and safely as the sea would allow, and then on getting the Kami-forsaken doshi-gatai to do her bidding once they'd reached land.

It was the latter part that she was struggling with.

She closed her eyes, letting the sway of the horse beneath her and the sound of dozens of horse hooves clipping the dirt road wash over her for a moment, and took a deep breath. Then immediately wished she hadn't. Her nostrils filled with the smell of hot horses, dust, and men who hadn't bathed in over a moon, and she coughed, her eyes shooting open as she did her best not to gag. She recovered quickly enough, glad that she was riding at the front of their column of horses with nothing but empty road ahead of her and over a dozen men behind her. It was unlikely anyone had noticed.

Her eyes refocused on the woods that lined the road and her mind returned to the problem of the men behind her.

With two more days of steady riding, they would reach the woods that their quarry called home. It should not be a complicated mission. Ride as fast as they could without damaging the horses, avoid drawing any attention on the way there, scout out the target, collect the scribe, and then do it all again in reverse. It should have been simple; with her own crew, it would have been. Instead, she had a band of criminals so vile even the Kaigun justice system had given up on them, and only her healer—and a blood mage she couldn't possibly trust—for backup.

She reminded herself, as the dappled light from the forest to either side of the road played across her vision, that her father had known the charges against every one of these men and had still believed she could accomplish this task with them alone. He hadn't sent her here to die by betrayal, which meant that there *had* to be a way to make this work.

That didn't mean her own mistakes wouldn't get her killed, though. Her father trusted her to be competent.

That morning, as they had left the Wind Serpent behind and gathered horses from one of the Saito family hostlers that had stations in every port in Gensokai, she had been surprised the doshigatai hadn't just ridden off into the distance the moment they'd mounted up. She hadn't thought her little speech reminding them of how Admiral Saito would hunt them down if they betrayed her had helped. Even when she had also reminded them that the Admiral had promised them freedom if they carried out their duties to her satisfaction, even when they had all sworn their loyalty in exchange for possession of the weapons they had claimed on the night they'd been escorted to her ship, they had seemed merely bored.

By the time she was done speaking, she had assumed she would have to track them down and kill them all one by one after they decided to escape. It would be tedious, and it would probably mean failure of the entire mission, or worse, it would mean she'd have to endanger her own crew. The Admiral would be furious, and she'd risk her inheritance. At least this time it would be her own fault. She could do nothing to control the rumors the Landers spread. Keeping the doshigatai from abandoning her, though—that was technically within her power. If she could sort out what needed to be done.

Her first thought had been a show of power, but she had already killed one of them with her bare hands and it had done little to discourage them. She'd outsmarted them when they'd tried to burn her ship to the waterline, but that hadn't garnered any respect from them either.

She sighed. She had a feeling this whole thing was going to get ugly before she was going to succeed at commanding these men. They were not lured by the promise of freedom her father offered, and perhaps he had truly believed they would be, and that was why she would fail. But either they suspected the Admiral would renege, or else they could sense the ensuing danger of this mission and did not truly believe they would survive if they remained.

Of course, now that Kaiyo had read the scroll her father had given her with the details that were known about the scribe and her protection… she couldn't blame them for their concern. Indeed, likely though they were to put a blade in her back at the first opportunity, she was glad to have as many doshigatai with her as she did, even if she mostly wanted them as fodder for whatever was behind the legends of Sōryū forest. Kaiyo shivered just thinking of the accounts she'd read about what waited for them there.

She had only reluctantly shared that scroll with Tanaka the night before they'd reached port, not because she didn't trust him, but because she was worried that he would try to talk her out of the mission once he'd read it.

He hadn't. He had only frowned and looked thoughtful for a long while once he'd finished. When he'd asked to be excused so that he could look something up, she'd had to swallow the invitation bubbling in her throat that he should bring his reference books to her cabin. Instead, she'd let him go and had ignored the strange twist to her stomach that accompanied his absence.

That had been the last time that she'd had a chance to moon over her second in command.

Now, her thoughts were focused on the road, on the potential threats that could come from the woods on either side, and on the threats that could come from the men who rode along with her.

There had to be some way to convince these men to follow her lead for the few days it would take to complete this task. But if the promise of their freedom would not ensure their loyalty, she wasn't certain what could.

As it happened, an opportunity presented around midday when they stopped again to water and feed the horses.

Kaiyo had been standing next to her own horse after checking its hooves, and considering joining Tanaka by the small creek where the men and horses were getting their water, and where her second in command had settled himself onto a large rock in order to take some shade while he went through his healing supplies.

She was just about to grab her water-skin and some dried squid and go join him when one of the doshigatai approached her.

The man was short and broad, and Kaiyo thought she recognized him as the man who had stood behind the fire lighter on the night of their attempted mutiny.

She didn't reach for her throwing knives as he approached, but she wanted to.

"Uto-san," she said to the man as he approached, with a slight nod of her head. She had reluctantly committed all of their names to memory, mostly so that she would remember whose talents lay where. Her father had insisted that these men would be of use to her. Uto, she recalled from the papers, had been an archer before he'd been caught forcing himself on new recruits in the Kaigunjima holding facilities between guard shifts.

The memory did not make it any easier not to reach for a blade.

The man smiled as he approached, bushy eyebrows raising as his face contorted in a gesture that Kaiyo was certain contained absolutely no warmth at all.

"Captain, can I speak with you for a moment? I have concerns."

Kaiyo glanced behind the man to where the other doshigatai were grazing their horses. Six of them were checking their horses' hooves still, two were filling waterskins, three were eating, one appeared to have gone into the woods to piss, and Lyt was nowhere in sight. Perhaps xe had also gone to relieve xirself. Kaiyo took all of that in during a fraction of a heartbeat, and also noted the handful of eyes that flicked her way when she looked at them. She desperately wanted to check behind herself, but she kept her shoulders square with her horse and resisted the temptation, keeping her ears on high alert instead.

"You can talk to me right here, Uto-san," she replied, matching the shorter man's false smile. "I would hate to have your men thinking I don't trust them."

She watched the man's face to see how he responded to the implied leadership, wondering if it would make him more or less hostile.

The man's voice dropped conspiratorially, and he leaned towards her.

"*I* don't particularly trust them, Captain," he whispered. "I think they mean you harm."

Kaiyo made a point of not leaning in to hear him, and instead glanced briefly at the men by the horses, even as the man before her shifted another step towards her.

"I'm sorry to hear that, Uto-san. What have they done to breach your trust?"

She remained standing upright, her arms crossed casually across her midsection, but now, as he hesitated with his response, she *did* drop her voice to match his.

"Did one of them steal that katana you took from my cabin?"

It was a guess. It could have been any of the men who had taken the strange katana, and she still hadn't searched their belongings to see who had possession of it. But either her guess hit its mark or else he was simply done pretending, because the man's false smile dropped away, and his hand shot forward from where it had been tucked behind his left hip. Kaiyo didn't need to see the glint of sunlight on metal to know that a dagger was making its way toward her throat.

Luckily, she had already been reaching for her throwing knives before he'd even moved. Uto was too close of a target for one of the small blades to do much good, but that was beside the point. She sidestepped the shorter man's lunge with his dagger and launched one of the two throwing knives at the man who she'd heard crunching through the woods beside her after circling around from where he'd been pretending to urinate earlier.

Etai, she thought his name was. Or had been. He now had a small dagger embedded in his eye deeply enough that she did not think he would be getting up from where he had fallen with his wakizashi in his hand.

Uto, whom she had sidestepped, had overcommitted to the move, perhaps convinced he had the element of surprise, or perhaps just inept with close combat, and she collapsed his right knee with a swift side kick from her left foot, even as she launched a second dagger at the man who had just begun to sneak up on her from behind. She had just spotted him over her left shoulder as she'd shifted her weight for the kick to Uto's leg.

Soka was his name, and he might get a chance to use it again, along with the fire kisō he was known to wield, as she'd only hit him in the shoulder with the small jade-handled knife that had been part of her wedding present. She was going to have to think of an appropriate gift for Tanaka to thank him. These small blades were far more accurate at a distance than her daggers. Their balance was truly superb.

She put her foot against Uto's neck, drew her full-sized dagger and another throwing knife, and turned to look at the men by the creek.

Half of them had weapons drawn, and two were on their knees in front of Lyt with pained expressions on their faces and weapons on the ground beside them. Lyt, for xir part, stood protectively between the men and Tanaka as if xe were a one-person barrier to her second in command. Kaiyo made a note to ask Tanaka what had happened, if they survived long enough for conversation.

"Anyone else?" she called loudly across the glade, throwing as much disdain as she could into her voice. "Etai is already dead by my hand. Uto-san here would be easy to dispatch, and Sokasan," she jerked her head in the direction of the wounded fire kisōshi, "will die if I don't give him an antidote to the poison on that blade."

She looked into the eyes of the men who had clearly planned to kill her here and leave her bones for the animals, "Do you really want to see how many of you I can kill before you give up? Or would you like for at least *some* of you to make it to freedom? There is no bounty on this mission, so having fewer comrades in arms will only increase your chances of dying, it won't gain you more riches."

She spat, disgusted that she should need to tell anyone who had once been Kaigun that they had no chance of profiting from the deaths of their traveling companions.

"All you have to do to earn your freedom is help me collect a scribe, a woman, by all accounts petite. She is, apparently, somewhat heavily guarded, but I've been assured that your collective talents are just the ones that I need. Admiral Saito selected each of you for a reason. Are you so desperate to die by my hand? Or are you too cowardly to face down a mere scribe in the woods?"

She spat again, pulled her foot off of Uto's neck, and turned to stalk into the woods. It wasn't that she thought it at all safe to leave the doshigatai unattended, or even to turn her back on them. Indeed, she expected at any moment one of them would charge her with a blade drawn and attempt to bury it in her back. But if she stood there looking at them a moment longer she was going to *try* to kill them all, even if it was suicide to do so, because the very idea of the crimes they had committed and the lies she was promising them combined to make her stomach roil.

She pushed into the woods at a furious pace, on the brink of running, but just barely restraining herself. The only reason she didn't tear into the woods as fast as her legs would allow was the thought that she would need to turn around in a moment in order to go back for Tanaka.

Not that he couldn't take care of himself, and he did seem to have Lyt on his side, but… she'd left wounded men behind and Tanaka would try to heal them even though they were lying, betraying sacks of horse dung, and that would leave him open to attack. So she stood next to a large tree, stared at the sky for a moment, and considered screaming, but didn't. Instead, she threw all of her daggers—save the two that were still embedded in her enemies—at a single knot in the large tree and took satisfaction in the solid thunk that each blade made as it sunk into the wood. Then she pulled them all out, replaced them in their sheaths, and returned to the creek, flipping her hanko idly between her knuckles as she walked.

When she returned to the clearing with the horses, she was shocked to find all the men still present. Tanaka was, as she had expected, treating the injured men, and no one made a move towards her as she went to grab the waterskin from her horse and fill it at the creek.

Her nerves were alight the entire time she squatted by the water with her back to half the men, but no one approached her. Except for the blood mage.

"Captain," Lyt said from xir full height, while she was still squatting on her heels. "Would you like me to return these men's weapons?"

Kaiyo thought about that for a moment. She had wondered what had happened between Lyt and the two men at xir feet earlier, but she decided that now was not a good time to question xir.

After all, xe was doing an excellent job of giving the impression that xe was loyal to Kaiyo and Tanaka alone, and that wasn't an impression Kaiyo cared to contradict when Lyt had just demonstrated xirself to be a formidable opponent.

"If you think they won't give me cause to kill them with them, then by all means. I trust your judgment, Lyt."

It was, of course, a lie, Kaiyo did not yet trust anything about the blood mage, but she recognized that this small show of rewarding Lyt's loyalty might go a long way towards convincing the rest of the Kami-cursed doshigatai that they might have their freedom if they did as they were ordered.

"Would you care to get an oath of loyalty from them first?" Lyt asked, casually, as if xe were inquiring as to whether or not the horses should be permitted to graze for another quarter watch before they moved on.

At that, Kaiyo looked up. She was very careful to control her expression, but she feared her eyes might have widened slightly at the sight of Lyt's long arms entirely filled with weapons. Xe hadn't just disarmed the two men xe had been keeping away from Tanaka; somehow, between when Kaiyo had stormed off into the woods and when she had returned, Lyt had disarmed the entire crew.

Kaiyo tilted her head to one side.

"That may be a good idea," she said, seeing an opportunity she should not waste.

She held her water-skin beneath the water for a few more breaths, then when it was full, she replaced the stopper and stood next to Lyt.

She cleared her throat and spoke loudly, intrigued to see that the men's gazes had already turned in her direction. The only one who ignored her was Tanaka, who was still hunched over

Soka and doing something to his shoulder. She didn't mind—he was busy, and he was also the only person here that she actually trusted. Besides, Soka's attention was trained on her, despite the healer's ministrations.

"You've twice now tried to escape the fate set for you by Admiral Saito."

Her voice rang across the clearing even though she barely raised it.

"To be honest, I can't blame you for wishing to be free of your punishment, cowards though that makes you. Of course, when you have committed so many crimes as to be deemed doshigatai, you would not wish to suffer the consequences. And I do not even blame you for doubting the Admiral's offer of freedom in exchange for your services. But let me remind you of what you stand to lose, since perhaps you consider that you've fallen too far from grace to lose anything more. Uto-san," and here she turned to look the short, broad man in the eyes and hold his gaze. "Your uncle owns a small farm here on the mainland. He believes you dead, of course, but you asked for all your remaining pay to be sent to his home when you were sentenced. He's alive and well, you should know, but I can't promise he'll remain so if you succeed in killing me and making your escape. Admiral Saito knows his location, and there are orders in place to raze the farm and kill all its occupants, down to the last mouse, should I fail to make even a single report."

She could see the pallor take Uto's face, and she cursed her father's thoroughness even as she praised his ingenuity. Her stomach turned at even the thought of the threats she was making, but she kept her face hardened and pressed on.

"Gatō-san," she said, turning to one of the men that Lyt had first disarmed. "Your grandmother is one of the best weavers in

Kaigunjima. It would be horrible if her entire loom works were to be destroyed, her livelihood gone up in smoke, simply because the grandson she's already publicly renounced, but whom she secretly still smuggles mochi to on his birthday, even in the dungeons of the doshigatai, had failed in his duty."

Gatō-san's face hollowed in a way that suggested she had effectively removed his heart. She felt ill. Why couldn't these vermin simply take their offer of freedom and follow orders? Why couldn't they have believed her when she made general threats about the Admiral destroying everything that they held dear if they betrayed her? Why did she have to spell out the details of these threats on innocent lives in order to get them to comply?

But her father's information was good, and as she turned to every one of these men and revealed their secrets, she could see something inside of them crumple. None of this was good, but it was, sadly, necessary. When she'd made it through to the last of them, the only one left was Lyt, but Lyt was the only doshigatai her father had found no connections for, no remaining loved ones, no hidden valuables, no former comrades in arms, nothing. The only information she had for Lyt was what had already proven to be a sufficient lure, a true offer of freedom. She gave Lyt a significant look, and tilted her head to one side, hoping that the rest of the doshigatai would take this as a conversation they'd already had. In a way, she supposed it was.

"You risk far more by attempting escape than you do by following orders. Obey me, and, yes, you may die fighting our opponents. But, should you survive, you will have a chance at freedom, and the assurance that those you still care about will be looked after."

That last part at least was true. Admiral Saito's last encrypted message, tucked into the scroll she'd been given explaining their quarry's location and defenses—which she'd immediately burned after she'd read it—had made it clear that, just as the doshigatai's betrayal would ensure their loved ones' demise, so their loyalty would grant them the Kaigun's protection for the rest of their days. It was only the truth of that promise that kept her stomach from rebelling entirely at the lies that preceded it.

"So, you have a choice before you. Promise to follow my orders from now until we return to Kaigunjima and be rewarded accordingly, or attempt to flee like a coward, die like a coward, and lose everything like a coward."

She didn't think it was much of a choice, really, but she wanted them all to fully understand what their betrayal would cost them.

Uto was the first to bow—not deeply, not from the ground as he probably should have, but she didn't expect these men to act like true Kisōshi even though some of them had been trained as such.

"I'm not a gambling man," he grumbled, a statement that Kaiyo found strange from a man who had risked blowing up a ship he was still standing on. "But even I know terrible odds when I hear them. You have my bow, if you'll give it back to me."

Kaiyo nodded to Lyt, who handed an unstrung longbow that Kaiyo had noticed sticking out of Uto's saddlebags earlier. She wondered briefly why the man hadn't simply hidden in the woods and shot her from there when he'd been trying to kill her. Even the folio her father had given her claimed the man was an excellent shot. Perhaps the doshigatai's plans of escape hadn't been that well devised this time around.

Uto's acceptance of the terms seemed to tip the entire crew into compliance. One by one, they all bowed to some degree and reclaimed their weapons. Of course, she didn't take it as any sort of sign that she could trust them, and she knew that arming them was a risk, but they were headed into a forest that had more than one legend told about it, and none of the legends claimed it was a healthful resting place for bandits.

As the last man—Kentaro, she thought his name was—took his weapon, she recognized the blue scabbard of the katana that had been stolen from her cabin, but said nothing. She had guessed that Uto had stolen the blade from her cabin, but it seemed she'd also guessed correctly that one of the other men had in turn stolen it from him. The lack of honor among these particular thieves was almost entertaining enough to be worth not interfering on its own, and now wasn't the time to bring up more of their treachery anyway. Besides, she didn't want to carry the Kami-cursed blade herself for the rest of their journey, which would be her only choice if she confiscated it from him now.

Instead of speaking, she spat again, thinking of how she shouldn't have to worry if a place was safe for bandits or not. She was an officer of the Kaigun, loyal captain of the Wind Serpent, faithful daughter of Admiral Saito... and she was absolutely headed into Sōryū forest in order to abduct a scribe from her lawful home with the help of a band of the worst criminals she'd ever met.

She sighed and turned towards the horses.

"Let's get moving," she said, unable to meet Tanaka's eyes even though he'd stood and looked to be walking towards her. "Delaying won't make this mission any easier."

7日 6月, 新議 8年

7th Day, 6th Moon, Cycle 8 of the New Council

⇒ Torako ⇐

TORAKO WATCHED ITACHI jump with both feet into the swiftly moving creek, feeling the cold flecks hit her skin with something between irritation and joy. As the dappled sun trickled past the forest canopy and warmed her skin, a voice in her mind suggested that hopping in with both feet was the correct choice, because it would be fun, and it would be cool, and the sun was only going to get hotter as the day wore on. Another voice suggested that *she* was not three cycles old, and that while she was happy to let Itachi play in the creek, Torako was an adult, and technically she was at work.

"You know, Itachi-chan, the only reason your mother lets me bring you on these patrols with me is so that I can teach you how to move through and live in the woods on your own. If you don't even try to learn how to hide your tracks in a creek, she may tell me I have to leave you behind next time."

There, that was what an adult should say, wasn't it?

Itachi turned her green eyes to her and smiled. Then she sent a jet of water squirting straight at Torako's face.

Torako dodged the unnatural stream, barely, and laughed.

"Oh, now you've done it," she called, abandoning the rock she'd been standing on to jump into the cold creek with both feet, even as she bent over to scoop water with her hands and launch it at her daughter.

The wave flew through the air with a precision she was proud of, then split in two to pass harmlessly to either side of Itachi's head.

"This," Torako observed, "is not a fair fight."

And Itachi's giggle was the only warning she had before glancing up to see a giant bubble of water hovering over her. It burst the moment she looked at it.

She spent a few moments coughing and spluttering before she collapsed into a pile of laughter on the mossy bank of the creek.

"Itachi-chan, you are going to have to dry us off. I refuse to hike in wet boots all day."

"Yes, Mama, I promise."

Torako was still smiling when she opened her eyes and turned to look upstream to where Itachi still stood in the middle of the creek, creating a series of water globes like the one that had soaked Torako a moment ago, only smaller. She was making them dance.

Her mind skipped back to a conversation she'd had with Taka-san one moon earlier.

"She'll need more training. Yanagi-sama is powerful and an excellent teacher, but he won't teach her how to fight. She's interested in more than just healing, you know, and you'll only be able to teach her how to wield a sword."

Torako had brushed away the reminder that she wasn't a true Kisōshi and focused instead on the rest of her friend's message.

"You think she needs to go to that school?"

"That school, as you call it, is the passion project of your own mother, and the primary reason we are no longer under the thumb of the Rōjū. My best friend grew up there and learned everything she knows there, so yes. I think she would benefit from Kuma Academy."

Torako blinked in the sunlight and pushed the memory away. It wasn't that she didn't understand the logical merit of the argument—she did. It was just that she had no interest in sending her daughter away from her. Curse it all, she got choked up when she went on patrol and left Itachi with Raku for a tenday. She wasn't about to send her off to study for ten cycles without her parents.

Of course, Taka'd had an answer to that objection too, hadn't she? *"You could go with her, you know—both of you."* But that was another suggestion that Torako was unwilling to entertain. Just because there weren't as many bandit attacks in the valley as there used to be since the fall of the Rōjū didn't mean that she could leave Sōryū Valley without protection. The fall of the Rōjū had done many things to help Gensokans of all kinds, but it still hadn't awarded Kisōshi protection to the areas where no Kisōshi showed an interest in living. This was her Valley, damn it, and she wasn't about to abandon it just because her daughter was shaping up to be one of the most powerful Kisōshi any of her very powerful friends had seen.

"Mama?"

Torako snapped out of her reverie at the sound of Itachi's quiet voice. She was half-convinced that she was about to get another water globe to the face, but when she looked over to where Itachi stood, the girl had dropped all of the globes back into the creek and was focused on something on the bank instead.

"What's that?" Itachi asked, pointing at the mossy bank.

Torako stood and went to inspect the thing that Itachi pointed to.

Not a thing, she realized, as she reached the spot the child had indicated. An impression.

Indeed, there was a sharp slash in the moss that covered the rest of the bank, the mud and rock beneath it exposed in stark contrast to the surrounding green.

"That, Itachi-chan," Torako said, reaching for her wakizashi without even thinking about it as she looked around the woods that surrounded them, "is a boot print."

And as she looked around the banks nearby, she saw signs that made the hair on the back of her neck rise and sent her clambering back to the place where she'd left her walking staff.

"What is it, Mama?" Itachi asked, even as Torako ushered her into the wrap that allowed her to ride comfortably against her back, her small face looking over her shoulder at the forest before them.

"Strangers," Torako said, not yet certain that there was anything to be worried about, but feeling in her gut that she ought to be worried anyway. "Half a dozen strangers wandering our valley."

Then she and Itachi fell into silence as she followed the tracks of men she didn't know leading off into the woods that she called home.

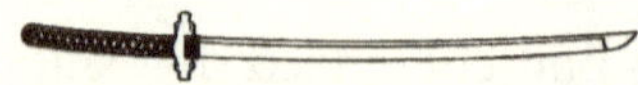

Torako had only half expected the trail to lead to actual bandits. The sun was low enough in the sky that the sunlight through the trees was dramatic, lighting some things and leaving the rest in shadow. She'd ignored her usual loop in order to track these men, and now she crouched in the shadow of a large boulder that she'd taken cover behind when the incautious tracks of six men had abruptly led her to voices much closer than she would have liked. If she'd been paying closer attention, she might have recognized the rise above her as a likely place for the men to make camp, giving themselves the high ground against any potential opponents. Instead, she'd practically blundered on top of them because she'd been trying to figure out how to answer Itachi's shower of questions about where baby deer came from without including some of the more horrifying details. By the time she'd realized they were so close to the strangers, the only option had been to dash behind these boulders and hope the men hadn't set an observant watch. It seemed they hadn't.

"Where'd that Kami-cursed tracker run off to anyway? Shouldn't xe be back by now?"

"Said xe'd go until the trail ran cold, or night came. I'm starting a fire and roasting these hares."

Murmurs of agreement all around made their way to Torako's boulder as the men searched through packs and gathered wood from nearby deadfall.

"Mama?" Itachi whispered beside her.

Torako turned to her daughter, eyes blazing. Itachi knew not to speak when she'd been told to hide. They were not far enough from these men for them to get away with even a whisper.

Itachi gestured to the woods, made the sign for tree, and the sign for looking.

Torako took a quiet breath and ducked behind the boulder next to her daughter.

She took in the forest behind them, dappled in afternoon sunlight, and looked for the familiar face of Yanagi-sama in the woods. She found no such thing.

She shook her head, and Itachi bit her lip and looked back to the woods herself. She was making the sign for tree again, pulling on Torako's sleeve, when Torako heard a twig snap on the other side of the boulder.

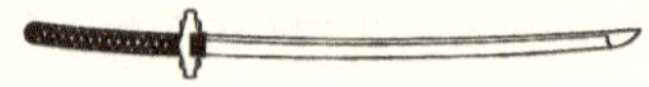

"Kuso," she whispered as she stood up, bringing her staff with her. She made a silent gesture with her right hand that would tell Itachi to stay hidden no matter what—if the girl was paying attention and not looking for trees with eyes, that is.

On the other side of the boulder stood a man preparing to piss.

Torako smiled and raised the hand that wasn't holding her staff.

"Lovely weather, isn't it?" she said, looking at the sky and giving the man a moment to stow his more vulnerable body parts.

The man, clearly too stunned for speech, grunted and reached for the dagger on his belt as soon as he'd put himself away.

"I'm not here to fight," she protested. "Just wondering what six men are doing in these woods so far from any signs of civilization."

But the man didn't reply, just drew the dagger from its sheath. Which his five friends clearly took as a sign that there would be no conversation, because she heard more steel on leather beyond the first man, and a quick glance told her that the men who had been seated on a few fallen logs around a softly crackling fire were now standing and arming themselves.

"We don't have to do this," Torako tried again. "You could all still walk away from this. I just want to make sure that you're not here to cause trouble for—"

But then the man standing in front of her shifted his gaze to something over Torako's shoulder, and he raised his dagger in preparation for a throw.

Itachi!!! Torako's mind screamed. She moved before she could think.

One moment the man stood before her poised to throw a knife, the next he was falling lifeless to the ground as blood poured from his opened neck. She heard the thunk of metal hitting rock as his knife missed its mark.

Torako still held the base of her walking staff in her left hand, but her right now held the katana she'd pulled from it, still dripping the blood of the man who had tried to throw a dagger at her daughter.

From there everything was chaos.

The familiar tingle of a fire kisō calling flame to life brought her attention into the sharp focus of battle that made the rest of the world fall away. She dropped the staff sheath for her katana and rolled forward, her mind focused on bringing the attacks and attention away from the boulders that hid Itachi's small form. She had to trust that Itachi would hide properly. There was no room for anything else in the wild dance that Torako was now committed to.

The fire came at her in a steady stream, which she just barely stayed ahead of. She could hear the rustling of a wind kisōshi as well, but she focused on the fire, rolling twice more to bring herself right up under the kisōshi's legs. She reached out and grabbed his ankle briefly with her left hand, then slashed up with her blade in a single fluid move as her legs came up under her. The man died looking startled, as most kisōshi did after she got close enough to touch them.

She did not linger over the kill. She had more blades closing in on her now, and somewhere a wind kisōshi would be planning something sneaky. She turned from the dying fire kisōshi to block the running charge of a man who seemed like he'd never used a katana before. He hacked at her with wild downward strikes that would have probably only offended the log he seemed intent on cutting. She had run him through before she could even wonder if he'd thought he was holding an axe instead of a katana.

The man who tried to cut into her side even as she'd been pulling her sword from the would-be wood cutter's gut actually *was* holding an axe, but he wielded it like someone who'd actually fought with one before.

Still, his cuts, though less telegraphed and better aimed, were not difficult for her to dodge. If the wind kisōshi hadn't chosen that moment to attack her with a wind blade, she would have handily dealt with the axe-wielder and the man who launched at her with two daggers at the same time.

As it was, she had to turn away from the wind blade, a narrow miss, and one that may have caught the axe-wielder, judging by the scream. Then she was rolling towards the kisōshi who'd sent the wind blade after her, hoping to dispatch him before the other two caught up to her.

She rose from her roll too close to the wind kisōshi to use her katana, so she punched him in the face with her off hand. The man had clearly been in the process of doing something fancy with the air around him, arms raised, leaves tousling angrily through the air at his sides, but contact with her fist put an end to that. He valiantly shrugged off the pain of having his face punched, which suggested he'd had some actual experience in close combat before—unlike the man who'd tried to chop her into kindling—but clearly whatever he'd planned to do next involved a kisō attack, because all he managed to do was raise his arms and look confused before she shoved her katana into his throat.

To be fair, no one was supposed to be able to do what she could, so it wasn't exactly sporting of her to run kisōshi through before they could figure out that she'd stifled their kisō, but being sporting wasn't the damned point.

She turned from the dying wind kisōshi just in time to catch both a dagger and a small battle axe in the same parry, but she took a small slash to her side at the same time, since the man with two daggers was getting desperate and was trying to take advantage of her blade being locked with two others.

Unfortunately for him, that left his off hand trailing as she sidestepped the worst of the slash, and she grabbed his wrist even as she pushed back against the dual press of their weapons. She dug her thumb so hard into the man's wrist that he screamed, even as he dropped the dagger. Then she dropped his wrist and pulled her wakizashi free from her belt and plunged it into his chest.

The man with the axe was already stumbling backwards, as she'd pushed towards them both to plant the wakizashi, and she could see that the wind blade had indeed caught the man's left arm earlier; it bled freely and hung limply at his side.

"Surrender," she said, even as she kept her fighting stance while the man circled her. "You don't have to do this. I'll let you live if you just tell me why you're here."

But the man just spat on the ground and rushed her once more.

Torako frowned, but didn't toy with the man. She still remembered how the first man had tried to throw his knife at Itachi. Rage coursed through her, and in two quick moves, the man was dead on the forest floor with his companions.

Torako blinked and looked at the six bodies spread out around her.

"You'd think bandits would be better at fighting in groups," she announced to no one in particular.

And with that, she turned to the nearest bush and vomited.

Torako wiped her mouth, grimacing at the smell and taste of bile that followed, and made her way back over to the boulder where she'd left Itachi, hoping there might still be water in their skin when she got there. She spat once more, but it barely helped. Her stomach's reaction to robbing anyone of their kisō never got any less vile, no matter how often she did it.

As she crossed the small rise where the bandits had been cooking their supper, she stopped to check each of the bodies along the way. First, to make certain they were all dead, and then to see if anything in their possession might explain why six bandits intent on killing the first woman who popped out from behind a boulder at them were wandering her valley.

The first three had nothing that even identified where they'd come from, let alone why they were there.

"Kuso," Torako muttered.

"Mama, that's a bad word."

"Itachi-chan! I told you to wait in those rocks!" Torako did her best not to shout, but fear always made her surly.

"I'm sorry, Mama. I did wait. But then I heard you talking, and I thought it was safe."

The girl had climbed to the top of one of the lower boulders, and perched there watching Torako.

"Itachi-chan, just because you hear me talking does *not* mean it's safe to stop hiding. I still haven't checked to make sure there aren't more of these men hiding nearby. You should have waited. You know it's not safe until I come to get you."

Itachi's small head hung in shame, and Torako took a deep breath.

"I'm sorry, Itachi-chan, but this is important. Your safety is important. Your mother would never forgive me if I let something happen to you, and I would never forgive myself, either."

Itachi nodded sadly, and Torako walked to her and then opened her arms to the small girl. She stood on the boulder and wrapped her arms around Torako's neck.

"You're yucky," she mumbled into Torako's shoulder.

Torako dropped her back on the boulder.

"Ah, yes. I suppose I am. Sorry." Torako had forgotten about the blood. "Is my cloak still there?" Torako gestured to the other side of the boulder with her chin.

Itachi beamed and nodded.

"It's with the rocks! I'll go get it."

Torako smiled in turn.

"Wait for me with the cloak, Itachi-chan. I need to take a closer look at these men. I'll join you in a moment. Don't leave the boulders again unless you're in danger, understand?"

Itachi agreed with a small smile on her lips and slid back over to the other side. Torako let out a long breath, trying not to think of all that Itachi might have seen today. She hated the idea of Itachi watching her kill these men, but she hated the idea of letting anyone harm her daughter even more. After a moment of staring at where Itachi had been and worrying her lip between her teeth, she turned and focused on collecting whatever information she could.

She couldn't change what was already done.

She didn't honestly expect there to be more men hiding in the woods, although she kept in mind that the men had talked of waiting for someone to return. But whether more men were on their way or not, she was glad to have Itachi safely behind the boulders and out of sight. She didn't particularly relish having her daughter watch her search these bandits. Seeing dead men was one thing. Seeing dead men having their pockets emptied by one's mother was another.

Torako consoled herself with the idea that Raku would be more than a little bit disappointed if Torako didn't find out why these men were here, or at least bring back some kind of clue.

There hadn't been actual bandits in their valley for cycles now. Torako's reputation was generally sufficient for them not to take the risk.

Another corpse with no identifying papers, features, or even particularly interesting taste in food. So far all of the men had the same uninteresting provisions of dried squid and uncooked rice, along with a few sheets of nori. She sighed and moved on to the next corpse.

None of this made sense. These men hadn't even tried to talk to her before they'd attacked her.

Torako went out of her way to appear like an odd but non-threatening woman wandering the woods. The staff, the cloak, the hunting leathers, they were all practical for a number of reasons, but they also served to help her play the part of bumbling forest lady. One that most ne'er-do-wells were all too happy to believe, most of the time.

The few thieves who'd ever tried to summer in the valley—usually while attempting to avoid ranging Kisōshi—generally tried to figure out if Torako was worth robbing before they tried to kill her. Most of them didn't think she was worth attacking, and more still thought they would "have some fun" with her before they tried to run her through.

They all learned the hard way that those were outdated ways of thinking. More importantly, they learned that if they were going to behave that way, they needed to do it somewhere other than Sōryū Valley. Not that it was a lesson they got to sit with for very long. Most often they were dead by the end of it.

If it had only been Torako and her family that would suffer repeat offenders, she might have been more lenient. But she'd learned early on that it wasn't *she* who usually paid the price when she gave bandits a second chance. Torako was ashamed to admit that it had taken more than one village burned to embers, its people displaced or worse, before she'd realized that mercy wasn't a luxury she could afford.

So, she had learned to be brutal, and the warning had spread on its own after that. Bandits might enter her valley, but they never left it again, and that wound up being lesson enough for all but the most desperate.

After enough cycles, even the desperate steered clear.

Consequently, she wasn't overly concerned with the dead men who lay at her feet. Or she wouldn't have been, if they'd tried to rob her before they'd tried to kill her. Instead, they'd seemed to be waiting for her, and they'd fought her without provocation.

That hadn't happened in so long that it made the hairs on the back of her neck prickle. The last time someone had been focused on attacking *her* personally had been when the Rōjū still ruled and they'd tired of Torako's justice running unchecked in the mountains they couldn't be bothered to protect.

She grumbled a bit, as yet another searched corpse rendered not a single answer to her questions. She moved on to the last corpse.

When she came to the last man's body, the one who had tried to chop her like firewood with a katana he didn't seem to know how to use, her eyes were drawn instantly to the blade still gripped in his hand.

It was a fine blade, at least as fine as her own, but that wasn't what caught her eye. It wasn't even the deep blue of the saya that caught her attention. Rather, a small detail that she could barely see between the man's fingers stopped her in mid-search of his pockets. A small amber stone was glinting in the afternoon light from somewhere on the hilt of the blade. For a moment, Torako could look at nothing else.

Torako's hand, as though moving on its own, reached out and pried the tsuka from the dead man's fingers, her eyes still focused on the glinting light. Her thumb ran over the small amber jewels that glowed together in the late afternoon sun. They were set into the face of a silver wolf, its features placid but stern, its fur looking almost real enough to move in the breeze that ruffled the trees around her. Before she could stop her hands, or even question what they were doing, she had removed the saya from the man's belt, cleaned the blade on his trousers, sheathed it, and hung it from her own belt.

Then Torako blinked, wondering what had possessed her. She had been fighting and killing men for two decades, and she had never once taken a sword off of a fallen opponent before.

She moved her hands to her belt, planning to untie the saya she'd just added to it, but found her hand stilled at her side. She could not make them move any further.

She shook her head, a strange fog filling her eyes and ears, and she frowned. Her eyes traveled to the deep blue katana on her belt again and the frown deepened.

"Perhaps Raku-chan can make something of it," she muttered. "It's a distinctive enough blade. It may even tell us something of the man who wielded it, of these bandits and where they've come from."

She nodded to herself, as if her words were justification enough for stealing from the dead. Then she abandoned her search of the bodies on the forest floor. There was no other useful information left there.

With that thought, she finally cleaned off her own katana, which she had been carrying from corpse to corpse in case any unwelcome visitors arrived while she was trying to find clues. Once the blade was clean of the worst of the blood, she walked to where the staff sheath was still lying on the ground and shoved the blade home. Then she cradled the staff in her hand, using it as the walking stick it so often masqueraded as.

It was time to head home.

She stretched her shoulders and arms then, trying not to grimace at the thought of how sore she would be tomorrow from all those ukemi.

"I'm too old to be rolling in the dirt so much," she muttered, heading over to where Itachi was waiting.

"Mama!" Itachi shouted, popping up from behind the boulders as Torako approached.

"Thank you for waiting, Itachi-chan," Torako said, leaning down to hug her once more. She was still covered in more blood than was ideal for hugging, but they would not reach the nearest creek where she could clean up for a long while yet, and if Itachi didn't object, she needed the small moment of shared affection.

"Can you walk for a bit?" Torako asked, once Itachi pulled back from the hug. "If my clothes dry a bit more before we use the wrap you won't get quite as dirty."

Itachi nodded but said nothing, and Torako suspected she was all too happy to walk. She tried not to think about how bad she must look if her daughter preferred to walk rather than get too close to her.

As they turned once more to the forest trails, though, Itachi reached up to take Torako's hand, her bright green eyes looking hopeful and full of an adoration that Torako felt was completely unearned on her part. Yet she felt the responding pull of her own heart whenever Itachi looked at her that way, and knew it didn't matter that she hadn't earned it.

Itachi was a compass for Torako's heart. Wherever she went, Torako pointed and followed.

Torako held her small hand tight while they moved as fast as Itachi's legs would allow over the rough forest terrain.

It was only later, when she'd tucked the girl into the wrap again, in hopes of covering a bit more ground, while Itachi might even get some sleep, that Itachi finally spoke once more.

"Mama, I saw the tree again," she yawned, tucking her head against Torako's shoulder.

Torako frowned and tried to remember when Itachi had mentioned the tree. Oh yes, right before the man had tried to piss on their hiding spot.

"Was it Yanagi-sama?" she asked.

Itachi's head shook slightly, even as her eyes drooped closed.

"No, not Yanagi-sensei, but… the tree seemed nice."

Torako reached up and caressed Itachi's cheek softly, trying to fathom what a new tree-person might possibly mean, but before she could ask any questions, Itachi was sound asleep against her back, her head lolling awkwardly against Torako's shoulder.

⟢ *Kaiyo* ⟣

KAIYO STARED INTO the flames and wondered for the hundredth time if she had made the right choice. The smell of rabbits roasting slowly above the fire should have been a pleasant distraction, and watching Tanaka tend the food and the fire was another form of distraction altogether, but no amount of rabbit, smoke, or handsome men she'd suddenly found herself married to was distraction enough to keep her from assuming the worst.

"They've run off," she muttered in Tanaka's direction, hoping the doshigatai she'd set to keeping watch were far enough off not to hear her. "I've lost us half our team before we've even gotten to the target."

"Possibly," Tanaka said, in his usual even voice. "Or perhaps they've already found our quarry and are tracking her home as we speak."

Kaiyo let out a humorless laugh.

"You don't believe that any more than I do."

Tanaka merely shrugged and turned the rabbits once more.

"They were told to return here by sunset."

Tanaka remained silent.

"You think I should have sent you with them," she said, sighing and rubbing her hands over her face.

"I didn't say that," Tanaka replied quietly.

"Not since this morning," Kaiyo retorted. "When you damned near insisted on it."

Tanaka prodded the fire with a stick.

"It wouldn't have helped," Kaiyo insisted. "They would have just killed you and left your body for the wolves before abandoning me anyway, and then where would I be?"

Tanaka smiled.

"Probably seated on that same log but having to cook the rabbits for yourself," he admitted. Then, after a longish pause in which the rabbits were given another turn, "At least Lyt is with them."

"You really think the blood mage we know nothing about is going to keep them from deserting? The only thing we know for sure is that xir foremost desire is escape."

"Yes, but xe wants true freedom, not freedom with a dash of you and the Admiral chasing xir down for the rest of xir days."

"Perhaps."

Kaiyo couldn't find any more energy to argue with Tanaka, nor could she find the enthusiasm for agreement. They had discussed every potential downfall the night before, after they'd made camp in Sōryū forest for the first time, and again this morning, when the two crews had gone separate ways.

As they'd gotten deeper into the forest, it had become clear that the horses were becoming more of a liability this far into the woods, where the trails had all but disappeared and were as much rock and gnarled roots as they were even ground. Between the slowed pace and the animals' frequent and daunting feeding requirements, it didn't make sense to bring them any farther. But since they would need them for their return journey, they'd left them to graze with hobbles in an open field about a half day's ride from the road.

The only problem was that someone needed to stay close enough to the horses to check on them periodically and that person needed to be trusted not to run off with all of their mounts.

In the end, Kaiyo had decided that the sensible thing to do was split their group into two crews: a scouting group of seven, consisting of the three trackers and four men who were decent fighters but still fairly swift over rough terrain, and a group that remained behind to mind the horses.

When Kaiyo had expressed her concern that the scouting group might not come back, Tanaka had volunteered to go with them to ensure their loyalty.

Kaiyo should have said yes. A pragmatic leader would have trusted her second to keep the men in line or die trying. It was the latter part of that she couldn't abide. The thought of Tanaka being overwhelmed by six doshigatai who didn't share his scruples and lacked even a shred of the barest loyalty… her stomach turned at the thought. She'd insisted that she needed him here so that the two of them could divide the duties of checking the horses and making smaller scouting patrols with the remaining doshigatai.

Lyt had stepped forward and promised to keep the men in line if xe could. Of course, xe had already been assigned to the other group because xe had been listed as one of the top trackers amongst the doshigatai. Kaiyo would just have to hope that xe had some influence on the doshigatai she'd sent out.

"Did I see that sword on the back of one of the trackers earlier?" Tanaka's voice pulled her from her thoughts, and she realized that she had been staring into the fire and flipping her hanko between her fingers for long enough that the rabbits were almost entirely cooked.

"Which sword is that?" she asked, even though she knew.

"You know the one. The—"

But she didn't get to hear Tanaka describe the katana that felt like a coming storm, because just then Lyt stepped from the shadows into the firelight, xir approach completely undetectable until xe was already there, blue eyes twinkling, head bowing slightly, before Kaiyo could even reach for her daggers.

"I'm sorry, Captain. The other men are dead."

⇒ *Torako* ⇐

AS SHE MOVED swiftly and sure-footedly through the woods with Itachi nestled tightly against her back thanks to the wrap, Torako tried to piece together how she would explain all of this to Raku. It wasn't as though Raku wouldn't understand her need to fight mountain bandits—that was what Torako *did*. It was mainly that she'd fought six of them by herself with their daughter watching from behind a rock and… that was going to take some explaining.

She sighed.

"What's wrong, Mama?" Itachi's small voice asked from behind her shoulder.

"I'm just trying to figure out how to explain to Raku-san how I wound up fighting those men with you so close by," she muttered. She did her best not to lie to Itachi whenever she could, and she didn't see any particular benefit to it in this case. The girl would hear the whole conversation that she and Raku would have anyway—it wasn't as though their small home afforded them any privacy where heated discussions were concerned.

"But those men attacked *you*, Mama," Itachi said. Torako could easily picture the girl's brows knit together in confusion even though she couldn't see more than her profile.

"Yes, but I should have kept you farther away from it. You didn't need to see me fight them."

Even in profile she could see Itachi's frown deepen.

"But that was so COOL!"

Torako laughed then. She couldn't help it. She didn't wish for Itachi to see that kind of violence, and she worried about how it might affect her, but if she couldn't stop it from happening, she was glad that her daughter seemed largely unfazed by it.

"You weren't frightened?" Torako asked, trying to ignore the warm spark of hope in her chest.

Itachi shook her head.

"*You* weren't frightened, Mama. So I knew I didn't have to be frightened either."

Itachi's smile was so broad as she said that, Torako could barely hold onto her worry about what Raku would say. Itachi's smile could set fire to Torako's deepest fears, just as her pain and fears cast the deepest shadows in Torako's soul. It seemed impossible that someone so small could hold so much power over her heart and mind, but it was true regardless.

"I'm glad that you weren't frightened," Torako admitted after a while. "I'm still sorry that you had to see me fight those men, though. Battles like that are never pretty. They're much less common than they used to be, even in these hills, so your mother will not like that I forced you to see that."

Itachi frowned again.

"I was behind a rock, Mama. I didn't *have* to watch."

Torako kissed the top of her head.

"Raku-san may not see it that way," she replied eventually.

"Don't worry, Mama. I'll tell Kaa-san what happened."

Torako took a deep breath and attempted to center herself, the way she usually did before battle. She was certain that Raku would forgive her in the end, but... she wasn't sure how long it would take.

⤝ Kaiyo ⤞

KAIYO LOOKED AT the bodies strewn over the ridgeline clearing and wondered if she should pretend that she was sorry that these men were dead. The wind was blowing north, so where she stood amongst the boulders was clear of the smell of death, at least for the moment. But she could see flies already set to feasting on the dead men at her feet in the low, golden light of late afternoon.

"How long had they been dead before you found them?" she asked Lyt, who stood between the bodies, searching for Kami knew what in xir attempt to piece together what had happened. The other six surviving doshigatai, along with Tanaka, stood behind her amongst the boulders.

"Almost no time at all, I think. Their wounds were still running when I inspected them the first time."

148

Kaiyo frowned.

"You didn't see anyone leaving here when you returned?"

"I was focused on my quarry right up until I stepped onto this ridge again. To say I was singularly absorbed would be an understatement."

Kaiyo snorted.

"So, you didn't happen to see anything useful. How convenient."

Now it was Lyt's turn to frown.

"Captain, I believe I can track the person responsible for this attack," xe said. "If you would like me to?"

Kaiyo inclined her head slightly and tried not to breathe too deeply. She supposed she didn't actually have to pretend to be sad that these men were dead, in the end. They had all been killed by a single attacker, a legend that she had an entire scroll dedicated to, one whose reputation had to be more than half-fanciful retellings if it was to be believed at all, and which even still made her shudder. She was going to need all the men she could get to overcome this opponent, and now half of her crew were dead.

She was lucky that her best tracker was still alive. If it truly was luck.

Kaiyo couldn't shake the impression that Lyt wasn't telling her everything. Xe had returned to their camp as soon as xe had found the men dead, and if xe had killed them xirself, xe could not possibly benefit from returning to Kaiyo instead of simply disappearing into the woods. Lyt was the only doshigatai the Admiral had no extra hold on. As far as anyone in the Kaigun knew, Lyt had no family connections, no friends, no person or place that could be used as leverage.

Which meant there was no reason for xir to be here still. Even if xe hadn't killed these men, xe had been given the perfect opportunity to disappear without a trace, and Kaiyo and her father had nothing they could do to xir if they never managed to find xir.

Kaiyo *wanted* to shake xir until xe explained why xe had stayed, why xe was still offering to help with this crazed mission. Half-formed images of Lyt killing these men in order to perform some horrifying blood ritual flitted through Kaiyo's mind, but she shook that thought away.

She didn't need wild children's tales to account for these deaths. She was no tracker, but even she could see that the wounds in all of the men were the same even slashes and puncture wounds left by a katana. Lyt was completely unarmed currently, and Kaiyo had never seen xir carry a weapon. Meanwhile, these men's deaths fit perfectly into the pattern of the protector of Sōryū forest. The scroll her father had given her was full of stories exactly like this one. Whole groups of supposed criminals found dead by the hand of a single attacker. Occasionally one of them survived, and the legend grew further. A cloaked giant of a man who moved like midnight and struck like lightning. A man who could fight two dozen bandits alone, with nothing more than a walking staff, or a katana, or a katana and the strongest kisō in all Gensokai, depending on who you asked.

Kaiyo shook her head, found her fingers tipping her stone owl from one knuckle to the next, and realized that Lyt had moved to the far side of the ridge. The other doshigatai had started moving among their fallen comrades.

"Hey, Kentaro-san's new toy is gone!" shouted Soka.

"Did you check Uto-san's body?" asked Gatō, beside him.

They did. Uto had one dagger in his hands—the other they found lying uselessly in front of one of the boulders. His bow was beside the fire, untouched since the men had made their impromptu camp, it seemed.

Kaiyo took one last look at the carnage in front of her and then motioned for Tanaka, who was the only person still standing with her at the boulders, to follow her over to where Lyt stood looking out from the ridgeline to the forest below.

"You know where we're headed?"

"No, but I believe I can find the trail, Captain."

"Do you know who did this?" Kaiyo asked.

"Not exactly, though I have some guesses. Would you find it interesting to know that there was a set of very small footprints tucked behind those boulders behind you?"

Kaiyo frowned.

"Are you suggesting this was all done by a kappa?"

"No, Captain, nothing so sinister. There is also a set of footprints leading this way that would fit someone as big as you or Tanaka, though perhaps a bit heavier than either of you. Those footprints, however, are accompanied by a set of small ones, for as far as I can see from here at any rate."

"You're saying the person who killed those men brought a child along with them?"

"I'm saying that, if we hurry, we might just be able to catch up to a person who was walking with a companion whose footprints are that small."

Kaiyo only hesitated for a moment before turning back to the doshigatai who were still offering farewells to, or perhaps simply looting the corpses of, their former comrades.

"Hurry up. We need to move if we're going to find our mark before dark."

Perhaps it was because the men were spooked by the slaughter of their companions, perhaps because the most contentious of them were now dead on the forest floor, but for whatever reason, no one argued with her orders, and in a handful of heartbeats they were moving quickly down the deer trail that Lyt picked out of the thick underbrush.

⤆ *Torako* ⤇

THE SUN WAS low in the sky, already dipping beneath the tree line, when Torako finally arrived at their cave with Itachi fast asleep against her chest, head tucked into the upper portion of the wrap that held her close.

Torako smiled as she thought of Tenshi then, grateful for the wrap she'd gifted them when Itachi was born, as well as the lessons she'd given Torako as a young girl on how to use the wrap to carry the newest rescues at Kuma-sensei's school. Torako had put in hundreds of hours with the delightful device in her cycles at that school, and even after almost twenty cycles of disuse, it had all come back to her in the first weeks of Itachi's life. She'd been a still-healing wreck then, and everything had hurt except walking (and even walking had hurt, just slightly less than everything else) but Torako had been so tired and pain-ridden that even holding the baby while standing had seemed like more than was feasible. The wrap had saved her sanity, and Raku's. They had taken turns with Itachi wrapped close while they slid through the hazy tasks that marked the sleepless days and nights of every new parent.

These days the wrap barely held the three-cycle-old child, but it still worked well enough to keep Itachi from having to walk when her short stride could not keep up with Torako's. Itachi was growing stronger every day, and could spend more and more of Torako's patrols walking alongside her mother, but she was still small enough that she would inevitably ask to be carried for at least half of a circuit, and Torako would have long ago gone mad if not for the wrap.

Itachi was still sleeping when Torako walked through the mouth of their cave, warmth and the scent of tea and drying ink hitting her in a quiet blast of home. Consequently, Raku—who had been hunched over their low table amidst a pile of scrolls and loose papers when Torako walked in—merely raised an eyebrow at the blood that spattered Torako's clothes and the extra sword she'd tied onto her belt.

Torako leaned her walking staff beside the cave mouth, alongside Raku's bow and an assortment of cloaks and jackets that hung on pegs mounted into the rock. Then she turned to help Raku extract Itachi from the wrap without waking her, a process that was a thousand times easier with two sets of hands. She felt her chest ache as she watched Raku tuck Itachi's still-slumbering form into a thin blanket atop a futon on the other side of the cave, and she wondered how was it possible for her heart to exist almost entirely outside of her own body.

After Raku had whisked Itachi to her bed, perhaps cuddling her a bit closer than the short trip strictly required—and who could blame her after a tenday's absence?—she returned to Torako and wrapped her arms around her neck. For a moment, Torako just gazed into Raku's deep brown eyes and mentally traced the heart-shaped face that held them. She still wondered sometimes how someone as lovely as Raku had decided she was a worthy companion.

"You're surprisingly attractive covered in blood," Raku said, her voice just above a whisper.

Torako smiled, wrapping her arms around her wife's waist and pulling her closer. She hated to get blood on the beautiful blue and gold kimono Raku wore, but it was mostly dry, and besides, she knew for a fact that Raku was excellent at removing every kind of stain from silk, especially blood and ink.

"And *you* are gorgeous as usual, even with ink on your nose," she replied, kissing the nose in question.

Raku's warm smile was all the answer Torako could hope for, and she couldn't suppress a smile of her own as she leaned down to press her lips to Raku's. She thrilled at how the contact warmed her entire body, even after seven cycles of practice. She doubted that she would ever grow tired of it. Then Raku deepened the kiss, and for a little while they sank into the passion of reuniting after a tenday's absence.

When they finally came up for air, Raku's eyes were all fire and interest. Then she frowned.

"Why are you covered in blood, though?" she asked, putting a tiny bit of distance between them even without releasing Torako's neck.

Torako sighed. She'd practiced this conversation in her head a hundred times, from the moment she'd left the ridge where she'd killed six men, until the moment she'd arrived at the cave they called home, but she was still certain she would get it all wrong somehow.

"I was attacked by six men on a ridge out towards the eastern pass. I tried to talk them out of it, but they didn't even try to rob me, they just went straight from 'Oh look a lady was hiding behind a boulder I tried to piss on,' to 'Let's all try to stab her, shall we?'"

Yes, she was doing an excellent job of this.

"I might have attempted not to kill them all, but one of them tried to throw a dagger at Itachi-chan, and after that, I rather lost all thoughts of mercy."

Ah yes, much better. That explanation made her sound entirely competent as a parent, didn't it? *I wouldn't have killed ALL of the men, but one of them threatened the daughter who I'd recklessly left a bit too close to their camp, so then I turned into a rage monster and cut them all down.*

Raku blinked at her for a moment, long enough that Torako feared she'd said some of that last thought aloud, and then pulled her gently out of the cave.

They both took a good look at Itachi's sleeping form as they stepped outside, but when they'd reassured themselves that the girl was sleeping soundly, they pushed the leather flap aside and stepped into the swiftly fading light of sunset.

"Do you have any idea who these men were? Did they say anything to you at all? Did they... look strange, or act odd, or give you any kind of clue as to why they might be here?"

Torako frowned and swallowed the defense of her own sanity she had prepared a moment earlier, certain that Raku was about to call it into question. She wouldn't even have blamed her.

"You don't care that I killed six men while our daughter hid behind a boulder?" she asked, too shocked to actually answer the question.

"Of course I care! But you and Itachi-chan seem unharmed, and she fell asleep curled against your back as usual, even though you were covered in blood, so I can only assume she hasn't decided you're a monster. As to the rest, if you ever fail to slay ANYONE who threatens our daughter's life... well, I guess I'll just have to kill them myself, but really, you're much better at it than I am. It would save a lot of time if you'd just take care of that part."

Torako couldn't help it. She pulled Raku to her and kissed her again, fiercely this time. How had she gotten so lucky? This time when they broke apart, she spoke before her mind could stop her.

"I also took a sword off of one of the bandits I killed," she admitted, her voice tinged with shame. "It was a very strange sword, and the man who attacked me with it didn't even seem to know how to hold a katana properly. I thought maybe it could tell us something useful. I couldn't find anything else on them that helped."

Torako pulled the blue katana from her belt as she spoke, then she held the sword up for Raku's inspection.

Raku said nothing as she looked at the katana in its sheath, but when she reached for it, Torako had to fight the urge not to pull it away.

"That *is* very odd. And this sword… feels wrong. Did Itachi say anything about it?"

Torako shook her head and took another look at the katana's intricately wrapped hilt. The beautifully detailed wolf head stared at her with its amber eyes.

"Itachi didn't really see it. I had already slipped it into my belt before she came out from behind the boulder. Why?"

Raku frowned but didn't reply immediately. After a while, she said, "I'm not sure, but…something strange is going on, Tora-chan. First I found something very strange in this latest scroll, and then your mother and Yanagi-sama were here a few days ago and they—"

"My mother came to visit?" Torako asked, returning the sword to her belt even as she spoke. For some reason, she didn't like having it too far from her body.

"Yes, along with Yanagi-sama. They were both acting a bit oddly, to be honest, and that combined with your woodland bandits and that sword…"

Raku's voice trailed off for a moment, and Torako tried to be patient, but in the end, she couldn't help asking.

"What did my mother tell you, Raku-chan?"

"Hmmm? Oh, yes. That. That will take some explaining. Why don't we get supper cooking and I'll tell you while the rice boils?"

Torako let out an exasperated sigh at the delay, but she smiled as she did it. Raku's storytelling was legendary, and if whatever message Tenshi had delivered was worthy of enough time to boil rice, then she would likely enjoy Raku's rendition of it enough to warrant the wait.

"Fine," Torako said, turning towards the cave. "Do you need me to hunt something?"

"I've already snared us a few hares," Raku replied. "But we're almost out of water."

Torako nodded and popped into the cave to fetch their larger, family waterskin, as well as Shiken, her staff. She moved the strange blue katana from her belt to her back, strangely unwilling to leave it behind, and kept Shiken in her hand. She was a bit overarmed for a trip to the creek, but after the bandits she'd found on the ridgeline she wasn't sure that was a bad thing. When she returned to the small clearing in front of their cave, Raku was surveying the woods, her gaze half-focused and her eyebrows drawn together over her nose.

"Are you alright?" Torako asked, stepping up beside her.

Raku nearly jumped, which told Torako quite a bit more than the muttered, "Yes, fine," that dismissed her concern.

"I'll be back to help with dinner, and you can tell me all that's worrying you, Raku-chan. Whatever is going on, we'll sort it out.

Together."

Raku smiled distractedly and offered another quick kiss, which Torako gladly took.

"Better come back quickly then—I can't even decide what's worrying me most," she replied, when the kiss ended.

Torako smiled, even though that statement was far from reassuring.

"I'll be so quick you'll hardly know I'm gone."

⇜ *Kaiyo* ⇝

KAIYO WATCHED THROUGH the glass as a tall woman with a katana strapped to her back and a walking staff in her hand kissed a petite woman briefly and passionately and then picked up an empty waterskin and walked off into the forest.

She turned to Lyt.

"Is that our killer?" she asked.

Lyt gave a noncommittal shrug.

"It could be. That person is the right size for the footprints I saw, and she has a blue sword strapped to her back. Beyond that… I cannot judge from here if she looks like she's recently killed half a dozen men."

Kaiyo still couldn't shake the idea that Lyt was hiding something, but she had no idea what it was. She looked to Tanaka.

"Tanaka-san, what are your thoughts?"

Tanaka was on her right side, Lyt on her left, and the three of them were all tucked neatly behind a very large fallen log a short distance up the mountain that loomed on the edge of this valley. A half a watch's swift walking had gotten them to this clearing, seemingly just after the larger woman had returned.

Kaiyo wondered how slowly the other woman must have moved for them to have caught up with her so easily. She hoped that didn't mean this was a trap.

Behind her, the six remaining doshigatai had set up a perimeter, partially because Kaiyo did not want to take any chances of the legendary Night Stalker, if that's indeed who they were dealing with, sneaking up on them, and partially so that she could speak with Tanaka and Lyt without them overhearing.

Tanaka still held his own glass up to his eye as he spoke.

"If the larger woman is the one who killed Uto-san and the rest, then we should move in quickly while she's gone."

Lyt objected, however.

"The woman carried a waterskin with her. I can smell clean water from here. If she's just gone to fill that skin, then she'll be back so soon that attacking now will just leave our backs exposed to her enraged return. We should wait until they sleep."

Kaiyo considered her options. Tanaka and Lyt both made good points.

"Let's watch them for a while. Perhaps we'll learn of a way to lure the Night Stalker away and then move in on the scribe."

There had been no sign of whoever had been responsible for the tiny footprints Lyt had described, and Kaiyo felt unaccountably relieved. Would the presence of a child change the facts of her mission?

Raku

RAKU WATCHED TORAKO walk into the woods and felt her chest tighten. Torako would be back soon with the water for the rice and then Raku would have to figure out how to relay all the strange things that Tenshi had revealed to her a few days earlier.

Raku took a deep breath and let it out slowly as she tried to decide how to word things and where to start. Should she explain the scrolls that she had been working on first? It might help, especially since she would need to explain that she had to return to New Council City right away. But then again, as far as she could tell Tenshi and Yanagi's absence had nothing to do with what she had uncovered in the scrolls.

She couldn't help but wonder if the men Torako had been forced to fight earlier were somehow related to whatever strange errand Tenshi was on to help her father. But how could that be? Torako hadn't said anything about them seeming like Kami.

Not that she'd given Torako much of a chance to explain, or even asked any reasonable questions once Torako had told her the basics.

Oh, she was getting this all wrong, but she had no idea what getting it right might look like. How did one tell their wife that she was one-quarter moon Kami and that her heritage was likely the reason their daughter was an incredibly powerful Kisōshi?

"Mama?" a small voice called from behind Raku.

"Itachi-chan!" she turned and found the small face and bright green eyes of the second love of her life. "Did you have a good nap?"

Itachi smiled.

"Yes! I dreamed of Mama! She was fighting bad men in the forest."

Kaiyo worked to keep the smile on her face.

"Did she win?"

"Of course!"

Kaiyo's smile was more genuine then.

"Well, why don't you help me cook these rabbits and tell me all about it."

She moved to the cave mouth and opened her arms wide so Itachi would know that a hug was welcome if she wanted one. The little girl's arms wrapping tight around her neck as she picked her up and carried her into the cave were enough to push almost every negative thought out of her head.

But one last look over her shoulder as she walked into the cave showed a setting sun, and no sign of Torako, who should have already returned by now with a skin full of water for their supper.

⟞ *Itachi* ⟝

ITACHI YAWNED AND watched Kaa-san spoon more rice into the small bowl that she had been using for as long as she could remember. When she saw her add the bit of rabbit on top, she could feel the saliva drip down her chin a bit. She wiped at it and clicked her hashi together impatiently. Her mother chuckled.

"Coming right up, Itachi-chan, have some patience."

Itachi laughed.

"I have patience, Kaa-san. I'm just hungry!"

Raku laughed too.

"I'm not sure you know what patience is. Here you go!"

Itachi ignored everything but the rice and rabbit her mother had put before her.

"Oishii!" she exclaimed after the first few bites.

Kaa-san laughed and filled her own bowl. Then she turned to stare out of the cave mouth into the distance again.

"Kaa-san, what's wrong?"

For a moment, Kaa-san said nothing, and didn't even turn towards Itachi. Itachi frowned and was about to ask again when her mother spoke.

"I'm just a bit worried about your Mama, that's all."

Itachi thought that was odd, since Mama was sometimes gone for days and days without Kaa-san worrying about her, and right now she had only been gone since just before sunset.

"Why?"

Kaa-san finally turned back to Itachi and smiled.

"No reason. I'm sure she's fine. Let's eat supper, ne?"

Itachi knew that her mother was lying. She also knew it was the lie her parents most often told her. It was the most confusing lie because it was always true. Every time her mother or mama told her things were fine it was true. But almost every time they *said* that things were fine, her kisō told her they were lying. She still didn't understand how it was possible, and when she'd asked Yanagi-sensei about it once, his answer hadn't helped.

"Ah. It is the lie that parents always hope will be true, and most of the time, it is true. But often, at the time they say it, they don't believe the words themselves," Yanagi-sensei had explained.

Itachi thought grown-ups were silly sometimes, and tree spirits too, for that matter.

But, since Kaa-san had told the lie that was always true, she didn't ask her mother why she was lying, she only refocused her attention on the food in her bowl.

She was always hungry for supper, but she was extra hungry after a tenday out doing patrols with Mama. Mama's legs were so long, and hers could barely keep up. Even when she napped in the wrap against Mama's back on the way home like she had today, she often felt sleepy halfway through supper. She yawned again, blinking a few times at what was left of her rice.

"Just a few more bites, Itachi-chan, then bedtime," Kaa-san sang from across the fire. Itachi managed to shovel the last three bites of rice, miso, and rabbit into her mouth, and then her eyes started to droop. Kaa-san grabbed the bowl from her hand just as her eyes lost the fight against sleep.

She woke up hearing unfamiliar voices outside their home. She could tell that Kaa-san lay completely still beside her, but she wasn't sure if she was still sleeping.

Itachi did not like the noises she heard. They were muffled but decisive, like the sounds of animals hunting. Itachi liked hunting animals. She was friends with some hawks and foxes in Yanagi's wood. But she did not like *being* hunted.

"Kaa-san?" she breathed, the barest whisper of a whisper.

Kaa-san's hand reached for hers and gripped it gently, then tightened. She must be awake, and she must hear the noises too.

Itachi did her best to stay still. She wished that Mama was here. A quick scan with her kisō told her that Mama was not nearby, though. The strange absence of kisō that represented her Mama was unmistakable. She tried not to let Mama's absence scare her. Mama could fight anyone at all and win. Kaa-san had said so more than once. Mama could protect them from anything that tried to hurt them, and if she wasn't here that could mean that… Itachi blinked and remembered that Kaa-san could also protect her. Kaa-san could shoot arrows at rabbits from very far away, and she had seen her practice throwing Kusuko around when she and Taka visited. Kaa-san could fight. Not with a sword like Mama, but she could still keep them both safe.

So Itachi tried to stay quiet and calm, and silently promised that she would listen and that she wouldn't get in the way.

She nodded to herself. This was their home. They would be alright in the end.

Her mother seemed to be waiting for something, because for a long time she just lay still as the noises outside got louder and louder. Then, she realized that her mother was trying to let Itachi read her thoughts. She could tell because she felt her mother squeeze her hand again and then she felt thoughts brush against her mind. Kaa-san didn't have any kisō of her own, not more than any person who wasn't a Kisōshi anyway, but Kaa-san understood that Itachi could use her kisō to read her thoughts if she concentrated hard enough. Yanagi-sensei had taught her how to do it. She wasn't very good at it yet, but she was practicing every day.

Even so, the images her mother let her see were clear. Kaa-san wanted her to hide, using her kisō if she could, so that whoever was outside couldn't find her. Kaa-san planned to make a fuss so that the people would pay attention to her instead of Itachi. Itachi squeezed her mother's hand to let her know she understood.

Itachi waited. She was a little bit afraid now, because Mama still wasn't back, and Kaa-san seemed very serious. Kaa-san was almost never serious.

Itachi took a deep breath, the way that Yanagi-sensei had taught her. Then she took another. And another. Soon, she found herself falling into the well of energy that Yanagi-sensei called her fuchi, the place where she felt water all around her, warm and comforting.

She thought about not wanting the people outside to see her. Hiding was what Kaa-san had asked her to do, and Kaa-san was very serious, so she would do it. She didn't want Kaa-san to be mad at her, and she didn't want whoever was making noises outside their cave to see her. She asked the water to help her hide. When she went deep inside her fuchi and asked nicely, the water usually helped.

When she opened her eyes, her mother was staring at her, but her eyes looked as if they were staring past her. She felt her mother squeeze her hand. She squeezed back.

Her mother smiled.

"That's my girl," she whispered, her voice little more than a breath on the wind.

Then Kaa-san let go of her hand and stood up. She gestured for Itachi to stay where she was and Itachi nodded. Her mother didn't wait for the reply though. She was already heading for the mouth of the cave.

Kaa-san stood just inside the leather flap that acted as a door in all but the coldest seasons, and tilted her head to one side, like she was listening to something.

She waited. Still, as stone.

Itachi was just beginning to feel itchy, like not moving for a moment longer was going to hurt, when someone who was not Kaa-san put a hand on the leather flap. Her mother waited one breath longer. Then she grabbed the hand, turned her body, and bent her knees in a way that had Itachi's jaw dropping almost as quickly as the man the hand belonged to—he had flipped right over Kaa-san's back and landed with his face staring at the top of the cave!

Kaa-san didn't hesitate. She stepped on top of the man on the floor, shouted, "Now!" and sprinted out of their cave.

Itachi didn't hesitate either. She leapt to follow her mother, planting a foot firmly on top of the man on the floor to do so, and then she ran out into the night.

There were too many adults outside. Itachi couldn't even tell which one was her mother. At least, not with her eyes.

She didn't have time to use her kisō yet. She had promised Kaa-san she would hide, and Kaa-san would be worried if she didn't. If Mama had taught her anything while they'd been ranging the valley looking for bandits, it was that worrying about something other than fighting could get you killed. Itachi had promised to always listen to Mama or Kaa-san whenever they said there was danger. She would do as Kaa-san asked.

The adults were all shouting at each other, moving quickly through the darkness. The moon was the only light to see by, but Itachi saw that Kaa-san had grabbed one of the strangers by the arm and twisted it until he cried out. Itachi, still hidden by her kisō, slipped between adults who were running towards her mother, and found a tree that had grown into two trunks just low enough off the ground that she could reach one foot up into the place where they joined. She curled into the split of the trunks, drawing her legs up and wrapping her arms around her knees, making herself as small as she could. She could still see her mother, and the person her mother was fighting, but she couldn't see much else in the moonlight.

She watched Kaa-san grab a knife from the belt of the latest man who had tried to grab her, and she watched with horror and awe as her mother shoved the blade into the man's gut.

He collapsed and Kaa-san spun out of his grasp, and out of Itachi's view.

She tried to shift so that she could see more of what was happening, but the low brush around her was thick, and there wasn't enough moonlight to make out what was happening beyond it. But now that she was out of the way, she didn't have to use her eyes to see. She closed her eyes and focused her kisō on Kaa-san instead.

It took a few deep breaths for her to focus. Kaa-san was moving quickly, and she was upset. Itachi didn't understand why her mother felt sad as well as angry, but those emotions were big and easy to follow, so Itachi held onto them.

In a handful of heartbeats, her mother's emotions were dulled so thoroughly that Itachi almost gasped, afraid of what that sudden dulling meant.

She took another deep breath. Leaving her hiding spot would be dangerous, and Kaa-san would be upset with her if she did something dangerous, so she needed to try to stay calm and think.

Suddenly a nearby rush of emotions overwhelmed her. Anger, fear, and sadness, but not her mother's. Then she felt a surge of something like kisō, something almost like when Yanagi-sensei healed the plants in his forest. Whatever it was, it made the emotions that weren't Kaa-san's go away, at least a bit.

Then, she felt her mother again. Fear and sadness again, but also confusion. All of those emotions were getting fainter, and then they dulled to the quiet hum of someone sleeping. Kaa-san was unconscious, and she was getting farther away by the moment.

Itachi wanted to run after her, but she thought of the men who had attacked Mama that afternoon. They hadn't wanted to talk to her, they had only wanted to fight. Itachi couldn't fight them. Not yet. Not alone. She needed Mama. Or Yanagi-sensei. Or Tenshi-san. Or even Taka and Kusuko, who sometimes visited. They would know what to do. They would help her fight the bandits who had taken Kaa-san. All Itachi had to do was wait.

So she waited.

And waited.

And didn't even notice when she fell asleep, still tucked into the crook of the tree.

❧ *Torako* ❧

TORAKO STOOD ATOP the granite ledge and blinked into the distance. The valley lay before her, a cloak of evergreen covering its shoulders, small streams joining up to form a moderate river where the mountains met between. She took a deep breath of crisp mountain air with just a hint of the warmth of summer coming on and wondered what she was doing here.

She hadn't meant to climb the peak above their cave. She recalled, now, that she had set out to fill the waterskin and had meant to return to help with supper. That was unlikely now. The sun was dropping behind the horizon, even as she watched.

"Kami curse it, what am I doing here?"

She didn't recall ascending the peak. She didn't recall choosing to abandon their waterskin. She didn't recall anything much, after kissing Raku and walking away. She sometimes made this climb to help her think, when she was worried, and she knew that Raku had planned to tell her something worrisome, but it didn't make any sense for her to come up here now. She was meant to be getting water to boil rice.

She looked down at her own hands and saw that she held her walking staff in one hand and the still-empty waterskin in the other.

"I'll be tripping my way down in the darkness now," she muttered, angry with herself and more than a bit worried. She could be absent-minded sometimes. If Itachi needed something, or wanted to play in the creek, Torako had more than once left rice cooking for too long and come back to find it burned to the bottom of the pot. But this… hiking an entire mountain so lost in her own mind that when she got to the top, she had no memory of the journey? That was something she'd never done before. But she could feel the slight strain in her legs that came from the ascent, she *had* made the climb herself, she just couldn't remember it. She shook her head, turning away from the impressive view in order to follow the small goat trail that she knew would lead her home.

But the trail wasn't there. Nothing was behind her now but fog. Fog, and a small glow coming from somewhere in the distance. The glow shifted, not quite flickering, but getting dimmer and brighter without ever going completely dark, as though it were both right in front of her and infinitely far away. She peered more closely into the distance and dropped the empty waterskin so that she could put her right hand on Shiken's hilt, ready to draw the blade if necessary. Instead of Shiken's wooden hilt, however, her hand met the wrapped hilt of the katana she had looted off the bandit's corpse that afternoon. Feeling a quick jolt of panic, she released it as soon as the wolf jewel grazed her palm, but the ever-changing glow intensified, and the fog only grew thicker around her. She looked around for Shiken, but she couldn't see the long wooden staff anywhere. Her right hand patted frantically and finally calmed slightly when she found Shiken slung across her back, where she'd sworn the pilfered blue katana had been only moments before. Had she somehow switched the blades and then forgotten?

She turned back to the horizon to see how much sunlight she had left before nightfall, but there she found only fog as well.

"Must be in a cloud," she muttered, gripping the strange katana's hilt firmly as a prickle of fear ran up her neck. She turned towards the distant glow once again, since it was the only thing she could see besides the fog.

"You are not in a cloud."

The voice, a low growling voice that reminded her of rocks tumbling under water, came from all around her, and she muttered a few curses at herself and at whatever had made her come all this way so late in the day. She was friends with a tree Kami, yes, but she didn't think that made her immune to the ill will of other Kami. If she'd somehow angered some other spirit by being here, she didn't think Yanagi-sama would be rushing to rescue her.

"Who is speaking?" she asked, attempting to keep her tone polite. It wouldn't help her to be rude to a mountain spirit, and if it wasn't a mountain spirit, if it was someone playing some kind of trick on her, there was no rule saying she couldn't stab them after she'd been polite to them.

"You have something of mine," the voice said. "Something I would like returned to me."

Torako looked down at her person. She was wearing the same leather pants and silk tunic she'd been wearing for the past cycle. She'd taken the hides of a few deer to one of the tailors in a nearby village to have them sewn, and Raku had bought her the silk tunic to celebrate their anniversary the cycle before. It was red, and sturdy, and didn't show blood easily. She didn't think the spirit was laying claim to her clothes. Her eyes settled on the katana her hand encircled instead of Shiken.

"I assume you mean this sword," she said aloud, deciding there couldn't be anything else on her that belonged to a foggy, growling, disembodied voice.

"It has been trying to make its way back to me for a long time," the echoing, growling voice said.

"Well, would you like me to leave it here? It feels a bit wrong to just throw in on the ground, but I won't keep it from you."

Torako realized that she was being overly flippant with someone she suspected might be a spirit. Especially when that spirit seemed to have the power to lure her up a mountainside without her knowledge or consent. But it wasn't often that she found herself frightened, and the experience always sharpened her tongue a bit.

"I'm afraid that will not be sufficient," the voice growled.

"Well, you'll have to tell me what to do with it, then. This blade didn't come with instructions, and I killed the man who was attacking me with it before he had a chance to mention creepy voices on mountaintops."

The voice made a noise that sounded like something between a bark and someone choking.

"Come closer, human, let me see you."

"Let me guess," Torako said, starting to wonder if the shock of being addressed by an unfamiliar fog had addled her brain. "You're near the disconcerting glow that keeps changing how far away it appears?"

"More or less," the voice breathed all around her.

"Of course you are," Torako muttered. "Why wouldn't you be?"

"I can hear you, even when you mutter," the voice said.

"Which does make one wonder why you can't see me," she replied, even as she began making her way towards the strange glow in the fog.

It wasn't that she thought approaching the glow was a good idea. A rather loud part of her was yelling that it was a terrible, terrible idea. Perhaps the worst she'd ever had. It was simply that refusing a spirit was a costly affair, and this one had already lured her up here against her will and without her conscious thought. That was powerful. Anything that could do that was not a thing to be trifled with. She'd spent enough time with Yanagi to know that angering spirits was a poor plan in the best of circumstances, and alone in the dark on a mountaintop was *not* the best of circumstances.

So, she pressed forward into the fog, worried that at any moment her feet would find the edge of the granite peak and she would tumble forward to her death before she could stop herself. Yet, the edge never came. She couldn't see the terrain on which she tread, but it felt soft with leaves or dying grass, and flat. Not like the sheer mountainside she had stood atop when she could still see.

"Excellent. I'm not even on the mountaintop any longer," she muttered.

"Ah, you noticed, did you? Very good."

"Is this some kind of test?" Torako wondered aloud, not convinced the spirit would answer her.

"Isn't everything?" the voice replied.

"You know, if you'd caught me five cycles ago, I'd have assumed I was simply losing my mind. Luckily, time in the company of a walking tree spirit has broadened my ideas of what counts as 'possible.'"

"Ah, is Yanagi-sama still roaming the valley below? Delightful."

"Are you friends with Yanagi-sama?" Torako asked.

The fog roiled around her, but it still revealed nothing. She saw no hint of the ground she walked upon, nor any sign of what was causing the distant glow that brightened and faded with every beat of her heart. She didn't truly expect the spirit to answer her, but asking nosy questions she didn't expect to have answered was better than walking silently through an unending fog.

"Friend is not a word I use to describe anyone in this world," the voice replied.

Torako stifled a bitter chuckle.

"That sounds familiar," she said, mostly to herself.

"Do you have a tale of woe to tell me, human? Are you all alone in this world?"

"Not anymore," Torako, admitted. "But for a long time, I could have said those words myself and been telling the truth."

"Oh? Is it a redemption story you've come to tell me then?"

"I'm just here to give your sword, Kami-sama. I'm not here to bore you with tales of human trifles."

Torako wondered at the confidence in her voice as she spoke. Judging by every story she'd listened to as a child, every legend she'd heard the Rakugoka tell, teasing a mountain spirit was the height of folly. But the silence of the fog surrounding her was unnatural, and the sound of her own voice was the only thing keeping her from jumping at every Kami-cursed shadow that rolled through the mist.

"Is there any chance you can speed this up?" she asked the void around her. The glow in the fog didn't seem to be getting any closer. It just brightened and faded as she walked, making it impossible to judge its distance.

"If only," the echoing voice called. Was it her imagination or did it sound wistful? "But I have waited ages for this moment. I can wait a trifle longer."

"Yeah, well, immortal beings have time to be patient. Some of the rest of us have to get home in time for supper."

"Yes, about that…" said the voice, as Torako's feet stopped without her instruction. She squinted into the fog, trying to make out the glow once more, and finally she was able to see that the glow was not one light, but two.

Two glowing orbs that were now distinctly getting closer. They no longer faded and brightened at random, but instead grew steadily brighter with each moment that passed.

She counted eleven heartbeats, and then the glows were directly in front of her, set in the face of an enormous wolf.

"I'm not so sure you'll be home for supper," the wolf said, and pounced.

⇒ *Kaiyo* ⇒

KAIYO SAW NOTHING but blood, smelled nothing but blood, and felt nothing but blood. Which was ridiculous, because she was surrounded by trees and moonlight, and men whose fear stank worse than the metallic tang that refused to leave her nostrils. Lyt was carrying the Kami-cursed scribe. Soka, Koshi, and the other surviving doshigatai were fanned out around them keeping watch on the woods that seemed alive with a malevolence directed firmly at them, and she half-carried, half-dragged a stumbling Tanaka who had one hand pressed tightly to his abdomen in an attempt to keep his insides where they belonged. She wasn't sure he was succeeding.

"Why the fuck didn't any of the scrolls tell us that the scribe could fight?" she growled, at no one in particular.

"Are you really so shocked that the wife of the woman who killed six of our men single-handedly didn't lay down and let us take her from her home?" Tanaka wheezed.

Kaiyo wanted to shake him.

"Stop talking," she snapped.

She caught sight of Tanaka's face in a flicker of moonlight as she spoke, and stopped in her tracks.

"Everyone stop!" she called. The damned healer was as white as wind-whipped waves, and if he bled to death she was going to kill him. As soon as her feet stopped pulling them forward Tanaka's legs gave out, and she found herself half-falling with him, just to keep him from hitting the ground too quickly. She managed to arrest his fall right at the end and lowered his head into her lap.

"Tanaka-san," she growled. "You have to stay awake to heal most of the bleeding. You know I can't."

"Don't have enough kisō," he murmured, his eyes fluttering closed.

Kaiyo swallowed, refusing to let the weight of panic that was settling on her chest keep her from thinking properly. It was her job to keep them all alive. Especially Tanaka.

"What do you need?" she asked.

"Kisō. Don't have enough."

She couldn't tell if Tanaka's speech was muddled from pain or from blood loss and she honestly didn't know whether it mattered. The man had a gash in his stomach as long as her hand and she didn't have an ounce of healing kisō in her body.

"Knives…" Tanaka murmured.

Kaiyo blinked. That made no sense. He didn't need knives. He needed the damned scribe not to have put a knife in his gut. He needed the opposite of knives.

When she blinked again, Lyt was beside her, the scribe still in xir arms.

"Captain, I believe he is asking you to remove your knives from their sheathes so he can borrow some of your energy."

Kaiyo looked at Lyt and blinked again. Perhaps if she blinked enough times, words would start to have meaning once more.

"I believe your knives interfere with kisō. Tanaka-san took

them off of you in order to bring you back to consciousness on the Wind Serpent a few days ago."

Kaiyo had no idea how her new throwing knives could interfere with kisō, but she didn't care. If Tanaka needed them gone, then they would be.

She removed them as quickly as her blood-slicked hands would allow.

Then she put her hand on Tanaka's and panicked when it didn't move in response.

"Tanaka-san," she said, loudly.

Nothing.

"TANAKA-SAN," she shouted.

She took a deep breath, because she could still see his chest moving. It wasn't time to panic yet.

"Captain," Lyt said, and now xe was kneeling beside her and the scribe had been laid out flat at xir side. "I believe Tanaka is too weak to heal himself, even if you managed to give him what little kisō you possess. I also believe we are running out of time to help him properly. He is bleeding rather badly. Our scribe here knows how to inflict a gut wound properly. I have a suggestion, but I fear you will not like it."

Kaiyo said nothing but looked into the clear blue eyes of the former doshigatai. Xir eyes were full of concern, and something else that Kaiyo could not name. It was the first time that Kaiyo had taken a good look at xir since the fight to abduct the scribe. It was the first time that Kaiyo noticed xe was bleeding rather badly xirself.

"I can help Tanaka-san. I'm… well known for my healing where I come from. But, well, your people locked me into a dungeon the last time I tried to heal someone my way."

Kaiyo swallowed. She knew where this was going.

She pressed her fingers to Tanaka's wrist, lightly, trying to feel his pulse. It was there, but it wasn't strong.

"Do it. Whatever you need to do to heal him, you have my word I won't report it to the Kaigun."

Lyt bowed xir head in acceptance and then looked up again.

"I will also need your blood," xe said, holding her gaze.

Kaiyo gave a single nod and lifted her wrist to xir.

"Take what you need."

Lyt smiled.

"It isn't much, but it will hurt a bit."

And then, without any further preamble, xe took a finger, which Kaiyo was horrified to see suddenly resembled a stick sharpened to a very fine point, and plunged it into her wrist until blood welled dark and warm against her skin. It did hurt, but it was over quickly, and Lyt pressed xir mouth to the wound for just a heartbeat, before pressing a normal-looking finger over the wound for another beat of her heart.

When xe removed xir finger, there was no mark on her skin.

Kaiyo looked into Lyt's eyes again, and, for just a moment, she saw skin that looked more like bark, papery and thin, eyes that were a blue so vivid they could have been gemstones, and features far more stark and angular than the face she had come to recognize over the past few days.

When she breathed out again, Lyt's face was returned to normal.

And then xe went to work.

Xe ignored Kaiyo entirely, but of course, Kaiyo was right there, Tanaka's head still perched in her lap, so she saw everything, and Lyt made no move to hide xir work.

Xe inspected the wound, xe placed xir hands on it, and then xe closed xir eyes and went very still for a long time.

Kaiyo watched in silence, dreading what she had agreed to even as she was fascinated watching it done. Blood magic. This was the crime that Lyt had committed, and this was what half of the wider world abhorred so strongly that legends of its evil had even made it to the Kaigun.

It looked an awful lot like healing with kisō, to Kaiyo.

Tanaka, when he was not the one tempting death, often went into a trance like the one Lyt now appeared to be in, while he coaxed the water in a person's body to do his bidding and move where it was needed. Convenient, when so much of people seemed to be made of water. How was what Lyt was doing any different, aside from the fact that xe'd needed to stab Kaiyo in the wrist first to do it?

When Lyt opened xir eyes and leaned back from Tanaka, Kaiyo suspected she knew how it was different. Lyt looked changed again, xir skin like bark once more, xir eyes like jewels, but jewels that had been hollowed out inside.

"Do you need more blood?" Kaiyo asked.

Lyt raised a papery eyebrow at her.

"You would offer it willingly?"

Kaiyo nodded. She would. Gladly. Because she still had her hand on Tanaka's wrist, and she could already feel how much stronger his pulse was beneath her fingers. Tanaka was going to live, and Lyt looked as though xe was on the verge of collapse.

"It would help me recover quickly enough that we could resume walking immediately."

Lyt's voice sounded hesitant, so Kaiyo raised her wrist once more.

"You saved his life."

She didn't think any further explanation was necessary.

Lyt seemed to accept this because xe once more punctured her wrist with an oddly sharpened finger and then drank quickly from the wound before healing it over.

Kaiyo stared at the unblemished spot on her wrist for a moment before looking up at Lyt once more.

"You'll have to tell me how this works sometime," she said.

Lyt bowed, slightly more than was appropriate for someone who had just done *her* a favor, and then stood up and walked over to the unconscious scribe.

Kaiyo let herself ignore them for a moment and instead stared at Tanaka's face. His breathing was deep and even, and his face was full of color once more.

She sucked in a sharp breath, leaning down to look more closely at the spot where his wound should have been. Smooth skin over muscles looked like they had never met a blade at all.

She glanced at Tanaka's face, wondering how long he would need to rest.

His eyes popped open.

He said nothing, but smiled so wide she wondered if he was drunk.

She only realized how close her face was to his when he brought his lips to hers and kissed them.

8日 6月, 新議 8年

8th Day, 6th Moon, Cycle 8 of the New Council

⟩⟩ *Torako* ⟨⟨

TORAKO AWOKE TO the kind of headache that usually only followed a long night of drinking sake with Raku.

"What in the name of Tanuki's sweaty balls did I do to myself?"

She looked around the granite mountaintop that was just beginning to glow with the soft light of dawn and wondered how she had gotten there. She stood, her muscles aching, most likely from the climb to get here—not that she remembered it—and her neck as sore as if she'd been grabbed by the throat in battle.

"Ugh," she rubbed her face, took a deep breath, and flinched at the crisp morning air hitting her throat. Summer was already taking its hold in the valley, but mountaintops have never given three shits about the weather anywhere else. Part of the ache she felt was undoubtedly from having slept in near-freezing temperatures. She was actually impressed that she could feel all of her extremities. And that she'd managed to sleep at all.

"You're too old to sleep on bare stone anymore, Torako," she chided herself, cracking her neck and shoulders.

The valley extended below her in the shadows that early dawn cast across the mountains opposite her, and the cold morning air nipped at her exposed skin. She was glad she wore her leathers, but she should have worn a cloak. What had possessed her to stay the night here?

Interesting choice of words.

Torako nearly jumped out of her skin.

"Who said that?" she asked, crouching into a fighting stance and reaching for the hilt of her sword.

Go ahead, draw the sword, the voice urged her. She wanted to comply, but obeying a voice inside her skull that wasn't her own struck her as questionable.

Wise, Torako-san. You were an excellent choice for a Claw.

"Claw?" she muttered, only belatedly realizing that she was answering the voice, even if she hadn't heeded its advice to draw the blade at her side.

Or Blade, if you prefer.

"Are you calling me a weapon?"

Aren't you one? the voice asked. *We're all weapons in our own right, in the end. Someone's foil. Someone's folly. Humans can always be used against each other, if you know the right tricks. But I know you're not actually a sword, if that's what you're saying.*

"Who are you, and why are you in my head?"

She shook her head as she spoke, as if the effort might dislodge the strange presence from her mind.

Don't you remember anything from last night? the voice asked.

"Last night? How long have I been unconscious?"

Sundown to sun up. Unsheathe the sword and I will explain—

But Torako didn't wait to hear what the voice in her head might explain before she turned to the goat path that led back to her cave, and began as hasty a descent as her feet would allow.

Where are you running off to? the voice asked, as she tore down the narrow trail. The mountainside was steep, and the trail doubled back on itself again, and again, to make the angle more manageable, but she skipped turns when she could, if the terrain wasn't too cluttered, whipping past boulders and careening around trees at a speed that was probably reckless, but she didn't care. If she'd been unconscious all night, then she had been gone at least that long, and Raku would be sick with worry. She'd left to fill a waterskin, she remembered that much. How could she have been gone for so long? Raku would be sure she was dead, and Itachi? Was Itachi sitting at home, sure that her mother had left her?

She ran faster.

Torako felt like she was falling as much as running down the side of the mountain. She whipped past trees at speeds that would have had branches cutting her skin if not for her protective leathers. The wind whipped the few tendrils of her hair that weren't contained by her braid into her face, and she blinked often to keep her eyes clear. Her lungs burned with the strain; even though she was running downhill, the effort of dodging trees, rocks, and anything else in her path at a flat run was enough to wind her.

Although her lack of breath may have been at least in part due to her exasperation with the strange voice in her head that would not stop talking as she descended the mountain.

We should speak before you see your family once more.

This is a dangerous pace for a mortal. One wrong step and you could fall to your death.

I can't believe I've finally been reunited with my full power after a thousand cycles only to have my wielder die running down a hill.

If you would stop for just a moment and draw the sword, you would find I can be of assistance.

They will not die of worry if you are gone for the time it takes me to explain this.

She brushed off the increasingly irritated thoughts that were not her own, and continued down the mountain.

It wasn't that she thought Raku would die of worry. It was more that the longer she ran, the more she remembered of her conversation with Raku after she'd arrived home. Raku had been so distracted by her own concerns that she'd brushed off Torako killing six men in front of their daughter. Not that she'd expected her wife to hold it against her for long, but she had expected her to at least be mildly concerned. Instead, she had been more worried about whatever it was that she'd planned to tell Torako.

If Torako had been in her right mind, she would never have walked away from Raku for longer than it would have taken to fill the waterskin. Instead, she'd somehow walked up a mountain and slept atop it. She had no idea how she would explain it, but

—

I could help you explain it, if you would give me a moment.

"If you can talk inside my head, why do you need me to draw my sword?" she panted, slowing only slightly to get those words out, but still hurtling down the trail as she did it.

I would rather you see me in my true form as I explain things for the first time. We technically met last night, but it is normal that you wouldn't remember without drawing the sword again. The rite isn't quite complete.

Torako had no idea what rite the voice was referring to, and she didn't feel particularly inclined to finish a ceremony she hadn't meant to start, so she ignored the voice and kept moving.

You are tied to me, whether you like it or not, human. If you have complaints, you should level them at your grandsire. But I am not about to go back into exile because you do not have the patience to walk down a mountainside.

Torako did nothing to slow her stride, but she did direct her thoughts to what the voice was saying.

"Tied to you?" she huffed. She was still running flat out and didn't have much breath to spare. She had just reached the flatter woodland trail at the base of the mountain and it wouldn't be long at all before she was back home with Raku and Itachi. She put on a final burst of speed, preparing to jump the creek.

Yes. If you would pause for a moment so that I might explain, you could unsheathe the sword and I would—

But Torako didn't hear what the voice would do, because at that moment she burst up the final rise that separated her from her home, and into the small clearing where she had left Raku the evening before.

Then felt her chest tighten in agony, as she took in the devastation and blood.

— Itachi —

ITACHI WOKE TO the sound of birds singing, the sun just poking through the forest canopy. She was surprised to find herself still curled into a ball between the two main trunks of the small tree she had hidden away in the night before.

She blinked and rubbed her eyes.

She hadn't meant to sleep in the tree. She had meant to wait for Mama.

She looked around the clearing that led to their cave and tried not to cry.

There was no one there. She used her kisō to be sure. But the ground was covered in unfamiliar footprints, Kaa-san's papers were strewn around the ground, Mama's cloak was trampled into the dirt, branches of nearby trees were broken, and there was blood in the grass not far from their cave door.

She could feel tears run down her face. Mama would say that it was ok to cry when she was scared. Kaa-san would say there was nothing to be scared of. But they were both gone, so Itachi thought that being scared was ok.

She had never been alone before. Not like this, anyway. She played in the woods sometimes while Mama and Kaa-san made food, or cleaned the futons. But they were always close by, and if she needed them, they would come running.

But no one was running to her now.

She sniffled.

She wiped at her face. Her back hurt from the branches poking her all night. And she needed to pee.

She was afraid to get out of the tree, in case the people who took Kaa-san came back, but she did not want to pee in the tree.

She had just decided to climb down from her perch when she heard the loud thump of footsteps coming fast from the creek. Her heart pounded to match the steps and she scrambled to pull her legs back into the crook of the tree.

Then she closed her eyes, asked her kisō to keep her hidden, and waited.

⁔ Torako ⁔

TORAKO COULD BARELY breathe. Her chest felt like it might never allow her enough air again. She could already tell that there was no one here—Raku would never have left her own scrolls and papers strewn about outside like this. If she were here, she would have been carefully collecting her work, or perhaps comforting Itachi after… whatever had happened here. But Torako could hear no sounds coming from the cave they had called home for the past five cycles, or from the woods beyond their clearing. Only the sounds of birds, squirrels, and other creatures going about their business. Which Torako knew meant that whoever had done this had been gone for some time.

She had to look, though. Her mind would not allow her to leave this place without checking every inch of it for signs of her daughter and wife.

Allow me to help you, please, child.

Torako was so devastated by what her eyes took in that she had forgotten about the voice.

Unsheathe the sword. You should be on your guard anyway, and I promise I can help you find your loved ones. My nose is far more effective than yours.

And why not do as the voice said? Torako had already lost her wife and her child, why not her mind as well? Besides, the voice made a good point about being on guard. Just because Torako felt as though she'd been hollowed out inside didn't mean she didn't have more to lose. Her family was missing. They needed her now more than ever. She couldn't find them if she let whoever was responsible for this catch her unawares and run her through.

She drew the katana from its deep blue sheath, and gasped when an enormous wolf appeared before her.

⫸ Itachi ⫷

ITACHI KEPT HER eyes shut tight, even as she heard the footsteps slow and then stop. She knew that closing her eyes didn't make *her* any harder to see, but she thought that if she kept her eyes closed it might be easier to stay quiet, because she wouldn't cry out if she saw a stranger in her woods.

She was just about to reach out with her kisō to figure out who stood in the clearing now when she heard a gasp. Her eyes flew open before she could stop them, and what she saw made her scream.

⪢ *Torako* ⪡

"PUPPY!!!"

TORAKO'S HEAD snapped up, her gaze jumping from the enormous wolf to the spot where the high-pitched squeal of delight had originated.

"Itachi-chan?" she asked, her heart in her throat.

She heard the sound of something small hitting the dirt and then the pounding of tiny feet, but she still couldn't see her daughter. She blinked and thought that she saw a strange shifting in the light not far from her, like heat rising off a rock in the sun, but when she tried to focus on it, nothing was there.

"Mama!" shouted a voice just in front of her.

And then she almost fell over when a small but solid weight launched into her legs and wrapped itself around her knees. As soon as the weight made contact, she could see that it was Itachi, her own daughter, suddenly right there, hugging her legs.

Torako pried the girl off of her knees and brought her up to her chest, hugging her tight and kissing her cheeks, nose, hair, anywhere she could.

"Itachi-chan," she whispered, with tears streaming down her face. She hadn't let herself truly consider what might have happened to the girl until this moment. She had rejected every horrible possibility her imagination had thrown at her, because to consider any of them for more than a heartbeat was to give in to absolute despair.

But now that she held her heart in her arms again, all the horrors that she had rejected made themselves known once more, and she couldn't help but sob with relief, knowing that none of them were real.

"Itachi-chan, what happened? Where is Kaa-san?"

When she looked at Itachi's small face, pressed against her shoulder, she saw that Itachi was crying too. Her eyes and nose were red and puffy, her face was wet, and she was smiling and shaking with sobs at the same time.

"Mama, I don't know where they took her. She told me to hide. They came while we were sleeping, and Kaa-san showed me her thoughts and told me to hide. I asked my kisō to help, and then not even Kaa-san could see me. She attacked the strangers and made them run after her, and I ran to the tree and stayed there and no one saw me. I was waiting for you to come home but I fell asleep. And then I was going to get up and pee but I heard you coming and thought it was more bandits so I stayed hidden and then—Mama, when did you get a wolf!?"

The entire explanation came out in one giant stream of words, and Torako let it wash over her like a healing spring. She hugged Itachi tighter and then turned to the wolf, who had apparently taken their distraction as an excuse to enter their cave and was just now coming back outside.

"My name is Sairō," the wolf said.

And Torako decided that now might be a good time to sit down. So she did.

"Your wolf talks?" Itachi squealed with delight.

The wolf indeed appeared to be talking.

"The wolf is not mine," Torako said, frowning. She was too stunned to even care that she was sitting in the dirt, but she was also starting to remember fragments of the night before.

"Accurate," Sairō agreed. "I belong to no one but myself. However, we are tied to one another, Torako-san. I did try to explain on the way down."

"YOU are the one who lured me up the mountainside," Torako growled.

"Yes. I had to. There was no other way to get my sword to my shrine."

"YOU are the reason I wasn't *here* last night."

Torako's voice was low enough that she could feel it vibrate her hands through Itachi's chest.

"I had nothing to do with whatever took place here last night, I swear to you. I called you to me because I cannot be whole without my sword, and it has been more than a thousand cycles since I was myself. The timing is strange, but it is a coincidence."

"And the fact that I found your sword on a bandit who attacked me yesterday is a coincidence too, I suppose?"

Sairō let out a huff of breath through their nose that Torako thought might be a snort of disdain.

"Hardly," they said. "It took quite a bit of maneuvering to get that katana anywhere near this mountain. As it was, you were the only worthy wielder within a reasonable distance. It was my luck that you stumbled upon that group of bandits. If the idiot who'd carried me that far had made it to this mountain, he would not have survived the rite, and I would be stuck all over again."

"So you *did* bring those bandits here." Torako probably would have risen and been taking threatening steps towards the enormous wolf by now, but Itachi was still clinging tightly to her chest, even as she ogled the "puppy," and Torako could not bear the thought of setting the girl down.

"I did not. They were headed here anyway, I simply encouraged them to bring my sword along for the ride."

Rather suddenly, Torako felt a headache coming on. She held Itachi to her and closed her eyes for a moment, wishing that she didn't have to think any of this through.

The bandits had taken Raku. It may or may not have had anything to do with the wolf spirit trapped in a sword, but it was done, and it could not be undone by arguing. They were wasting time.

She took a deep breath. Kissed the top of Itachi's head and set her down on the ground beside her.

"Itachi-chan, can you go and get our two warmest cloaks, and our two warmest blankets?" she asked, looking into her daughter's deep green eyes.

"Yes, Mama!"

Itachi's voice was bright and she smiled, wiping her face as she said the words, but Torako could tell the girl was still a ball of mixed emotions. Fair enough. So was Torako.

When Itachi was inside the cave, Torako turned to the enormous wolf once more, finally taking a good look at them. They had white and grey fur, with almost black markings on their head and back. Their eyes glowed, seeming to waver between bright yellow and amber.

"Sairō-san," Torako said, trying out the wolf's name, and feeling an unsettling hum pass through her as she did so. "I don't trust you."

Sairō said nothing to that, and Torako sighed.

"You said, earlier, in my head… you said that you could help me find my family. My daughter is here, thank all the Kami. But you heard her. They took Raku-san, my wife. She… I can't live without her, so if you don't want to wind up trapped in that sword again without a human to let you out, you're going to have to help me."

Sairō's face was, well, a wolf's face, and Torako didn't know much about how wolves expressed their emotions, but nothing she had said seemed to particularly ruffle the creature.

"I have said already that we are tied, Torako-san. You are a worthy Claw, or you would not have survived the rite that joined us. I am bound to protect you, and, unlike some, I recognize that physical injuries are not the only threats that humans need protecting from. I will do all that I can to help you regain your heart."

Torako felt too numb to appreciate the sincerity in those words, so she simply nodded at the wolf and then stood. She sheathed the sword in its scabbard, tucking the saya into her belt. When she looked up, Sairō was still there, watching her from just in front of the cave mouth.

"I thought the sword had to be drawn for you to… be here," she said, gesturing at the wolf.

"The first time, yes. It was the final part of the rite that bound us. Now that it is done, so long as you are in possession of my Claw, the blade need not be drawn for me to wander freely."

Torako shook her head again, as if doing so would chase away this strange new reality in which she was bound to a talking wolf spirit.

With Sairō's katana safely tucked into her belt, she had a brief moment of panic, then remembered finding Shiken on her back the night before. She still wasn't certain if most of that had been a dream of some sort, so she reached over her shoulder with frantic hands until she felt her walking staff tied in place.

She was amazed that she hadn't caught it on a tree when she'd been running at top speed down the side of a mountain.

She rubbed the top of the katana that had gotten her through more than twenty cycles of guarding Sōryū forest fondly and then she went inside to pack a few essentials for their journey.

When she and Itachi returned to the clearing a little bit later, they were dressed as they had been the day before. They both had small bedrolls strapped to their backs, in the center of which they'd packed minimal provisions and the means to boil water and skewer rabbits easily. Torako had Sairō's blade tucked into her belt, along with her wakizashi and a hunting knife, and the wrap slung around her waist like a sash, but with all the knots in place for her to easily arrange it on her shoulders to carry Itachi when she grew tired.

Torako tried not to think about how far ahead their quarry would be. Leaving unprepared would only slow them down in the long run. She had managed to resist the urge to clean up Raku's papers properly, resorting to quickly grabbing the ones outside and placing them on the low table within.

"You can find her?" Torako asked.

Sairō looked at her and dipped their snout in what Torako took to be assent.

"I have been gathering the scents of all those who went through your home and the nearby woods here last night. I can follow any of them you like, but for now, our choice is simple. They all went in the same direction. One of them was bleeding quite a bit, and if we are lucky this will have slowed them down. Follow me."

Sairō didn't wait for a reply. The wolf simply padded silently into the woods, away from the cave that had been home since Itachi was born, and Torako and Itachi had to run to catch up.

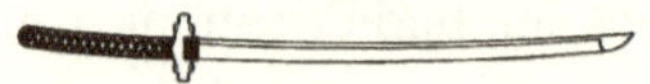

Torako let her gaze rake over the forest that surrounded the thin trail they followed, breathing in the warm air of early summer, full of the scent of damp leaves, new growth, and fresh dirt. She tried to think of anywhere safe she could leave Itachi that wouldn't make it impossible for her to catch up with whoever had stolen Raku away. She wasn't coming up with many options.

"Itachi-chan, can you call Yanagi-sama?" she asked, when the sun was still low in the sky.

Itachi was quiet for a moment beside her on the trail. They both walked as fast as they could to try to keep up with the enormous wolf ahead of them, but Itachi had been telling her what little she could about the people who had taken Raku when she had the breath for it. Eventually, she shook her head.

"No, Mama. I can't hear him. Kaa-san said that he and Obaa-chan came to say goodbye while we were on patrol."

Torako frowned at that news.

"Raku-san mentioned that Tenshi-san had come by to talk to her, but she didn't say that she'd gone on a trip."

Of course, she hadn't really had the chance. Torako had disappeared up the side of a mountain before Raku could tell her what she'd wanted to say.

Well, there were her two top choices for watching Itachi gone in a single breath.

She sighed, then turned to look at Itachi, with her serious face and little legs struggling to keep up with Torako's long stride and the wolf's graceful gait.

"Hold on a moment, will you, Sairō?"

She didn't look to see if the wolf waited, only knelt and started adjusting her cloak and bags.

It didn't take long for Torako to pull the wrap into place and have Itachi climb onto her back, wriggling into the crossed layers of fabric so that she could see over Torako's shoulder without needing to hold her own weight up.

"Your pup should learn to run faster," the giant wolf grumbled.

"She's half my height and *I* can barely keep up with you," Torako replied mildly, making a final adjustment to the bedroll and waterskin that were now slung across her chest. She pulled their straps snug so they wouldn't bounce off of her as she practically ran to keep pace with the unnaturally large wolf.

Sairō only grunted.

Once all was in place, she leaned heavily on Shiken and stood up. Then she turned back to the wolf.

"Let's go," Torako said.

The wolf turned and trotted down the path once more, and Torako started after them.

"Mama, I need to pee," Itachi said.

"Itachi-chan, you—"

Torako cut herself off and took a deep breath. She hadn't reminded the girl to pee before getting in the wrap. She had been too intent on moving faster, hoping against all odds that they would catch up with the bandits who had taken Raku and make them release her.

"Yes. Ok. Just a moment."

She didn't have to yell after the enormous wolf ahead of her, who had already stopped in the trail. Torako knelt down and helped Itachi extract herself from the wrap.

"Go quickly, please," she said, once Itachi was on the ground.

When they were finally ready to resume their pursuit, Torako looked at Sairō and said nothing at all, but the wolf turned on the trail and bounded away in a proper run. Torako let out a rueful laugh and followed after.

The sun was high in the sky, though barely visible through the thick green canopy above them, when they reached the place where the trail widened and Torako fell to her knees.

"Mama, what's wrong?" Itachi's voice asked quietly.

Torako couldn't form words around the lump in her throat, but she didn't have to. Sairō turned to her and let out a low growl.

"Horses," the wolf said. "More horses than these men could possibly need, but they took them all anyway."

Torako swallowed to try to keep the emotions at bay.

"Mama? What is it? Are horses bad?"

Torako blinked at the obvious hoof prints, at the recently devoured grass that now covered only half of the clearing just ahead. They'd moved as fast as they could. She'd carried Itachi on her back while running, damn it all. She had a wolf that could smell how many horses these people had, and she *still* hadn't managed to get here in time to matter. They had horses. The road was just on the other side of the foothills before her, and they had horses. Once they reached the road they could ride hard and go anywhere in Gensokai, and Torako would simply have to guess.

She could feel the tears streaming down her face, and she still hadn't answered Itachi's increasingly insistent questions.

"Mama? Why are the horses making you sad?"

Torako wiped her face with one of the more-sueded patches on her arm leathers.

"Torako-san."

Suddenly there was a pair of glowing amber orbs in front of her.

She blinked.

Ah yes. Eyes. Sairō's eyes.

"Torako-san," the voice repeated. And now, when Torako blinked, she thought the eyes were much closer than they had been a moment earlier. No that wasn't right, they weren't any closer. They were just bigger. Much bigger. How could the wolf's eyes be that big?

She stood up.

And stepped back.

"How did you do that?"

Sairō made a sound that could have been a bark or a laugh.

"I may have had half my power trapped in a katana for an age, but I'm still a Kami, child. The rules as you know them don't entirely apply to me."

Torako simply stared at the wolf for another long moment.

"Well, what are you waiting for, Claw?"

Torako was about to ask what they meant when Sairō clarified.

"Get on."

Torako's heart skipped in her chest. The wolf was the size of a large horse. She didn't think Sairō was in the habit of letting people ride them. She hated the necessity of it.

She refused to think of anything but reaching Raku.

She got on.

"Are you sure—" Torako began, as she adjusted her seat so that she was balanced astride the wolf, with Itachi still wrapped to her back. But Sairō took off at a full run before she could finish the question, and Torako barely restrained a shriek as she worked to keep her seat. Riding a wolf was *not* the same as riding a horse. Sairō might have been as tall as a horse now, but that didn't mean they were as comfortable as a horse. Wolves were tall, lanky creatures without broad backs for riding, even when they suddenly made themselves horse height.

If it hadn't been for the thick fur covering Sairō's body, the repeated jarring would have been unbearable. As it was, Torako was worried that walking would be a challenge the next day.

And even still, it was one of the most exhilarating things Torako had ever done. Sairō kept a pace that would have exhausted most horses. Of course, a normal wolf couldn't hold a candle to a horse for long, but this wolf, this enormous, horse-sized wolf, could bound as a wolf could, but with legs the length of a horse's.

The road disappeared beneath them at an alarming rate. Wind whipped Torako's face hard enough that she eventually leaned low behind Sairō's head, glad that her body acted as a windbreak for Itachi.

Of course, since Sairō was *not* a horse—bred for endurance as well as speed—the sun was only halfway to setting when they came to a rather abrupt halt.

"If you would be so kind as to find me a deer, or two, it would be appreciated," Sairō requested, as Torako and Itachi dismounted on shaking legs. Then the enormous creature stretched out in a grassy clearing to the right of the road and promptly closed their eyes.

Torako didn't say anything in reply. A part of her wished to argue, but how could she? A horse would have stopped to graze by now. It only made sense that Sairō would need rest and food.

As much as she chafed at the idea of stopping when the bandits who had taken Raku might still be riding away, she was fairly certain they had been moving faster than most horses could. She had to hope they were gaining on their enemies fast enough that they could catch them even if they stopped for a few hours here and there. As soon as they had hit the road headed northeast, she could easily guess where the enemy was headed—Sairō's excellent nose was hardly needed at this point—and her stomach tightened at the thought of the bandits getting there before she caught up to them. This road led to Sakata, and a ship leaving from Sakata could head anywhere in Gensokai.

Torako pushed away those worries and pulled Itachi from the wrap as gently as she could. *How had the girl fallen asleep while riding a wolf?* And then she nestled her daughter into the crook of Sairō's front paws. She hesitated only for a moment as she did it. She'd had her doubts when the wolf first appeared, and it wasn't as though she didn't suspect the Kami of having its own agenda, but… she couldn't imagine the creature meant them any harm after everything it had done for them that day. Besides, all things considered, was there a safer place to leave her heart than under the guard of a horse-sized wolf?

She placed her bedroll beside them both, picked up the waterskin and Shiken, checked to be certain that Sairō's blade was still in her belt, and then set about deciding how best to hunt a deer with a katana.

Torako cursed herself for not bringing Raku's bow with her, but there was only so much she could carry when she was also carrying Itachi in the wrap, and a bow and arrows had seemed like too much. She had expected to fish, or stick to the dried provisions she and Itachi had packed. She had not expected to have to feed a monstrous wolf who was too exhausted from carrying her on its back to catch its own food.

Then she had decided that hunting a deer with a sword would pose an interesting challenge. It had.

But now she was covered in blood dripping down her arms, and her back felt like it was about to cramp up, and she really wished someone had told her that she was going to have to hunt deer, because she definitely would have brought the Kami-cursed bow, and a quiver full of arrows. She would have.

She had needed to search nearly a full league into the forest in order to find a deer; a distance that she had probably taken longer than usual to cover thanks to the pain in her crotch and thighs. Wolf riding certainly had its drawbacks. But she'd followed the lone buck long enough for it to become fully distracted by a tasty bit of underbrush, and then snuck up on it with an already drawn blade in hopes of decapitating it. Decapitating it had not quite worked on the first try, and she had been forced to make multiple cuts. At least she'd killed the poor thing with the first blow. She was intent on removing the head because, small though the buck was, it would be hard enough for her to carry without the small rack of antlers and skull attached to it. The entire process was messy, and made messier still by the act of carrying the thing over her shoulders. At least the blood had stopped flowing freely by the time she reached their camp.

"Here," she said, throwing the buck in front of the still-slumbering wolf when she finally reached them. "Save us a leg," she added, when Sairō blinked themself awake to the smell of freshly killed deer.

She felt a hundred times lighter as soon as the animal was off of her.

"I'm going to wash off in a stream I saw on the way back. It's not far. I'll fill our waterskins as well. Keep an eye on Itachi-chan, would you?"

"Always," the wolf replied, as Torako turned back to the woods once more.

Torako moved quickly through the sun-dappled woods to the small stream she'd passed earlier, trying to think about anything other than how the blood covering her clothes and skin felt. She tried to decide how she felt about the enormous wolf who had lured her to the top of a mountain just when her family had needed her most.

She certainly appreciated Sairō allowing her and Itachi to ride on their back. It was getting her to Raku far faster than she would have been able to move on her own, especially with Itachi in tow. In addition, because the wolf could still scent the bandits on the road, she didn't have to guess where they had gone. She was grateful to be moving, to be doing something to get Raku back, to reach her before… she wasn't sure what unnamed clock they were racing to beat, but she was certain that if they took too long, rescue would cease to be an option. So she was grateful. Definitely.

But she also had to wonder at the timing. Sairō might insist it was coincidence, but how could it be? Something about their presence had caused Raku's abduction. Torako had run into some bandits, killed them, taken the katana that held half of Sairō's power, and then more bandits had shown up and taken her wife. The idea that the two events were unrelated was preposterous. And Sairō even admitted that they had used the bandits to bring the sword to her valley. So why wouldn't the bandits try to recover it? But then why take Raku instead of Torako? Why take a *person* at all? If they wanted the sword, why wouldn't they keep looking for it instead of running off with her wife as fast as they could? None of it added up. Raku had wanted to tell her something before she'd wandered up a mountain against her own will, and she would bet a whole moon's rice that whatever it was would be the key to all these pieces. But she didn't have the key. She didn't have Raku. Nothing felt right anymore, and Torako couldn't make sense of it without her wife.

She looked down and found that she had reached the stream already.

She sighed as she set about washing the blood from her face, hands, and arms, and she was so absorbed in the task of getting clean that she didn't even notice the flash of a face reflected in the water behind her shoulder.

Sairō must have fallen back asleep as soon they had finished consuming the small buck she had brought them. The enormous wolf was snoring softly, with a slightly bloody muzzle curled against the length of Itachi's small, still sleeping form. Torako felt her chest loosen somewhat at the sight of it. She wasn't sure why —it's not as though she had expected Sairō to harm Itachi at all, she would never have left her there if she had. It was only that Itachi's small hand was clutching a handful of the thick fur that covered Sairō's neck, and the wolf had tucked a protective paw over her legs.

She smiled, despite her other misgivings about the creature. She had always had a soft spot for anyone who was kind to her daughter. It seemed that enormous wolf spirits were no exception.

Torako was delighted to see that Sairō had left her a deer leg too, as she'd requested.

By the time she had collected wood, roasted the leg, and divided up the meat into portions for her, Itachi, and rations for the next day of travel, both Itachi and Sairō were starting to wake up.

The sun was dipping behind the horizon by the time Torako and Itachi had finished eating.

"Allow me to stretch a bit, then we'll be on our way," Sairō said, getting to their feet by way of what looked like a deep bow, followed by a move that dragged their massive hind legs through the tall grass for a moment before bringing them up to standing.

Torako was almost too stunned by the suggestion to speak, but she decided not to question her luck. Even taking the time to hunt and prepare food had eaten away at her, necessary though she knew it to be. She was ecstatic to think they might gain even more ground before they stopped for the night.

She did her own quick series of stretches, then made sure to coax Itachi into peeing one more time before she donned the wrap, helped Itachi climb inside it, on her chest this time, and slung their bedrolls and waterskins in place across her back. She wasn't certain that switching Itachi to her chest would make things more comfortable, but she thought that simply shifting things around might ease some of the chafing.

"Well, come on then," Sairō grumbled, even as they bowed once more to allow Torako to get on.

Just as she was putting her hands in the wolf's thick ruff in order to pull herself up, an idea occurred to her.

"Just a moment," she said, sliding down to stand next to Sairō again. "Would you object to a blanket across your back, just here?"

She patted lightly at the place where she and Itachi had been sitting.

"Hmph. I'm hot enough as it is, Torako-san."

Torako hesitated.

"Never mind. I only thought some extra padding might make it easier for me to walk and hunt when we stop for the night."

Sairō huffed out a breath, but before Torako could reach for their ruff to mount, they lay down.

"Quickly, we don't have much time. And if you go sliding off because of the blanket, it's your own fault."

Torako didn't reply, she simply removed her bedroll, pulled the blanket from around her belongings and rerolled them all into her cloak before putting the roll on her back once more. Then she positioned the blanket, folded over twice, right where she planned to sit.

This time, when Sairō rose with Torako and Itachi in place, she didn't quite feel like crying, and decided that would have to count as an improvement.

⇒ *Itachi* ⇐

ITACHI WOKE UP screaming for Obaa-chan.

Mama was right there, instantly clutching her tight with one arm and kissing her face and head, whispering that everything would be alright. But how could everything be alright when she'd seen Obaa-chan disappear?! One moment she had been standing there, shouting something at the creatures who held her arms, and the next moment she had been gone. The creatures—who had looked like something out of a nightmare, shifting and changing shape every time that Itachi tried to look at them—had been laughing and shouting, cheering that they'd got her, and then, when Itachi had desperately tried to reach for Obaa-chan again, she had found nothing. Nothing at all. Not even a trace telling her that Obaa-chan had returned to the human realm.

Then Yanagi-sama had been there, she wasn't sure where he'd come from, telling her it wasn't safe to stay, that she needed to leave. To return to the human realm right away.

She hadn't wanted to, and when she had started to cry out for Obaa-chan, Yanagi-sama had somehow *pushed* her back into her own body. Where she was wrapped tight to Mama's chest, with a giant wolf running down the road beneath them, helping them try to catch up to the people who had taken Kaa-san.

So, no. Nothing was alright.

But she cried quietly against her mother's chest and didn't even try to explain, because she didn't know how to explain it. Mama wasn't supposed to know about her dreamwalking. Obaa-chan had taught her how, after the first time she had wandered into Obaa-chan's dreams when she was little. After that, she had been able to visit Obaa-chan whenever she wanted, even when Obaa-chan was far away. Itachi had loved dreamwalking, and she had always worried that if she told Mama or Kaa-san about it, they would ask her to stop. So instead it had been her and Obaa-chan's secret.

Itachi hadn't meant to visit her tonight. She hadn't even meant to fall asleep again. But somehow the pounding of wolf paws had lulled her to sleep, and she had wound up in the dream world without meaning to go.

And then she had witnessed her grandmother being torn away from the world.

9日 6月, 新議 8年

9th Day, 6th Moon, Cycle 8 of the New Council

⇒ Torako ⇐

BY THE TIME they stopped for the night, Torako wondered if the blanket had made any difference at all. Every step was painful. She helped Itachi out of the wrap and set the girl to collecting firewood and filling the waterskins solely to give her something to do. She had stopped crying after a while, but she still seemed upset, and had barely spoken since whatever nightmare had awoken her in the middle of their ride. Honestly, Torako wasn't surprised she was having nightmares, after everything she'd been through in the past two days. She only hoped that the nightmares would stop once they'd gotten Raku back safely. Itachi seemed determined to collect firewood and water despite everything though, so Torako decided she could worry about the rest later.

Sairō, for their part, had immediately lain directly in the creek that ran past the clearing where they had stopped, and after a few mouthfuls of water, the giant wolf seemed disinclined to get up.

"Another deer, please, Torako-san," they had asked before closing their eyes.

"Itachi-chan, promise me you will stay in the clearing with Sairō-san," Torako had said, checking both her katanas. She would have to use Sairō's blade this time, instead of Shiken, she thought. She hadn't had time to sharpen and clean Shiken properly since the last deer, and she'd rather not have to make multiple cuts again.

The mere idea of tracking and hunting another deer right now, when her daughter seemed haunted by a nightmare and her entire body was begging her to simply lie down and rest for the night, made her ache, body and soul. But she didn't allow that to stop her. She couldn't.

Sairō had covered enough ground that they must be near to catching the bandits by now. As long as their enemies stopped for their own rest—and if they were relying on horses, they would have to—then the gap between them had to be closing. In return for that advantage, she would do anything she could to aid the enormous wolf. She would hunt a hundred deer if she had to.

She groaned as all the chafed spots on her body throbbed unpleasantly in unison with every careful step she took along the moonlit path that led into the woods.

Hopefully one deer would be enough.

Torako almost cried with relief when she came across two does nibbling some of the long grass next to a small pond not far from where Sairō had laid claim to the creek. They stood, heads bent to the ground, unconcerned despite being clearly visible in the dappled moonlight that poured through the canopy above. It made her wonder if a spirit wolf had any scent to speak of. The two creatures seemed utterly undisturbed in their meal, despite the proximity of a giant wolf. Of course, they hadn't noticed her yet either, and while she was normally quite adept at walking quietly through the woods, her legs were so sore that she felt like every step she took was a barely controlled slap of her feet against the ground. She had been amazed to find them still munching quietly by the time she had tucked herself behind a fallen log on the far side of the pond.

Still, the does paid her no mind.

The grass must have been truly delicious.

She had just drawn Sairō's blade in order to start her final approach toward her quarry when she saw a flash of something in the pond beside her.

She turned, glad to already have a blade in hand, to see what might have caused it, but she saw nothing but moonlight reflecting on the water. After checking the woods behind her to be certain that nothing was there, she returned her focus to deer-stalking.

She was getting better at killing large animals swiftly with only a katana, but it was still messy. At least she'd managed to take the doe's head off with a single cut this time. Sairō's blade was quite a bit sharper than Shiken, with its poor, battered edge. The second doe had gone running as soon as she'd struck the first, and Torako was relieved to find that there were no fawns hiding nearby as she knelt and prepared to hoist the still-warm body of the first doe onto her shoulders.

It wasn't until she stood up, with the animal draped across both shoulders, that she sensed motion directly behind her, this time complete with the shuffle of feet in leaves. She whirled, deer and all, to see... a ghost? No, that wasn't right.

The figure, bathed so entirely in moonlight that it appeared to be made of it, simply stared at her for a moment through glowing eyes before finally speaking.

"Torako-san, I must speak with you."

"Right. Well, lucky for you, I have a deer on my shoulders and reaching for my katana will be a literal pain in my ass right now, so sure. Go ahead. I promise not to stab you unless you say something I don't like."

The figure bathed in moonlight frowned.

"I'm afraid what I have to tell you will not please you at all."

"Well, you'll have a head start by the time I put this deer down, so go ahead."

"Did your mother ever talk to you about her father?"

That had not been anywhere close to what Torako had guessed this might be about. She had been running scenarios that might tie this moon person to Raku's capture through her head since the moment they had appeared, but she had not anticipated talking about her mother's father.

"No," was the only answer she could give.

"Then you have little reason to trust me, but perhaps that is for the best. After tonight, you should not trust me at all."

That made so little sense that Torako could do nothing but stand there, being bled on by a deer corpse.

"I am your grandfather, Tsukuyomi," the figure in moonlight declared. "Your mother was the product of my union with a human woman."

Tsukuyomi hesitated for a moment then, and Torako's mind had just enough time to snag on his use of "was" before he continued, his voice sounding broken compared to only moments ago.

"She is gone. Tenshi-san is no longer in this world, or the next, and… I am so sorry."

Torako simply stared and blinked.

"It is all my fault. I thought I could protect her, but… I'm sorry. And there is more to come. I've sent you what protection I can, but it may not be enough. You must not trust me, if you see me again. I wish I had more time to explain, but—"

The shining figure of Tsukuyomi turned to look over his shoulder then, before turning back to her.

"Do not trust me."

And then he was gone. He didn't leave, he did not walk away, he simply vanished, as if he had never been there. And perhaps he hadn't. She had heard the name Tsukuyomi before. The god of the moon. Her mother had never mentioned him, though. In fact, she had never spoken of her father at all.

But she had told Raku something important, something that Raku had then planned to tell her.

Torako felt hollow inside. She had no interest in believing that Tenshi was dead. She and her mother had had their differences over the cycles, and for good reason, but since Itachi had been born, they had been mending all that was broken between them, and Torako had been learning to love her mother again. Perhaps she had never really stopped.

She did not wish to believe this random being made of moonlight, who showed up and warned her not to trust him.

But Itachi had called out for her Obaa-chan when she'd woken from that nightmare.

And for a long while afterwards, she had whispered a single phrase over and over again.

"She's gone."

Torako drifted into an aching sleep with Itachi curled in her arms. She had somehow managed to go through the motions of eating—probably because her body was screaming out for food —even though the meat moved through her mouth like mud and ash. She doubted she would have slept at all, were it not for the combined exhaustion of the leagues she had covered on foot with Itachi on her back and the strain of riding wolfback for half the night.

She awoke to a kick in the face. She blinked blearily at the offending foot for a moment, wondering how Itachi had found enough room to flip upside down while still curled in her arms, and why she'd felt the need to thrust her heel into Torako's jaw. She took some comfort in realizing that Itachi was still sound asleep, and probably wouldn't have applied her heel quite so enthusiastically to Torako's chin if she'd been conscious.

"Tiny demon," she whispered, rubbing her jaw and staring at the early morning sky. They were still in the clearing just beyond the road where Sairō had collapsed into the nearby creek. The sky was just lightening with the first hints of dawn above the thick green canopy of the forest. For a moment, it was almost peaceful.

Then, everything came back to her. Waking up with a strange voice in her head, racing home to find Raku missing, then the moon Kami, the deer, the news about her mother. She still didn't want to believe it was true, but when she had returned to their camp and dropped the doe in front of a slumbering Sairō, she had seen the look in Itachi's eyes again and gone to comfort her.

The little girl had come undone in her arms, pouring forth a story about how she'd had a dream in which she'd seen Tenshi die. She couldn't quite explain it all, and Torako did not ask her to. Instead, she'd held her tight until there were no more tears. Then she'd brought out some of the leftover venison from her earlier hunt and cut them both enough to fill their bellies quickly.

She'd been too exhausted to contemplate what any of it meant last night, and she still didn't feel as though she had any idea what was going on. Too much was happening at once, and all of it was awful.

She could do nothing for her mother and she could do nothing for her grandfather, if he truly was who he said he was. She knew nothing of the spirit realm, and even less of what conflict her mother had gotten wrapped up in.

But she was filled with a steadily growing rage that she could not quite stifle. Her rage needed a target, and if they were quick, it could have one.

She woke her companions and prepared for the road.

≮ Kaiyo ≯

KAIYO SMILED INTO the morning sun that filtered through the trees lining the road. She had never been more grateful to be contradicted, and struggled even now to contain her joy that Tanaka was well enough to be obstreperous.

"You can't mean to follow through on your father's orders," Tanaka continued, from where he rode beside her. The only reason he wasn't yelling at her was that even he understood that having this conversation within earshot of the doshigatai would put both their lives at risk.

"I don't particularly *want* to. But I'd rather not have them on the Wind Serpent for the return trip. I don't trust any of them, and Admiral Saito made it perfectly clear that the scribe is our top priority. What if they decide to try to blow us all up again?"

She was whispering even though the men were all riding ahead of them and the wind blew in their direction. The breeze already carried the faintest trace of the sea with it, and she expected that the next rise they climbed, a little over a league distant, would reveal Sakata, the ocean, and her ship. She told herself it was the proximity of the sea and her ship that made her giddy, and not that Tanaka was beside her, alive, and arguing.

"They are people, Captain. You can't simply dispose of them now that you've used them to your liking."

Kaiyo thought about that for a moment. She wasn't fond of killing, for all that she didn't shy away from it when it was necessary. But what else was she meant to do with a half a dozen men who had been deemed completely irredeemable by her (typically very forgiving) justice system?

"I won't risk you, my crew, my ship, or even this scribe," she nearly spat the word *scribe*, "for these men, just because they've finally made themselves useful after a lifetime of murder, rape, and arson."

"You sound reluctant about protecting the scribe," Tanaka noted.

"She gutted you," Kaiyo growled. "If it weren't for Lyt, you would have died."

Tanaka turned to look at her.

"Captain, we pulled her from her own home in the dead of night, without so much as a word of warning. What did you expect her to do, start writing us love poems?"

Kaiyo only grunted in response.

She knew it wasn't rational to hate the woman for defending herself. If their positions had been reversed, she would have done the same, only to even greater devastation. Tanuki's balls, if the woman's wife had returned home before they had gotten away, Kaiyo was fairly certain not one of them would have escaped with their lives. But that didn't mean she forgave the woman for shoving a knife into her second's gut.

"Returning to our original topic, I don't see how you can, in good conscience, follow your father's orders."

Kaiyo sighed. She wished she didn't see Tanaka's point. She blamed Lyt.

"What do you blame me for, Captain?"

Kaiyo's eyes snapped up as the doshigatai tracker rode alongside them, and she wondered if she had said her last thought aloud without noticing.

Tanaka smiled at xir.

"The Captain was just wondering how expendable you and your compatriots truly are," he said, blithely.

Kaiyo frowned.

"That's not it," she objected. "I've been given strict orders."

"Ah, have you really grown so fond of us that you're actually questioning whether or not you should kill us the moment we reach the Wind Serpent? Getting soft, aren't you, Captain?"

Kaiyo knew that xe was mocking her, but she also wondered how xe could so easily joke about it.

"You're the only one whose fate I'm questioning, Lyt," she growled, then shuddered because it was true. For all that the remaining doshigatai had fallen in line and done as ordered, after half their number had been killed. Kaiyo wouldn't have hesitated to send them to the bottom of the sea as soon as they reached the Wind Serpent. Lyt, on the other hand, had saved her life and her ship, and then xe had saved Tanaka. How could she repay that with death?

"Ah, I see."

The three of them rode beside each other in silence for a long moment.

"If I may plead for my fellow prisoners, Captain?"

Kaiyo said nothing, which Lyt seemed to take as permission.

"I know that Kaigunka pride themselves on their justice system, and how it's more rehabilitative than punitive. It is indeed superior to the justice offered here on the mainland, and even superior to a number of other nations. You may have guessed by now that I was not raised among your people. Would it surprise you to know that there are places in the world where imprisonment forms no part of justice for any crime?"

"Just because some other nation refuses to lock up their rapists doesn't mean that we should follow suit."

"And I wouldn't expect you to singlehandedly change your entire system of justice between here and the ship. However, it is worth considering that just because these men were condemned to rot in a cell does not mean that their lives are inherently devoid of worth."

"They raped people. Murdered people. Set fire to a ship with fifty people locked in the hold!" Kaiyo objected.

"Let me ask you this: does killing them help the people they have harmed?"

"It might. Some of them repeatedly harmed the people they were closest to. Setting them free on the world would be a disaster for their victims, or the families of their victims. Some crimes cannot be forgiven."

Lyt was silent for another moment.

"Perhaps not, but does the Kaigun's system of justice ever ask *why* these crimes were committed? Do the men and women locked away ever have a chance to fix the broken parts of themselves that led to such terrible choices?"

Kaiyo wanted to scream at Lyt, but she remembered at the last moment that she did not wish their conversation to be overheard.

"It does. These men have been given more than one chance to make changes, but it hasn't happened. Even those who commit awful crimes don't get locked away in the doshigatai dungeon for a single offense. They are put there for committing heinous crimes repeatedly and without remorse, even after going through our rehabilitation programs."

"Really?" Lyt asked, raising a single eyebrow.

"Of course!"

"And what about me, then?"

Kaiyo's mouth snapped shut, as she realized what Lyt was saying. Xe had been locked up after multiple 'offenses,' but the first five of those were simply attempting to escape. Which was not in itself an offense that would ever put someone in the doshi-gatai dungeon. The reason xe had been locked away without re-habilitation had been xir use of blood magic. The report that Kaiyo had read didn't even specify what Lyt had done with blood magic, only that xe had used it, and for that, xe had spent the last five cycles locked in an underground stone cell, away from every-thing.

"What exactly did you—"

But she cut off her own question when she looked at the tracker's face. Xir eyes were trained on the road behind them, widening in a surprise Kaiyo had never seen there.

"I think we should consider hurrying," Lyt said, xir voice only slightly higher than normal.

"Why?" Tanaka asked, as he and Kaiyo both peered over their shoulders to try to see whatever had caught Lyt's attention.

"Because I believe our scribe's protection might be catching up to us."

Torako

TORAKO IGNORED THE pain in her thighs, legs, and crotch. She ignored the blur of trees, mountains, and foothills that faded into the distance with every ground-eating stride that Sairō made. She ignored the growing scent of saltwater on the wind that whipped at her face and hair, and focused instead on the smoldering rage inside her.

She tried not to think about what Itachi might be forced to witness when she finally caught up to the bandits who had taken Raku.

Itachi clung to Sairō's thick neck ruff even though Torako had one arm wrapped tightly around her waist. As they had mounted up that morning, Torako had decided that having Itachi attached to her in the wrap might not be the safest choice. She wasn't certain what she would do if and when they caught up with the bandits, but she could guess that some of it might put her in direct contact with weapons. She would rather that Itachi stayed with Sairō and kept away from any swinging blades, if at all possible.

The sun wasn't even halfway to its zenith when Torako saw over half a dozen horses in the distance.

"That can't be them, can it?" she whispered.

She had no way to know how fast the bandits had been traveling, or when they had stopped to make camp. When she had first seen the signs that the bandits had mounted horses to make their escape, she had thought there were a dozen horses or more. The group ahead had fewer than ten. But they could have abandoned some of them along the way, once they thought themselves far enough ahead of any pursuit that they wouldn't be giving mounts to their enemies, couldn't they?

Sairō said nothing, but their pace increased noticeably.

There were nine horses moving at a solid canter, but not running flat out. Of course, they had no reason to suspect they were being pursued. No way to know that Torako—who would have had to walk half a day's journey to procure a horse of any kind—instead rode an enormous wolf at a blistering pace, and had somehow managed to make up the twelve-hour lead they'd had in just over a day.

Torako tried to keep her breathing even, but she noticed Itachi's small face looking up at her with apprehension and excitement.

"Can you sense Raku-san?" she asked. "Is she ahead of us?"

Torako made sure she wasn't touching Itachi's skin so she wouldn't interfere with her kisō.

Itachi closed her eyes and frowned a bit, an expression Torako associated with the three-cycle-old trying to focus. Eventually, she nodded.

"Kaa-san feels like she's sleeping, but she's there."

Torako nodded. Probably sedated. It would make sense. It's not as though Raku would have gone quietly. She would have fought tooth and nail to stay with her daughter and to keep these brigands from stealing her away. She hoped, rather coldly, that she'd hurt some of the men who'd taken her.

The rhythm of the giant paws slapping the road beneath her increased its tempo yet again and Torako briefly worried that Sairō would do themself harm, but the thought was almost immediately forgotten when she looked up and saw that the horses in the distance were speeding up too.

"Damn!"

Sairō shot forward, as though driven by Torako's own desperation, but just as likely sick of running and wanting this to be done with one way or another.

The distance between wolf and horses was closing now and Torako did her best not to whoop with glee as she saw faces turn over shoulders and then back to the road ahead in a panic. Many a kick was being applied to an already suffering horse, but the mounts the men used were not racing horses, so they were not meant to keep the kind of pace that Sairō was now pushing them towards. Besides, they didn't have the motivation that Sairō did.

At least, not until one of the beasts finally noticed the giant predator running it down. Then it was only moments before they all took off at a full gallop.

"Tanuki's balls," Torako muttered, more loudly than she'd meant to.

Sairō had been gaining steadily on the bandits, and she was certain they would have overtaken the bastards if their horses hadn't suddenly noticed the enormous wolf behind them.

The horses were sprinting now, attaining speeds that only an animal with death on its heels can achieve, and though Sairō sped up as well, the gap between them was no longer closing. They couldn't beat the horses in an all-out sprint for their lives.

But, maybe they wouldn't have to, Torako thought, as she saw the outskirts of Sakata materialize in the distance. The port city was large and bustling, and it would be full of traders, citizens out shopping, and Kami knew what else. There wouldn't be room for the horses to continue their gallop.

Torako clung desperately to that notion as she saw the horses start to gain ground.

It was less than a hundred heartbeats, though it felt like an eternity, before the horses reached their first obstacle. A large, trundling hay cart was taking up the majority of the road ahead of them, leaving only a single horsewidth on either side. The steep ditches that ran on both sides of the road would easily break a horse's leg.

So the bandits' nine horses—which had earlier morphed into a sprinting ball of chaos taking up the full width of the road—

were now forced to run single file. But with an enormous and increasingly irate wolf chasing them, none of them seemed inclined to let the others go first.

The horses bucked, bit, and kicked to try to make their way through the two narrow slots, and nothing their riders did could convince them to behave calmly, or decline to exert violence on their fellows. It was chaos, and Torako reveled in how quickly Sairō devoured the distance between them while the horses fought over who would go first.

By the time the horses had finally allowed themselves to be organized into a line, Sairō, Torako, and Itachi were close enough that Torako could finally tell which horse carried Raku. She was unconscious, draped lengthwise across the lap of one of the bandits. Or she had been. Even as Torako watched, the person riding with Raku's unconscious form was pulling her into a seated position in the saddle, probably in an attempt to make her sleeping form seem less suspicious to the people of Sakata.

Torako growled at the sight, and she heard a low growl echo in Sairō's chest as they surged forward yet again.

They were so close.

The last horse was finally past the hay cart just as Sairō got within striking distance. If the final horse hadn't been the one carrying Raku, Torako was fairly certain Sairō would have sunk their teeth into it. As it was, they barely restrained another growl. Torako could feel it in their chest, even though she couldn't hear it. She was grateful it hadn't been loosed. They didn't need the horses to run any faster than they were already running.

They were now so close to the final horse that Torako could see the panicked whites of its eyes, but the chase took on an almost comically slow pace regardless. The bandits' horses and Sairō were all forced to dodge obstacle after obstacle now that they'd reached the outskirts of Sakata. Torako was furious with the people who dragged their various carts through the streets, the families out strolling. Every single one of them was someone who stood between her and Raku. Between her and vengeance.

The rage that had been building in her since learning of her mother's death had only grown hotter and harder to contain.

The only thing that kept her from lashing out was knowing that the people in her way were also providing obstacles for Raku's abductors. Torako found herself wishing to hug them in the same breath as she wished to curse them.

She grunted, holding Itachi close as Sairō leapt over a low cart full of daikon that happened to trundle in front of them just as the wolf had put on another surge of speed. The terrified cart owner screamed loudly before tripping over their own feet in their attempt to occupy a space uninhabited by enormous wolves.

Torako was tempted to shout an apology over her shoulder, but what was the point? The horses ahead of her and the giant wolf she rode were leaving havoc in their wake, and no words from her mouth could make up for that. Maybe once she had recovered her spouse she would volunteer to help repair the damage. For now, her rage and desperation drove her onwards without sparing more than a glance for those whose property they damaged.

The horses ahead of her were spreading out now, weaving through dozens of obstacles that appeared at any given moment in the increasingly crowded streets.

If Torako hadn't been chasing down the people who had abducted the love of her life, she might have paid some attention to the way the buildings around them had changed from houses to businesses, and now to warehouses and storage facilities. She *did* notice that they had been running downhill for the last short while, and she eventually looked past the horses for long enough to see the ocean looming before her.

She gasped. She had seen the sea before, but it always took her breath away. Then she blinked and refocused on her quarry.

Ever since she'd realized the bandits were likely headed for Sakata, she'd feared this eventuality. They were already in the warehouse district. They were clearly headed for the docks. She could no longer afford to chase her quarry and hope for a chance to grab Raku. She needed to make her own chance.

"Itachi-chan," she said, bending down to the girl's ear. "I need you to hold on tight and stay with Sairō-san, alright? Don't let go, no matter what."

Itachi turned her head to meet Torako's gaze. Her eyes were wide with what could have been fear, but she nodded.

"I promise, Mama."

"Good. I love you. Hold Shiken for me," she said as she handed her walking stick to Itachi. She also tucked the straps of the two bedrolls onto Itachi's shoulder. The girl was riding low enough, and holding onto Sairō's neck ruff tightly enough, that she kept her balance even with the cumbersome gear. Good.

Torako was going to need both hands for this next part, and she still had Sairō's blade tucked into her belt along with her wakizashi. She was well enough armed for what she hoped would be a brief fight.

Torako watched the gap between Sairō and the last rider close until there was less than half a horse length between Sairō and the bandit holding Raku. She barely looked at the rider, whose short hair and odd clothing, most notably a red tunic, had only made them easier to track amongst the crowds. Beyond that first dismissive glance, her eyes were only for Raku's smaller form in the same saddle.

Torako took a moment to breathe and to bring her legs up underneath her so her feet were centered on Sairō's back. Inhale, balance, exhale… spring.

She flew through the air towards the red-shirted rider. Even if she knocked all three of them to the ground when she connected, the obstacles of the city had slowed them enough that the fall would be unlikely to do more than bruise them.

She was so focused on the rider who held Raku that she didn't even see the one that intercepted her flight.

Her legs caught on a horse that hadn't been there a heartbeat earlier, and the momentum she had used to reach the red-shirted rider carried her forcefully across the back of the newly arrived horse, just behind its rider, where she found herself barely clinging to their saddlebags. The man in the saddle leaned back with a knife in his hand, no doubt hoping to free himself of Torako's unwelcome weight, but Torako was not so easily dissuaded. She had already managed to hook one arm through the strap attaching the saddlebag, and she took the strain of her weight on that arm and reached wildly for the arm swinging a dagger at her.

Her wild reach connected and she grabbed the man's wrist before the blade could connect. In the same movement, she jerked his forearm down and away, conveniently plunging the blade into his thigh.

The moment he let go of the knife in order to scream, she grabbed the hilt and used it as a handhold to help her gain the top of the horse, which had the added benefit of making an even larger wound in the man's leg. His scream had turned into more of a wet rasp by the time she pushed him out of the saddle with the blade planted in his ribs for good measure.

It always amazed her how few men were able to focus through any amount of pain. Torako had continued to fight with arrows and daggers in her arms and legs before, because the alternative had always been death, and death did not appeal to her. Then again, she had also spent three days laboring with Itachi, so perhaps women were simply made of sterner stuff. Regardless, even after twenty cycles of fighting, she was still surprised when a single wound was enough to undo a man. Of course, she hadn't had much occasion to see how many women kept fighting with severe wounds, but if conversations with Taka and Kusuko were anything to judge by, she wasn't the only one who could keep fighting with a blade in her.

As soon as she was balanced in the saddle Torako looked all around her to find the rider who held Raku. Her stomach dropped when she saw a flash of red ahead of her. The rider who held Raku had clearly made use of the time Torako had been distracted by trying not to get stabbed and then gaining control of the horse.

She was now a few cart lengths behind the red-shirted bandit. She dug her heels into the horse she now rode, ignoring the people in the streets shouting their displeasure at the half-dozen horses riding pell-mell through the crowds.

She did her best not to run over any bystanders, but she was riding fast now, trying to close the distance between herself and the red-shirted rider, and she would not be able to react fast enough if some witless pedestrian stepped in front of her.

Which was probably why the next bandit tried to unseat her by riding their own mount into her mount's flank. Or perhaps they were trying to crush her leg, a feat they would have accomplished if her own mount hadn't partially sidestepped the incoming horse.

At least the animal had been paying attention.

Sadly, the bandit didn't give up when their first attempt to dislodge her failed. She had just enough time to brace herself and get low in the saddle before the rider of the other horse launched himself at her with a dagger drawn.

Could none of these men shoot a bow from horseback? Some of them were dressed as kisōshi—were they truly unable to attack from a distance?

Not that she was complaining.

For example, the man who had just landed on her back and tried to put a blade in her shoulder quickly discovered why jumping from horse to horse was meant to be a move of desperation. He'd misjudged the distance, or perhaps the distance had changed suddenly—after all, the horses were still busy dodging traffic—and instead of landing squarely atop her back as he had probably planned, he landed across her mount's back instead, and almost slipped off without finding a handhold before he caught triumphantly onto the same saddlebag strap that she had used.

Unfortunately for him, he'd had to drop his dagger and grab hold with both arms to stop his descent. Torako wasted no time in shooting her elbow back hard into the man's face. He cried out, but held tight to the strap, so she reached her right hand to her belt, grabbed her wakizashi, and shoved the blade into his neck.

Between one breath and the next, the man fell to the road, in all likelihood with a few horse hooves to the head for his troubles.

Torako winced and then reminded herself that these men had taken Raku in the dead of night and were now trying to kill her before she could get her back. They deserved none of her mercy.

She looked up and cursed loudly.

They were in sight of the docks now.

And the red-shirted rider was already racing down the pier at a speed that was causing dockworkers and sailors to dive out of the way (some into the water) to avoid being trampled. Four more bandits rode alongside the red shirt, keeping pace except when they had to dodge carts, barrels, or crates.

She didn't know where the remainder of the nine horses they'd first chased after were now, and she didn't care. She was fairly certain the two men she'd fought wouldn't be fighting again soon, if ever. With five ahead of her, that left two more riders unaccounted for. If they caught up to her, she would deal with it. For now, she only cared about Raku.

Torako didn't hesitate. She couldn't afford to. If the bandits sailed away with Raku right now, she was certain all was lost. She dug her heels in harder, tucked herself low to the horse's neck, and hoped that enough people had been scared out of the way by Raku's captors that they would stay out of her path.

Soon, all she could hear was the rush of wind in her ears and the pounding of hooves against wooden planks. The animal was clearly tiring, but so were the horses she chased. Her mount jumped more than one pile of crates and barrels as she urged it down the pier. She was gaining on the horses ahead of her.

"Come on," she hissed, not sure if she was addressing herself, the horse, or the world at large.

Then, suddenly, the five horses ahead of her disappeared, and she had to look a second time to realize that they'd made a sharp turn to the right. Torako didn't have time to pace the turn at all. She put her whole body into the turn while hauling on the reins, wrenching her mount to the right. Her horse's legs slipped out from under it—she felt a pang of guilt for the fall it would take—but she wasn't going down with it, because she had started dismounting the moment she felt the horse's weight shift, launching herself from the saddle to the dock in a ground-eating roll that she knew would leave her in agony tomorrow. She came up gasping. Turned out, it was agony right now. She was running as soon as her feet were under her, despite the pain, charging down the dock where five horses had just ground to a halt in front of a ship bobbing against its moorings, while a frantic crew did a number of things with rope that Torako could not identify but was certain meant it was preparing to sail.

She ran flat out, ignoring the searing in her legs, thighs, and back, and launched herself at the bandits, who were still dismounting even as she reached them. She drew Sairō's blade as she closed the distance, aiming her first cut at the back of the bandit in the red shirt, who was still pulling Raku from the saddle.

Instead, a blade from her right pulled her cut short and had her turning to face one of the other bandits who had dismounted unencumbered by hostages. Rage had narrowed her focus so that she couldn't see beyond the next move, but she couldn't seem to draw a breath that didn't fill her with greater ire. Some monsters she'd never heard of before had taken her mother, and there was nothing she could do about that, but these bastards had taken away the love of her life, and they were right in front of her, and if she could just get past this asshole and his friends she could hold Raku again.

She slashed wildly at the man before her, but he wasn't a poorly trained mercenary like the men she had killed two days ago. This man had trained as kisōshi, as she had, and he moved his katana deftly enough that her anger alone wasn't going to break down his defenses.

Then a second man joined the first in trying to push her back from the red-shirted bandit and Raku.

Torako let out something that was half growl, half scream, and she parried the new opponent who'd arrived on her left with such force that the man's sword clattered from his grip. She charged through the opening, leading with a front kick that sent the man into the water and moved to follow the red-shirted bandit who now had Raku halfway up the ramp to the bobbing ship. She felt the man who had first intercepted her reach for her trailing wrist, but whatever he had planned must have involved kisō, because he let go in an instant and was clearly too shocked at his own lack of power to attack her as she pushed her way towards Raku.

She was halfway up the ramp when another bandit rushed past the redshirt in order to challenge her.

"I. Don't. Have. Time. For. This," she gritted through clenched teeth as she parried the first attack and then practically bludgeoned the bandit to death with her katana. It wasn't that the blade wasn't still sharp, it was just that she slashed at him with such force that she may as well have been using a club. He went down with a sickening crunch as the blade bit into his collarbone so deeply that his shoulder nearly detached.

She knew that her rage was still getting the better of her, she knew that fighting with this much anger driving her could lead to lethal mistakes, but there was nothing she could do to quell the emotion. She did her best to harness it instead, pushing herself farther up the ramp and nearly gaining the top before the next bandit threw himself at her.

Even still, she had enough momentum to push both herself and the bandit over the final lip of the gangplank and onto the deck of the ship. The bandit lost his footing as they reached the deck, falling flat. But she wasn't here to slaughter bandits, no matter how much anger drove her forward. She leapt over the splayed bandit and sprinted towards where she could just make out a flash of red disappearing down a hatch.

Which was when over thirty cycles of martial training saved her life, even though her fury was doing its best to get her killed.

She didn't see or hear the blades that flicked through the air towards her throat and chest—at least, not that she was conscious of—but some part of her sensed the danger, and she dropped into a low dive towards the hatch. She was grateful for her leathers, as the few patches of exposed skin she sported got smeared across the textured finish of the deck. Tomorrow was going to be excruciating, if she lived that long.

It was only as she hit the deck that her ears registered the sound of the blades flicking through the air. It was only the muffled scream of someone behind where she had been standing that confirmed that she had barely missed being the target of those blades.

She was just reaching for the edge of the hatch the redshirt had disappeared into when she felt the wind whip her hair out of its simple braid and into her eyes. She blinked, grunted, and continued to reach for the hatch by feel.

Someone grabbed her ankle, but she lashed out with a firm kick and felt a satisfying crunch as her heel connected with what felt like a nose.

She expected a blade in her back at any moment, but she could hardly give up now. Her fingers had just found the inside edge of the hatch when the wind picked up another notch and she noticed that the deck was tilting.

More than tilting.

"Tanuki's balls."

If she hadn't had one arm half inside the hatch already, she would have slid down the opposite side of the deck she'd come from and into the ocean. As it was, she had been flung to the opposite side of—and was now clinging with a very bruised arm to —the hatch she had just been attempting to enter.

She supposed this was why no one had put a blade in her back. They'd been too busy preparing for whatever was happening to the ship.

She could already feel her grip slipping, but she was so close. She couldn't let go. She wouldn't. Raku was just on the other side of this hatch. She couldn't fail Raku, fail Itachi, fail herself. She had already failed at so much. Tenshi was gone and nothing was right, and this was the thing she was supposed to be good at. She was supposed to be able to protect the ones she loved. She'd trained her whole life to do just that. She'd already failed Raku once. She wouldn't do it again.

She shouted something unintelligible and hoisted her weight a bit higher, pulling up so that she could just make out the darkness on the other side of the hatch.

Her legs lay against the deck, but most of her weight pulled towards the water. She could see a froth of waves lashing against the rail below her.

How had they set sail so quickly? How had they reached a speed like this so fast? She tried not to think of Itachi and Sairō somewhere behind her in Sakata, probably wondering if she was dead yet. She had to get to Raku. She had to pull herself inside, she needed time to think. She screamed into the wind and pulled herself a tiny bit higher. If she could just gain another handspan, she could pull herself into this thrice-cursed hatch and gain herself a moment to think.

Then pain was shooting through her forearm. Her eyes went white with it, and she wanted to vomit. Suddenly, she couldn't think of anything, not even her own name.

"Time for you to go,"a voice she did not recognize muttered from within the hatch.

Her grip slackened, then failed her completely, and she scrabbled desperately against the deck as she slid all too quickly towards the water, but all she managed was to lose more skin as she went. She barely managed to get her feet between her and the railing. It did nothing to stop her fall, only helped her change the angle. She saved her head and back from the worst the rail had to offer, then fell screaming into the cold, dark sea.

⇒ *Raku* ⇐

RAKU BLINKED. Blinking hurt. Not blinking, sadly, was not an improvement. Her stomach lurched, and she swallowed to keep from vomiting. Swallowing also hurt, and caused her head to throb. She wondered if she had hit her head somehow.

"Itachi-chan?" she whispered, or tried to whisper. She barely managed to force an incoherent hiss past her lips.

What in the eight hells had happened to her?

She tried to take a deep breath, hoping that it would lend her a calm she did not currently feel, but the air smelled of kelp, mold, blood, and bile. Her stomach heaved again, and before she could do anything to stop it she was turning to her side and vomiting.

Much to her surprise, the vomit went mostly into a large metal pail positioned an arm's length beneath her. Further inspection showed that she was laying in a hammock. The design was odd. Three sides were raised, the fabric beneath her was stretched taut by wooden slats and so was fairly level rather than curved to hug her, and the fourth side, which she had just vomited over rather easily, was lowered and rolled beneath her.

She must have hit her head if she was vomiting this readily.

She decided to close her eyes and think for a moment.

When she woke up again the scents of blood and bile were almost gone, although the scent of mold and kelp remained strong. She was able to take a deep breath this time.

Blinking, though still uncomfortable, no longer caused a throbbing pain in her skull.

She decided to open her eyes long enough to inspect whatever was above her, which turned out to be a wooden ceiling that was much closer than she would have expected. She thought she might be able to reach it with a toe, if she could lift her leg straight above her. She decided that test could wait.

She took another deep breath, instead.

"Itachi-chan?" she whispered, and this time she could hear her own voice.

Dread clutched her chest when silence was the only answer.

She lay staring at the wood panels above her for a moment and let tears slide down her cheeks and past her ears.

It was then that she noticed the ceiling was swaying.

No. Wait.

She was swaying. Why was she swaying? Was it an earthquake?

Then she heard a rush of footsteps above her, shouts that she couldn't quite make out, but which she was certain included the word sail.

She was on a ship.

"Kuso."

"Ah yes, a reasonable sentiment, all things considered," said a deep voice from her right.

She turned her head again, but was swamped with another wave of nausea and had to close her eyes for a moment.

When she opened them, a man with deep brown eyes and long hair pulled into a tail at his neck looked down at her from just past her shoulder.

"If it had been up to me, we would not have drugged you that whole time. I'm afraid I wasn't consulted at the time, though."

Raku found that her mind was beginning to piece together memories of how she had gotten here. Or rather, how she had been taken from her home. She had no memory of a journey of any kind, but if she had been drugged, as this man suggested, then she was unlikely to remember anything beyond when she'd lost consciousness.

One memory in particular leapt out at her.

"Where is my daughter?"

The man's face was now close enough that she could feel his breath on her skin. Which of course, was directly related to the fact that she'd grabbed the collar of his tunic and dragged him down to her in a motion so swift he hadn't even had time to react.

"WHERE. IS. SHE?!"

The man swallowed and she could see that his face had paled a bit. She wondered if that was because he hadn't seen her move, or because she had reached for his belt in hopes of finding a weapon there, but had found nothing more than latched pouches.

"She's safe," he gasped. "Or, at least, we didn't do anything to her. We couldn't find her, and she was never our target to begin with. Our orders were just to bring you."

Raku released the man's collar and then sank back against the hammock, exhausted from that small exertion.

She wanted to berate the man for leaving a child alone in the woods, but since the alternative would have meant Itachi being here with her, she said nothing.

She desperately wished to ask about Torako, but she held her tongue. She couldn't bear hearing that they'd killed her. That the reason she had never come home that night was because they had ambushed her alone in the woods.

She only realized that her eyes had fallen closed when they jerked open in response to the man's hand touching her wrist. She tried to pull away from his grasp, but he held her firmly between his fingers.

She looked up into his face to find his eyes closed. His eyebrows were furrowed in concentration, and he was muttering something to himself that she could not hear.

"What are you doing to me?" she asked, her voice a harsh croak. At least it was louder than the whisper she'd managed earlier.

"Making sure that the drugs are leaving your system," he replied, without opening his eyes.

"Are you a healer, then?"

"I am."

"Is it not against some oath of yours to heal up prisoners just so they can be killed later?"

At that, the man's eyes opened. He stared at her for a moment before answering.

"The Captain tried to order me not to heal you."

"You ignored your Captain?"

"She wasn't thinking clearly."

"That doesn't seem like the kind of a thing a healer is supposed to say to a prisoner."

"You know little of how the Wind Serpent is run."

"So your Captain is an unreasonable woman?"

"She is not reasonable where you are concerned."

"Oh? And what did *I* do to *her*?"

"She didn't take well to you gutting her second in command."

Raku saw a brief flash of steel in moonlight in her memory and frowned.

"Perhaps her second in command shouldn't have tried to take a mother away from her child."

"A fair assessment," the man replied. He had already closed his eyes and returned to whatever he was doing with her wrist.

"Good thing you were there to heal her second, I suppose."

Raku was fishing now, unsure if she hoped that she had killed the second or not.

"Alas, I was not able to heal him."

"Were the wounds too grievous?"

"I probably could have managed them if I'd been conscious. But I'd recently been gutted."

Raku didn't have time to panic about the man who was healing her most likely wishing her dead. Her vision darkened before she'd drawn her next breath, and then the world faded away.

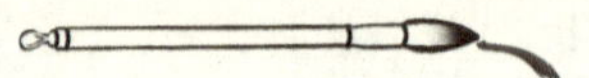

Raku woke to the sound of humming. She opened her eyes, and for a moment she was not at all certain why there were wooden planks above her instead of rock. She took a deep breath in and the smell of saltwater, kelp, and a hint of mold brought it all back to her.

Her stomach roiled once more and she swallowed, desperate to avoid vomiting again if she could help it. She turned her head just in case, finding the same metal pail in place beneath her. Or perhaps it was a new pail. It was clean and dry, in any event, and the deep breath she had taken in had smelled like the interior of most ships, not like bile, or blood.

When her eyes traveled up from the pail, she was surprised to see that the healer who had tended her earlier now had his back to her and was tending someone else. A woman was lying on a hammock identical to hers on the other side of the cabin, and the healer was inspecting her legs. Or he was inspecting what remained of her legs, at any rate.

The other woman was looking directly at Raku, and so she did what she always did when she met strange women in vulnerable situations—she smiled.

The other woman frowned in reply.

"Not the reaction I was expecting," the woman muttered in a gruff tone.

"Did *I* cut your legs off in a fit of rage, then?" Raku asked, wondering how many of these bandits she'd managed to damage when they'd taken her from her home.

That startled a laugh out of the other woman. The healer ignored them both and continued with whatever he was doing.

"No. My legs have nothing to do with you. But I can't say I expected you to smile at any of us, given how you got here."

Raku shrugged and tried to sit up. Her stomach instantly rebelled, and she found herself adding to the bucket against her best wishes.

"Not much of a sailor, then," the woman said.

Raku wiped at the sides of her mouth and spat.

"I suppose not. It's not normally this bad, but I also tend to stay away from boats."

"Did you smile at me out of pity?"

Raku blinked a few times. Her brain still felt slower than usual. She had said and done things in the first few moments of talking to the healer that she normally would have held in reserve. She was usually much better at subtlety. It had gotten her through many tough scrapes. She couldn't fight the way that Torako could, but she generally didn't need to. Overcoming one's enemies didn't always require cutting them in half. She had smiled reflexively at the woman because it was a thing she did to put people at ease.

"I rather think I smiled to keep you from wanting to kill me," she said after a moment. "The face you were making when I first caught your eye wasn't entirely reassuring."

It was true. She wasn't convinced that the expression had been directed at her, but the woman had been looking slightly murderous.

"Ah, well. It's not exactly pleasant to have Tanaka-san prod at the ghost of these legs. Sorry if you took it as anger directed at you."

Raku nodded but said nothing. She had already spoken too much without thinking. She needed to start pulling her usual protections around her. She wasn't going to be able to convince these people that she was completely harmless after all she'd done when they captured her, but perhaps she could make them think it had been adrenaline and panic that had won the day. It might still be possible to convince them all that she was weak and a bit helpless, especially considering how awful she felt at the moment.

Just as she decided that laying back down and pretending sleep might be in her best interest, Tanaka-san—as the other woman had named him—called for someone through the open doorway. No, she was on a ship, they weren't called doors on ships, were they? Hatchways. That was it.

"She's all done, Lyt-san. You can take her now."

Raku had to look up at the figure that entered when Tanaka finished speaking because they were incredibly tall, and could not stand up fully in the low-ceilinged cabin.

"May I offer my services as transport, Suzuki-san?" Lyt said.

The woman, who Raku assumed was Suzuki, frowned.

"You don't have to ask every time, Lyt-san."

"Of course I do. I would not touch you without your consent."

Suzuki rolled her eyes.

"You're doing me a favor hauling me all over the ship, you have my consent."

"Which you may revoke at any time. And you are doing me a favor by explaining how this ship is run."

"Pick me up before I stab you, Lyt-san."

Lyt smiled, and then carefully collected Suzuki in a two-armed carry.

"We should really rig a harness so that I can just ride on your back," she muttered.

"Then you would be constantly hitting your head on these low ceilings, as I do."

"Still, at least I could be sure of where we were going," she replied.

Lyt's own retort was lost to the general hubbub of the ship as the pair moved out the hatchway and down the passage that led to who knew where.

Raku blinked a few times.

"Xe is always very adamant about consent," Tanaka muttered to the room at large. His tone made it sound like Lyt was something of a puzzle to him.

"I'm surprised xe took up with your band of ruffians, then," Raku replied, before she could think better of it.

Tanaka turned to her then and she would have sworn he looked embarrassed.

"Believe it or not, we don't spend most of our time stealing mothers away from their children," he said, as if that somehow excused the fact that they had done precisely that to her.

"Oh? Should I feel special then? Lucky me! What won me that particular honor?"

Tanaka's mouth formed a hard line and he said nothing.

Raku wanted to stand up and spit in his face, but even attempting to sit up had caused her stomach to heave. She knew it would do little good, as satisfying as it would be to vomit on the man's feet.

She chided herself for thinking that way. Tanaka already had good reason to hate her. After all, she had shoved his own dagger into his gut. She didn't need to antagonize him further.

As though sensing some of what she was thinking, Tanaka said, "I can give you something to soothe your stomach if you like. You'll recover faster from the sedatives if you can keep food and water down."

Raku only nodded, but Tanaka turned to the small workbench that ran along half of the far wall, then turned back to her holding a small green tab in one hand.

"I'll need water," she said as she took the tab from his hand.

Tanaka grabbed a small flask from the workbench and handed it to her. Then he helped her to sit up a bit so that swallowing wouldn't be an absolute disaster.

She looked at the tab and the flask for a moment, and it did occur to her that he might be trying to kill her. After all, she had shoved a knife in his belly, for all that he seemed to be entirely healthy now.

But she knew that he and his fellows had brought her this far without killing her, and that had to have been quite a bit more trouble than killing her in her own home would have been. So she put the tab in her mouth and swallowed it down with water from the flask.

The water felt cool and soothing going down her throat. She waited a few heartbeats, but nothing terrible happened.

"Thank you," she said, after taking another long swig of water and handing the flask back to him.

Tanaka was quiet for a long moment after he took the flask.

"You have no reason to thank me. I may not have agreed with our orders, but I did nothing to stop your abduction. More than your life or mine is at stake in this."

He paused for a moment and Raku couldn't help but laugh.

"Do you expect to convince me that I ought to accept my fate because whatever you people deem my life to be worth, it's less than whatever you think is at stake? If I were going to let anyone else define my worth, I would have rolled over and died a long time ago. You're not the first people to think I'm worthless, and you won't be the last."

"I didn't mean—"

"Didn't you?" Raku thought the drugs must still be addling her mind. This was the opposite of her usual strategy. She survived by convincing the world she wasn't a threat, by hiding in plain sight, by letting them make assumptions about everything—from her brightly colored kimono, to her decorative hairstyles, from her petite form, to her dazzling smiles. She was a walking contradiction, but almost no one ever found the sharp-edged truth of her. Whatever drugs they had given her had stripped away her defenses, and now she was all sharp edges and pointy truths.

Tanaka was silent for so long that Raku lay back down and closed her eyes for a moment, half convinced that he'd left the room rather than respond.

"I did everything I could to make sure that your wife wasn't killed. She took out almost everyone sent to collect you and got within a hand's breadth of reaching you before we got you belowdecks. The thing my people want from you… it's not up to me to decide if it's right or wrong, but leaving your daughter without a parent was not something I was prepared to live with. If she's a strong swimmer, there's a good chance she's still alive."

It was Tanaka's voice. She was certain of it. But when she opened her eyes a heartbeat later, the healer was gone.

Tears—joyful, angry, anguished tears—eventually carried her to sleep.

Torako

TORAKO WOKE TO the sensation of very large teeth in her shoulder. She blinked and sputtered, was slapped in the face by the cold salty hand of the sea, and then heaved what felt like half of the ocean out of her throat. She was still sorting out which way was up when she abruptly felt her back and legs dragging through wet sand.

By the time she could actually see anything properly, she was far enough onto the beach that the sand was only damp. The teeth released her and she rubbed her shoulder, surprised to find that there was no blood there. She let her head sink into the sand for a moment, and when next she opened her eyes, two sets of eyes stared back at her. One set huge, amber, and looking rather disgruntled. The other set small, green, and full of tears.

She immediately sat up and wrapped her arms around Itachi.

"Mama, I thought you died."

Torako, unsure what else to say, simply made comforting cooing noises into Itachi's ear as she held her close and rubbed her back. Eventually, she tried, "It takes more than a ship full of bandits and a cold ocean to stop me."

Sairō's low huff beside her made her turn to look at the wolf. They looked smaller than they had a moment ago, though still twice as large as any wolf had reason to be.

"You're lucky the child and I were watching from the pier," they growled from where they now lay in the sand with their side curled against Torako's legs. "I barely reached you before you started going under as it was."

Torako shivered at the memory. Only one of her arms had been responding to her call by the time she hit the water, and swimming had been far too slow to keep her warm. Her body had lost its heat more quickly than she would have expected for a warm day in early summer, and soon none of her limbs had been responding to her call. She didn't really remember Sairō arriving to save her. She did recall thinking she was about to drown.

"Even if you saw me go over, I'm surprised you reached me in time. That ship was sailing faster than any I've ever seen."

Sairō let out another huff.

"You can thank your daughter for that. She said we couldn't let you go alone. I think she had plans for us to somehow join you on that cursed boat. Luckily, they sent you swimming before we had to test *that* plan."

The daughter in question was curled up against her chest, and her quiet breathing and peaceful, tear-streaked face suggested she had fallen asleep.

"She used a lot of her kisō to make the swimming easier," Sairō grumbled, in what sounded like reluctant admiration.

For a long while, Torako just sat there with her good arm wrapped tight around her daughter, feeling her warm little body pressed tight against her chest and thanking all the Kami that they were both still alive.

"I lost her, Sairō-san," Torako whispered, after what seemed like an age. "She was right there. I was so close at one point I could have leapt the distance between us. I tried. But… I couldn't reach her in time."

Sairō was silent for a long while and then eventually rumbled, "Did you see them harm her?"

"No." She shook her head and wondered if she was trying to reassure herself as she did it. "No, when I saw her she was unconscious but she seemed… well, she wasn't wounded anyway."

It was one small relief in the sea of worries that now crowded her thoughts.

"Perhaps they don't intend to harm her," Sairō suggested.

She thought even the wolf sounded skeptical as they said it.

"If they meant her no harm, why would they have taken her at all? People don't steal other people away against their will for a friendly conversation after which they let them go on their way. They must need her for something, but I can't imagine they plan to simply return her once they've got what they wanted."

Sairō's silence was telling.

Torako cradled Itachi closer for a moment.

"Thank you for keeping her safe," she said, without looking at the giant wolf.

"Hmph. Don't expect me to play childminder every time you plan to throw yourself in harm's way. Small humans only get underfoot."

Torako buried her face in Itachi's hair to hide the grin that she couldn't keep from her face.

"She likes you, you know," Torako prodded.

Sairō snorted.

"She can like me all she wishes, it won't be mutual."

"I thought wolves were natural caretakers."

"Wolves naturally take care of their own young."

"Human children aren't that different from wolf pups."

"Human children are cats without dignity."

"Does that mean you're fond of cats, too?"

Sairō's growl was loud enough to wake Itachi.

"Mama, I'm hungry."

Torako swallowed and hugged Itachi close.

"I know, sweetie."

She looked at Itachi, and looked at Sairō, and asked the question she'd been dreading since she woke up.

"Did any of our gear make it?"

Itachi's face fell, and Torako didn't even hesitate to wrap her in another giant hug.

"It's alright, Itachi-chan. It's more than alright. You kept yourself safe and rescued me from the sea. The rest is just… stuff."

"Your sword. Shiken… I'm sorry, Mama. I couldn't hold onto Sairō in the water and keep the sword close. Sairō said maybe it would float."

"It doesn't matter, Dearheart. It was just a sword. You're far more important."

She meant those words with every fiber of her being, even though the loss of the blade that Kuma-sensei had gifted her all those cycles ago left a dull ache in her heart.

"Come on," she said, standing up. Her whole body protested as she unfolded herself from the sand, but they had already wasted more time than they could afford, so her body would just have to save its complaints for later. The ship carrying Raku would be leagues away by now, and she had no idea where it was headed or how she would find it.

"We need to get you some food." She held out her hand to Itachi, hoping that the girl had enough energy to walk for a bit because she didn't think she could hold her.

And your wife? Sairō asked within Torako's mind.

"We need help, preferably from someone with a very fast ship."

She thought for a moment, then sighed.

"I may know just the man."

"Who?" Sairō asked, aloud this time.

"An old friend."

Torako looked at Itachi for a moment, her brilliant green eyes sparkling in the late afternoon sunlight in an expression that was all too familiar. The vision sent a thousand worries into a cyclone in Torako's head until she couldn't even pick one to start with.

"I hope."

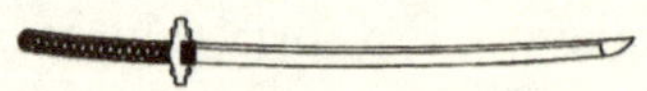

Torako followed the young serving woman through the warm hallway, trying to keep her stomach from loudly acknowledging the smell of steamed rice, savory meats, and warmed sake that teased her senses.

Just as the young woman gestured her through a sliding door towards the end of the hall, Torako opened her hand in the woman's line of sight, tilting the silver fox pin that sat there so that it caught the light.

"Do you have a message?" the young woman asked.

"Tell him Shiken is missing."

The young woman said nothing to that, but slid the shoji closed behind Torako, who folded herself into place at the low table in the center of the small room. She simply had to hope that Kitsu would keep his word.

As Torako waited for the serving woman to return, she stared at her forearm and marveled at the fact that she could still move her hand. The stab wound that went all the way through from one side to the other was what made the simple act of opening and closing of her fingers seem impressive.

How did I not bleed to death before we even reached land?

She flexed her fingers again. It hurt, quite a bit really, but the fact that her fingers responded, and that the wound was no longer bleeding, did not at all match with her—not inconsiderable—experience with stab wounds.

Our connection is capable of lending you my kisō at times. Torako nearly jumped up from the table when Sairō's voice sounded in her mind. Her injured arm clutched her chest for a moment before she got her breathing in order.

I hadn't thought I was speaking with you.

Sairō continued as if she hadn't "said" anything.

To be honest, I'm surprised there is still a wound. Most of my Claws healed much faster than this.

Torako frowned at her arm as a hundred questions rose to her mind at once.

Kisō doesn't affect me. No kisōshi has ever been able to use it to heal or harm me.

Sairō was silent long enough that she wondered if the wolf had somehow dropped their connection. She had left Sairō and Itachi at the oden cart that sat just beside Sakata's most popular izakaya, with assurances from Midori—the first person that she had shown the silver fox to—that she would feed Itachi-chan to bursting and keep both girl and "dog" warm while they waited. Torako had worked very hard not to laugh at the murderous expression on Sairō's face while Midori explained where Torako should go next in her search for the Silver Fox.

Luckily, Midori had also loaned her a cloak that covered Sairō's blade well enough that she had been able to bring the katana inside with her. She assumed that was how the wolf was speaking to her now.

If something prevents kisō from affecting you, then that would explain… much.

This time Torako managed not to jump when Sairō's voice returned to her.

It sounds like we need to talk.

Torako tried not to send her irritation along with the thought, but she assumed she failed. She was grateful for everything Sairō had done for her over the past two days and she didn't want to seem unappreciative. But all of this had started with Sairō's blade, and she wasn't at all convinced the wolf wasn't somehow at fault. The idea that they had useful information that they hadn't told her yet was maddening. She knew it was ridiculous to think that the wolf would have had energy to spare on explaining things when it had been chasing bandits flat out for days, but…

She took a deep breath, closing her eyes. Apparently almost drowning in frigid waters hadn't been enough to cool her rage.

If you could tell me a bit more about what you—

But Torako missed the rest of Sairō's question because that was the moment that the screen door slid open and a face that she hadn't seen in nearly four cycles flashed a mischievous grin at her and said, "Torako-san, bearer of my heart, to what do I owe this great pleasure?"

Torako knew that punching Kitsu wasn't the way to get what she needed from him, and she also wasn't certain that he deserved to be punched, but that didn't reduce how much she wanted to smash her fist into his face as he folded himself beside her at the low table and took her hand as though there was no reason for him not to.

She ignored his instructions to the serving woman and focused very hard on relaxing the fist she'd made with her off hand, just as she ignored the questions that Sairō was peppering her with from inside her own mind.

"Stop," she said, more forcefully than she'd meant to, as she leapt to her feet.

To her dismay, Kitsu rose with her, his face the perfect picture of concern.

"Torako-san, are you well?" he asked.

She hated that his voice sounded sincere. That he was visibly concerned for her well-being. She desperately needed him to hate her.

"I need your ship," she blurted.

Damn it all, she'd rehearsed this conversation a dozen times in her head since the idea had come to her, and none of them started that way. It was the second worst way she could have started things off. But if she didn't get this right, he could turn her away and then she would have nothing. Kitsu was the only person she knew with anything more than a dinghy. Not only that, he was the only person she knew who might have some idea of where Raku's captors had taken her. A lancing pain shot through her as she longed for Raku's presence. Raku was the one who always knew how to charm someone into helping, or talk them into helping so subtly they never even noticed it, perhaps even deciding it had been their idea all along. Raku could make a squirrel give over its winter nuts if the squirrel could understand Gensokan.

Torako took a deep breath. She needed to start over. She needed to say something that would make him think she wasn't just here to use him for his ship. She needed—

"Alright, you have it. Where are we going?"

"What?"

"If you need my ship, Love, you have it. Where are we taking it?"

It was as if two days' worth of exhaustion and emotion hit her all at once. Her legs no longer held her weight. She sank to the tatami floor and sobbed with her face against her knees. When Kitsu wrapped a comforting arm around her shoulders, she didn't even want to punch him.

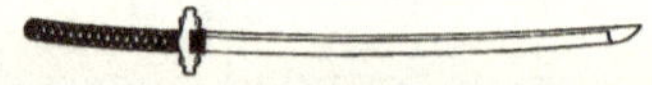

The sea spread out before Torako, the hull of the Trickster cutting quickly through the rolling waves, the sky disappearing where it met the sea in an invisible embrace. She stood with her face to the wind, the sea spray curling the tendrils of hair that had escaped her braid, the tang of the ocean filling her lungs, and she laughed. They hadn't been on the Trickster long—she could still see Sakata behind them if she squinted—but she was already in love with sailing.

What's funny? growled Sairō's voice inside her mind.

Torako looked down at the giant wolf and the smile fell from her face.

Sairō was curled tightly against her legs, but with their muzzle just poking out between the railings so that they could more easily loose their stomach into the sea. The wolf had been ill from almost the moment they'd left port, and Torako felt more than a bit guilty that she hadn't asked them how they felt about sailing. Although to be fair, it hadn't occurred to her that a wolf Kami who spent a good portion of their existence inside of a sword could get seasick. She had brought Sairō to the bow of the ship with her even before they had taken ill, hoping that here she, Itachi, and the very large wolf would be mostly out of the way as the crew set about their business.

"Is there anything I can do to make it better?" she asked, as Sairō groaned once more. "Are you sure you don't want me to dismiss you back into the sword?"

A low growl was Sairō's only response.

Torako sighed. She'd suggested it earlier, when Sairō had vomited over the side before the crew had even finished raising the sails. But Sairō had insisted all would be well and she hadn't questioned them.

I don't trust that pirate of yours.

Torako snorted in contempt. "He's a smuggler, not a pirate, and he *isn't* mine."

If you say so. But if I go back into the sword now, I won't be able to come out again until we reach land. You'll be left without my help if anything happens.

"Your help? Yes, because you'll be so useful to me vomiting over the side and too dizzy to stand."

Torako glared at the wolf for a moment, trying to think of some argument that would let her give them some ease, but she was distracted by the sound of Itachi's laughter spilling across the deck behind her. She turned in time to see the girl run across the deck, giggling madly while a smiling crew member made monster noises and lumbered slowly after her. Torako dropped to her knees just in time to wrap her in a warm hug when the girl ran all the way into her arms, still squealing.

"Mama! That lady says that I can't play on the barrels."

Itachi stated this as though she had just learned a very interesting fact that she was now sharing, rather than as some sort of complaint.

Torako smiled.

"Is that why the monster was chasing you? To keep you away from the barrels?"

Itachi nodded solemnly.

"Yes, but she wasn't really a monster. Just pretending."

Torako's smile widened.

"May I tap your nose?" she asked, still grinning.

Itachi grinned back.

"Yes."

Torako tapped Itachi's nose and then the girl jumped at her with another hug.

"Mama trap!" she shouted.

"The best kind," Torako conceded, as her eyes slid closed to allow herself to savor the small moment of affection and try to push away the grief that welled up alongside it. Ever since she had come unraveled on the floor of the izakaya, her emotions felt all too near the surface. Every moment of joy was tinged with a sadness she did not care to name.

The sound of Sairō vomiting over the side once more ended Itachi's giggling embrace. The young Kisōshi slid down from Torako's arms and sat down beside the wolf, spreading her small hands into their thick fur.

Then she closed her eyes.

A few heartbeats later, Sairō's eyes slid closed and their breathing evened out.

Torako quickly clamped down on the panic that tried to rise in her as she saw the wolf go still, realizing that Itachi must have done something to allow the wolf to rest.

"I took some of the tummy pains away," Itachi said, still running her hands through Sairō's thick fur.

Torako simply smiled and did not bother to ask how Itachi had done it. It wasn't that she wasn't curious, it was only because she'd noticed that Itachi got very self-conscious when she or Raku asked her about her kisō. She always wished to know how her daughter's connection to water allowed her to do such wondrous things, but she found that asking seemed to take some of the joy from Itachi's accomplishments, and she hated seeing some of the light leave her eyes whenever she asked.

"Thank you, Itachi-chan," she said instead. "I'm certain Sairō will appreciate being able to rest properly."

"Interesting rescue party," said a low voice behind her.

Torako turned, and instantly berated herself for the heat that flushed her cheeks and neck at the sight of Kitsu standing there with his head tilted slightly to one side. She ignored the implied judgment on her rescue party. She supposed most people would think her mad for bringing her three-cycle-old child along to rescue the child's own mother, but she wasn't sure what else she could have done. There had been no time to take her to any of the few people she could trust. Tenshi and Yanagi would have been the only ones close enough, usually, but Raku had said they'd left the Valley. The only others she would have trusted to protect Itachi when a host of bandits were potentially after her were Taka and Kusuko, or possibly Taka's friend Ryūko-san. But the trek to reach any of them would have taken so long that Torako was certain she'd have had no one to rescue by the time she'd left Itachi in their care. She'd considered leaving Itachi with the Silver Fox network, in the hope that they could secret her away to Taka, but if there were more bandits looking for Itachi, the danger to the Silver Fox's people was too great. In the end, she had decided that being surrounded by Kitsu's more than capable crew while Torako flung herself at whatever danger lay between her and Raku was the safest place the girl could be.

She didn't have to explain any of that to Kitsu, however.

"You know I hate it when you sneak up on me," she said, her voice clipped.

"Which only increases my enjoyment of it. However, I promise I haven't come here to vex you."

He raised his hands, which held a length of sturdy-looking rope.

"I thought your friend there might prefer not to risk sliding into the sea if our ride gets a bit more exciting."

The way Kitsu's eyes flashed as he said the words made Torako suddenly certain that more exciting would probably not be the words Sairō would wind up choosing to describe whatever was about to happen to their ride. Still, she could only assume that if Kitsu was offering to secure an enormous seasick wolf, it was because not doing so would have awful consequences. Kitsu's propensity for mischief rarely extended to actual harm.

"I would say you should ask them first, but they're finally sleeping…"

"If they object to the treatment, I promise to take full responsibility," Kitsu said, already leaning down to wrap the rope around Sairō in a makeshift harness that would ensure they did not slide out, no matter which way the ship tilted. "I have to say, I'm surprised they're managing to rest at all, given how ill they were earlier."

"Itachi-chan did something to let them rest," Torako said, unable to keep the pride out of her voice. "She's learned a lot of healing from… her instructors."

Torako cursed her voice for breaking, but of course Itachi had been learning healing from both Yanagi-sama and Tenshi, and the thought of Tenshi brought too much emotion with it to be contained.

Kitsu either didn't notice the break, or else was too distracted by the notion of a small child having the power to help an ailing wolf Kami. The way his eyes locked onto Itachi's face suggested the latter.

"That's some impressive work, Little One. You must have very good instructors."

Itachi smiled and nodded.

"Yanagi-sama is a tree Kami, he knows more about healing than anyone! And Obaa-chan is—was…"

Itachi stopped speaking abruptly and began to sniffle.

Torako didn't say anything, but sat down beside her daughter and opened her arms. Itachi crawled right into them.

"I'm sorry," was all that Kitsu said as he finished securing Sairō's sleeping form.

When he was done he turned, still on his knees, to Torako and Itachi, and the mischievous glint had returned to his eyes.

"Now, Itachi-chan, tell me how you feel about sea serpents."

Torako stood at the bow of the ship once more, Itachi clinging excitedly to her back with the wrap securing her in place, Sairō still secured and slumbering at her feet, and felt her eyes widen and her jaw drop in awe. No matter what Kitsu had said about these two creatures being friends of his, she couldn't quite shake the hint of fear that crawled along her spine as she watched two sea serpents, each as big as the Trickster itself, drop below the waterline and then rise to take hold of a loop of the thickest lines she'd ever seen (she'd been corrected calmly but firmly when she'd called them ropes a moment ago) in their enormous, sharply fanged mouths, and then pull them taut. The lines split at multiple points along their length, and each new split was secured to a different portion of the ship. When all was said and done, the Trickster looked like a rather cumbersome spider dangling from a very convoluted bit of its own webbing.

The crew that had rowed out to pass the massive lines to the serpents had included Kitsu, who had seemed to deliver some kind of lengthy speech to them before they'd taken up their positions. Now, as the last of the returning crew of the Trickster climbed aboard once more and the longboats were hauled up and secured back onto the deck, a signal was given. She wasn't certain what the signal was, because she heard nothing, and she was too focused on the massive water dragons ahead of her to see anything that might have been done on deck. But the sea serpents shot forward as one, and then, a heartbeat later, the Trickster surged forward with them.

In the span of a few breaths the ship was moving faster than Torako had ever seen a ship move, even the one that had tipped her into the sea that morning.

"We'll catch the bastards that took your woman yet, I'll wager," said an unfamiliar voice from beside her.

Torako turned to see a woman, as tall as she was and twice as wide, raise a commiserating eyebrow.

"Uso," the woman said, with a small bow. "Captain said you were after the Wind Serpent. Fast ship, the Serpent. No match for real serpents, though."

The woman spat after she spoke and Torako didn't know what she should respond to first.

"Torako," she said, deciding introductions were probably safest. "And this is Itachi-chan, my daughter."

She hoped that pointing out the presence of the small child on her back might keep Uso from some of the less savory topics that a smuggler might choose to raise, but she didn't hold out much hope. She hadn't met very many of Kitsu's crew over the cycles, but the ones she *had* met had seemed to have a competition going to see which of them could upset her with bawdy or bloody tales. They had all been disappointed. Torako was not at all put off by such things, but that didn't mean that she wanted Itachi to listen to them.

Torako was soon distracted from wondering what Uso might say next as her stomach dropped away and she turned to see the bow of the Trickster slide down the steepest swell she'd ever seen. Torako let out a whoop of excitement, Itachi giggling loudly in her ear, as she gripped the rail and felt the spray of the water slap her face, driven by a wind that whipped away all other sounds.

"Captain was right about you," the other woman shouted over the wind.

Torako turned and did her best to glare at Uso through the hair that whipped loose from her braid and repeatedly covered her eyes.

"What is that supposed to mean?" she asked. She was unused to people smiling in response to her glare, but then again, she usually loomed over people as she did her glaring, and there was simply no looming over Uso. Uso's smile was alluring, for all that Torako wanted to smack it off her face. Instead, she raised an eyebrow until the woman chose to reply.

"He always said you would love the sea," Uso explained when she'd smirked long enough.

Torako tried to push away the memories that accompanied that truth, but it wasn't easy. The cycles she'd spent with Kitsu dipping in and out of her life had contained a thousand variations on that particular conversation. How he was certain she would love the sea. How she thought he might be right, how she couldn't abandon her valley to the bandits that were always trying to make a home there at the expense of the many small villages that no one else seemed willing to protect.

"Pity you decided to leave him high and dry," Uso continued, as the wind died down somewhat while the ship climbed the next swell. "I don't think he's ever quite gotten over it."

Now Torako couldn't help but laugh.

"Kitsu-san has done many things in his life," she said. "But pining after a lover isn't one of them. Least of all me."

Uso's face darkened as Torako spoke, and Torako wondered which of them was missing something.

"Oh? Would you care to explain why the Captain hasn't taken anyone to bed in the past nine cycles then?"

Uso was still smirking when Torako turned and walked away from the railing with Itachi still wrapped to her back.

"Keep an eye on the wolf," was all she'd said to the woman.

She barely noticed the steep incline of the deck as she made her way towards the stern.

"Stay here a moment," was all she said to Itachi when she placed her in one of the hammocks in the cabin they'd been assigned when they first boarded the ship.

Silence rang in her ears, along with a slowly building fury, as she stalked the short distance from where she'd left Itachi to the great cabin.

"What in the thirteen hells is that woman talking about?" was what she shouted when she burst into Kitsu's quarters without so much as knocking.

"Am I supposed to know which woman you're referring to?" Kitsu asked, his eyes glittering and his head tilted to one side in curiosity, as though she hadn't just barged into his personal quarters without permission.

"Uso-san. The… I don't even know who she is. But she just said that you haven't taken anyone to your bed for nine cycles! That's… That cannot be true."

Kitsu's eyebrows rose eloquently, and he stood and crossed back to the door she had just barged through and slid it closed once more.

"Tora-chan, you *know* that's not true. But I assume your concern is that there's been no one *else*." Kitsu's eyes flickered with… something… as he returned to where she stood. "You believed her?" he asked, as he settled himself in front of the low table where he'd been sitting when she'd entered.

Torako took a moment to look around the room now, as she felt heat flush her neck and cheeks. Had she believed that woman? Or had she assumed the whole thing was part of some elaborate ploy? Kitsu sat calmly before her now, legs crossed on a brightly decorated zabuton before a low table barely containing a haphazard arrangement of maps, charts, and Kami knew what else. She took a breath and folded herself to the floor across from him.

"I don't know if I believed her but… the idea made me so angry that I didn't really think about it. I just…" Her voice trailed away as she realized she couldn't complete the sentence. Then she sighed. "I needed it not to be true."

"Well, congratulations. It is false. Not that it's any of your business, either."

Torako laughed then. Nothing was funny, but she couldn't stop herself.

"You're right, of course. I know it's not my business. I just couldn't fathom why she would have told me that if it weren't… I thought she was trying…"

"To make you feel guilty enough to take back up with me?"

This time Torako laughed out of humor.

"I hope she doesn't think that little of either of us."

Kitsu sat calmly on the other side of the desk for a while and then sighed before he spoke again.

"Did you know that my crew took bets on when we'd tire of each other?"

Torako felt her neck flush and shook her head.

"It was a great amusement to them for a long time. I wouldn't be surprised if Uso-san had money staked on how you'd react to what she just told you."

"She lied, then?"

Kitsu frowned for a moment.

"Not exactly," he replied.

And just like that, the fury rose in Torako once more.

"Kitsu-san, you can't just—" and then she stopped herself, because there was no good way to end that sentence.

"I can't just what? Are you going to suggest I can't stop being intimate with people whenever I choose? You're a bit rash sometimes, Tora-chan, but you've never said anything truly foolish before."

Torako swallowed the anger that had been driving her first statement and tried again.

"You can do whatever you want, obviously, but I know what your preferences are. Or what they were, anyway. I just… I want you to be happy."

Now Kitsu smiled at her and the light in his eyes sent a pang of guilt right through her heart.

"Then you will be pleased to hear that the reason Uso-san suspects that I haven't taken anyone to bed since you and I parted ways is that, after a few cycles of my entire crew placing bets on my love life, I decided I would be more circumspect with any of my future partners."

Torako felt one knot in her chest loosen a bit.

"You, I take it, have found a more permanent arrangement?" he asked after a moment.

Torako swallowed. She was not looking forward to this part.

"Yes, I'm married to a brilliant scribe." For a moment, Torako struggled to come up with words that could accurately convey Raku. "She's fierce, brilliant, and much better with people than I am."

"And you have a daughter together," Kitsu said, his voice only mildly curious.

"About that," Torako said, unsure how best to proceed, but knowing that Raku would never forgive her if she didn't make good on her promise right now. "She's your daughter."

Kitsu laughed.

Torako frowned.

"That's impossible," Kitsu explained when he finally regained enough breath.

"I assure you it is quite possible. In fact, it's the only possibility. Raku-san and I chose you expressly for the purpose, and there were no backup plans."

Kitsu was still smiling.

"I'm truly honored that you would choose me for such purposes, but I can guarantee you that it wasn't me."

"Kitsu-san, there was no one else. Raku-san is an excellent lover in every respect, but she is decidedly lacking in the equipment it would take to impregnate me."

"Well, in that regard, so am I."

"Then I have hallucinated every single one of our sexual encounters?"

"That's not what I meant, and you know it. But believe me, I can't have impregnated you. It's impossible for me to impregnate a human by accident."

"That is not how pregnancy works, Kitsu-san."

"Not normally no, but I assure you, for me it does. You're a null. I can't possibly have impregnated you."

"Just because my mother stole away my kisō when I was still in the womb doesn't mean that I can't have children, Kitsu-san. I have a daughter and nine moons of misery to prove it!"

"Of course it doesn't stop you from having children, Tora-chan. That's not what I'm saying. But—wait, did you say your mother stole your kisō?"

"Yes. She drained me of any power I might have had before I

was born. It's why I wasn't on speaking terms with her when you and I were together."

"But… that's not… that shouldn't be possible. I can't think of a single kisōshi who has the power to take another's kisō, not even in the womb. Especially not in the womb."

Kitsu's expression had gone distant, losing the mischievous twinkle it generally held, and instead shifting to some faraway idea that, by the looks of it, was decidedly unpleasant.

Torako's frustration was just reaching its limits when Kitsu's eyes came back into focus and his gaze locked with hers.

"Torako-san, may I touch you? I need—I need to check something."

Torako had no idea what Kitsu could check simply by touching her, but if it would keep him from arguing about the provenance of her own daughter with her, she would let him touch her as much as he liked.

Then she shook her head. No. Maybe not that much.

She swallowed.

"Yes, you can touch me to check for whatever it is that will keep you from insisting Itachi-chan isn't your blood."

Kitsu's bow was quick but solemn and then he placed his hand gently against her neck. She would have been suspicious of the placement, but most of her skin was covered in deer hide, and she knew from experience that skin to skin was the best way to interact with another's kisō. Of course, as Kitsu was well aware, using kisō on her would simply end with that energy pulled away to Kami knew where.

She hoped he didn't hold the contact long enough to make her lose the oden Midori had fed them.

It was only a heartbeat before he dropped his hand away, though.

Kitsu's eyes popped open, and his face paled.

"It's true," he whispered. "I got you pregnant."

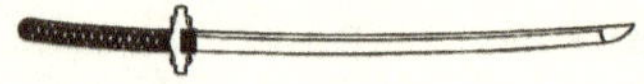

"Don't sound so glum, she's a pretty great kid," Torako said, trying to keep the edge of anger out of her voice. And then, before she could stop herself, the words she'd been holding in ever since the last time she'd seen Kitsu came tumbling out in a torrent. "Also, Raku-san and I don't expect you to be involved at all. I suggested you never needed to know, but Raku-san wanted me to tell you what we were doing before I slept with you that time. I told her it was none of your business, if you'd been willing to sleep with me and then walk away, especially since it was possible the pregnancy wouldn't stick anyway, but she insisted that since we *planned* to keep the child you deserved some choice. I told her we weren't *really* planning it because I wasn't planning to see you that night, that I'd actually thought you were dead, and that just because you'd been on the top of the list of hypothetical men I'd be willing to sleep with in order to make a family didn't mean that our reunion gave you any right to the child. She made me promise I'd tell you if I ever saw you again, though."

Torako blinked and wished she'd stopped herself around the words "pretty great kid."

"That is… a lot."

"Are you angry?" Torako asked. "I think I would be angry if I were you, but I'm also not sure you have any right to be angry."

Kitsu simply blinked at her a few times. When he finally spoke, his voice was the least certain she'd ever heard it.

"Itachi-chan, is she… What's she like?"

Torako smiled. This was a subject she generally enjoyed.

"She's delightful. Of course, I'm incredibly biased, but she's always trying to help. She's a fast learner, and she's endlessly curious. The other day I almost ran straight into a group of bandits we were following because she'd asked me an uncomfortable question about how deer made more deer."

Torako realized she was rambling again, but she didn't care as much this time.

"And she's the most powerful water kisō that Yanagi-sama has trained in an age."

"Didn't he train Taka-san?"

Torako nodded and felt her stomach drop a bit. That was one of the primary things that she and Raku were concerned about. Yanagi-sama was not prone to exaggeration, and he insisted that Itachi would be more powerful than Taka was. It was a frightening thought for two parents with less than no kisō between them.

Suddenly, she was hit with a wave of rage and sorrow as she thought of Itachi's life without Tenshi in it. And right on its heels was a wave of longing for Raku that almost unraveled her.

"I should go check on Itachi-chan," she murmured, standing up. "I left her in our cabin on the way here."

Kitsu sprang to his feet beside her.

"Why don't I check on her? You can take a moment for yourself on deck. The serpents have been hauling us at an excellent clip. We may yet catch up to Itachi-chan's mother tonight."

Torako could barely fathom the possibility, but she felt off enough, between the grief, longing, and hope that Kitsu had just offered her, to take his suggestion and head out onto the deck for a moment to gather her thoughts.

⚛ *Itachi* ⚛

ITACHI SAT IN the corner of the small cabin with her knees tucked tight against her chest and tried to make the spirit go away. She hadn't minded being left in the little cabin when Mama had dropped her there. There was a small lamp hanging on the wall that made the room feel warm and cozy, even though the air was damp, and Itachi actually liked the damp air because it meant she could feel water everywhere and water was her friend.

But the spirit that had slunk into the room as soon as Mama had left was staring at her like a hungry animal, grinding its rather large teeth, and she was worried that if she looked at it again it would start talking to her, and the talking spirits usually said horrible things. She missed Sairō. There hadn't been any spirits around ever since the big wolf had shown up. Why couldn't Mama have left Sairō in here with her?

She kept her eyes on the wooden planks under her feet, and tried to count the knots she saw in the wood. Yanagi-sensei said that the knots were where branches had grown out of the tree when it was alive, and she liked thinking of Yanagi-sensei and living trees. They were much better than angry spirits.

But thinking of trees did not make the spirit go away.

It moaned.

Itachi pulled her legs tighter and considered closing her eyes. She didn't know if that would make the spirit more or less likely to talk to her. She wished she had asked Yanagi-sensei how to get rid of the spirits, but she had worried that he would tell Mama and Kaa-san about them. Itachi didn't want Mama or Kaa-san to know about the spirits because they always seemed to worry every time they learned about some new thing that Itachi could do with her kisō. Itachi didn't think the spirits came to her because of her water kisō, but she also didn't think Mama or Kaasan would understand that, they would just be sad that they couldn't help her make the spirits go away.

She hated making them sad.

But right now she wished she had risked asking Yanagi-sensei, because the spirit was starting to growl.

"Go away, go away, go away," she whispered.

Telling the spirits to leave had never worked before, but mostly she wanted to not have to listen to the growling.

"Is this gentleman bothering you?" asked a low voice from the other side of the cabin.

Itachi looked up and was surprised to see the bright yellow gaze of the captain of the Trickster.

"Who?" she asked, trying her best not to look at the spirit. It wasn't growling now.

The captain tilted his head to one side and looked at her again. Then he looked directly at the spirit. Then he looked back to her and raised an eyebrow.

"You can see them too?" she asked, unable to keep her voice from squeaking.

"I can."

For a long moment, he just looked at her, as if she was a bit of wood and he was trying to figure out where all of her branches had been.

"Would you like me to teach you how to make them leave you alone?" he asked.

And, before she could even open her mouth to agree, he made a flicking motion with his hand, and the spirit disappeared.

❧ *Torako* ❧

TORAKO STOOD AT the bow once more, trying to let the wind in her hair and the salt spray on her face calm the turmoil in her heart. It wasn't working. She tried staring at the majestic forms of the sea serpents frothing the sea beyond her, their enormous bodies breaking the water and pulling the ship at such speeds she couldn't fathom how anyone could outrun them. That didn't work either. Her mind couldn't even settle on what was upsetting her, there were too many options. Her lingering resentment of the choice that Tenshi had made for her before she was even born warred with the anguish she felt at knowing Tenshi was gone. Her love for Raku and the life they had built together battled with her annoyance at Raku's insistence that Torako needed to tell Kitsu about Itachi's origins and offer him the opportunity to be a part of her life. Her cycles-old anger at Kitsu for reappearing in her life when she'd half expected him to be dead wrestled with her own emotional attachment to what they had once been to each other.

Her stomach twisted. She needed to focus on something. This maelstrom of emotions was making her dizzy.

She should never have told Kitsu that he was Itachi's father. Why did it matter? He wasn't her father in any way that mattered. He hadn't been involved in her life at all until today. Torako and Raku were her parents. She didn't need anyone else.

No that wasn't true. She needed Tenshi, and Yanagi, and Taka, and Kusuko. She needed as many loving adults in her life as she could get. Torako was being foolish if she thought Itachi wouldn't benefit from having another loving adult in her life. So, why was she feeling so raw now that Kitsu knew the truth?

Probably because she expected him to be angry with her once he had time to think about it a bit, and she didn't think he had any right to be angry with her. Did he? No. She hadn't lied to him when they'd slept together nearly five cycles prior. She'd been happy to see him, delighted he was still alive and, yes, perhaps a bit nostalgic for what they'd been to each other. She and Raku had never been possessive about who else they went to bed with, but even beyond their usual arrangement, Raku had been encouraging her to find a man whose company she enjoyed so that they might start a family. Torako had teased Raku about how if she wanted a family so badly she should seduce a man herself, but Raku had never been even remotely interested in anything a man could offer her in the bedroom, so it had fallen to Torako. And just when she'd been despairing that there were far too few men she found alluring in the world, Kitsu had reappeared in her life, by chance, as she'd been finishing one of her longer patrols. One night in the inn where'd they'd first met was all it had taken. He hadn't done anything to prevent pregnancy and neither had she.

Even so, she was astounded that it had worked. She was the daughter of a midwife and friends with the most powerful healer in Gensokai, and she knew that for every woman who despaired because one night of carelessness left her with a lifetime commitment, three more women could not make all the carelessness in the world into the child they longed to have.

So she'd had no reason to tell Kitsu anything beforehand. There was nothing to tell. What would she have said? "Oh, by the way, if this little reunion gets me pregnant, AND that pregnancy lasts all the way to term, my wife and I will actually be very happy because we've been wanting a child, so thanks in advance?"

She actually laughed at the thought of it.

Then she sighed.

She didn't think Kitsu would actually be angry with her in the end. He'd never been particularly judgmental and… well, he'd probably wind up becoming good friends with Raku. Her head thunked down onto the rail as she realized she had probably just roped the man into her life for the remainder of it.

"Kuso," she muttered.

Then she blinked, as she noticed the empty length of rope at her feet. Sairō was gone.

Just as she was about to turn and start looking for the enormous wolf, a voice from above shouted, "Sail!"

Torako's heart leapt in her chest. Could it be? Could they truly have caught up with Raku's captors already?

❐Itachi❐

"SUGOI!" ITACHI BLURTED as soon as the spirit was gone.

The captain of the Trickster was still standing just inside the little room, near the lamp, but when she looked at him again his eyes flashed a bright yellow.

"Why are you glowing?" she asked.

"Am I glowing?" he asked.

"Your eyes were."

"Ah, yes. I suppose you *would* be able to see that. Most people don't."

"Why can I see it, then?"

"Probably for the same reason you can see spirits," he replied. "You and I have some things in common, I think."

"Oh? Is that because we're related?"

The man's smile flickered like the lamp beside him and Itachi wondered if she had said something wrong.

"Mama said you were family."

The captain's eyebrows went very high up his forehead when she said that, so she tried again.

"Well, she said you were family if you wanted to be, and otherwise you were a good friend."

"And when did Torako-san say that?"

"When she was explaining who she was searching for in Sakata."

"Do you know who I am?" he asked.

"You are the captain of the Trickster," Itachi said, smiling because she knew the answer.

"And my name is Kitsu," the captain replied, returning her smile.

"That sounds like kitsune," Itachi replied. "Are you a fox?"

"Are you a weasel?" Kitsu replied.

"I don't think so. Weasels are even smaller than me."

"And much furrier," Kitsu agreed.

"But you could turn into a fox!" Itachi suggested.

"Could I?" Kitsu asked, and she noticed his eyes glowed again.

"Could you?" she asked, truly curious now.

"That's not someth—"

But she didn't get to hear what it wasn't because just then a voice from somewhere nearby shouted, "Captain, Sail ho!"

"Ah," said Kitsu. "They'll need me on deck. Would you like to come?"

Itachi wasn't sure what to say, because she knew that she was not supposed to wander off with people she had just met. But they were on a ship, so where could they wander off to? And

Mama had said this man was family. That wasn't the same as someone she had just met. Not really.

Itachi moved to follow the captain, but just as she stepped into the passageway, something huge and furry stepped in front of them.

"I'd prefer if the child stayed with me," Sairō growled.

Kitsu opened his mouth. Maybe he was going to argue. Then he shrugged and said, "Fine. I'm needed on deck. As long as you keep her safe, you'll get no argument from me."

"Are you still sick?" she asked the wolf. They didn't look well.

"I vomited twice on the way here."

"Then why did you—"

"Something is coming, child. And we need to be prepared."

❧ Torako ❧

TORAKO COULD BARELY breathe as she watched the other sail take shape against the moonlit clouds. When the sailor from the crow's nest had called out, she hadn't been able to see anything like a sail in the distance, but she had watched in a dazed hope that she was almost afraid to kindle as nothing transformed into a speck, which became a dot, which finally became a sail-shaped blot against the low-lying clouds that caught the moon's errant rays.

Lighting up the horizon so that her enemies were visible and growing closer by the moment, the moon had never been more beautiful.

Perhaps it was that thought that ruined everything.

Perhaps she would never know.

She felt the hair on her neck rise even as she watched the ship on the horizon loom large enough that she could make out how many sails it carried, along with their shape. She was loath to pry her eyes from the other ship, as if looking away would somehow allow them to escape, but she had not survived twenty cycles as a warrior by ignoring those hairs.

She turned to see the thin, glowing man she had met by the deer pond.

"Torako-san, flee."

Torako simply blinked at the man made of moonlight. To where, precisely, was she meant to flee? She was on a ship. In the middle of the sea. There was nowhere safer than where she stood.

But the moon being who had called himself her grandfather, and warned her not to trust him the last time that they had met, did not wait for any response from her before flickering out of existence again.

And then as she looked out over the bow of the ship, Torako at last understood *why* Tsukuyomi had told her to flee, even if she had no idea how he'd expected her to manage it.

The left-hand sea serpent, previously indistinguishable from its fellow, now had eyes that glowed the same bright silver-white as the moonlight that lit the clouds. And those eyes were now visible to her because the enormous head that housed them was turned halfway towards the Trickster. The reason for which was soon made obvious, as it released the line from the ship it had held in its enormous teeth and instead attempted to sink those teeth into its companion. Its companion, of course, dropped the line it carried to defend itself.

The ship did not slow. The lines were still looped haphazardly around the serpents' bodies, so they would have still been pulling the ship, but the serpents had stopped moving forward. However, the ship had nothing to slow it but the wind and the waves. And those appeared to be moving with them. They were headed towards the sea serpents very quickly.

Which would have been bad enough, given that the sea serpents were incredibly large, and probably quite solid.

It was made infinitely worse, however, by the fact that the serpents were fighting each other, writhing in the water so violently that they threw large swells and splashes of water in every direction. Some of which headed straight for the Trickster. Just for extra fun, the Trickster was still tied to the serpents by the lines they had carried earlier, but which now encircled their long bodies. In other words, they couldn't steer around them.

Not that they would have had time to, anyway.

The serpents had been at least ten ship lengths ahead of the Trickster at the full length of lines that they pulled. Torako didn't wait to see how long it would take to reach the place where they churned the water into an angry torrent. Instead, she took her grandfather's advice.

She fled.

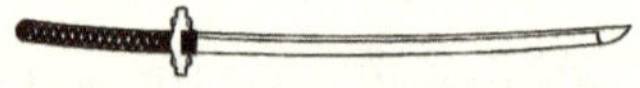

Torako's very first thought as she turned from the bow and began running across the deck was that she had to find Itachi. The crew had exploded into action behind her as she had watched the violence between the two sea serpents unfold. They moved across the deck like hundreds of angry insects, their movements a finely tuned and coordinated chaos to her untrained eyes. Everyone seemed to have some specific task, though it wasn't at all clear to Torako what each of those tasks might be. But people carried things, pulled things, tightened some things and loosened others. She thought she saw a few men and women with axes rush to the sides of the ship and drop over, and she wondered if they were hoping to cut the lines that attached them to the serpents. That seemed reasonable.

She was too busy dodging bodies and looking for Itachi's tiny figure to worry about what anyone was doing with their axes though.

She didn't see Kitsu anywhere, but she assumed he was busy doing whatever a captain did to try to save his ship from enormous serpents having a wrestling match in a location it was impossible to avoid. She wasn't really looking for him anyway, she was looking for a flash of green eyes in a tiny face. Kitsu had gone to check on her, but he would have come on deck the moment the lookout called the sail. Had he left Itachi alone? Her chest was just starting to tighten with worry as she neared the stern of the ship and the hatch she would need to climb down to see if Itachi was still in their cabin when a flash of fur caught her peripheral vision.

She turned, and the tightness in her chest eased entirely as she saw Itachi astride Sairō's back. The wolf wasn't in their horse-sized form anymore, but that hardly mattered for a rider as small as Itachi. Even at only double the size of a normal wolf, Sairō was more than large enough to support the three-cycle old's weight.

She took one step towards them before a cracking louder than anything she'd ever heard before rent the night and Itachi and Sairō disappeared from view, along with everything else. Shards of wood flew through the air around her, and enormous scales replaced the ship that had been before her, under her, behind her.

She was falling, for the second time that day, into the arms of the frigid ocean below.

As she fell, for one instant, a part of her mind shrieked that she had been SO CLOSE. So close to Itachi. So close to getting Raku back. So close. She wanted to scream. Perhaps she was screaming. It was impossible to tell with the wind whipping past her filled with wood, blood, and the sea.

Then she hit the water. It was colder here than in Sakata harbor, even though the air had seemed just as warm out of the wind. The combination of the force and the cold took her breath away, and she realized that she had indeed been screaming, and it had probably saved her life, because it had kept the water from filling her nose and mouth as she went under.

She waited until her momentum stopped pushing her down and then she pushed up to the surface. She gasped for breath as soon as her face hit the air, and she tried to clear her eyes well enough to find Itachi.

But even once she could see again, her brain took a long moment to piece together what was before her. The Trickster had been smashed into more pieces than she could easily count. She thought she saw movement that might have been other people, but she couldn't be sure. The sea serpent whose body had crushed it was no longer visible, and she hoped that it had swum away instead of sticking around to pluck its supper from the water.

Of course, it didn't matter if it had—she'd kill a dozen a sea serpents if they got between her and Itachi. Just as she started swimming for the wreckage to search for her daughter, something wrapped firmly around her ankle and pulled her under the waves.

⟩⟩⟩ *Itachi* ⟨⟨⟨

ITACHI HAD NEVER held on to anything so tight in her life.

Her fingers gripped Sairō's fur so hard that her hands were white.

Or maybe that was the cold.

The water was much colder than she'd thought it would be. Her teeth were chattering, and she thought her whole body shook, but that could also have been because she was afraid. The water had gone up her nose and into her mouth when they had fallen into the water. It had left as soon as she asked it to, though. So she could breathe now.

It wasn't the fall that had scared her, or the waves that carried sharp bits of wood too close to them. It was mostly the sea serpents.

The large one that had crushed the ship had been very scary. But it was the little ones that kept trying to pull her and Sairō into the water that scared her most.

Sairō's head dove into the water again and came up with another of the smaller serpents between their teeth. Itachi hoped that the blood that coated the wolf's muzzle was the serpent's. The serpents were each twice as long as Itachi, and there were more than Itachi could count from her perch on Sairō's back, but they were all trying to pull Sairō below the water.

"Hold on tight, child! I need to dive again," Sairō growled.

Itachi closed her eyes and mouth and pushed air into her nose and ears. Then she felt water all around her and for the first time in her life, it didn't feel like a warm hug. She kept her eyes closed. She didn't want to see the serpents attacking Sairō and it was probably too dark to see much anyway. She held tight to Sairō's long ruff and tried to wrap her legs close to Sairō's body. She could feel the wolf turning and snapping at the smaller serpents. She tried not to think of anything except holding tight. She wanted to cry. She wanted to call out for Mama. But she knew that Mama could not hear her under the water, and crying would make her want to breathe again, so she didn't do either.

Just when Itachi was worried that she was going to breathe in water, Sairō brought them both to the surface.

"Can you swim, child?" Sairō asked, as soon as they'd gotten their breath back.

"Yes," Itachi answered, though her voice was barely more than a squeak.

"You may need to soon. I'm getting very tired."

Itachi said nothing, because she could hear the wolf's voice getting weaker as they spoke. She reached out with her kisō and sensed a dozen cuts all over Sairō's legs and face.

"Keep your kisō, child. You'll need it to keep warm." Sairō sounded like they were falling asleep, and Itachi did not like that at all. "My magic… doesn't like the sea… moon's a bit of a bastard… Don't let…"

Itachi gasped as Sairō dipped beneath a wave and started to pull her under too. She kept one hand wrapped in Sairō's fur and used the other hand and her legs to tread water.

"Stay with me," she begged, trying to pull the wolf above the water. Sairō was very large, even for a wolf, and they were mostly muscle, which Yanagi-sensei had once told her was very bad for floating.

Itachi felt something brush her leg and she screamed, but she did not let go of Sairō's fur.

"Stay!" she shouted, even though she was fairly certain Sairō could no longer hear her.

She knew the serpents were going to try to pull them both under. Sairō had said to save her kisō, but save it for what? If the serpents pulled them both to the bottom of the sea her kisō wouldn't do them any good.

She closed her eyes and held on tight to Sairō's fur. The next time she felt a serpent in the water she used her kisō to move the water like a whip. She couldn't see the serpent, but she thought she hit it. Sairō sank a bit more and she used her kisō to try to push them up out of the water. It worked, but just as she did it, another serpent wrapped around Sairō's paw and pulled down.

Itachi tried to whip it with water like the last one. It let go. But another serpent wrapped around a different paw and pulled down. Itachi gasped as both she and Sairō sank beneath the waves.

She wanted to cry. It wasn't fair. She was so little and the stupid serpents were so big. She couldn't fight them off and hold Sairō up at the same time. And now they were both going to be dragged to the bottom of the ocean because she wasn't strong enough to save them.

She gritted her teeth, held back a scream that would only let water into her mouth, and pushed very hard against the water.

Itachi and Sairō popped up above the waves and she breathed deeply before they crashed back into the sea. She could see the serpents waiting for her as soon as they touched the water again, and Itachi wanted to scream.

And then she did scream.

Because one of the enormous sea serpents that had been pulling the ship broke out of the water right beside her.

She was so scared she let go of Sairō's fur. The wolf began to sink immediately, and Itachi screamed again and dove after them.

She grabbed their ruff and tried to kick upwards, but Sairō was so much bigger than she was. She used kisō, asking the water to push her. It did.

They rose to the top again and Itachi wondered if she should have let them sink. Being eaten by a sea serpent probably hurt worse than drowning.

Then something grabbed her arm from behind and she gripped Sairō's fur extra hard, prepared to fight. But before she could even turn around to look, that something hauled her out of the water, and all she could do was scream Sairō's name as they sank once more into the sea.

≈ *Torako* ≈

TORAKO HATED THE little sea serpents. When she managed to get above the water long enough to breathe, she cursed them soundly.

"Not worth the sweat off Tanuki's balls," was her favorite so far. Not that she'd taken any time to appreciate the turn of phrase, as she'd had to immediately return to cutting the heads off of sea serpents.

She wanted nothing more than to swim into the nearby wreckage and search for Itachi, but the serpents would not leave her be. For every three that she killed, three more were doing their best to wrap her ankles and drag her below the water.

It was much harder to kill the ones that were attached to her legs, so she had to hold her breath while she jabbed at them cautiously in order to avoid cutting her own legs open. She was getting tired.

Tanuki's balls, she had *started* tired. The only reason she hadn't been dragged to the bottom of the ocean already was that the sea serpents were too large to all attack her at once, and because they seemed to understand that the katana could kill them. If they had been the mindless animals she had originally suspected them of being, they would have simply overwhelmed her at the sacrifice of a few dozen of their kind, but after she'd decapitated the first few, the remainder had given the katana a wide berth whenever they could and she had been able to keep both of her arms free so far, as well as alternating legs.

For animals that didn't enjoy being stabbed, they were remarkably persistent in trying to drown her, though. Perhaps they were pack hunters and they knew they would eventually tire her out. They weren't wrong. She was already flagging.

She slashed at one serpent and then turned to slash at a second that she caught in her peripheral vision. She felt a third and fourth wrap her ankles and she cursed just before they pulled her under again.

She couldn't see much, even just below the surface—the moonlight didn't penetrate the way sunlight did—but she kept her eyes open against the slight sting of salt water even so. She slashed at the two serpents on her ankles first and was gratified when they released her quickly. She kicked up as soon as they'd let her go, but another serpent wrapped around her waist before she'd even broken the surface.

Cutting at her own waist with a katana was practically impossible, in addition to being a terrible idea. She reached for her wakizashi with her left hand, but before she could bring the blade to bear, another serpent wrapped around her arm.

The serpents might have been learning how to fight her more effectively, but she could still cut at her own arm well enough. She neatly decapitated the serpent holding back her wakizashi and then drove the smaller blade into the serpent wrapped around her waist.

She didn't wait for the creature to release her before she started kicking towards the surface again. She needed air. She had been under for too long already.

She burst above the waves for just a heartbeat, long enough for one quick lungful of air before she felt serpents all around her. She wasn't even certain how many were there, but they must have been waiting for the moment her head went above the waterline and she wouldn't be able to see them approach.

Both her legs, her waist… she managed to stave off the first few that came at her arms, just by striking out wildly as soon as she felt the first serpent connect, but it was only a temporary victory. The serpents on her legs dragged her under and when she finally saw the mass of writing creatures that waited for her she wanted to scream out of sheer frustration.

Kuso, she thought, forcefully, just on principle.

She put her blades through as many of them as she could. She became a whirlwind of blades and fury. She knew it was pointless, there were too many of them, but it provided her with a small amount of satisfaction to know that she'd killed a few dozen more of the bastards that were going to drown her.

She wasn't sure when the pressure on her arm grew so tight that she dropped her wakizashi. Probably just before she dropped her katana. She wondered if Sairō would be able to get the damned blade back after this, or if they would be trapped at the bottom of the sea. She didn't like that thought. She tried to thrash against the serpents again. She couldn't die now. She had to save Itachi. She had to save Raku. She wanted to avenge Tenshi.

Fucking serpents.

She hoped she'd killed a lot of them.

Her lungs were on fire, but she was nowhere near the surface.

It didn't matter, she had nothing left to fight with. She took a breath, and choked because it wasn't air that filled her lungs. She retched, but couldn't stop.

Thankfully, that was when everything went black.

⮜ *Itachi* ⮞

ITACHI HADN'T SEEN just how large the scales on the enormous sea serpents were until she'd been stuck between two of them. Now that she was using them to keep her and Sairō in place while she did her best to heal the wolf's wounds, she was very aware that the scales were each as tall as she was and half as thick.

She was very glad the *something* that had grabbed her had turned out to be Kitsu. She was even more glad that Kitsu seemed to be friends with the sea serpent she was now riding, along with what looked like a hundred men and women from Kitsu's ship. At least, Itachi assumed the serpent was his friend, because why else would she allow a hundred tiny humans to prance around on her back?

Kitsu had hauled Itachi from the water and shouted at her to grab one of the huge scales before he had dived in again to surface with Sairō a moment later. Sairō had looked more like a drowned cat than a wolf, but they were still breathing when Kitsu had shoved them beside her, so Itachi had immediately pushed her hand into Sairō's fur and tried to remember everything Yanagi-sensei had taught her about healing cuts.

She didn't look up when Kitsu returned to sit beside her for a moment. She didn't look up when the serpent started sliding through the waves again without managing to dump any of the people off her back. She was focused on telling all of Sairō's blood where to go, because it kept trying to go all the places it shouldn't. Thankfully, her kisō knew that the blood was mostly water, and water was happy to listen to her.

She *did* look up when Sairō growled, "Torako-san, wait!" without opening their eyes.

Kitsu-san also looked at the wolf when they spoke, then looked to the water.

Sairō was silent for a few awful heartbeats and then they lifted their head and glared very hard at the water.

"There, Fox-boy. Hurry!"

Kitsu didn't wait. He jumped.

Itachi swallowed, watching the water where Kitsu had just disappeared, but she kept her hand on Sairō and kept their blood where it was supposed to be.

She was just beginning to worry when Kitsu finally broke the surface of the water with Mama in his arms. She enjoyed one breath of relief when she saw Kitsu pull Mama onto the back of the serpent a few scales away from where she sat with Sairō. But that relief quickly turned to a sick fear when she saw that Kitsu was crying.

Itachi hadn't realized that she'd let go of Sairō, or that she'd asked the water to carry her from the middle of the serpent's back where she and Sairō had been safely tucked away to where Mama was. She didn't realize she was doing anything strange at all until afterwards, when Kitsu pulled her aside to speak with her. In that moment she just saw Mama looking pale and far too still, and knew that she needed to be by her side.

Itachi had known that she needed her mama. She hadn't realized that Mama needed her too, until she got there.

Kitsu was saying something, but Itachi barely heard him. Her kisō was telling her everything he was saying, but without her needing to understand the words.

"Lungs are stopped."

"I can't get her to breathe."

"I was too late."

Itachi did not let those words into her head. She also didn't let herself think about how she'd never been able to heal Mama before. About how the fact that Mama sucked kisō from people meant Itachi could never help her the way she'd just helped Sairō. She ignored that thought, because that thought meant that Mama was dead, and Mama could not be dead. Itachi needed Mama to smile at her, and teach her how to walk through the woods without leaving tracks, and hug her when she was scared, and fight bandits in the woods to keep her safe. Mama could not be dead. So, Itachi ignored what she knew, and she sent her kisō diving into Mama's body. She might have sobbed when she realized that no spark of kisō waited for her own, not even to snatch it away from her, but she did not stop. She looked for the water, just as she had with Sairō, only this time she wasn't trying to keep the water in, she was trying to pull it out.

Too much water. Water where water shouldn't go.

She pulled, and pushed, and pumped.

Water came out of Mama's mouth and nose. First in a trickle, then in a rush. Itachi kept pulling it out until she couldn't find even a drop left in Mama's lungs. But still, Mama didn't move.

Then Kitsu leaned over Mama, almost pushing Itachi out of the way, and put his hands on her chest. He pushed, and pushed, and pushed again. He looked like he was making bread, but instead of dough he pushed on Mama's heart. Itachi wanted to look away, or to help him push, or do something, anything, but…

"Torako, come back!"

That was Sairō's growling voice, she was sure of it, but what did they think—

Mama gasped and Itachi gasped with her, as if she hadn't breathed since Kitsu had started pushing on Mama's chest, and maybe she hadn't.

Mama vomited seawater over the side of the serpent, and then Itachi didn't know who had moved where or when, but she was hugging Mama, and Mama was hugging her, and they were both crying, and then Kitsu was hugging them both and tears were running down his face too, and Sairō let out what sounded like a celebratory howl, and she thought maybe the crew of the Trickster were cheering, but Itachi was too busy leaning into Mama's arms to know, and then she let her eyes close and sleep took her.

Torako

TORAKO CAME BACK ready to kill something, but instead found herself vomiting from the edge of a giant serpent into the sea.

Once she'd freed the ocean water from her stomach and returned it to its home, she blinked. She heard a tiny hitch of
breath behind her and turned to find Itachi watching her with
eyes as wide as scallop shells and tears running down her face. In
a single heartbeat, the distance between them closed and Itachi
was in her arms and holding her tight.

"Shh… I'm here now. I'm here. Shhh…"

Torako wasn't certain who she was reassuring. Her own heart
was hammering in her chest and her body felt strange, as though
she wasn't quite connected to her own limbs.

She hadn't even noticed that Kitsu had wrapped them both
in his arms until she heard him sobbing into her shoulder. Maybe
she was reassuring him too.

For a long moment, she just sat there and let sounds and
smells wash over her with no meaning. Voices around her shouting or perhaps cheering, a wolf howling, none of it mattered
when compared to the steady beat of the tiny heart pressed
against her chest.

Then she looked down into Itachi's small face and felt a stab
of panic when she saw the girl was still and her eyes were closed.

"She's fine," Kitsu whispered, still pressed into her shoulder
with his arms around them both. "She's asleep. She used a lot of
kisō tonight. I don't even know how she did it all, and… I have
no idea how she saved you. Kisō shouldn't work on you, but
she…"

Kitsu let his voice trail off, but Torako had some inkling of
what he meant. Itachi had never been able to heal her before.
She had tried many times. It always ended the same way, with
the little girl losing all her kisō for a few moments and with
Torako vomiting into a bush. It shouldn't have been possible, and
yet.

Sairō-san, are you well? she asked, sensing the wolf was close by but not knowing if they were close enough to hear her if she spoke aloud.

Well is not the word I would choose to describe myself at the moment. But I'm alive, thanks to your daughter. You and I both owe her a debt I hope we're never able to repay.

Torako shuddered at the thought of needing to save Itachi's life the way that the girl had saved theirs tonight. She agreed with the wolf completely.

I believe I owe more than Itachi for my life, Sairō-san.

Somehow the wolf managed to grunt in her mind. She thought they might be scoffing at the idea.

What happened, Sairō-san? she tried again. She had a guess. All that water, everything had gone dark, and she had heard one voice through the darkness, but…

"You were dead, Tora-chan," Kitsu said. She didn't know if he was somehow answering the question that Sairō refused to acknowledge, or if he was simply continuing the conversation she had been having with him a moment earlier.

She finally looked up into the bright amber of Kitsu's eyes and saw that they were still filled with tears.

"I didn't reach you fast enough. You were so still. And nothing worked. I tried hitting your back to clear the water, but it wouldn't budge, and your heart, your lungs… everything had stopped."

Torako swallowed.

"I think… I think Sairō-san did something… I… everything was black, I felt nothing, heard nothing, saw nothing, but then I heard them ask me to wait. And then I heard them ask me to come back."

It was woefully shy of everything that she had gone through, but she didn't know how else to explain it. She wasn't even certain any of it was real. But…

Her gaze caught Kitsu's again and before she knew it his hands were holding her face, his eyes begging a question they hadn't asked in cycles and she was nodding as his lips pressed to hers and their tears mingled along with their tongues.

Torako wasn't even embarrassed when a gruff voice from behind Kitsu cleared its throat.

"Captain, we found this in the water just now. Thought Torako-san might want it back."

Torako's eyes widened when she saw what the sailor was holding in her hands. It was Sairō's katana.

Torako laughed.

"Steel doesn't float," she said, accepting the blade and sheathing it in the scabbard that was still tied to her belt.

"Damnedest thing," said the sailor. "Wasn't even pretending to be stuck to some bit of flotsam from the Trickster, just hanging there as if it were made of balsam. I almost didn't grab it, but Uso-san said it was yours."

Torako didn't know what to say, so she simply thanked the woman and bowed until she clambered down the serpent's scales again to where a knot of crew huddled together between some of the largest spines.

Kitsu was frowning at the katana when Torako looked up again.

"What?" she asked.

"That's not a normal katana."

"No shit."

"You know it's possessed?"

"Of course I do. It's Sairō-san who possesses it. Although, I'm not sure I'd call it possession, more like they've been cursed into it."

"Cursed?"

"Or something. Honestly, we haven't had much time to talk about it."

And with that, Torako felt a surge of guilt and desperation as everything about the serpent attack returned to her.

"Raku-san," she whispered, wanting to scream in frustration again and barely containing it. They had been so close. "We were almost on top of them when the serpents started fighting and… damn it all. My grandfather. Did you see that bastard when you were… whatever it was you were doing during the attack?"

Kitsu tilted his head to one side. He had released her earlier to give her enough space to sheath the sword, but he'd looked ready to resume their embrace until she'd mentioned her grandfather. Now he just looked… curious, suspicious? She wasn't sure.

"Am I meant to know who your grandfather is?" he asked.

"Ah. I suppose not, considering I didn't know until two nights ago… although with everything else going on, I'm honestly not certain who knows what at this point."

"Tora-chan, you're babbling."

Torako glared at him. But she knew he was right, so she took a deep breath and tried again.

"Well, I'm not entirely certain, but a moon Kami named Tsukuyomi showed up the other night to tell me that he was my grandfather. Among… other things."

She swallowed, not yet ready to talk about Tenshi again.

Kitsu's head remained tilted to one side and now he added a single raised eyebrow to the expression.

"And you believed him?"

"Not exactly, but… I can't quite figure out why he would lie about it, and… well, having a Kami for a grandparent would explain certain things about Itachi-chan, don't you think?"

She gestured to where Itachi lay cradled in her lap still, and Kitsu's face blanked of all expression for a moment.

"Indeed," he muttered.

"Kitsu-san," Torako took a deep breath, steeling herself for an argument. "I can't give up on Raku-chan. I know… I know you've just lost your ship and probably most of your crew, but…"

Kitsu's eyes refocused on Torako's face then, and he smiled, which surprised her.

"You'd be surprised how many people can fit on a sea serpent's back, actually. We managed to save most of the Trickster's people."

That eased the ache in Torako's chest more than she would have expected. She'd hardly known the Trickster's crew, but the idea that many of them might have died solely for trying to help her rescue Raku had hurt.

"The Wind Serpent," Torako said, looking towards the horizon and wishing that she could see anything against the dark waters.

"I have a very good guess as to where The Wind Serpent was headed," Kitsu said, his voice soft behind her. "And I've already communicated with our serpent friend about heading that direction as soon as my crew is accounted for."

Torako swallowed back the tears that were trying to burst forward, not because she was embarrassed by them—she'd been bawling a moment ago and hadn't cared—but simply because she was too tired. She didn't have the energy for more crying. Come to that, she didn't have the energy for much of anything else, either. Kitsu made an inviting circle with his arms, and even though she was bursting with questions, and fears, and the need to make some kind of plan, she pulled Itachi close to her chest, leaned into Kitsu's embrace, and let sleep carry her away.

⤙ *Raku* ⤚

RAKU TRIED TO enjoy the fresh air and moonlight that greeted her on the deck of the Wind Serpent, but it was difficult when she took her newfound permission to wander the decks as a sure sign that they planned to kill her. "They" being whoever had orchestrated this whole thing. Probably not Tanaka. Perhaps the woman who stood on the other side of the stern deck glaring at her whenever she thought Raku wasn't looking.

Raku sighed and looked out over the stern rail. She held tight to the words Tanaka had spoken to her earlier about Torako likely being alive. If Torako was alive and chasing her, then Itachi was probably alive and safe somewhere. She didn't plan to let these people kill her, but knowing that the other parts of her heart still beat on made escape seem more like a problem to solve and less like a distant wish that would never come to pass.

She *almost* regretted whatever Tanaka had done to her to keep her stomach calm. It would be far easier to feign weakness if she were still vomiting every time she tried to move. Instead, Tanaka's ministrations had made her able to keep down food and water, and as the day had worn on, she'd felt well enough to stand on her own. Shortly after that, Tanaka had suggested she go on deck to get some fresh air and stretch her legs.

When she'd slowly climbed her way up the hatch that led onto the main deck and then stood watching the crew move with the coordinated efficiency generally reserved for military units, Raku had realized that it was the first time she had ever stood on the deck of a ship and not been ill. Not wishing to be in the way, she had climbed a short set of stairs leading to a raised deck at the very back of the ship. Not long after that, the short-haired, sharp-eyed woman who looked ready to kill her had climbed the same stairs and then looked downright murderous when she found Raku there.

"Tanaka-san told me to get some air," Raku had said to the cold-eyed woman.

The short-haired, oddly-dressed woman hadn't replied, but something about Raku's statement had caused her mouth to snap shut, and then she'd turned to look over the side rail instead of… whatever violent thing she'd been planning before Raku had spoken.

Swiftly moving clouds and patches of rolling fog made it dark enough, despite a nearly full moon, that Raku couldn't see many details of the crew, or even of the woman who stood on this smaller, raised deck with her. So she focused on the water instead, wondering how long it would be until they reached their destination. They could be heading anywhere. She looked at the stars for a moment and wished she had spent more time studying the constellations. She'd read enough to know that sailors could navigate by the stars, but not enough to know how to do so herself.

Raku saw movement in her peripheral vision and turned just enough to see that the woman on the far side of the stern deck had been approached by another crew member.

She heard the word, "Captain," in the earlier part of the crew member's report, but the rest was whispered too quietly for her to decipher.

She wished she were a wind kisō so she might pull the words towards her, but alas, she had almost no kisō at all, let alone enough to align with a particular element. She was good at watching without appearing to do so, however, and so she took careful note of the body language between the two people—the young man who had come to report clearly subordinate to the woman who had already been there—while they spoke.

It was a short conversation, and it ended with the woman and the young man both descending from the stern deck.

Raku watched them head to the largest of the three masts on the ship and then was surprised to see the woman, who she was now fairly certain was the captain, climb the mast all the way up to the crow's nest.

Raku looked out to the water again, but saw nothing save waves and moonlight.

She kept her eyes and ears open, even as she returned to her thoughts.

She didn't *have* to know where they were headed to start preparing an escape plan. Clearly this ship was not her final destination, or else she would already have been speaking with whoever it was that had ordered her capture. So they would, at some point, be moving her from this ship. She hoped they would be moving her to land, though she supposed it was possible they might move her to another ship. Either way, being moved would present an excellent opportunity for distraction, and thus escape.

She would simply have to do her best to make them underestimate her, something she typically excelled at, and then take advantage of whatever opportunity presented itself.

A commotion from above caught Raku's attention.

She thought she heard someone mutter a few expletives, and then there was a rush of activity on the deck below.

She looked to the water again to see what had caused it all, and was surprised to see a dark smudge on the horizon. Nothing definite, barely even a shape. Merely a spot that was somehow darker than the night sky and the ocean it bled into.

Raku had assumed whatever the lookouts had found would not be visible without a telescope, but whatever this was, it was approaching quickly. Even as she watched, the shape loomed larger and became more defined.

Not that the definition made any sense.

Because the definition made the shapes look like two enormous dragons half-submerged in the sea.

As they drew closer, that impression only became stronger, and then it was made stranger still by the shape of a ship with its sails furled being pulled along behind them.

A flash of white light drew Raku's attention back to the deck of the Wind Serpent.

She turned, and saw a being made of moonlight standing in front of the captain, whose face made Raku suspect she was as surprised as anyone to see such a person appear on her deck. Raku could not hear the words exchanged between them, and before she could even decide to step forward to try to eavesdrop, another flash of white light left the deck in front of the captain empty, as if the being of moonlight had never been.

Then a distant flicker had Raku turning to the rail once more, where she watched in horror as one of the serpents' eyes flashed white just before it turned and attacked its comrade.

Her lungs froze, along with her muscles, as she watched the scene play out like the most horrific mummers' act. One serpent collided with the other, as the ship moved at dizzying speeds towards them. The white-eyed serpent thrashed against the other, only to abandon it and fling itself down into the middle of the speeding ship.

She watched the distant ship cleave into a hundred pieces and felt her heart cleave with it.

It could have been anyone, she knew that. Theoretically, any ship in the sea could have been approaching the Wind Serpent. The fact that she knew no one who might have harnessed two sea serpents to pull a ship in pursuit of the Wind Serpent only made it *less* likely that it had been a ship carrying Torako towards her, not more. Who knew what enemies the people who had taken her might have? And yet… somehow, she was absolutely certain that Torako had been aboard that ship.

So, she wasn't acting when her knees gave out beneath her and her vision clouded.

She wasn't pretending when Tanaka's voice—suddenly behind her but sounding strangely distant to her ears—could do nothing to rouse her from the despair that crawled over her entire being.

She wasn't feigning weakness when she let them carry her to the healing berth again without even an ounce of resistance, or when she ignored Tanaka's quietly offered condolences as she turned to face the hull of the ship and cried herself into unconsciousness.

10日 6月, 新議 8年

10th Day, 6th Moon, Cycle 8 of the New Council

⚬Kaiyo⚬

KAIYO BREATHED IN the slightly damp wood smell that always suffused her great cabin and tried to find something to look at that wouldn't leave her glaring at Tanaka as she tried to come up with a response that wouldn't make her sound petty. She failed. In her defense, she'd been on edge ever since an embodiment of Tsukuyomi had shown up on her deck and offered direct assistance with the problem of the swiftly encroaching sea serpents towing an enemy ship.

It wasn't that she hadn't appreciated the help in dealing with the creatures straight out a fantasy tale getting far too close to her ship. It was more that she hadn't expected the moon Kami to offer help in person, or to deliver such devastating aid when he did.

Watching the sea serpents destroy the other ship so quickly had been terrifying. Fear made her angry. Now, on top of everything else, Tanaka was insisting on risking himself again just to protect his latest patient.

"She almost killed you. She deserves a little rough handling."

"She just saw her wife killed by a sea serpent. She doesn't need rough handling, she needs a healer."

"I won't risk my crew just because you've got a soft spot for the woman who stabbed you."

"I'm not asking you to risk your crew, I'm asking you to risk *me.*"

"You *are* my crew, Tanaka-san, and you're the least expendable person on this ship. You can't just volunteer for every dangerous assignment."

"As a general rule, I don't. But just because you've taken a disliking to her doesn't mean you can risk her well-being. The Admiral requested an interview with her. Presumably she needs to be able to speak when she gets there."

Kaiyo glared some more because if she opened her mouth she would say something that Tanaka would consider damning. For the first time since he'd joined her crew, she regretted how much she valued his good opinion of her. She had been the first person to balk at what might need to be done to the scribe, even in the name of preventing war. She knew that Tanaka would not appreciate the fact that her inclination to protect the woman had dissolved the moment she had shoved a knife into Tanaka's gut. So, instead of speaking, she flipped her owl hanko through her fingers and stared at one of the charts she had pinned to the bulkhead, pretending it held her interest while she gutted the scribe in her imagination.

Unsurprisingly, Tanaka interrupted her musings.

"Captain, I am not the only healer in this fleet. I'm not even the only healer on this ship. If something happens to me, I can be replaced by—"

"Tanaka-san, you idiot, I cannot possibly replace my best friend."

She was tempted to throw the owl hanko at his head as she said this, but thought that might undermine her point.

"I… that is…"

Tanaka was stammering, and when Kaiyo turned to look at her second in command she saw that, for reasons beyond her comprehension, he appeared to be blushing.

"I thought we'd been over this," Kaiyo muttered, turning to pace her quarters. "The entire reason that I was willing to marry you, instead of say, quietly killing every man my mother brought forward to try to salvage my reputation, starting with you and continuing for as long as needed, was because you are... Kami curse it, Tanaka-san, you may be my *only* friend."

Kaiyo took a deep breath and, because she hated conversations like this and really did not wish to keep having this exact one every time Tanaka put himself in danger, added, "When you almost died because that woman shoved a knife in your gut, I realized just how awful it would be if I lost you. Not for the damned ship, our crew, or the fleet, but for *me*. I have no interest in experiencing that feeling again. Or anything close to it."

Tanaka swallowed. She could see his throat bob in her peripheral vision, and she tried to ignore the answering flutter in her stomach by refocusing on the chart on her wall.

"I..." Tanaka's voice trailed off, but he was suddenly standing right behind her. She could feel the heat of him against her back even though he wasn't touching her, and all at once, her whole body was alight with the possibilities of what might happen next.

Kaiyo had never been particularly interested in men. She hadn't been that interested in women either. She'd tried both, just to make sure. Before she'd earned her captaincy she'd been party to enough bawdy conversations with her crewmates that she'd been curious what all the fuss was about. She'd been slightly more satisfied with the women who'd joined her bed than the men, but overall, the experiences hadn't been pleasant enough to warrant her time and attention. In the end, she'd just assumed that her body simply didn't respond to sex the way most people's did. She'd never felt the tingling anticipation her crewmates had described. Her experiences had been more exploratory than passionate, and none of them had been superior to what she could accomplish by herself. All of that was yet another reason that she hadn't wanted to marry. She'd been certain that she and her future spouse would only be disappointments to each other.

But when Tanaka's hand touched her shoulder, ever so gently, in a gesture that asked her to face him but assumed nothing, her nerves felt alight. Her breath caught when she turned to him and his eyes caught hers, and she felt her mouth open slightly—in anticipation or surprise, she wasn't sure.

Tanaka's hand traced from her collarbone to the base of her neck and then along her jawline to her chin.

"Kaiyo-san," he whispered, and she wondered if it was the first time he'd ever used her name to address her, even as a warmth pooled in her stomach and spread towards her toes. "May I kiss you?"

Kaiyo didn't answer, but stepped forward, closing the distance between them, and had one moment to see Tanaka's eyes flare with want and anticipation before his lips met hers and their arms pulled each other close, seeking confirmation of a truth they'd both harbored like a secret for Kami knew how long.

Suddenly, Kaiyo was more than curious about what sharing a bed with Tanaka might be like. Every scrap of her body wanted her to draw out this kiss until they were both breathless, and much, much closer than clothing would allow.

Which was perhaps why she threw a knife at the door to her cabin when someone knocked on it a moment later.

"Captain, I believe I can be of assistance," said Lyt through the sliding door that remained closed but now had a small owl-topped blade sticking through it.

Kaiyo cursed silently when Tanaka leapt away from her as if she'd singed him.

She glared at him for a moment and he blushed again, either from embarrassment or enjoyment, she couldn't be certain. He was smiling, though, which she took as a good sign.

She took a moment to straighten her shirt and then called, "Come, in Lyt-san," even as she reached forward to pluck her owl hanko from the door.

"Do you usually throw knives at those who knock on your door, Captain?" Lyt asked, eyeing her calmly as xe ducked to enter the cabin.

"Do you usually take knives blooming out of doors as a sign to enter?" she returned.

Lyt shrugged.

"I am not familiar with all of your culture's idiosyncrasies."

"I would think a knife at eye level was a signal that crossed cultural barriers."

Lyt smiled.

"Do you still need someone to escort this scribe from the ship?"

"I'll have the marines do it," Kaiyo replied.

She glanced at Tanaka and wondered if he had enlisted Lyt to dissuade her. His face was back to its usual blank mask, though, so she couldn't be sure.

"I don't believe she will be able to answer any questions your people may have for her if she isn't treated very carefully for the next few days."

"You think the way that she is walked off this ship will make a difference?" Kaiyo asked, incredulous.

"Yes. And more than that, I believe that I can help her heal enough to restore her to something of her former self if you'll give me some time with her."

"Go see her now if you're so concerned with her well-being," Kaiyo huffed.

"We'll be in port in half an hour," Tanaka said. "Not quite enough time to make the assessment and treatment she probably needs."

"She won't be allowed visitors once she's in the detainment center," Kaiyo said. "If you need time with her, now is all you have."

"If Lyt-san is made a guard and posted with her, xe and I can escort her. We'll have half an hour now, plus the hour it will take to move her from the docks to the detainment center, and if you'll sign the papers, Lyt-san can be made part of her guard rotation. Hopefully, by the time she's called to interview with the Admiral, she'll be well enough to speak with him."

"Why not simply make xir a healing assistant and insist xe be allowed to tend her in the detainment facility?"

It didn't even occur to Kaiyo to ask why Lyt would be able to provide assistance that Tanaka could not. She had watched Tanaka's skills at healing both mental and physical wounds for cycles. He truly was the best the Kaigun had to offer as a healer. He'd even spent a moon studying with Taka-sensei, the famed healer from the north. But it hadn't taken more than witnessing the single healing Lyt had performed on Tanaka's gutted abdomen to understand that Lyt had abilities even Tanaka could never aspire to. And anyone who had spent time in Suzuki's presence since Lyt had returned to the ship could tell you that Lyt's healing abilities were not limited to the physical.

Kaiyo hated to admit it, but the Kaigun had made a mistake where Lyt was concerned. Kaiyo still didn't fully understand what blood magic was, and there were many questions she planned to ask Lyt when the opportunity arose, but she knew what it wasn't. It wasn't the abomination she'd been told it was ever since joining the Kaigun. Sadly, her word and a few signed papers would not be enough to change anyone's opinions on that matter. Not overnight, at any rate.

"The scrutiny on a new healer would be far more than cursory, Captain. I don't know that there are any papers you could sign that would enable Lyt-san to tend Raku-san as a healer. I'm not even sure a paper from the Admiral could do it."

Kaiyo sighed. She knew that Tanaka was right. The scrutiny for a new guardsman on the other hand was… negligible. Guard duty in the detainment facilities was a frequent assignment for fresh recruits, mixed carefully with senior guards, of course, but no one would even blink if she made Lyt a guard now that they were newly reinstated to the Kaigun. If any of the other doshigatai had survived the mission to capture the scribe, it was probably where they would have been assigned anyway. She winced at the thought. She didn't much mourn the doshigatai who had fallen to the blades of the Night Stalker, but she felt a pang for the ones who had fallen to the enormous wolf.

She shook the distracting imagery away and then sighed.

"Fine, you'll both be assigned to her escort, Tanaka-san as healer and Lyt-san as a newly reinstated guard. If anything goes wrong I will personally see you both court-martialed."

She wondered briefly, as Tanaka and Lyt filed out, if it was inappropriate to threaten to court-martial your husband only a few minutes after you'd kissed him for the second time.

❧ Raku ❧

RAKU HAD DONE everything she could, and now it was time to see how well she'd misled the enemy. She stumbled as they led her from the healing berth to the main deck. She kept her gaze distant and unfocused, even in the bright sunlight, despite the temptation to see where in the hells they'd brought her. She didn't let the humming sounds of a bustling port, or the fresh ocean breeze, or even the warm sunlight on her face pull a reaction from her.

It was barely an act.

Certainly, the hours she had spent limp, defeated, and feeling as though her insides had been scraped away by horror and grief were not an act. A tiny voice in the back of her mind insisted that Torako might still be alive, that even if she had been on that ship, perhaps there had been some wreckage she had clung to, a long-boat that had somehow slipped unseen into the water, *something* that might have saved her. But she didn't believe that voice.

That voice wasn't why she was making herself seem almost catatonic with grief. That voice wasn't why she was listening much more carefully than her deliberately slack features let on. That voice wasn't what had her counting the guards around her, even with unfocused eyes and a lolling head.

No. It was Itachi that was keeping her just on this side of despair.

Raku was almost certain that one-third of her heart was now missing, never to be returned. But she had to believe that Itachi was safe somewhere. That Torako had done everything she could to protect their daughter. The world could not possibly be cruel enough to take them both from her.

And for Itachi, she would pull the last threads of herself together and keep them wound. For Itachi, she would pretend to be more hollowed out and broken than she actually felt. For Itachi, she would make the devastation inside her visible to the world and hide away the tiny spark of hope within her.

She stumbled again, as though she no longer had the will to make her legs move her forward, and the guards around her caught at her arms.

She listened. Waited. Watched without seeing.

There.

"Urgent message for you, Captain!" shouted a rather exuberant voice.

Her guards had just maneuvered her to the top of the gangplank. She was delighted to find that the gangplank was only wide enough for two people at a time. One guard walked in front of her, alongside Tanaka the healer, another held her elbow, and two more followed behind her. She couldn't have asked for better timing.

She had felt the eyes of the captain on her from the moment she'd been brought on deck, and she had wondered more than once if the woman planned to throw a knife at her if she so much as stepped out of line. But more than one careening step into the men guarding her had made it perfectly clear that no one was going to kill her just for her "natural" clumsiness. Still, the more eyes that were focused on her when she made her next move, the harder all of this was going to be.

The messenger at the bottom of the gangplank made an aggravated gesture and started pushing their way up, forcing those who were descending to walk single file.

Raku could hardly believe her luck.

"Captain," the young woman repeated, and Raku noticed, even with her eyes unfocused and mostly trained on the docks beneath them, that the woman calling out to the captain was wearing some kind of uniform, although it was unlike anything Raku had ever seen before.

Raku let her head loll almost against the guard who held her, allowing the jostle of the passing messenger to push her hard into the guard's chest. Then she hastily stepped away from the guard as soon as the messenger was clear.

She waited one more heartbeat, taking two shaking steps towards the bottom of the ramp, as the messenger said, "Captain Saito, you must come at once!"

That was when she tripped with the full weight of her body, and threw a bit of extra momentum granted by the angle of the ramp into it. She sprawled heavily into the bodies of the guard and Tanaka. They did their best to catch her, and if she'd truly been in the almost catatonic state she was mimicking, they would have succeeded. Instead, she used her weight, momentum, and the angle of the gangplank itself to pull them both down with her, as she went sprawling painfully across the damp wood of the docks.

The key difference, of course, was that she had been expecting to fall, and they had not. So, it shouldn't have surprised anyone when she rolled to her feet, and then dashed quickly into the thick crowd of the docks.

Raku had never been to this city before, but she was familiar enough with the basic layout of most ports and piers to have a decent sense of where she needed to go to avoid the notice of the ship that had captured her. She didn't know where she was in relation to Sakata or the rest of the mainland, but that hardly mattered. All she needed to do was find someone attached to the Silver Fox, and she would be given directions as well as a means of escape. She hoped she wouldn't have to get on another ship. She doubted whoever might be willing to sail her home would have access to whatever medicine Tanaka had given her for her stomach. No matter. She would deal with that when the time came. First, she needed to get out of sight.

Unfortunately, the more she looked around the booming port city, the less she felt confident that she would be able to blend in. She had already stopped running. In fact, she had barely run at all, besides her initial burst of speed to get out of sight of the ship. But once she'd stepped behind a large stack of crates, she had come out on the other side walking calmly, having pulled the combs from her hair and shifted the bow of her obi. They were small changes, but she knew that anyone looking for a running woman with her hair up and a large vertical bow would skip right over her. Especially since she was walking at the same speed as the rest of the crowd and not making a fuss.

In any other port, she might have worried that her brightly colored kimono and hakama would cause her to stand out too much to let her slide into the crowd as she normally would, but wherever this port city was, it was full of people wearing brightly colored clothes of all kinds. In fact, in the very short time since she'd started walking, she'd noticed a series of fashions unlike any she had ever seen.

She was briefly furious with her kidnappers for having brought her somewhere so interesting but forcing her to run and hide instead of having the liberty to look around and enjoy whatever she found. It was a strange thing to be angry about, with everything else going on, but still.

She didn't dare look over her shoulder, but the mere fact that she heard no shouts or pounding footsteps made her think that her pursuers hadn't spotted her yet. She did her best to appear as a woman walking through the stalls at the pier out to buy some food for her household.

She had reached the market stalls at least, which was useful. The men and women carrying crates, barrels, and sacks filled with all manner of supplies were already behind her, and now she was wandering past stall after stall selling fish, rice, and other grains. Some of the food was very familiar to her, but some of it she had never seen before.

She wished she had time to ask about any of it.

Instead, a flash of light reflected on steel caught her eye and she found herself walking towards a stall filled with women gutting fish.

"Have you received any offerings for the Silver Fox recently?" she asked the grey-haired woman who was selling large cuts of tuna to any passerby showing the slightest interest.

"Oh yes. Every tenday. Here, let me see if I can find something suitable," replied the grey-haired woman. Then she turned and exchanged a few whispered words with one of the other women in the stall. A moment later she turned back to Raku and said, "Why don't you come around back?"

≫ *Kaiyo* ≪

KAIYO REALLY WANTED to stab someone, but she was surrounded by civilians, and worse, the people she wanted to stab consisted of her best friend/husband, and a blood mage. Of course, she probably could have stabbed the Sansa who had inadvertently created the perfect distraction for her wayward scribe, but that seemed a bit harsh. The woman had only been trying to tell her something about the new prisoners that Kaiyo had delivered before her father had sent for her. Unfortunately, Kaiyo hadn't heard any of what the Sansa had been trying to tell her, because she had immediately set off running after the scribe, who was supposed to be so unwell that she needed careful handling instead of a full complement of marines.

And that, Kaiyo thought, as she stared around the crowded docks in the early morning sun, after completely losing track of the scribe somehow, *is why I want to stab Lyt and Tanaka. They were the ones who fell for her act. They're the ones who should be out here overturning every crate on the docks to get her back.*

Of course, they were there. Both of them were within her peripheral vision still, searching out the missing scribe who had somehow jumped behind a stack of crates and then disappeared from sight like a sprite in a children's tale.

The file her father had given her about Raku (she wanted to spit every time she thought the name) had been the slimmest of them all and had described her as a pint-sized scribe and historian who excelled at research. It hadn't said a damned word about her ability to gut people, or to disappear into a crowd like a fading mirage. She'd been suspicious of the woman's abilities ever since she'd stabbed Tanaka, but mostly she'd just been angry with her. It wasn't particularly difficult to run a knife into someone's gut if you were desperate. Especially, if that knife had previously been in Tanaka's hands. The man was a competent fighter, but he mostly specialized in saving people's lives, rather than ending them, and he'd probably been bending over backwards not to hurt the woman they'd been sent to abduct. It was no wonder he'd gotten himself stabbed.

But now that she'd seen the woman, still dressed in her fine kimono and decorative hakama, disappear right in front of her simply by ducking behind some crates… Kaiyo was beginning to suspect the woman was more than she seemed, and that thought had Kaiyo back to wanting to stab someone. Tanaka had chased the scribe behind the crates and then come round the other side with nothing.

"Captain, if I may," said a voice from behind her.

Kaiyo turned to see Lyt, who she had been certain was searching the docks to her right a moment ago.

"Yes, Lyt-san?" she replied, hoping that xe could not see how disconcerted she was by xir sudden, silent arrival behind her.

"I know that you have little reason to trust me after Raku-san's recent escape, but I believe I can track the woman fairly easily if necessary."

Kaiyo narrowed her eyes at the blood mage.

"Of course it's necessary," she growled. "Your orders are—"

"Ah," Lyt said, cutting her off. "I believe you've forgotten our arrangement. You offered me true freedom when we returned from this mission. I realize that you may have been working on the assumption that meant until the scribe was in the Admiral's custody, but I think you can understand why I might not want to wait until I'm standing in the midst of a few dozen Kaigunka before you tell me I'm free to leave."

Kaiyo swallowed. Her initial reaction was to loathe Lyt for their willingness to betray her and their mission so easily, but she took a deep breath and remembered that Lyt had been locked away in the worst dungeon the Kaigun possessed, a fate that most of the Kaigun considered too ill for the majority of criminals, for the simple crime of wanting to return to their home, and for practicing blood magic to try to get there. What loyalty would she have for a group of people who had treated her with the same contempt?

And she knew Lyt was as good as xir word. Xe could have sabotaged Kaiyo's mission a hundred times by now, most easily when the other six men in xir unit had been killed and xe had been alone in the wilderness.

"Fine, what do you want?" She had already promised Lyt xir freedom, she didn't know what else she could offer xir, but—

"I will capture her for you if you'll give me your word that you'll try to spare her life."

"Lyt-san, I can't possibly keep—"

"I recognize she may do any number of things that will cause you, or one of the guards perhaps, to kill her over the course of her confinement, but… she does not deserve to die for simply knowing something you wish unknown. You manage to keep hundreds of captives from the ships you sink every cycle, surely you can try to figure something out."

Kaiyo's stomach turned at the proposition. It wasn't that she hadn't had the same thought at the start of this mess. Her father had insisted that war might be the consequence of the scribe's continued freedom and even then she had balked at the idea of killing her. But then the woman had almost killed Tanaka and now…

She heard the soft footsteps of her second in command just as she had the thought.

"I agree, Captain. We should do all we can to keep her alive. At this point, she is likely the only parent left to that child, and making that girl an orphan seems a particularly cruel price for the little one to pay because her mother read the wrong scroll."

Kaiyo wanted to shout at both of them that people paid cruel prices all the time. To ask them what they thought was happening every time they sank a foreign vessel for the crime of entering uncharted waters. But she knew that there was cruelty and there was *cruelty*. And she knew that part of what drove her was a silent rage that had been kindled at the prospect of losing Tanaka.

What rage had she kindled in Raku by tearing her away from her family? Was it any less deserved?

She took a deep breath and nodded.

"Fine. Find her. I'll do my best to see she isn't executed."

⇒ Raku ⇐

THE RELIEF THAT had flooded Raku when the grey-haired fish-monger had invited her into the stall had been slowly overwhelmed by the challenge of not losing her stomach to the overwhelming scent of fish guts.

Raku had cleaned fish before—hundreds of them, probably. She and Torako often prepared fish for their evening meals, and while Torako might be better at killing things, Raku was better at the small, precise motions that were needed to prepare a fish for human consumption.

Raku swallowed, as the memory of Torako wasting large amounts of perfectly good fish flesh because she didn't have the patience to separate it from the bone properly threatened to make her a sobbing wreck. She pushed the memories away and focused on the motions of her hands, breathing through her mouth in hopes of keeping the worst smells at bay.

No, it wasn't that she was unused to the task of cleaning fish, it was simply that the difference between preparing one or two fish for a meal and dumping their guts into an area set aside for the local hawk population to come and help themselves was quite a bit different from systematically emptying the guts of hundreds of fish into a barrel filled with nothing else.

She decided that, in addition to ignoring unhelpful memories, she would also ignore unhelpful smells.

She let the voices of the women working beside her wash over her, letting her hands practice the quick efficient motions of fish cleaning without slowing herself down by thinking about it.

In little time at all, her hands were moving on their own and her mind was wandering to other things.

She had known about the Silver Fox for most of her life—in a way, she owed her entire career as a spy to that network. As soon as she'd finished her scribe's apprenticeship and gotten away from the bastard who'd trained her, she had run into the Silver Fox network almost immediately. It turned out that women seeking aid to escape various threats, most often abusive partners, but also hundreds of other dangers, were often in need of a scribe. In the very first town where she'd offered her services— wandering scribes were often the only chance some smaller villages had at legal paperwork, and sometimes even the larger towns had more need of people who could read and write well than the local scribes could accommodate—she had been approached by one of the older women in charge of the local arm of the network. She hadn't even considered saying no when she'd been asked to write up divorce papers for a young mother in hiding, and she'd turned down the older woman's attempts to pay her for it, too. She'd been helping the Silver Fox ever since.

This was the first time *she* had needed their services, though.

She hadn't been certain there would be a branch here. After all, she had no idea where she was, and so much of what she'd seen since she'd stepped off of the boat had seemed odd enough that she'd begun to wonder if this place was so far removed from the places she knew that the Silver Fox would have no home here. But she'd been certain that if anyone were to be involved with the Silver Fox, it would be among the dock market, as the network always kept an eye on the ships coming and going. When she saw a fishmonger's stall staffed entirely by women, she thought they would at least know where to point her, if they weren't part of the network themselves.

Now all she had to do was hide here, in plain sight, until the network found her safe passage out of this port.

Raku wondered, later, if the almost meditative state that she'd entered whilst gutting fish and trying to ignore the scent of it had saved her. For all that she'd been a spy for a dozen cycles, she'd never actually trained for the position. She was observant, and she was good at research, and when the Silver Fox had been approached about a potential contact to take a closer look at the library in Rōjū City, she had been the obvious candidate. So, when cycles of careful listening and snooping around indexes finally paid off in uncovering the location of a scroll that ultimately wound up bringing about the end of the Rōjū Council, she left her career as a spy with cycles of experience—including a few dozen very close calls with the Rōjū's hishi—but no actual instruction. Nothing in her conscious mind noticed anything strange as she was slicing open the belly of yet another unremarkable fish, but some part of her must have registered a silence where there should have been conversation, an intake of breath that was sharper than normal, or perhaps even the focus of the people around her shifting slightly, towards the front of the stall.

It wasn't training, but *something* had her ducking beneath the counter on which she had just been opening fish bellies, and she had only the soft thunk of a dart sinking into wood to prove that she hadn't imagined the threat to begin with.

Raku cursed under her breath as she began crawling on all fours, shifting behind the barrels set up to catch fish innards, shimmying between those barrels and the planks of wood that made up the stall, doing her best to move silently while also moving quickly. She was grateful at least for how tightly packed the stalls were, and how narrow the alley behind the line of stalls was—where she spilled unceremoniously into the dirt once she cleared the barrels under the fishmonger's cutting table. It would be more difficult for her pursuers to move through the alley than it was for her. She hoped the women at the stall didn't do anything to put themselves at risk attempting to keep the captain of The Wind Serpent away from her.

She was already running, doubled over, with her hands grazing the ground occasionally for stability, a few stalls past the fishmongers who had hidden her, when she heard her pursuers burst into the alley behind her.

Luckily, a heartbeat later she saw a small, poorly rendered fox carved into the wall of a warehouse, and without thinking, she turned towards it. The clearance between that warehouse and the one beside it was slight enough that she felt her kimono catch on the corner as she slid sideways between the buildings, but it was just wide enough that if she skipped sideways down it, as though she were dancing, she made quick progress. She had already cleared the two buildings before she heard the shouts of her pursuers. She wondered if any of them would be small enough to follow her, but she didn't stick around to find out.

To her delight, there was another roughly rendered fox on the wall to her right, so she turned that way and ran as quickly as she could down a shaded cobbled street that seemed just large enough for a wagon, but which was currently empty. When she reached its end, another tiny fox carving pointed her towards another narrow gap, this time between a ryokan and what looked like a ramenya.

She kept running, grateful that she'd spent so much of the spring walking to local villages that might need her services instead of riding horses to and from New Council City. A series of the tiny fox illustrations, some mere scratches in wood, some fully detailed paintings hung artfully on doorways and in arches, led her on an erratic but efficient trek through whatever port town this was.

Eventually, the trail of fox icons led her out of the town, up a hill, and into a delightfully thick forest. The shade of the trees was enough to cool her, and now that she was tucked into a bit of woods she felt confident enough to catch her breath and turn to look for her pursuers. She saw no one behind her—not on the hill and not coming out of the last street that she had sprinted along.

She did, however, see the ocean in every direction. She could just make out the port behind her, full of more ships than she'd seen even in Atsumi, Gensokai's busiest port city. Which is why a creeping certainty came upon her, even as she looked in every direction and saw nothing but water, that she was not in Gensokai any longer.

She closed her eyes, trying not to let that thought overwhelm her. She was on an island, yes, and that island was not one that she had ever seen on a map, because none of the islands she knew held a port that was larger than Atsumi, but that did not mean that all was lost. They clearly had a branch of the Silver Fox here, and if that was true, then there *had* to be a way off of this island. The Silver Fox always had an escape route—it was what they did.

She took a few more deep breaths, trying to appreciate the stark beauty of the azure waters that surrounded the busy harbor with its strange rock pillars topped with odd metal contraptions.

Then she turned and followed the remaining fox carvings, these mostly scrawled into the bark of the trees, and wound her way through the forest until she finally found herself standing before a small cabin with a tiny curl of smoke wafting from its chimney.

Afraid to call out, even with the fox signs leading her here, Raku waited in the shade of the trees for a time, hoping that whoever lived in the cabin would come out and give her some idea of just who she was handing her fate to.

Then a voice that was far too close to her back said, "And what are you doing here, young one?"

Raku turned to see a petite woman with slate grey hair and a piercing gaze staring at her with an intensity that made Raku wish her preferred armor were made of leather instead of silk.

"I'm here to see about a fox," she said.

The woman's eyes brightened immediately at that.

"Ah, of course. Best come inside for some tea, then. Foxes can be a bit capricious in these parts."

Raku frowned. She'd never heard that particular response to the code words, but the old woman hadn't thought she was crazy or tried to run her off, and besides, Raku thought she might strangle someone for a good cup of tea at this point.

Raku followed the grey-haired woman out of the clearing that smelled of damp earth and green leaves and into the overly warm cabin that smelled of fresh rice and strong tea, more out of a sense of desperation than because she was certain it was safe to do so.

She didn't think it likely that the much older woman, who was even smaller than Raku, would pose much of a threat if it came down to it, but the cabin could be full of armed guards, for all that Raku knew. Or the tea could be drugged. Or the woman could just be trying to stall her until her pursuers caught up. But in that moment, Raku almost didn't care about any of that. She'd been running all morning, she'd barely recovered from the drugs the bandits had used to sedate her before she'd been wrecked by grief, she felt numb to her own emotions and exhausted beyond measure. She would probably let a host of guards cart her away at this point if she could just be allowed to rest for a few moments first.

She almost laughed at herself for that thought. She knew it wasn't true, the moment she thought it. She wouldn't give up that easily, warm tea or no. But the woman… well, it wasn't that she couldn't be a threat. Raku knew all too well that underestimating someone for being small and female was a mistake. Underestimating someone because they had a few decades *more* life experience seemed like absolute folly to her. It was just that, as far as Raku could tell, the woman's cabin in this small clearing of forest was the end of the Silver Fox's trail. Raku had trusted in the Silver Fox network for cycles now, and this didn't seem like a good time to stop.

Which is why she wasn't prepared to block the dagger that rested against her throat the moment she stepped through the door. Luckily, the woman didn't seem inclined to cut her throat yet, because there was nothing Raku would have been able to do to stop her in that moment.

"Who are you?" the grey-haired woman asked.

"Raku," she replied, her voice sounding far more casual than she had expected. "And you?"

The older woman chuckled.

"Bold. I like that. You may call me Fubuki."

"Fubuki-san, it's a pleasure to meet you. Does this mean you're rescinding your offer of tea?"

That had the woman cackling outright. The dagger disappeared and Raku couldn't even track the motion that hid it. One moment it had been at her throat, and the next it was out of sight and the woman was shuffling towards a small pot hanging over a fire.

"It's rare that I get someone looking for the Silver Fox here, and more so alone. Someone from the stall usually comes along. You smell like fish guts, but no one's here with you…"

"You're concerned that I've harmed someone in the network?" Raku tried to keep the incredulity out of her voice. After all, the woman had no idea of her long history with the Silver Fox. The entire system functioned on anonymity. The women who used it were kept safe by the fact that no one in the chain knew anyone beyond the next link in either direction. So this woman had no reason to know that Raku would sooner cut off her own hand than hurt someone who helped the Silver Fox.

"I think that if you've harmed anyone you'll barely live long enough to regret it."

"As it should be," Raku replied solemnly.

That had Fubuki turning to stare at her. She did not laugh.

"I forget that women on the mainland have greater need of the Silver Fox than we do here."

Raku's chest clenched at the confirmation that they were not on the mainland.

"The people who brought me here didn't do me the favor of telling me where we were," Raku replied.

Fubuki smiled then, but the gesture looked more sorrowful than conciliatory.

"You're on Kaigunjima, Raku-san. Though I dare say you'll have no idea where that is."

Raku's stomach dropped at the thought. She was familiar with nearly every map of Gensokai made in the past thousand cycles. She'd been familiar with them before she started her research on the parts of Gensokai's history lost to the Rōjū—a wandering scribe would be remiss indeed if she weren't familiar with the terrain she covered—but over the past seven cycles, she'd become even more familiar with Gensokai's geography. She knew the names of every island that called itself part of Gensokai, but Fubuki was right. She'd never heard of Kaigunjima.

She realized, a moment too late, as the light reflecting off of Fubuki's face shifted in a way that had nothing to do with the fire, that she had left the door open behind her, too distracted by having a knife pressed to her throat, and then the prospect of tea, to close it. She briefly felt a pang of horrified embarrassment as she realized she had also left her boots on past the old woman's genkan. She would have apologized, but she was too busy turning to see who was blocking the light in the doorway.

They were lit from behind by the sun, and so she was unable to make out any of their features. Instead, she heard the soft snap of a wrist-mounted crossbow firing a dart, and though she tried to leap out of the line of fire, she still felt the pain of a dart piercing her shoulder as she dove towards the ground.

She landed painfully, but before she could even try to rise, she felt a foot step firmly in the middle of her back.

"Don't kill her, Kaiyo-san. She's under the protection of the Fox."

Raku thought that was the voice of Fubuki, but her vision was already darkening at the edges and everything felt far away.

"I'm doing my best not to, Fubuki-sensei. But damned if I know why everyone wishes to protect the vile woman."

Raku didn't hear Fubuki's reply. She didn't hear anything else as the blackness overwhelmed her.

Torako

TORAKO SHIFTED HER face away from the light trying to pry through her eyelids, burrowing herself into the shoulder of the arms that held her. She could smell the tang of saltwater on the air, and the shoulder underneath her cheek smelled of leather cedar oil. For a moment, that felt familiar and right, and then her brain jumped to the present and her eyes flew open.

"Kitsu-san?" she asked, not quite willing to look him in the eyes. Instead, she glanced behind her and felt the tension in her shoulders release as her gaze swept over Itachi's small form curled tightly in the circle of Sairō's legs. They were both snoring. She wondered when the girl had left her lap and headed for the wolf's.

"Yes, Love?"

She could feel Kitsu's voice through his chest.

"You shouldn't call me that."

"I won't, if you don't like it."

Torako thought about that for a long time. Did she dislike it? Or was she worried that Raku wouldn't like it? She almost laughed. She knew better than that. Raku loved her deeply, but she'd never been the jealous kind. Torako wasn't either. It was part of why their relationship worked so well. They cared deeply enough for each other that they trusted one another to follow their hearts, or their bodies, and keep coming back. Neither of them had much interest in pursuing other relationships, but whenever it came up they always felt comfortable seeing where things went. No, Raku wouldn't care one way or the other if Kitsu called her Love and Torako enjoyed it. The only thing that Raku would be hurt by was lies.

"I don't know if I like it or not," she said at length.

And that was the truth. She and Kitsu had parted ways for good reasons, and they'd parted as friends, but Torako had still been hurt by it. Beyond that, she wasn't sure why Kitsu caring about her after all these cycles made her uncomfortable, but it did. Cycles ago, when Torako had tried to explain her feelings regarding Kitsu, Raku had said it was because she was afraid. When Torako scoffed and asked what she could possibly be afraid of, Raku had replied, "That he'll take my place in your heart." Torako had said that was ridiculous, and she'd meant it— she had never even contemplated starting a family with Kitsu; Raku was the only person she'd ever trusted deeply enough to share that kind of partnership with—but she wondered now if Raku had been at least partially right.

Because her distaste for Kitsu's endearments had only increased the less likely it seemed that she would ever find Raku again.

She swallowed and shook her head. She had no intention of following *that* line of thinking right now.

She was saved from those thoughts by a cheer going up nearby, and she finally blinked her eyes open, skipping right past Kitsu's bright amber gaze and focusing instead on the horizon.

Which was no longer a horizon but instead a large, heavily forested island and a tiny beach surrounded by cliffs so tall it almost looked like the cross-section of a well.

"Welcome, Torako-san, to Kaigunjima. The island I believe your wife's captors have absconded to."

Torako had never ridden a sea serpent anywhere before, so it wasn't accurate to say she was disappointed. You couldn't be disappointed when you had no expectations at all. But, when she'd seen the cliffs shooting up from the tiny beach that were twice as tall as a ship's mast, she had wondered if the sea serpent was going to stretch her neck up to the top of the cliff and allow them to climb her scales and dismount from there.

Instead, the serpent had partially beached herself—there was no way her full length could fit on the tiny stretch of sand at the cliff's base—long enough for them all to slide their way down to the sand, filling the beach to capacity with the crew of the Trickster, an overly large wolf, a small child, and Torako, before Kitsu had engaged in some silent discussion with the creature and then she had swum away.

"Thank you!" Torako had called after her, even though she was fairly certain the creature did not speak Gensokan.

She'd faced the sea, watching the enormous serpent covered in vibrant green, blue, and purple scales swim her way into deeper waters and then disappear beneath the waves. Then Torako had let the sun warm her face a bit, taking a few deep breaths of salt-tinged air before turning back to the cliff face that shot up on all sides of the small patch of sand beneath their feet.

"She liked you," said a deep, familiar voice from beside her.

"Who did?"

"The sea dragon."

At that, she turned to look Kitsu in the eyes.

"Dragon?"

"Dragon, serpent, what's the difference?"

"I believe the difference is that if you say the word serpent to describe a dragon in its presence, you die horribly."

Kitsu's laugh warmed her almost as much as the sun had.

"Well, you make a good point, but a sea serpent doesn't make such distinctions."

"That's probably proof enough that they're not dragons then."

"Oh, I don't know. If you ask dragons about their aquatic cousins, they usually refer to them as dragons."

Torako simply stared at him for a moment.

"I'm not even going to ask why you know that."

"Mama! Look! That lady is climbing the cliff!"

Torako beamed down at Itachi, who was still clinging to Sairō's back, and wondered if the wolf ever planned to let the girl out of their sight again. Then she followed Itachi's finger and took a moment to appreciate the skill Kitsu's crew member was exhibiting as she scaled the cliff face as fast as most of the crew had climbed the rigging on the Trickster.

The memory of Kitsu's crew in the rigging sent a pang of sadness through her.

"Kitsu-san, your ship… I'm so sorry."

Kitsu, who had also been watching the woman climb, turned to her and shrugged.

"It's not the first time the Trickster has met a watery end, though that might be the most spectacular death she's ever endured. I'm just glad we were able to save most of the crew."

Torako didn't know what to say to that, so she went back to watching the woman climb.

She wondered, briefly, if they were all meant to climb to the top of the cliff like that, with no ropes or harnesses and a fatal fall for any who missed a hold, but once she took a good look at the cliffside she realized that there was a small cave about half-way up the cliff face. Not long after Torako had noticed it, the woman climbing had pulled herself over the ledge and into the dark space beyond.

"She's fast," Torako said.

"Oh yes, Yamori-san is our best climber by far, and that's saying something on a ship like mine. It's largely thanks to her that this cove is open to us."

Torako was about to ask what he meant by that when a flash of motion above caught her eye and she watched as a rope ladder was flung out of the cave mouth and then unrolled itself in mid-air before whipping harshly against the cliff face.

"There we are, time to move," Kitsu gestured forward with one hand as though it was the height of courtesy to allow her up the swinging rope ladder first.

Torako was about to object, but Itachi was already giggling and moving up the first few rungs. Sairō was watching her and looking decidedly non-plussed.

"Sairō-san, can you climb something like that?" Torako asked, hesitantly.

Sairō growled, but didn't reply.

"Would you like me to dismiss you into the sword and then summon you again once we're up?" she offered.

Sairō plastered their ears to their head and whined once but finally replied, "Yes, but be quick about it. I still don't trust your fox."

Torako wasn't certain if she wanted to object more to the idea that Kitsu was hers or that he was a fox, but decided that the kindest thing to do was simply dismiss the wolf and climb the ladder as quickly as she could. Itachi was already much too far ahead for her liking anyway. She grasped the hilt of the katana, imagined Sairō disappearing, and hoped that was enough to do it.

When she opened her eyes the wolf was gone.

"That's a neat trick," said Kitsu.

Torako ignored him and followed Itachi up the ladder and into the cave.

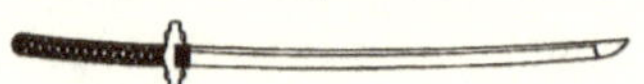

The climb up was not as harrowing as Torako had expected. She was fairly used to scaling short cliffs around her valley when necessary, but the key there was that they were short. She wasn't afraid of heights per se, but she had hated the thought of trying to mimic Yamori's skilled ascent of the sheer face, especially with Itachi.

Itachi, for her part, seemed to find the whole exercise delightful. The rope ladder was easy enough to climb, as it was made of a thick, stiff rope that barely gave at all, and Itachi clearly thought nothing of the fall and simply scampered to the cave ledge, where Yamori offered her a hand up over the ledge and inside.

Torako however, could not ignore the danger a fall from that height would pose. Even from halfway to the cave mouth the fall would have been fatal. From the cave ledge, it would have been doubly so.

"I suppose that's not actually how it works," she muttered to herself. "You're not twice as dead if you fall from twice the height. Just equally dead and in more pieces."

She heard a chuckle from below that made her realize that Kitsu was just behind her.

Not for the first time, Torako was glad that the boots she wore had supple soles covered in a hardened shell of the sap from a tree that grew in the south. They were soft enough that she could easily feel the rungs of the ladder beneath her feet, and they gripped well enough that even the sea spray she could feel coating everything around her didn't make her slip. Still, she was all too aware of the distance between herself and the beach by the time she was up and over the ledge.

She moved quickly towards the back of the cave.

Or, she would have, except that the back of the cave wasn't visible from where she stood.

"Mama, it's amazing!" Itachi called. Torako had to agree.

Her mind took a few moments to understand what her eyes were seeing. What had looked, from below, like a small cave sunk into an almost sheer cliff face, was in fact...

"Welcome, to the Smuggler's hideaway!" announced Kitsu, as he stepped beside her.

She supposed that was the best description for it. The cavern itself was huge. The narrow mouth they had crawled through was more like a window than anything. The space widened up to the size of a large tavern almost immediately, and then went on and on, past where Torako could even see. And the entire space was lined with crates, bags, bedrolls, futon, a wall of weapons, ropes, gear, and what looked to be enough extra sails to rig an entire ship.

"How did you know of this place?" she asked, turning partway towards Kitsu.

"Well... I built it," said Kitsu, looking altogether too pleased.

Torako thought about that for a moment.

"Kitsu-san, where *are* we?"

"That, Tora-chan, would take a very long time to explain in any meaningful way. We're on Kaigunjima. I would bet my ship that your wife was brought here. And, as you may have now guessed, I'm somewhat familiar with the area."

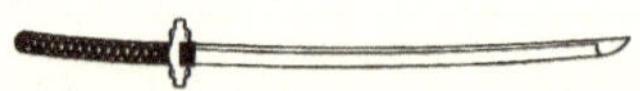

Torako wasn't certain if she wanted to laugh, cry, or scream, so she opted for drawing her sword. Kitsu jumped back, which was gratifying, but she'd only done it so she could call Sairō.

"Come on out then," she said, not sure yet what the rules were about bringing the wolf out and dismissing them.

"You've been standing in this cave long enough to be annoyed with the fox, and yet you just now drew me?"

Sairō walked immediately to Itachi's side and laid their head on top of her feet. Itachi gave a delighted squeal of, "Puppy!" and then sat down and threw her arms around the oversized wolf's neck.

Torako chuckled.

"I was distracted by the size of this place," she said, walking over to where the wolf was now attempting to look disgruntled—but also leaning very enthusiastically into the scratches they were receiving behind their ears—and sat down so that she could glare at Kitsu with a few hundred pounds of wolf behind her.

"You're familiar with this place?" she asked, her eyes still narrowed in suspicion, as behind Kitsu his entire crew was slowly making their way up from the beach and into the cavern. They all seemed perfectly at home in the large space, immediately bustling off to some familiar task amongst all the gear that was carefully organized against every bit of rocky wall.

"Smugglers need hiding places, Tora-chan, it's a professional requirement. And this one is one of our best. First of all, Kaigunjima doesn't get visitors from the mainland, so it was the perfect place to evade the Rōjū when that was one of our primary concerns. Second of all, this cave is high enough up the cliff wall that even though it's exposed to the sea, even the tallest Tsunami is unlikely to ever flood it. And, third of all, the Kaigun, for all their flaws, have always done their best to help us avoid the Rōjū."

"So, what you're telling me is that you have a business relationship with the people who abducted my wife."

Kitsu frowned for a moment.

"Technically yes, but you make it sound much—"

Torako had crossed the space between them, wrapped her fingers around Kitsu's throat, and pushed him up against one of the few expanses of rock that wasn't covered in crates before he even had time to react.

"Swear to me that you knew nothing of this," she snarled, ignoring the alarmed shouts of Kitsu's crew behind her, and Sairō's answering growls.

Kitsu's face was surprisingly calm for a man who was being held by the throat, but he still couldn't answer unless she released her grip, so she lowered him to the ground and stepped back.

"Of course not, Torako-san. How could you even think it?" he replied between coughs.

"Because I have no idea who took her, but you seem to have a comfy thieves' den ON THE SAME ISLAND THEY CALL HOME."

She hadn't meant to shout, but her voice rose anyway.

The commotion behind her seemed to have quieted down, at least.

"I can assure you that my association with the Kaigun is strictly professional and that I had no idea that they had taken her until you told me a ship called The Wind Serpent had sailed off with her. Since then, I've done everything I could to get you to her as quickly as possible. I don't know what more you want from me."

He said that last bit as though it pained him, and Torako flinched slightly.

"I'm sorry, Kitsu-san. I…" she took a deep breath and let it out. "I don't know what to do. I haven't known what to do since this started, and, at every turn, it seems like I'm the last person to find out what's happening. First Raku-san, then Tenshi-san, then my grandfather, or whoever that damned moon Kami is, and now… I'm just tired of being the last to know everything. It's starting to seem like a conspiracy."

Kitsu's frown deepened and he stepped closer to her.

"You may find that it *is* somewhat of a conspiracy, but it's not a new one, and I promise you it hasn't been made for the explicit purpose of making you feel stupid. The Kaigun has much to answer for, not least of which is taking Raku-san from her family. Now, as I am familiar with the lay of the island, I have some suggestions to make for our rescue plan."

Torako blinked at Kitsu for a moment.

"*Our* rescue plan?" she asked. "Kitsu-san, I can't possibly expect you to sacrifice anything more for this. You and your people should stay here where it's safe and I'll—"

"Tora-chan, please. I promise not to endanger any of my crew, but you cannot expect me to sit idly by while you risk your life again."

Torako wanted to argue, but it dawned on her that every moment she spent arguing with Kitsu was a moment longer for her enemies to harm Raku. It wasn't her job to protect Kitsu from his own folly. It never had been. If he wished to risk himself, he was welcome to. She needed to go after Raku, and soon.

"Fine. Tell me about this island then," she said, and Kitsu's eyes flashed with something she couldn't quite place as he led her over to a very large map.

⫸ *Itachi* ⫷

ITACHI WANTED TO cry, but crying would prove Mama right so she wouldn't cry. She would not. She took a deep breath and dug her fingers into Sairō's neck fur.

"You can't leave me behind, Mama," she sniffed. She wasn't crying. She just had a runny nose.

"I know it's hard, Itachi-chan, but where I'm going will be full of people trying to stab me. They won't be careful about not hurting you too, and I don't know what I would do if someone hurt you, Itachi-chan."

Itachi looked into Mama's eyes for a moment. The brownish-green of them was made brighter by the tears that filled them. Those tears did *not* make Itachi feel any better.

"It will be ok, Itachi-chan," Mama said, trying to sound like she believed the words.

But Itachi knew that she didn't believe them, and that was the problem.

"You're lying, Mama," she whispered. "You can't leave me here. What if you never come back?"

Mama's arms wrapped around her then and pulled her tight. She hadn't asked, and Mama was usually good about asking, but Itachi didn't mind this time, because she wanted the hug. She wanted it so much that she never wanted it to end.

"Itachi-san," said the low grumbly voice of the wolf whose fur she'd been wrapped up in a few moments earlier, "I find that I'm far too tired to go chasing after angry humans again. Would you stay with me and keep me warm? Almost drowning was far more excitement than my old bones have had in centuries."

Itachi thought about that. Sairō was telling the truth. Which was odd, because Sairō didn't *look* all that tired. Well, they *had* curled up at her feet again. And they *were* closing their eyes a lot. Maybe that's just what wolves looked like when they were tired.

"I promise to bring Kitsu-san with me to help keep me safe," Mama murmured in her ear as she held her tight. "And I'll do my best to get Raku-san back and bring her to you as quick as I can."

Mama was telling the truth now, and that was better than the lie that was always true. After all, if the past few days had taught her anything, it was that the lie that was always true *wasn't*, and she thought she might never believe it again.

"I'll stay with Sairō and keep them safe," she said finally, wiping at the tears on her face. "But you have to come back, Mama. You and Kaa-san *have* to come back."

Mama nodded, and held her tight, but didn't say anything else. Then she sat back and wiped at her own tears.

"Don't let the smugglers cheat you at cards," Mama said, before kissing the top of her head. "I love you to the moon and back, Itachi-chan."

And then she turned on her heel and followed Kitsu-san deeper into the cave, until the darkness ate them up.

"Can you scratch a little bit lower?" Sairō rumbled, as she leaned hard against them and buried her fingers in their fur. "My left shoulder is covered in salt and itches like a demon."

Itachi laughed, even if tears still wet her cheeks, and focused on getting Sairō comfortable.

━ Kaiyo ━

"ARE YOU REALLY going to just stay here until she wakes up?" asked Tanaka, from across the wide expanse of Tatami that separated Kaiyo from the door.

She took a deep breath, full of the smell of sun-warmed tatami mixed with a sea breeze, tried to stay the hand that reached for her hanko, and failed. In moments the tiny seal was flipping between her fingers once more, as she stared out of the open window that looked out across Kaigunjima harbor. She didn't need to look to know that the Lander scribe at her feet was still unconscious, or that Tanaka was fretting about the whole thing from the doorway, since he hadn't been granted entrance to this newly secured room.

"Admiral Saito will be here in a few hours, and I can't trust anyone else to guard her at this point."

She didn't even *try* not to glare accusingly at Tanaka when she said this, and he at least had the decency to look away as his cheeks reddened with what she could only hope was embarrassment.

"The holding cells would be—"

"The holding cells aren't made to keep actual prisoners contained, and you know it. They're meant to convince survivors that we don't mean them any harm. Someone hell-bent on escaping would only need a handful of minutes to break out of there, and then woe betide the new recruits on duty who try to stop them." Tanaka opened his mouth as though he was about to object, so she pressed on before he could actually start speaking. "How many of our least experienced marines do you wish to see gutted like you were, before my father arrives for this interrogation, Tanaka-san?"

At that, Tanaka's mouth snapped shut and Kaiyo felt some of the tension leave her shoulders.

"I'll guard her with a complement of raiko until the Admiral arrives to question her," she repeated. "It will undoubtedly be quite boring, but it's better than the alternative."

Tanaka snorted.

"You'll be throwing daggers at raiko for target practice long before the Admiral gets here," he said.

Kaiyo wasn't sure if she should laugh or throw her hanko at him, so she settled on glaring.

"If you think I can't—"

But before she could finish stabbing Tanaka with words instead of daggers, a white light flashed through the room, almost blinding her. Without thinking, Kaiyo placed herself between the light and the scribe's unconscious form and drew two of her throwing knives, leaving her hanko somewhere at her feet.

She blinked until a glowing silver-white form took shape in front of her.

"You again," she whispered.

"Sorry to interrupt your vigil over the very dangerous slumbering scribe," the tall, thin man wearing robes that seemed made of pure moonlight said, in a voice that sounded something like rolling waves. "But I thought you should know that you have a problem. Some of your pursuers may have survived the little accident I arranged the other night, and it would be in your best interest to collect them."

Kaiyo was torn between insult and intrigue, so she didn't fling any of her small knives at the moon person.

"Why would you warn me of such a thing?" she asked, unable to keep the suspicion from her voice.

"For much the same reason that I informed you that you were being pursued by your prisoner's wife last night. Unlike then, however, there is little I can do about it, besides warn you. My powers do not extend much beyond the sea."

Kaiyo frowned. She recognized the man as the same one who had arrived in a flash of white light on the Wind Serpent the day before and then done… something… to cause one of largest sea serpents she had ever seen to destroy a perfectly good ship, presumably taking its entire crew to a watery grave. She shuddered at the memory, but the real reason her mind was screaming some vague warning at her finally slid into place as she took a closer look at the man's kimono. She'd seen that pattern somewhere.

"You were at the wedding," Kaiyo muttered.

"You have a functioning memory, congratulations. I recommend sending someone you trust after the intruders. There's a good chance anyone else will make a hash of it, and you've already come too close to ruining this mission, haven't you?"

Kaiyo felt the insult like a blow to the face, but the reminder of people she trusted had her looking around the room to see why she was the only one who had moved to put herself between Raku and the man made of moonlight.

She was somewhat horrified to see that everyone else in the room appeared frozen in place, as though time had stopped, or else something more powerful than she had ever experienced had grabbed hold of them.

"The sun is still up and my powers aren't what they could be. I didn't feel like dealing with a half-dozen raiko trying to interrupt us."

That was hardly an explanation at all, but Kaiyo was starting to put a few things together. A being made of moonlight, who had been powerful enough to control a sea serpent, and had managed to freeze all of her raiko and Tanaka in mid-motion…

"Do you have a name, Kami-sama?" she asked, more than a little concerned about who she faced.

"Oh, you've grown suddenly respectful, have you? You've little to worry about. You're enough like your father that I've come to expect a certain level of incivility. But you've much to worry about without my continued interference. Search to the east, near the caverns, and remember what I said about sending someone you trust."

And with that, and a single flash of light, the moon Kami was gone.

Kaiyo blinked again and everyone started moving at once. Tanaka was halfway across the room and she could feel the change in pressure as five raiko all prepared themselves for battle, when she yelled, "STOP."

"You're too late," she added, in a less commanding tone, after everyone paused in their tracks. Unlike when the moon Kami had frozen them, this time they still fidgeted and breathed after they'd stopped themselves.

Kaiyo instantly knelt to check the unconscious scribe. She was just as she had been. The moon Kami hadn't done anything to her that Kaiyo could sense.

"Tanaka-san, would you check her? I've no idea what that creature is capable of."

The raiko all looked puzzled as they inspected the room, clearly confused by the sudden flashes of light and Kaiyo's anger.

Tanaka didn't hesitate to move to the scribe's side and check her over, but he spoke as he did so.

"What was all that, Captain?"

"I'm not entirely certain, Tanaka-san, but I'd bet a tenday's pay that we were just visited by a moon Kami."

"Another one?" Tanaka asked. Kaiyo saw that his face paled as he asked it, and she supposed he remembered the sea serpent attack just as well as she did.

"The same one," she replied, wondering how Tanaka had realized what the moon Kami was before she had.

"Tsukuyomi-sama, then," he muttered.

Kaiyo frowned again.

"How do you know that?"

"You don't spend enough time below decks if you don't recognize one of the primary patrons of the Kaigun, Captain."

Kaiyo said nothing, because she supposed that was true.

"What did he want?" Tanaka asked, even as he stood up from the scribe's side. "She's as well as she was when we brought her here," he added, before Kaiyo had a chance to answer his question.

She didn't ask how well that was, because she knew that Tanaka was still concerned about her fragility even after their harried chase of the woman across half the island.

"He wanted to warn me that we have unwelcome visitors on the island. He suggested I only send my most trusted allies after them."

She frowned pointedly in Tanaka's direction and much to her surprise, he smiled.

"I suppose I had better get moving then," he said, turning away from her and heading towards the door.

"Tanaka-san, you don't even know where you're heading, it could easily be a trap."

"Seems like a rather elaborate trap, especially without explicit directions."

"Tanaka-san…"

"May I offer my services?" offered a soft voice from the doorway.

Kaiyo and Tanaka both looked up to see Lyt standing there. Xe was smiling faintly in an expression that Kaiyo couldn't quite parse.

"Which services would those be?" Kaiyo asked, still unsure if she could trust xir, after this morning.

"As a tracker," xe said.

Kaiyo had to admit that Lyt's tracking had been crucial to her finding Raku at Fubuki-sensei's cabin. She was sure her old instructor would have managed to keep the woman from getting away if she'd known she was a prisoner, but something about the way Fubuki-sensei had asked her to keep the scribe alive made her wonder what would have happened if she, Lyt, and Tanaka had taken much longer to arrive.

In the end, the fact that Lyt had done nothing but offer assistance since their first agreement decided her.

"Fine. You and Tanaka-san will search out these intruders and bring them here," she said. "The moon Kami said to look to the east, near the caverns, for all the good that will do you."

Tanaka nodded and Lyt smiled.

"Saves us searching the entire compound first, doesn't it?" xe suggested.

Kaiyo merely scowled until they had both left.

She ignored the hollow feeling in her stomach as she watched Tanaka walk away from her again, and it was only long after he was out of hearing that she muttered under her breath, "Be careful."

≈ *Torako* ≈

THE CITY WAS unlike anything Torako had ever seen. It was as bustling a port as Atsumi, full of ships and people as one would expect, but the clothing people wore, and the styles of the ships… Torako was at a loss to describe most of it. The differences were difficult to place. The ships were made in much the same way as the Trickster, but the decorative flourishes were a different style entirely, and even some of the decks were arranged differently. And the fashion… some of it was at least based on the latest fashions in kimono, hakama, and uwagi. But some of it was more like her own leathers than she would ever have expected to see in a city, and much of it was even more odd than that. She felt a stab of longing for Raku, who she knew would be delighted by the different clothes and who would probably have some idea of where they had come from, and why Torako had never seen them before.

She brushed that longing away, refocusing on the problem before her. Which was Kitsu. Or more accurately, it was the challenge posed by convincing herself not to stab him in frustration.

"Why can't we just sneak in and start searching for her? That fence doesn't look too high."

"Because no matter how low the fence is, it isn't going to do you any good to try to sneak around from outside. You need to get all the way into the holding area of the complex and you won't get there from here before the guards call the alarm."

"Let them call the alarm. I'll just cut them down."

Kitsu stared at her for a moment with his head in its usual tilt while he blinked at her.

"It's not that I don't believe you, Tora-chan, it's just that it would save quite a few lives to do this my way."

Torako snorted.

"The lives of the people who stole Raku-chan away from her family are hardly worth preserving."

"Torako-san, you have every right to think ill of them at the moment. They have much to answer for, but... most of the people you would cut down have nothing to do with the decision to take Raku-san. Tanuki's balls, they don't even have anything to do with her actual capture. There are thousands of Kaigunka, and from what you've described, fewer than two dozen actually came after your wife. Do you really think fifty people deserve to die because you can't be bothered to engage in a bit of stealth?"

Kitsu's voice was quiet. They were, after all, hiding not far beyond one of the gates to the compound that Kitsu claimed would hold Raku. But his voice was surprisingly agitated, and Torako wondered who these people were, that Kitsu actually cared if they lived or died.

Then she shook her head. That was unfair. Kitsu had never been callous with other people's lives. He was a smuggler, not an assassin, and all of his biggest smuggling jobs had been about saving people, not getting them killed.

"Fine," she said after a long while lost in thought. "We'll do things your way, then."

"Excellent," said Kitsu, his eyes lighting briefly in the late afternoon sun. "And I'm sorry."

And then Torako saw Kitsu's hand dart forward, and she moved to block him, but it didn't matter because he wasn't aiming anywhere in particular. She felt something pierce the skin of her forearm and then, a few heartbeats later, the world disappeared.

Torako blinked herself awake and tried to remember why she was angry. It was an odd feeling, to be certain that she was furious but not know the reason. She looked around her to see if there were any clues.

She was lying on a futon much like the slim one she used at home. The futon was laid out on a tatami floor, and the smell of grass was strong enough to suggest the floor was relatively new. She wasn't covered by any kind of sheet or blanket, but then again, the room was warm and she was still dressed in all of her leathers. Her wakizashi, katana, and hunting knife were all missing. That was a problem.

The room was... odd. Alright, it was a perfectly normal room. It was six tatami in size, with a futon, a small low table, and a water basin attached to the wall, the likes of which she had only seen in New Council City.

But all of that *was* odd because she was fairly certain she hadn't expected to wake up in a normal room.

She pushed herself up from the futon and found that she was uninjured, which was something. A handful of steps put her in front of the sliding door that was the only clear entrance or exit to the room. She tried to slide it open but found it locked.

That was as she'd expected.

Then Torako jumped back from the door as she heard footsteps approaching from beyond it. She tucked herself into the one corner of the room that would be difficult to see for someone coming through the door, and she waited.

The footsteps stopped.

Keys jangled and pottery clinked.

The door slid open.

A man wearing a strange uniform entered balancing a tray on one hand, and Torako hesitated, because she didn't want to attack someone who might be here to help her.

Then he turned, his amber eyes flashing in the low light provided by the setting sun coming through the far window, and Torako recognized Kitsu.

She launched herself at him, knocking the tray from his hands and pinning him to the wall with enough force to knock the wind from him, as she remembered quite suddenly why she was furious.

Torako glared at Kitsu's startled expression as her hands clenched his throat and pushed him up against the blank wall of the room she'd been captive in until he'd unlocked the door. She could smell miso and fish over the scent of salt and pine that always tinged Kitsu's clothes.

"Hrkkk," Kitsu said.

She released his throat long enough for him to sink to the floor, but then she shoved him back against the wall with her forearm across his throat so she was one quick jab of her elbow away from collapsing his windpipe.

"You were never this interested in pinning me against the wall when we were together," Kitsu said, his customary smirk resuming its usual place.

Torako growled.

"You *drugged* me."

"You said you agreed to my plan."

"You said your plan was to pretend I was a prisoner and sneak us into the restraining cells."

"And that's exactly what I did."

"You didn't *say* you were going to drug me."

"You didn't ask."

"Kitsu-san..." Torako couldn't form a coherent sentence after that, but she thought she might be growling. Or maybe Sairō was growling in her head and she could hear it? Could it be both? She focused on glaring at Kitsu instead of worrying about who was growling.

"I'm sorry, Tora-chan. If you'll recall, I apologized right before I drugged you. But I half expected you to decide to start cutting down guards the moment we got through the gates and I didn't feel like letting you kill a few dozen people all for the prize of not even getting to Raku-san successfully."

"You seriously don't trust me to keep my temper in check long enough to run a rescue mission?" she huffed, her anger ebbing into something more like annoyance.

"You've... seemed a bit on edge lately," Kitsu muttered, with a pointed glance at her arm pressed against his throat.

Torako stepped back and walked towards the still-open door.

"It's a shame we can't trust each other anymore, Kitsu-san," she said, before she turned, slid the door closed, and used the keys she'd just pulled from Kitsu's belt while she'd had her body shoved up against his to lock it behind her.

"Torako-san, WAIT!" he shouted as she walked down the hall.

She could still hear him shouting when she turned the corner and ran into the first set of guards.

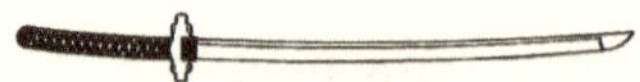

There were only three of them, but Torako didn't have any of her weapons. She considered turning the other way, but there was no chance they hadn't seen her. That was clear enough from the startled expressions on their faces. The only reason she was certain they were guards was that they were wearing uniforms identical to the one that Kitsu had been wearing, and they wore swords in their belts along with an array of keys and restraints that were probably familiar to every guard in history. Were it not for those giveaways, she might have thought they were all students. Two of them were sitting at a small table, laying out tiles for some kind of game. One was leaning against the wall behind them, her eyes trained on the hallway that Torako had just traversed. They could have been trainees passing the time between lectures.

They seemed very young.

Perhaps that's why she did her best not to kill them.

Or perhaps it was because they hadn't immediately moved to attack her the moment she'd turned the corner.

In fact, they were still staring at her, wide-eyed and unmoving, as she stepped behind the man whose hands were still holding a set of game tiles and gripped his neck, skin to skin, so that her fingers found an easy link to his kisō, and she *pulled*, leaving him limp in the chair. It wasn't a technique she often had time to apply in battle, as it required direct contact with a person's skin and enough time to concentrate on pulling their kisō from them hard enough to render them unconscious. Which, if they weren't a kisōshi, didn't actually take long. The man who now slumped dramatically in his chair had not been a kisōshi.

His sudden loss of consciousness finally set his friends into motion, however.

Which made it quite a bit trickier to avoid killing *them*.

Both of the women reached for the katana on their belts at the same time, and Torako had to flip the small table at them to give her the extra moment she needed to move around its edge and then roll inside the guard of the woman whose back was already against the wall.

Very young, she thought as she angled her body so that the momentum from her standing up slammed the woman into the wall even as Torako pried the katana from her hand and reared her head back so that the guard's head bounced off Torako's skull and then the wall.

She slumped to the ground limply enough that Torako focused her attention, and the blade, on the woman who had been sitting down to play a game and now found herself stuck between a blade and an overturned table.

"I don't particularly want to hurt you," Torako admitted. "But I can't let you sound the alarm either."

The other woman swallowed.

And then she collapsed.

Torako blinked and was only half surprised to find Kitsu reaching across the overturned table in order to remove the dart from the woman's neck.

"You should have waited," he grumbled.

"You had another key?" she asked.

"The day that I need a key to get past a simple room lock is the day you will need to set my body to the pyre and commend me to the Kami."

Torako shook her head. She should have known that Kitsu would have his lock picks on him. Silly to think that a costume change would have had him leaving his most useful gear behind. He was a charlatan, not an idiot.

"If you're done making far too much noise and leaving a trail of bodies in your wake, you could come with me. I happen to have spent the time you were unconscious learning as much as I could about Raku-san's whereabouts."

Torako merely glared at the man and set about untying the sheath for her newly acquired katana from the woman unconscious on the floor behind her. She flinched a bit at the blood dripping from the woman's nose, but there was little to be done about it. She might wake up, she might not. That was always the risk with head injuries. She was breathing evenly for now.

"I also happen to know where your sword is," Kitsu added.

Torako felt something loosen between her shoulder blades, but she didn't stop removing the scabbard from the woman's belt.

"I'll keep this until we get there," she said patting the hilt of the katana. It was a drastically inferior blade. Good enough for someone who always had access to an armory and whose life scheduled in time for blade maintenance every day, but nothing like the blade Shiken had been, or the one that Sairō was attached to. "Lead the way then."

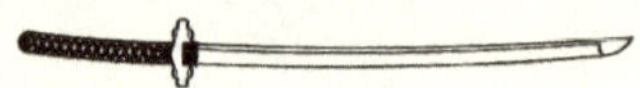

Retrieving her blades was easier than she'd expected. The hard part was trusting that Kitsu would return to her when he left her to collect them. She'd hidden in a small alcove filled with some large-leafed potted plants while Kitsu had gone striding confidently through an enormous antechamber and then through the doors to what he had assured her was an office dedicated to confiscated property.

She had sunk down low beneath the plants and counted out a hundred deep breaths while he went on his errand. She didn't know what was wrong with her. She still wasn't certain if trusting Kitsu was a good idea, but he was right to say that she'd been on edge recently. She felt jagged, broken, and raw. Like a glass bowl that had been shattered but was still holding its shape—it had just enough pieces missing to cut anyone who tried to touch it, but not so many that it was going to fall apart without another push.

Then she swallowed a noise that was half laugh, half sob as it occurred to her that she had good reason to fall apart, she just didn't have the time. Perhaps that was why she kept lashing out at Kitsu, even though he'd done nothing but try to help her since she'd shown up and asked him for his ship. It wasn't that he wasn't trustworthy, it was just that he made a convenient makiwara. Someone strong enough to take her anger without breaking. She let out her hundredth deep breath. He deserved better than to be her striking post, though.

"Feeling better yet?" he asked.

She popped one eye open and didn't bother berating him for sneaking up on her. She had been well-attuned to the room around her, and no one should have been able to approach without her notice. The fact that Kitsu had… only ensured that he wasn't an imposter, she supposed.

"I still hate that," she replied evenly. "How'd it go?"

Of course, that was a silly question, since Kitsu was clearly holding Sairō's katana, her wakizashi, and even her hunting knife.

"This is such a well-oiled bureaucracy that all it takes is the right piece of paperwork and not even the most stubborn property manager can resist my charms."

"Is it really your charms when it's paperwork?" she asked, even as she began untying her stolen katana so she could replace it with Sairō's.

"I like to think my charm is always a factor," Kitsu said quietly.

"Of course you like to think that," Torako replied. "That doesn't make it true, though."

"You wound me."

"I will absolutely wound you if you don't stop talking and start leading me to wherever these miscreants are keeping my wife."

"You wouldn't."

"You probably shouldn't have armed me, but it's too late now."

And with that, Torako stood up, all her weapons once more in place, and turned to see five guards standing at attention with their hands on their swords.

"Friends of yours?" she asked, as Kitsu stood beside her.

"I'm afraid not."

His frown wasn't reassuring.

"Well then, this will be fun," Torako said, as she leapt onto one of the large pots, drew her katana, and then threw herself at the five guards before they could overcome their shock.

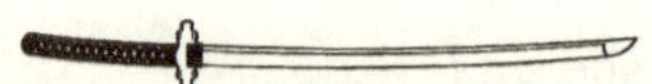

Torako wasn't sure why all of these guards were so easily stunned into inaction. All she'd done was climb a large plant pot and jump at them with her weapon drawn. Either they weren't much used to armed combat, which was a strange quality in a guard, or else they just weren't used to combat in strange contexts. She had been trained to fight absolutely anywhere and then had spent decades battling ragtag groups in the wilderness, along with the occasional warehouse, city street, or even the odd library when she'd been assisting Kitsu or Raku. There was no location that her mind considered off-limits for fighting.

These guards, however, seemed very put off by the idea of fighting in this large marble entryway. Or perhaps they just objected to someone climbing the decorative plants. Then again, maybe having a lone attacker jump at you when any sensible person would recognize they were outnumbered is what threw them.

Regardless, they took far too long to act, and Torako used that hesitation to her advantage.

She had landed squarely in the middle of the knot of guards because that would make it difficult for them to attack her without hitting their friends until they backed up. It also meant that her own reach was shortened, not because she cared about stabbing more than one target at once, but because she didn't have room to move her own blade without running into the giant ceramic vase behind her, or one of the guards.

None of which particularly mattered, because she opted for head-butting the nearest guard, a man who was so close to her that if he'd had his hand on his wakizashi instead of his katana he'd have been able to gut her already. Luckily, he didn't have room to even draw his blade, and once she'd smashed her forehead into his he wasn't likely to remember anything as sensible as pulling a shorter weapon until she was far out of reach.

She was already spinning to meet the blade of the next closest attacker as the first guard slumped to the floor with blood gushing from his nose. The next guard had moved faster than her fellows, stepping back enough to give herself room to fight, but by engaging Torako where she stood, she hindered the attacks of the other guards, putting herself between them and Torako.

Torako was, of course, intentionally keeping her back to the ceramic pots, as she easily deflected the hesitant slashes of the quick guard. The guards three companions were finally stepping back far enough to draw their own blades, but none of them seemed confident enough to strike while their colleague was in the way.

A problem which became less relevant once Torako disarmed her with an opportune slash to the wrist. The woman dropped her katana and immediately wrapped her other hand around the wound. Not wanting her compatriots to get any ideas, Torako used that moment to lay her blade at the woman's throat.

As expected, the remaining guards all froze in place.

"Can we skip to the part where you just let me walk away from here with this woman as a hostage?" she asked, her voice as steady as her blade.

"I don't particularly want to kill her, or the rest of you, but I find I don't have the patience to spare all your lives if you insist on getting between me and my wife."

The guards all exchanged looks that suggested they had no idea what Torako was talking about.

"I believe these underlings have little to do with your wife," came the gravelly voice from behind her that she'd been expecting to interrupt ever since she jumped into the knot of guards.

"Well, then they should be sensible enough to step aside," she replied, not even flicking a glance towards Kitsu. He was either coming forward to help her, or he was about to stab her in the back, literally, but there wasn't much she could do about it if he meant to betray her. "They should recognize this is well past their pay grade."

"Indeed," Kitsu said, as he dropped down beside her. "And they should also recognize that their Tiasa has everything under control."

Torako grimaced as she felt the point of a dart dig into the skin along her neck.

"You bastard," she mumbled as her vision darkened and then faded to black.

⚊Itachi⚊

ITACHI WATCHED SAIRŌ walk back and forth across the stone floor so quickly it made the giant stone room seem small. Every now and again, the wolf would growl something that Itachi couldn't quite understand. Once or twice, she thought she heard them say Mama's other name. She tried not to let Sairō's pacing scare her; she tried to remember that she thought it was funny at first, especially since she had still been on Sairō's back when they had started.

She had gotten down when the constant turns had started to make her tummy hurt and one of the nice people that worked on Kitsu's boat had given her a bowl of soup. That had been yummy, but the soup was gone now and Sairō was still walking in circles and growling a bit.

Itachi decided that she should try one of the breathing exercises Yanagi-sensei had given her to help her stay calm. She sat down with her legs folded under her and closed her eyes. Then she tried to take deep breaths and count them. It was easy to focus on counting, but sometimes when the numbers got big she would forget which number came next and so she would just start at one again.

By the third time she started over, she was hearing a distant voice in her mind.

That was strange, but it happened sometimes. Mostly it happened when she was asleep, but sometimes during the day. For a moment, her whole body went tight like a rope because she was worried that the voice might be one of the mean spirits, but then she remembered Sairō was close by, and the mean spirits never bothered her when the wolf was close to her.

She focused on counting her breathing again and then the voice came back, sounding louder this time, but still as if it was far away, maybe in the direction that Mama and Kitsu had gone.

Itachi-chan, help…

Itachi felt tears come to her eyes because she knew that voice.

She stood up without thinking and blinked her eyes open. Sairō was still walking in circles, still growling and mumbling something about stupid foxes. She didn't want to bother them, but the voice…

Itachi-chan, I need you…

Itachi turned towards the tunnel. It was dark, but she could still hear that voice.

Itachi-chan, hurry. You can't trust…

The voice faded in and out, but Itachi found her feet moving her down the dark tunnel almost without thinking. She knew she should tell someone where she was going, but what had the voice said about trust? Besides, Mama had gone this way, and wherever Mama was, was sure to be safe, because Mama could fight anything at all.

She was far enough into the tunnel that it was completely dark by the time she heard Sairō call out for her in the distance. Some part of her thought she should wait for them. Mama had said they were going to protect her, and she knew she trusted the wolf, but—

Itachi-chan, help!

Itachi started to run, how could she not? Tenshi-san, her Obaa-chan, needed her!

⟞ *Torako* ⟝

TORAKO AWOKE TO darkness, with Kitsu's body pressed all along hers, chest to chest, thigh to thigh. Even their knees touched. She hated that she recognized the weight of him before she'd even had a chance to open her eyes fully. Of course, there was also the smell of salt and pine, in case she'd had any doubt.

"You have the span of three breaths to explain yourself before I gut you, Kitsu-san," she whispered.

Her left hand had already found the hilt of her wakizashi, which was both reassuring and puzzling. However, the fact that she was still armed was a very large part of why Kitsu wasn't already dead. She didn't need a blade to kill a man, but her blades were still there, and she doubted the people who had stolen Raku away would have left her armed.

"You keep trying to fight everyone you see, but the easiest way across this compound is to pretend you're a prisoner and that I'm escorting you across the grounds. I had to look like I was knocking you out and carting you off to a superior officer to keep those five idiots from sounding the alarm. I carried you as far as I could, but you're damned heavy, and now we're lying behind some very nicely sculpted shrubs while you wake up so that we can finish this thrice-cursed rescue mission."

Kitsu's voice, though low and rumbling, as usual, was an unusually harsh whisper that came out in what sounded like a single breath.

When he was done, Torako couldn't help it. She laughed.

"Shhh!" Kitsu scolded, but his voice sounded less menacing than it had a moment earlier.

"Are you trying to get us killed?" he asked.

"Why are you lying on top of me?" Torako asked, ignoring his question.

"I didn't want you to have time or space to kill me when you woke up," he muttered. "I knew you'd be furious."

"Did you really believe lying like this would protect you?" she asked, voice mild, still whispering, but no longer laced with fury.

"Not entirely, no. I'm sure you know at least ten different ways to kill me from this position, but I thought it might slow you down, plus it made certain I'd notice immediately when you woke."

"So really you just wanted to make sure I couldn't sneak up on you," she concluded.

"You're not the only one who hates it," he replied coyly.

She finally turned to look at him. She had been rather thoroughly inspecting the shrubs Kitsu had mentioned, and the night darkened sky above, as they spoke, but something about his voice just then made her turn to see his eyes.

Which were glowing.

Any curiosity she'd had about what emotion had tinged his voice a moment ago was swept away by… whatever was making his eyes resemble lightning bugs.

"Umm… Kitsu-san?"

"Hmmm?"

His voice was a low rumble that she felt all the way through her chest. If she hadn't been so distracted by the light show in his face, she might have felt it lower down, too.

"Your eyes are…" she trailed off, not sure how to explain and hoping he would know what she meant.

"Oh? You can see it now? That's interesting."

"Is it?"

"To me, yes."

"Any interest in sharing why your eyes are glowing?"

"The answer might take longer than is sensible to spend here."

"Could you possibly come up with a summary?"

"Not really. There's no way to talk about it without you asking a hundred questions."

"You're really not going to answer."

"I promise I will, just not right now."

"You're vexing."

"I try."

Torako sighed and considered the rest of their plan. Or Kitsu's plan, at any rate. *Her* plan kept getting her knocked out by drugged darts.

"How long was I unconscious?"

"Not long." He tapped a pouch on the side of his belt. "I have an antidote that works almost as quickly as the sleeping draught."

"Where did you find draughts that work that quickly anyway? That shouldn't be possible."

"I am a man of many mysteries," he replied, finally standing and reaching down to offer his hand.

She ignored the hand and rolled to her feet. Then she cursed as her knees started to give out and Kitsu had to catch her.

"I know you can generally stand on your own, Love, it's just that getting hit with that draught twice in one night would be a lot for anyone. Here."

And then, in a move so surprising it wiped away her annoyance at the term of endearment, he offered her an onigiri, which he had pulled from yet another pouch.

She didn't even bother to ask where he'd gotten it—they didn't have time, and she didn't care. She ate the rice ball in a half-dozen swift bites.

"I don't suppose you've got a hot bath kicking around those pouches?" she asked, wiping her mouth and gazing speculatively at Kitsu's belt.

"Sadly no, but you'll be pleased to know that if we live long enough there are a number of hot springs hidden away on this island, and one of them can actually be reached through our little smugglers' cove."

Torako glanced around the courtyard and assessed the nearby threats. There didn't seem to be any, but she was fairly certain that only meant they were hidden.

"Well, you're the one who is suspiciously familiar with this place," she said, after a moment. "Where are we headed?"

"Are you suggesting you don't trust me?" asked Kitsu with a hand pressed across his heart.

Torako snorted.

"You have narrowly avoided my wrath three times tonight. Don't push your luck."

What Torako didn't say was that after this last drugging, she actually *did* trust him again. Possibly she'd never stopped. But he'd had her completely unconscious with five enemies, well three really, ready to assist him if he'd wanted to betray her. He hadn't. She still wasn't certain why she felt so angry with Kitsu, but she did trust him.

She felt something loosen in her chest at the realization. Perhaps it was simply one less thing to worry about, but something eased when she finally decided that Kitsu, at least, was not the enemy.

"Follow me," he replied. "And if we run into anyone, promise to act like a captive?"

Torako only grunted, but Kitsu simply rolled his eyes and led her out across the darkened courtyard.

⤙ Raku ⤚

RAKU BLINKED HERSELF awake, half expecting to find herself back in the gently swaying hammock of The Wind Serpent. Instead, she felt her back pressed into the familiar ridged smoothness of a tatami mat. She tried to get an idea of where she was before she made any obvious movement, so for a moment she did nothing but open her eyes and breathe as evenly as she could. Anyone paying close attention would probably notice the slight shift in her breathing before she had woken enough to try to feign sleep, but if she was lucky no one would be paying attention.

"Welcome back," said a wry voice from behind her.

Well, damn, that hadn't lasted long.

Seeing no point in pretending any longer, she took a deeper breath and got a lungful of the dry straw smell of well-aged tatami, along with the scent of an ocean breeze. It would have been pleasant if she hadn't been well aware that she was still a prisoner. She was dismayed to note that her wrists and ankles were bound. She hated when her enemies stopped underestimating her—it always made things more difficult.

"Where is that dear healer of yours?" she asked, even before she turned in the direction of the voice. She had recognized it as belonging to the woman who had been giving commands on the Wind Serpent, the one she was fairly certain was the captain of that vessel. She didn't need to see her to confirm that it was the same woman, and in fact, seeing her might have hurt more than it helped as she'd barely been able to make out any of the woman's features the few times she'd gotten a glimpse of her.

So she took her time rolling onto her back, a task that was slow to begin with, due to her bound wrists, and which allowed her to get a better look at the room she was in. It was large, with plain walls and well-maintained tatami floors, and there were three kisōshi guards standing at attention on the wall that she was facing.

Internally she drew on one of Torako's favorite epithets, involving a debauched Kami and his testes.

"And why exactly am I trussed up like an unruly bird?" she asked, mostly as a way to distract herself from the pain of pushing against the shoulder that sported a newly healing dart wound as she shifted her weight to glare at the woman who had spoken.

She gasped when she finally got onto her other side, but it wasn't because of the wound in her shoulder. It was because, in the bright light coming from the wall sconces that bordered the room, she could see very clearly the features of the woman who held her captive. It was indeed the captain of the ship, and... well, she was glad she hadn't seen her features clearly earlier, because they swamped her with a dozen emotions she couldn't place or easily push away. She took a few deep breaths and hoped that it would all come across as pain from her injury.

"The healer you asked for is off on an errand better-suited to his talents, since he utterly failed to hold you captive when given the chance. And the reason you are trussed up like an unruly bird is that I do not want you to fly away."

"You don't think six kisōshi is enough to keep me in my place?" Raku asked, eyeing the wall beyond where the captain sat in front of a low table. It matched the wall she'd woken up facing, down to the three kisōshi standing at attention across it.

"There are two more outside the door, as well," the woman replied. "And no. I don't think so. I'm afraid that I'm done underestimating you. My... Second in Command might think you too distraught to be restrained properly, but we all know how that turned out."

Interesting. "Too distraught to be restrained properly" was a rather different logic than she'd expected, even from the healer who had been kind to her in his way. These people were full of contradictions. They'd stolen her from her home and family, then healed her and seemed embarrassed about it. At least, Tanaka had. But this woman didn't seem embarrassed, she seemed angry. Which was something Raku could work with.

"Did you kill him for his incompetence, then? Or is he actually off on some 'errand?'" she asked.

The mark struck home, and she almost flinched when the too-familiar expression of guilt-tinged anger crossed the other woman's face.

"We don't kill people for their mistakes in the Kaigun," she bit out.

"Oh? You reserve that for innocent people you've kidnapped, after you've interrogated them, is that it?"

The flinch was more noticeable the second time, and Raku pushed away the need she felt to apologize just because the eyebrows and chin that the emotions were writ across looked familiar. This woman was not Torako.

"We don't plan to kill you," the woman replied.

The other woman's voice was monotone, and Raku wondered if that was how she hid her lies, or if it came from somewhere else. Feeling inspired by the similarities that haunted her in the woman's face, she guessed.

"You want to, though, don't you?"

That set the other woman's features into a hardness that was not at all familiar, and, for just a moment, Raku questioned the assumptions she'd made about this woman's face.

"You're not wrong," the other woman huffed. "I've wanted to put a blade in your gut ever since you put one into my Second's."

Ah, that explained many things, especially the way the woman kept almost saying a different word just before she said Second.

"Well, at least you're loyal, I'll give you that much."

"What would you know of loyalty, Lander? You've been raised in a society that long ago gave up any hint of communal strength. Your people turn on each other for the barest scrap of power, and it led to ten centuries of oppression and genocide."

Well, that was *very* interesting. This woman, this captain, this bandit and kidnapper, belonged to some group of people who considered themselves wholly separate from regular Gensokans. How very curious.

"I don't suppose you'd be willing to tell me your name? Thinking of you as the captain of the Wind Serpent is tiring, and I've been drugged too many times in the past few days to have extra energy to spare on it."

"I am Kaiyo Saito," the woman replied.

Raku wanted to laugh. Saito was perhaps the most common name in Gensokai. If the woman's name was actually Saito it did nothing to tell Raku who she might be. If it wasn't, well, it only told Raku that she wasn't particularly creative.

"Well, then, Kaiyo-san, can you tell me, perchance, why you look so much like my wife?"

⇒ *Torako* ⇒

AFTER THREE MORE sparsely guarded courtyards, across which Kitsu led her like a prisoner, followed by slinking around the sides of a dozen buildings that were unlike any Torako had encountered before—who built entire buildings out of shaped clay stones?—and far too many winding staircases later, they were finally close to where Kitsu claimed Raku could be found.

"Four guards, at least two of them raiko," Kitsu whispered, from beside her.

They both had their backs plastered to the wall, and Kitsu's head had just returned from its brief foray around the corner.

"You'll have to go first," he added.

Torako barely restrained a guffaw.

"Did you seriously just say there are *raiko* down there? Storm-callers? The kind that shoot lightning and bring hurricanes? And you want me to go first?" she whispered furiously. "What happened to me pretending to be a prisoner?"

Kitsu shrugged, offering her his usual lopsided smirk.

"We're past that part. If Raku-san is here, she's at the end of this hallway. That's why there are so many guards. I can't lie our way down there, but you can fight them before they know what's happening. Use your usual trick."

Torako frowned. The rest of their journey here had been easy. Suspiciously so. They hadn't run into any more guards after the group that she'd jumped into the midst of right after Kitsu had retrieved her blades for her. But either there was an ambush waiting for her in the room at the end of this hall, or Raku was waiting for her there. Or both. Both was always a possibility.

"I thought you wanted to stab things?" Kitsu asked, after she'd hesitated for just a heartbeat.

"I always want to stab things," she replied.

"You always *wanted* to stab things. I'd thought parenthood might've changed that."

"In my experience, parenthood doesn't make you want to stab things any less. It's more that it makes you want to be very certain of your reasons for stabbing things."

"Ah yes, you're a role model now."

"A role model who stabs things."

"Things that are people."

"Is now really the time for this discussion?"

Kitsu shrugged. "Are you ready to stab some people-shaped things, now?"

"Fine," she sighed. "I don't suppose you'll have my back?" she asked.

Kitsu winked at her. "I'll be there to clean up the mess, as usual."

Torako wanted to laugh, but they'd already made too much noise and spent too long talking. They were going to alert every guard in that hallway to their presence in a moment, if they hadn't already. It was time to move.

⋙ Kaiyo ⋘

KAIYO PUZZLED OVER that question for a moment, unsure what the devil the scribe was talking about. She had never seen the woman's wife, or at least, not well enough to mark any of her features. After all, she had been racing ahead of her on horseback while being pursued by a giant wolf the one time she'd 'met' the

woman, and that didn't exactly lend itself to a careful consideration of features. She'd noticed she was tall, broad, and angry, but
that was about it.

Now she stared at the scribe's petite form and wondered what
it was that made the woman think she shared features with her
spouse. Raku was nothing like what Kaiyo would look for in a
partner, if she had ever been interested in finding one. Raku was
short, pleasantly round—though she knew such looks were out of
fashion on the mainland, the Kaigun had never eschewed a full
female figure—and she wore her hair in decorative combs and
dressed in brightly colored kimono even though she lived in a
rather drab hole in the rock in the middle of a deep forest protected by a demon.

Alright, that last part wasn't accurate. It was actually protected by the same woman whose features Kaiyo hadn't noted thanks
to the enormous wolf she'd been riding and the threat of violence that had rolled off of her in waves, but it amounted to the
same thing. Her assessment of Raku was that she was entirely
frivolous, something that Kaiyo found completely unattractive.
She failed to imagine any kind of draw to the woman. She was
attracted to, well, until very recently she would have said she
wasn't attracted to anything, but she was struggling to deny what
Tanaka's kiss had done to her, so she was beginning to think she
was attracted to unadulterated honesty and unrelenting competence. The image of Tanaka's eyes flashing as he pointed out
some mistake he thought she was making came unbidden to her
mind and sent a shiver down her spine.

She didn't say any of this to the woman lying on the floor
with her wrists and ankles bound, but instead opted for, "You're
not my type."

The scribe laughed.

"I shouldn't think so. I would take offense, but I'm not particularly attracted to people who take me from my home against my will and then pretend it's my fault somehow. I'm also not attracted to women who order my wife killed in battle."

The scribe paused and swallowed for a moment, perhaps to hold back some stronger emotion, and Kaiyo suddenly found her memory pulling forth the image of the sea serpent turning that other ship into little more than kindling. Her hand gripped the hanko she hadn't even noticed pulling from her belt pouch until her knuckles turned white.

"I'm sorry about that," she said, and was surprised to find that she meant it. "It wasn't... I didn't order it. Not that I wouldn't have fought that ship off and potentially killed your wife anyway, but... That wasn't done on my orders."

Kaiyo thought of the moon Kami who had arrived to warn her of the so-called intruders and wondered if she had inadvertently sent Tanaka and Lyt to their deaths. She shook the thought away.

The scribe cleared her throat.

"Well, that isn't much comfort since the only reason she was in a ship following yours was to get me back after you took me. You'll forgive me if I continue to lay the blame squarely on your shoulders."

Kaiyo nodded. That much, she did forgive.

"As is only reasonable. It's my fault, even if I didn't order it. If I had done a better job of staying ahead of your wife, she'd have been too far behind to pose a threat."

She saw surprise in the scribe's eyes and wondered if the woman hadn't expected her to own her mistake, or if she simply thought she was owning the *wrong* mistake.

"You really think that's the problem with your actions? That you didn't do your job of kidnapping me well enough?"

"I'm sure you see no reason to think that you needed to be kidnapped, and I couldn't expect you to, but whatever reason the Admiral has for bringing you here, it's not just some whim. The stakes are much greater than your life or mine."

"Or my wife's?" the other woman's voice broke on the words.

"Or your wife's," Kaiyo agreed. "You must think that this is either some petty banditry, or even perhaps something strangely personal, but I can assure you, it isn't. You're here because the alternative was to let thousands of people die. I'm not proud that we had to take a scribe from her home and kill her wife to accomplish it, but my pride has no place in the equation. We're protecting all of Gensokai."

"From what?" the woman on the floor asked, her voice carrying a tone that made Kaiyo think the woman questioned her sanity. She couldn't truly blame her. Because Landers were so ignorant of the way the world worked, explaining the truth likely sounded insane.

"That's best left for you to discuss with the admiral," she replied.

She could tell that the woman was getting ready to sally another set of questions at her, but she fell silent and both of them turned to look at the door in the same moment, as they heard the unmistakable sound of someone running full-speed down a hall without any attempt at stealth.

Then a cry of pain came from just outside the door.

She had just enough time to pull both her knives from her wrist bracers before the door exploded inward.

⮘ *Itachi* ⮚

ITACHI KEPT RUNNING, even as the protests from Sairō got louder and more insistent. They still seemed distant compared to the voice of her grandmother, which sounded like it was getting closer with every step. She knew that her grandmother was gone—she had seen it happen—but she also knew that the spirit realm was a strange place and that she saw spirits in the regular world all the time. It did not seem strange to her that Obaa-chan's spirit would call to her, and she would answer that call no matter what.

So she ran, and she didn't look back, even when Sairō's low growl started to fill the tunnel behind her.

Itachi-chan, help…

The voice sounded frightened in a way that Obaa-chan never did, but that only made sense, after everything that had happened.

Itachi ran faster.

She was running so fast that when she burst out of the tunnel into a forest, she couldn't get her legs to stop before she smacked right into the very tall tree person that she recognized from the ridge where Mama had fought the six bandits and the man who had peed on their rock.

"Hello, little one," the tree person said. "What are you doing here?"

But before Itachi could decide if she should scream or not, she felt long thin fingers close over her arms, heard a loud low growl too far behind her, and then her legs stopped working, her arms wouldn't move, and her voice would not allow her to scream.

"She's a child," said the soft voice of the tree.

"She's got more kisō than I do, and she looks like the scribe's wife. Whatever is coming after her sounds angry," said another voice.

She could tell that she was moving, though she could no longer feel her arms and legs. Was the tree person carrying her?

"Do you think this is who the moon Kami meant?"

"It must be."

"What about the wolf?"

"If it's the same one that killed half our people in Sakata, then we'd better move quickly."

"I'll do my best to cover our tracks, then."

Itachi wasn't sure what any of it meant, but she was suddenly too sleepy to care. She blinked a few times, and the world faded completely.

⟞ *Torako* ⟝

TORAKO CHARGED DOWN the hallway and tried not to think about what a lightning bolt to the chest might feel like. She didn't shout as she went, she issued no frivolous battle cries—that would only warn her enemies that she meant to cut them down. No, instead, she kept her blades sheathed and ran like her life depended on it. Which it did.

The guards clearly weren't expecting an attack, not even from a woman charging down the hall at full speed, especially one who didn't have any weapons drawn, which is why she was able to drop into a roll at the last instant, come up inside the closest guard's defenses, and grab onto his neck before he'd even called his kisō properly. She didn't have time to draw so much of it that he'd lose consciousness. In fact, she wasn't certain she could drain a raiko that far even if she had all day. She'd never fought a raiko before—she'd never thought they existed outside of children's stories until a few moments ago—so what did she know? She knew that she didn't have time to find out, because she could already feel the gathering energy of the raiko on the far side of the door.

She turned, pulling the guard she held with her, using him as a shield against the woman whose hands were glowing with a power that Torako had no interest in experiencing firsthand. Of course, there was only one way to be certain she wouldn't.

She issued a silent apology to the guard whose neck she had grabbed, who was probably thoroughly confused as to why his kisō wasn't responding to his call and was about to feel quite a bit worse than mere confusion. Still, maybe as a fellow raiko he wouldn't feel it.

She slammed the man into the woman who was preparing to shoot lighting at Torako's chest, and then rammed them both into the far wall that formed the end of the hallway. It hurt. She'd needed enough momentum to drive all three of them hard into the wall, and the impact shuddered through her even with two other bodies to take the worst of the blow, but it had the desired effect. It stunned both the guards, knocked them about enough to disorient them, and allowed her to grab the bare skin of the second guard as well.

When she stepped back, they both moved as if to attack her with their stormcalling, but only blinked in confusion when it didn't work.

Two soft thuds marked Kitsu's arrival, as darts hit their shoulders.

"Nice shot," she whispered, as he arrived beside her and the two raiko fell to the power of his sleeping draught.

"You lined them up so nicely for me," he said, eyes glinting in the bright light issuing from the wall sconces. Torako pretended not to notice that they were glowing again.

"Do you need a moment?" Kitsu asked.

"A moment?" she repeated dully.

"To… you know."

She stared at him for a heartbeat before realizing that no nausea gripped her stomach.

"No. Which is odd. Two kisōshi that powerful should have me painting the floors."

She couldn't hear Kitsu's reply, however, because she was suddenly overwhelmed with a rage that didn't feel like hers and a fierce growling filled her mind.

"Tora-chan?"

She could barely hear Kitsu's voice right beside her, but the voice in her mind was a clamor of rage and snarling.

Sairō? she asked. But the howling rage that filled her didn't take on the form of words.

"Torako-san, we need to move."

She nodded, and Kitsu gestured towards the paper door in front of her.

She was suddenly consumed with a desperate need for violence, for vengeance.

Without thinking, she was pulling her wakizashi and Sairō's blade. She only barely restrained herself from turning them both on Kitsu. She had only the barest idea what had come over her, but she knew that letting it idle next to Kitsu could be a lethal mistake. So she did the only thing that made sense under the circumstances—she dove through the silk screen door and rolled into the room where they were holding Raku, looking for a fight.

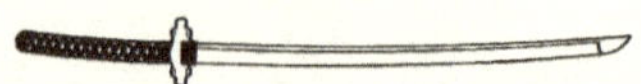

Torako was glad that she'd chosen to dive and then roll through the flimsy material of the silk and wood sliding door, even if she was going to regret the bruises that tormented her if she lived long enough to feel them the next day. She felt the crackling energy of a lightning bolt fly over her head and back before she stood up and threw herself sideways to avoid yet another bolt of searing energy headed for her. Clearly, a straightforward entrance would have made this a very short fight. She could hear Kitsu charging along behind her and had to hope he was somehow prepared for lightning.

Of course, she could barely think with all the rage and incoherent howling that was going on in her mind. Luckily, thinking had never been an integral part of her fighting style. Her body moved with the ease and grace of decades of training and experience, and she had already dispatched two of the nearest raiko without even a pang of regret when a cold voice stopped her in her tracks.

"Drop your swords, or I cut her throat," said the woman in the center of the room, the woman who was now holding a dagger to Raku's throat. Torako's vision narrowed to where the blade met Raku's skin.

The howling anger only got louder in her mind, and it wouldn't let her drop her swords, though she was finally getting some coherent words in there as well. She tried to shake the voice away, even as she kept her blade pressed to the throat of the third raiko, who she had been on the point of dispatching before this woman had placed a knife against Torako's heart.

"Let her go and I might not kill you," Torako whispered, unsure if she was growling under the words, or if that was merely Sairō continuing their rampage in her mind.

Summon me!

Torako shook her head again, trying to think around the rage, the howling, and the blade at Raku's throat.

"You can't kill me before I kill her. Lay down your blades, and we might all still walk away from this."

Summon me! Torako-san, you must—

Torako blinked. Kitsu was utterly still beside her and she thought the rest of the room was too, but her mind was spinning with Sairō's ire. She was fairly certain that her own rage was just as loud inside her; she couldn't think straight, she couldn't decide, she wanted to kill everyone in this room who might harm Raku, and she really desperately needed everyone to "JUST SHUT UP!"

She closed her eyes as she yelled the words, hoping she could use the brief darkness to summon the wolf to her side, and that must have worked, because suddenly her head was much quieter. In the same instant, she felt a blade hit her shoulder and heard a soft thud beside her as if someone had collapsed. Her eyes shot open and the knife was no longer at Raku's throat, but there was something painful in her shoulder.

She looked down at the blade. It was small and had lodged into the muscle of her shoulder. She would have to worry about it later. She felt Sairō coil in anticipation, to her right. She had to assume there was some kind of drug on the blade, as a similar one had rendered Kitsu unconscious immediately—that was the thud she'd heard—but she didn't have time to worry about that now, either, because the woman who'd been threatening Raku was the one who had thrown the knives, which meant that Raku no longer had a blade at her throat, and Torako could already tell that Raku was going to do something rash. She had that spark in her eye that always came before she did something most people would consider unhinged. So Torako pushed the blade of her katana into the throat of the raiko she'd been about to kill earlier, feeling more remorse than she had when Sairō had been filling her mind with their own brand of vengeance. Considering the throat Sairō ripped from the next closest guard, Torako thought that they were well past trying to protect the people who had stolen Raku away.

Torako heard a grunt from where Raku had stood and turned to be sure that it was the right person going down. Indeed, Raku had the other woman's wrist in what looked like a very painful lock, and Torako was already charging to where the raiko behind her were clearly deliberating whether they could get a clear shot at Raku without hitting their own people.

Sairō snarled behind her, then rushed past before she could finish closing the gap on the other raiko. She almost wanted to laugh. They were winning! They were actually winning, and for the first time since she'd come home to a ransacked cave and Itachi hiding in the crook of a tree, Torako started to believe that she and Raku and Itachi might all get to go home again. To be together as a family and live out their lives with little more than bandits to trouble them.

And then that dream faded to black with everything else, as her ears popped and eyes went black, and the world disappeared.

⟞ *Raku* ⟝

RAKU REGAINED CONSCIOUSNESS, surprised to find that she had a consciousness to return to. She had just managed to restrain the captain of the Wind Serpent, hoping to give Torako enough time to cut through the remaining guards, when a dozen or more raiko had swept into the room surrounding a man that looked vaguely familiar. When her vision had dimmed and she'd lost consciousness, she'd assumed that was the end of everything. Now she blinked in the bright light of wall sconces identical to the ones that had filled the last room she'd woken in. Perhaps they were the same ones. This room was the same size, from what she could see.

She was disappointed to find her arms bound once more, after she'd so carefully managed to free them while the captain and her guards had been distracted by Torako's onslaught. They were tender now, from the places she'd worked them loose, and whoever had tied her the second time hadn't given much consideration to her wounds.

She was facing the center of the room this time, lying on her shoulder with her back pressed against a wall, and she could tell that there were others lying near her head and feet, but she didn't have the range of motion to see who it was. She hoped it was Torako and Kitsu.

There was now a low table at the center of the room, with someone seated in front of it, and the remaining three walls were once more lined with guards, even more than had been present the first time Raku had awoken here.

Most disturbingly, there were no bodies littering the floor. She was wondering if perhaps this was a different room, after all, when the faint tang of blood met her nose and she saw that there were a few hastily washed stains on the floor.

"We didn't have enough time to clean properly," said a low voice. "When raiko use a pressure drop to knock everyone unconscious, you can never be certain how long they'll remain that way, and we're rather… shorthanded at the moment. I hope you'll forgive the mess."

Raku's eyes met those of the man seated at the low table and she tried to maneuver herself into a sitting position so that her gaze would be level with his, despite how much it hurt her bound wrists to do so.

"If you think the blood of a few guards' lives is no more than a mess to clean up, I'm not sure it's my forgiveness you need," Raku replied, as she finally managed to push herself to her knees.

"Ah. I did not say that *I* considered it nothing more than a mess, but I'm rather surprised to hear that you consider it anything more than that. Then again, it wasn't you who cut down five of my best raiko, was it?"

Raku wanted to scream at the man that he didn't hold the moral high ground. Torako had been desperate to save both their lives from whatever stupid plan he'd made requiring her abduction. But instead, she forced herself to take a breath and answer with as much calm as she could inject into her voice. It was difficult. She was already repressing all the emotions that had started to overwhelm her the moment she'd seen Torako alive and charging into the room to save her.

"No. But it also wasn't me who stole a scribe from her family just because I couldn't be bothered to arrange a formal meeting, Saito-san."

She'd just remembered why the man looked familiar. He was one of the New Council's merchant advisers. She'd never met the man before, but she'd seen him on the periphery of a few meetings that Tsuku-san had asked her to attend; never anything more than his profile or the back of his head, probably not even enough for her to make a connection to the man sitting here if the young Captain of the Wind Serpent hadn't introduced herself as a Saito, and reminded Raku of that family and their rather large fleet of ships.

If Raku were a normal historian, she *still* might not have made the connection to his name or his work with the Council, but she'd been a spy for too many cycles to start forgetting faces, or even profiles, and the ranks that went with them.

The man didn't quite raise his eyebrows or widen his eyes. In fact, he barely reacted at all, but he had the look of someone who had spent decades schooling his features to keep every reaction hidden, and the slight pause before he smiled told Raku that he hadn't expected her to know who he was.

"But let's not dither about the ethical implications of you sacrificing so many of your people to speak with me when you could have just asked Tsuku-san for an introduction. Let's talk about why the leader of Gensokai's largest merchant fleet wants me dead." Raku intentionally timed her jibe to cut the man off before he could reply to her first accusation, and watching him stifle a series of more aggravated emotions was very telling indeed.

"You aren't what I expected," the man said, after a moment.

"Sorry to disappoint you. If I'd been given my part in advance I could have studied the role better. Were you hoping for a frightened young innocent, or a scribe with interests so narrow she would have no idea what to do when faced with..." Raku glanced around the room and out the window towards the harbor and port city that were now lit by lampposts and shop lanterns, "whatever this is?"

The older man chuckled.

Raku's eyes had finally adjusted to the lights in the room, and the man had turned so that his face was illuminated in full for the first time since she'd awoken. A few details jumped out at her immediately: one was that his hair was greying at the temples, another was that he seemed to have made tea—all the accoutrement for a proper tea ceremony were laid out on the low table—and the third and final thing was that she realized the man looked far more familiar than a passing glance in a New Council meeting could account for, and her heart jumped into her throat when she suddenly understood *why.*

"I didn't say I was disappointed, I said you weren't what I expected. I'll admit I rather supposed you would be something like a frightened historian. Though I really should have known better. I believe, based on the account my daughter has given me, that I should not have spent quite so much time worrying about your protector, while failing to worry about you."

Raku ignored the implied compliment, and instead regretted that these people now saw her as a threat. She had spent cycles cultivating a persona that exuded competence at precisely one thing, and one thing only. It wasn't entirely an act—she was a historian and scribe, she *did* get absorbed in her work, and she enjoyed fashion and jewelry and very fine calligraphy brushes. All of those things did a great deal to hide the fact that she was also able to gut a man with his own knife if she was cornered.

"Oh you really should be more worried about Torako-san," Raku said. "She's got quite a temper on her. Then again, maybe you're already familiar with that."

Raku stared fixedly at the man sitting at the low table, determined not to look to either side, unwilling to draw attention to the faint movement she could hear beside her.

"I'm certainly impressed with her ability to take on a half-dozen raiko single—"

"No, I mean it must be familiar because I imagine it runs in your family," she replied. She wasn't certain if it was Torako or Kitsu, or even that giant wolf, that had started to stir beside her, but she was determined to keep the attention of Saito and all his guards on herself.

"I'm afraid I don't know what you mean," he said.

Raku wasn't entirely certain what she meant either, because she had never known who Torako's family was, beyond Tenshi. Even when Tenshi had told her about Torako's grandfather, she didn't mention a word about anyone else. But Raku had already been shocked to find that Kaiyo Saito shared all-too-many features with her wife, and she could see the same family resemblance here, in this man who seemed of an age with Tenshi-san, and who shared the same hazel eyes as Torako. She needed a distraction, and she figured this would do as well as any other.

"I mean that you shouldn't be surprised to find that your own daughter shares your temper. Or that of her sister."

The look on the man's face was more stubborn confusion than surprise, and Raku was sure he was about to object on perfectly reasonable grounds, but just then Torako sat up and said, "My what?!"

⚎ *Torako* ⚎

TORAKO HAD BEEN working quietly on removing her wrist binding while Raku distracted everyone in the room with her own brand of a full-speed charge. She'd assumed, from the moment she'd regained consciousness and been flooded with relief at the sound of Raku's voice berating someone for getting their own people killed, that her wife was planning to talk circles around everyone while Torako freed herself well enough to start slitting throats. Faint noises on Raku's other side made her hopeful that she wasn't the only one awake and focusing on escape.

Her efforts came to a rather abrupt halt, however, when her ears finally processed the last thing Raku had said.

"My what!?" she found herself shouting, even though she was only halfway free of her wrist restraints. They had decided to tie her arms behind her, probably to keep her from being able to strangle anyone with the restraints, but they'd also put her back against the wall. It had been easy enough to feign sleep while she started working the loops over her hands. Anyone who tied a person's hands behind them but didn't want to dislocate their shoulders while they did it had a tendency to leave a bit too much slack in the rope. Especially for someone who regularly practiced untying her wrists to entertain a three-cycle-old child.

But now she was sitting up on her knees, anger and surprise having moved her without conscious thought, and while she cursed the very temper that her wife had just mentioned for making her draw attention she didn't want, at least her wrists were still behind her.

She looked carefully at the man in question, sure that Raku had simply been trying to goad him, and disappointed that she'd allowed it to goad *her* instead, but found her jaw dropping as she looked at the man's features.

"What is this?" she asked, as if she expected someone to jump from behind a screen and explain that all of this was some elaborate joke.

"Tenshi-san?" the older man asked, at almost the same time.

That made Torako's blood run cold.

"What did you do to her?" she asked, her voice coming out more snarl than words. "Why did you kill her?"

"Kill her? I would never—who *are* you?"

"Tenshi-san's daughter, and your death if you don't answer me. What did you *do*?"

"I didn't do anything. I haven't seen her in decades. She… we…." The man's voice broke, and she could tell even from where she sat that he was overcome with emotion.

"Father?" asked a rough voice from the other side of the room.

The woman who spoke was just lifting herself from the floor, as though she too had been rendered unconscious, though her wrists and ankles were unbound. Torako realized from the clothes she wore and the daggers sheathed on her belt that she must have been the woman who'd been holding a knife to Raku's throat earlier, but the rage that swelled up at the memory was quickly twisted into something else as she finally took a good look at her face. A face that was disquietingly familiar, though she'd never seen it before Raku's abduction.

"What is going on here?" she asked, her own voice weak.

It was Raku who spoke next, and Torako thought that might have been the only reason she didn't charge the enemy—for all that they looked eerily familiar—bound hands be damned, simply to stop her mind from spinning.

"Tora-chan, I can't be certain, but… I think we may be talking to your father."

Raku paused for a moment after saying that, as though waiting for someone to argue with her, but no one did. When her eyes turned and caught Torako's she continued, probably sensing that if she didn't keep talking Torako might do something rash.

"I didn't notice it until today. Kaiyo-san led the attack against me, but I never had a chance to see her face in full light for more than a heartbeat or two until this evening. I suspected something was odd when I noticed how many features you two shared. But it wasn't until I saw Saito Kuzuri-san's face just now that it all made sense. I could have believed that Kaiyo-san was a more distant relative, perhaps a cousin, but, considering that the first name that came to Saito-san's lips when he saw you was your mother's, I can only imagine the connection is more direct."

Torako wasn't certain what to say to any of this. It seemed preposterous. The idea that this man, who had taken Raku away and tried to have her killed, even indirectly, might also be her father was… "beyond absurd," she heard herself mumble.

The woman who Raku had called Kaiyo now sat down at the low table on the opposite side from her father.

"Father?" she asked again. Torako thought her face seemed paler than it had earlier, and wondered if that was because she'd taken a wound somewhere, or if it was because she was learning some horrifying truths of her own.

Saito-san didn't answer her for a long moment. He was staring directly at Torako, with eyes as wide as someone who'd seen a long-departed spirit.

So the other woman slammed the table with her hands.

"Did you truly send me after my own sister-in-law, with orders to kill anyone who tried to stop me?" she snarled.

Torako almost wanted to laugh. It was rather like listening to herself when she was angry.

"I didn't know," the man gasped, as if he could barely breathe. "I didn't know."

His eyes snapped back to Torako.

"Tenshi-san and I, we were… I loved her. You must understand that. I loved her more than I had ever expected to love another person, and then…"

He glanced at Kaiyo, and Torako followed his eyes, then wondered if she wasn't the only one shattering under this revelation.

"My parents learned of the affair and had me married off. They didn't even give me a day to say goodbye, nothing, they simply told me I would marry, practically dragged me to the shrine, and then shipped me off to the Kaigun the same day. I was gone for two cycles."

He swallowed, and Torako almost felt pity for him. His eyes were no longer looking at her or his daughter, they were unfocused and distant. His voice sounded hollow when next he spoke.

"I tried to find her when they finally let me return home two cycles later, but she had disappeared. No one could tell me anything about her. Hardly anyone remembered her, and those that did had no idea where she'd gone. No one told me she was with child. I would have…. No. That's a lie. I couldn't find her, so I wouldn't have done anything even if I'd known, but if I had been able to find her, I would have done what I could for her, and for you. I would never have abandoned you."

Torako didn't know what to say. She had no interest in comforting the man, but she had also never wanted for a father. She'd had Kuma-sensei when she was young. She had Yanagi-sama now. She'd had enough paternal care in her life.

No, the rage that she felt boiling in her chest wasn't for herself—at least not entirely—it was for Tenshi. For her mother. Who'd had a great friend in Kuma-sensei, but who had never had a long-term lover again, at least not that Torako had ever known of.

"And *our* mother?" Kaiyo asked with a ragged voice.

"You've always known that your mother and I had an arranged marriage. I've never broken faith with her. I told her everything the night we were forced to marry. She had as little choice in it as I did, but we both did our duty to our families."

"And now?" Kaiyo asked.

Torako felt like she was intruding on someone else's private conversation as she watched the cold expression of her half-sister boring into Saito's.

"You know that I respect her. I even love her in some ways. But she's never replaced Tenshi-san."

Kaiyo's deepening frown suggested she didn't like where this was going.

"Before you decide to avenge your mother's honor, Kaiyo-chan, you should remember that she's not some wilting flower that I could easily discard. She had her own part in all of this, and she's never been a victim."

Kaiyo snorted and rolled her eyes.

Which Torako took to mean that the man had a point.

"So which of us *does* get to stab you, then?" she asked.

It was Kaiyo who turned to her and answered, "Well, it's your wife he abducted, so I believe you get first blood."

"Yes, but it seems he's been keeping secrets from you your entire life, so I'm willing to let you throw one of those little ones at him first if you like."

"Why did you ask what I'd done with your mother, child?"

Torako's gaze quickly shifted away from her apparent half-sister and fixed instead on Saito.

"Because she's *dead* and you're the only person I know who has been trying to take my family from me lately," she replied, coldly.

"Dead? How? What happened?"

"I would ask you the same thing, since the moon Kami who told me she was gone is the same one that you sent to kill me yesterday."

"What?"

"Tsukuyomi-sama? Tall, thin, made out of moonlight? Rather hard to miss."

That had Saito's mouth snapping shut so quickly that Torako noticed Raku and Kaiyo both turning to glare at him with her.

"I am familiar with the moon Kami of which you speak, but I did *not* send him to kill you," Saito said carefully.

Kaiyo snorted again, and Torako noticed that she now flipped a small red hanko between her knuckles while she spoke.

"He sent himself," she said, when everyone looked at her. "Showed up on my ship just long to tell me he would take care of my problem and then suddenly two sea serpents were fighting and one of them smashed through the Trickster."

"The Trickster?" Saito said.

"The smuggler's ship," Kaiyo replied.

Torako was about to ask why Kitsu wasn't awake yet when there was a rough rapping at the door. Kaiyo pulled one of her much longer daggers and went to stand before the doorway before saying, "Enter."

Torako's eyes locked on the door, some part of her mind telling her to pay close attention to what was on the other side, and she barely registered that instead of a sliding door there was now a hastily attached curtain as the only separation between the room and the hallway. Her memory of diving through the silk screen shoji that had been there earlier seemed like a lifetime ago. She ignored that thought, kept her breathing even, and focused on the curtain being pulled away. The man standing on the other side looked vaguely familiar—probably another of the bandits she'd chased through Sakata—but she recognized what he held in his arms all too well.

She jumped to her feet and charged halfway across the room, even with her ankles and wrists bound, even through the searing pain of the ropes straining against her muscles and tendons, before she noticed that Raku was right beside her, equally hobbled and equally uncaring, and Kitsu and Sairō were both beside her as well. They had risen together like a vengeful tide, and if they hadn't all been more than half restrained, Torako was certain the man before her would have been dead before even the raiko lining the walls could have rendered them unconscious again. Because in his arms was the small, too-still form of Itachi.

The only things that saved the man holding Itachi were the restraints that slowed all four of them, and a quick brush of fingers from the exceedingly tall individual to the man's right who ran a gentle hand along Itachi's sleeping cheek, which somehow caused the small girl to wake instantly, turn to Torako, and smile.

That smile stopped Torako in her tracks, and must have done the same for Raku, Kitsu, and Sairō, for their wave of vengeance crashed abruptly to a halt.

"Mama," Itachi said, her face full of wonder and relief, then tears as she turned and saw Raku. "Kaa-san!"

The man holding her set her gently on the ground, and she instantly ran to Raku's arms, bound though they were. Torako hopped over to them—thankfully it wasn't far—and sank down beside them. Her arms were still tied behind her, so she simply leaned against them.

She turned to glare at the approach of the man who'd held Itachi, but he raised his empty hands and then nodded towards her wrists.

"May I cut your bonds, Night Stalker?" he asked.

Torako wanted to laugh at the deference in his tone and the name he chose to label her with. The fact that the bandits who had taken Raku from her home had known enough of the local lore to realize that she was the legendary scourge to any who would harm Sōryū valley seemed strangely comical to her. She nodded, instead, then turned back to the only things that mattered.

⚬ *Raku* ⚬

RAKU HAD LIFTED her bound wrists, with no thought to the pain that went shooting through her arms, and managed to encircle Itachi's small sobbing form as the girl threw her arms around her neck. When Torako settled against them, leaning on Raku for support and somehow managing to cuddle Itachi with the gesture, Raku felt something settle in place inside her, as if some broken piece of her was returning to its proper spot, like a ceramic bowl that had shattered but had been puzzled back together—still fragile, and in need of some cementing, but once again the proper shape and ready to be made whole. It was a silly thought, but she let it flow over her along with the wash of emotions that came with her family being restored to her.

"Kaa-san, we were so worried," Itachi chirped between sobs.

Raku's own tears flowed freely and she wasn't certain she could make her voice respond, but she swallowed and managed to croak, "I knew you would find me."

And even though she'd known no such thing, even that morning, some part of her believed it. She'd never relied on Torako to rescue her, but they'd taken turns rescuing each other over the cycles since they'd first found each other, and now Itachi was part of that and she knew that she trusted them both to find her, even if they didn't have to.

Torako let out a small gasp and Raku's eyes flashed to her wife's, but Torako's face was too full of emotions for Raku to discern what had caused the gasp until Torako's arms, which must have been freed by Tanaka, wrapped around both her and Itachi and pulled them close. She felt Torako's kisses in her hair and she leaned desperately into that embrace, drunk with the feel of it after having been so certain it was lost forever only the day be-fore. She felt a gentle tug at her own wrists and was surprised to feel the cool touch water kisō flowing over her, mending the abraded skin and soothing the small aches that filled her wrists and arms.

Then she was distracted from that sensation entirely as a very large, very wet wolf nose inserted itself between her cheek and Itachi's, a warm tongue catching part of her chin as it worked its way in to lick away her daughter's tears.

Raku couldn't do anything but laugh at the sensation. She had no idea where the giant wolf had come from, what it was doing here, or what its intentions might be, but any creature that charged forward, with its legs still bound, growling at the man who held her unconscious daughter, and then made her daughter giggle with joy as its tongue removed her tears, was welcome to lick anyone in her family.

She turned her head then, and saw Kitsu, arms and ankles now free, rubbing the places where he'd been bound and staring at their little reunion with something like longing. Raku felt a smile come to her lips unbidden, and she glanced at Torako, who was still holding her and Itachi so tight that she had no notion of the look her old lover was giving them. Raku caught his gaze and tilted her head towards their awkward pile-on.

"You'd better get in here," she said, making an educated guess or two about the past few days. "Anyone who sacrifices their ship in an attempt to rescue me counts as family."

Kitsu's eyes widened briefly, but then a small smile crossed his lips and he knelt beside Torako, behind Itachi, and wrapped his arms around the three of them, though she noticed he was care-ful not to touch the giant wolf.

She leaned into the additional embrace, feeling particularly grateful for a wolf she'd never met and a man who still held some part of her wife's heart, knowing that whatever else might motivate them, they had loved Torako enough to help her, to come after Raku, and to protect Itachi.

Eventually, the uneven breathing of Saito Kuzuri caught her attention and she looked up from the strange family huddle she found herself in and locked her gaze on the older man's.

"I am sorry for everything I've put you through," he said, his voice rough. "But I'm afraid that I cannot pretend I would not do it again. You have uncovered some very dangerous truths about our past, and I cannot let you share them with the Council."

His gaze was haunted, and Raku heaved a sigh that broke apart their small huddle, Kitsu and Torako taking up positions on either side of her and the enormous wolf lying down between her family and everyone else in that room, a statement as well as a threat, Raku thought. Only Itachi remained in her embrace, though even she turned to face the room, her small form nestled tightly between Raku's arms.

"The entire history of Gensokai is but one dangerous truth after another, Saito-san," she said. "Why should this truth be any different than the others that have come to light?"

She cast her mind back to the text she'd been transcribing a few days before she'd been abducted. She had some notion of why the man who controlled more than half of Gensokai's shipping might be concerned with what she had learned, but she couldn't imagine how he could think it a problem worth killing over.

"Because the truths that have been uncovered until now have only helped to bring peace and prosperity to Gensokai, but the one that you are close to revealing will bring nothing but death, destruction, and war."

Raku raised an eyebrow at that claim.

"If what I've read is true, then there was a time when that knowledge did no such thing."

She'd finally realized, when she got through all of the scrolls she'd reclaimed from the depths of the restricted library, that she had been reading the outline of a very large trade agreement. An unlikely product of endless war.

"You say that only because you do not know the full extent of your ignorance."

"Then why don't you enlighten me," she said, her eyes hardening.

When Saito hesitated, she filled in the silence for him.

"You already planned to kill me for knowing too much. Now you realize you would have to kill your own daughter and granddaughter as well, and you're reluctant. But if what you say is true, then the situation remains the same. Either you can convince me not to share this knowledge with the New Council, or you'll be forced to try to kill us all."

"Try?" Saito asked, his voice incredulous as he glanced at the dozen raiko still positioned all around the room.

Raku smirked, exuding far more confidence than she felt.

"Yes, *try*. You've lost your biggest advantage, which was keeping all of us separated and a knife at my throat. Now that we're together, you'll have a hard time indeed, raiko or no. At the very least, we'll kill both you and your daughter before they can drop the pressure on us again, and then where will your empire be?"

Everything about Kaiyo's bearing told Raku that she was Saito's heir.

"Empire?" Saito huffed. "Is that what you think of me? You think I would send a dozen of my own people to die in an attempt to kidnap a scribe simply to ensure that I don't have to share trade with foreign vessels?"

Raku kept her gaze level.

"Men have done worse things for less."

Saito growled something but she couldn't make out the words. Raku was not terribly surprised to hear Kaiyo answer her.

"The Kaigun has been charged with keeping Gensokai safe from all foreign interference for the past oh... nine centuries now? Maybe more."

"So the Rōjū installed your predecessors, then," Torako spat. "Always a good sign."

Raku was surprised that Torako was taking the news of the Kaigun with such equanimity, but perhaps she didn't truly comprehend what Saito was saying. Raku wasn't certain she understood it herself.

"Yours sounds like an impossible task," she admitted. "If the scrolls I uncovered were accurate, there were dozens of other nations that were once our trade partners. You would have to have thousands of ships to keep them all away from us."

And now Kaiyo's chin rose and her eyes flashed with something like pride as she answered, "Over 5,000 ships, actually, over 200,000 crew, and double that on shore to support it all, working from a network of floating islands we've constructed over the centuries as well as all of the most remote islands actually under Gensokan control, and every raiko to ever be captured on the mainland."

"Impossible," Raku gasped. "How could you possibly support that many?"

"We've got a fairly constant influx of goods from the vessels that we capture, but we also take their crews whenever we can, so those supplies don't last long, and we can't always take the ships with little enough damage to keep their freight anyway. Still, this island and ten more like it supply most of our food, with supplements from the mainland whenever they've had a particularly good cycle."

Raku felt her mouth dropping open. That was… it was impossible, or it should have been. But was it really any *more* impossible than the existence of dozens of other nations that they'd never heard of thanks to the patrols of this naval force?

"How have you remained in secret for this long?" she asked, unable to fathom the conspiracy it would take to keep them hidden.

"My family claims to be the foremost shipping merchants in all Gensokai. We allow very few vessels to travel to the mainland, but those we do are always well disguised as merchant vessels. Honestly, even most of our outer patrols look like merchant vessels to the untrained eye—our people are very disciplined, but our uniforms are not anything like what most people would expect of a military force, not at sea anyway."

Raku frowned.

"Why?"

"The uniforms would stand out too much if we—"

"No, why exist at all? You claim to protect us, but the scrolls I read spoke of trade agreements with the people of dozens of nations. Clearly, peace was possible once, why do you claim that you protect us from war?"

"Because the world is not what it once was, and we have been a well-guarded secret for far too long. The other nations that seek us out now do not wish to do so for our own best interests. They wish to take what we have for themselves, or else they wish to punish us for the ships and people we've taken from them over the centuries. They cannot find us reliably, because we do not let any ship that enters our waters leave them, but if they could put us on a map, they would send their armies after us quickly enough."

"And surely, with a navy of 5,000 ships we must be able to deter them," Torako said, while Raku asked, "Did we burn all their maps before you started your task, then?"

It was Saito who answered that question.

"The short answer? Yes. We did. Early on, when we were first establishing ourselves, the Rōjū sent 'diplomatic' envoys to every nation we could gain entry to and many that we could not, and destroyed every shred of paper that could be found in reference to our location."

That dropped a few jaws around the room.

"But of course, they couldn't have gotten everything, including the memories of those who had been here, so the rest was down to us." Saito sounded as though this were a common history lesson and not the revelation of an enormous conspiracy against the people of Gensokai.

"And now you keep our people trapped in ignorance?" Raku asked before she could think better of it. "You've worked with the Rōjū for centuries, you yourself must have worked with them in your lifetime—they've only been gone for seven cycles—and you've just gone along with their wishes, keeping all of us apart from the rest of the world? A world that might have… oh I don't know, objected to the subjugation and murder of half our population of Kisōshi?"

Saito winced at this accusation, but Kaiyo raised her chin and leveled eyes bright with anger at Raku.

"You cannot know what we have done to help undo the worst of what the Rōjū ordered. We've been undermining them for cycles, and right under their noses! Did you not see my crew? Did you not count the number of women? More than half my crew are women, including my raiko. While you Landers let your people sacrifice girls to the Rōjū's power, we've kept our people safe. Stormcallers are free to live out their lives in peace with us, Kisōshi come from every level of society and aren't stolen away from their parents. We treat our women with the same respect we treat our men, and we don't lock people away for the crime of being poor, hungry, or desperate."

Raku felt her own anger flaring in response to Kaiyo's, but it was Torako who responded before her.

"And yet, you left hundreds of thousands of us to that very fate while you commanded the greatest military force Gensokai has ever *known*. You could have turned that power against the Rōjū at any moment and saved us all any damned time in the past nine hundred cycles!"

Torako's voice shook with just as much anger as Raku felt welling up inside of her and she was pleased to hear her own thoughts echoed in her wife's words.

Saito sounded tired beyond mere physical exhaustion when he replied, "We could not," he sighed. "Not without risking war on all fronts."

When everyone else in the room simply stared at him, he continued.

"If we'd turned away enough of our forces to depose the Rōjū, we'd have invited any number of other nations to attack us while our backs were turned, and we don't have enough ships to wage war on the mainland and at sea. Besides, how many people, Kaigunka and rikuka alike, would have died if we had? Would you truly have advocated the mass slaughter of our own people simply to depose the Rōjū? And then who should have remained in charge, the Kaigun? I love our people, but nations run entirely by their militaries do not end well."

He swallowed and took a deep breath.

"We could not have saved Gensokai from the Rōjū single-handedly, no matter how many ships we have. What Ryūko-san and her sisters did for Gensokai was the least-bloody transfer of power we could have hoped for, and the New Council seems well inclined to make Gensokai a far more equitable place."

Silence filled the room as people considered this, and Raku wondered if the guards lining the walls knew all of this history already, or if they were gaining some extra insight into their own governance as well.

"Fine. Let's pretend I agree that you couldn't have helped to overthrow the Rōjū. But the idea that war is the only option if we inform the Council of the truth of other nations is still absurd. Are you going to tell me that all of the world's nations are at war now? That there is no peace to be had, no allies to be found?"

Saito and Kaiyo exchanged a glance that Raku could not interpret.

"There aren't any major wars happening at the moment," Saito said.

"That we've heard of, anyway," muttered Kaiyo.

"But I can guarantee you that most of the nations that have lost ships to us would take our attempt to rejoin the world very poorly."

"How can you know that, if you've never allowed them to speak with us?" Raku asked, bewildered.

"Because they make up half of our fighting force. We live with them, they are our families, friends, and crewmates."

"Then surely you ought to trust them?" Raku asked, confused.

"We do," Kaiyo said.

"And so we believe them when they tell us that most of their nations have already signed a declaration of war against Gensokai," Saito added, his voice dark.

⚞ Kaiyo ⚟

KAIYO STARED AT the dumbfounded expressions of the people gathered around the room as her father revealed the truths about international waters that all of her people grew up knowing. She was unsurprised to see that the man her father had named as the captain of the Trickster did not look shocked by any of this. She had known he was a smuggler as soon as his ship had been named, but either his ability to control his expression was second to none, or else he was already aware of most of what they were discussing. Which made her wonder where exactly he smuggled things from.

Of course, the enormous wolf's expression was also very composed, but she would have been rather more surprised if it hadn't been. Did the creature even understand what they were discussing? Or was it simply there to bite the heads off of anyone its human companions disagreed with?

She did her best to keep her own face composed. It had been hard enough to keep the contempt out of her voice when the scribe had suggested that the Kaigun had a responsibility to protect the Landers from their damnable Rōjū. As if they hadn't brought that fate upon themselves by allowing the ruling body into power after the fall of the Yūwaku.

Her father was explaining the joint declaration still, and Kaiyo was struggling to keep her focus on a subject that she had studied thoroughly as a child, despite the fact that her fingers were already tipping her hanko idly between her knuckles while she listened.

Which was perhaps why she found her gaze focused on the warrior who still knelt beside the scribe, fingers clenching and unclenching into fists, as she listened to the explanation of just how many nations considered themself at war with Gensokai.

The woman *did* look a bit like Kaiyo's father, now that she had time to consider it. Something about the line of her jaw, the shape of her forehead, and definitely the color of her eyes. Kaiyo felt an itch of irritation at the thought that those features might make the warrior her sister. Half-sister only, but still. She did not like the idea of being related to any of these people. Partly because it made her feel a guilt she shouldn't have to bear, because she'd been sent after the scribe, and partially because she didn't like thinking that her father had an entire family she'd never known about. Not that he'd known about it either.

Kaiyo frowned.

At least her sister was a deadly warrior, that was something Kaiyo could respect, even when it was a talent found in a rikuka.

A rap on the doorway brought her quickly back to the present.

"Admiral," a familiar voice called from the hallway.

Her father glared at the doorway, where the curtain pulled back to show the same Sansa that had been trying to deliver a message when Raku had made her first escape attempt.

"I left orders not to be disturbed," Saito said, his voice brooking no argument.

The Sansa paled but did not retreat.

"I know Admiral, but the… there's a situation, and…" the Sansa shook her head, and then started again as though she couldn't quite remember what she was meant to say. "There's a situation in the detainment housing and you've been specifically requested by the prisoner."

Saito's eyes flared with barely concealed anger and she wondered if anyone could tell how close this Sansa was to being demoted.

"There is a problem in the detainment housing. And you need *me*?"

The Sansa swallowed, as if finally realizing that this was not the type of thing the Admiral was meant to deal with, but then she pressed on rather bravely.

"The prisoner is… she's taken so many hostages, Admiral, and the only word she seems to know in Gensokan is Admiral, and we… we didn't know what else to do."

Kaiyo was beginning to suspect that her father was losing his mind. To be equitable, she was wondering if she was losing her own. What else could explain the fact her father had agreed to interrupt his interrogation of the scribe who could potentially sink them all into war, only to drag them all, even down to the wolf and the child, across the compound to the detainment housing because one of the new recruits had started taking hostages and demanding to speak with whoever was in charge? And what else could explain that she'd come along?

She sighed and kept her eyes on the warrior, who was now armed with, of all things, the deep blue katana that she had pulled from the captain of the hundred-gunner. She supposed it only made sense that the woman would have taken the strange blade off of the men that Kaiyo had sent to kill her and whom she had slaughtered instead, but seeing the blade again made a spot between her shoulders itch, even though it no longer felt like a coming storm.

"Captain?" Lyt said beside her.

She almost startled. Lyt moved so quietly that even though Kaiyo had known xe was there, she'd half forgotten it until xe spoke.

"Isn't that Kentaro-san's blade?" xe asked, flicking xir gaze at the katana in the warrior's belt.

"No," Kaiyo said simply, but when Lyt raised an eyebrow at that, she continued, "Kentaro-san never owned that blade, he stole it. I've no idea who it belongs to properly, but it certainly never belonged to that thief."

Lyt's smile was wry.

"But you admit it's the same blade?" xe persisted.

Kaiyo only nodded.

"Interesting," xe whispered.

And then the enormous wolf that had been padding silently along next to the warrior stopped in their tracks and turned to face them.

"The blade is mine," the wolf said in a deep rumbling voice. Kaiyo's jaw dropped. Of all the things that had happened yet today, the wolf speaking in complete sentences was perhaps the thing her mind was least able to comprehend. She could feel Tanaka-san tense behind her. Even though he wasn't touching her, she felt his energy gathering, as if preparing a defense. "If you must ascribe it to some human, then you'd best think of it as Torako-san's. A fact I expect you to remember when we meet your latest *guest*."

Then the wolf pivoted and leapt down the hall to the warrior's side once more, where it calmly accepted an absentminded scratch behind the ears from the woman dressed in leathers with the small child wrapped to her back.

"Torako-san is her name, her wife is Raku-san, and the girl is Itachi-chan," Lyt said, quietly.

"What?" Kaiyo asked, her eyes suddenly snapping to Lyt's bright blue ones.

"You seem to think of them by *what* they are rather than who. They have names. They're people. Your family, in fact."

Then Lyt nodded curtly and moved to follow the wolf.

Kaiyo could barely understand what had just transpired.

"Did I *say* any of that aloud?" she asked Tanaka.

"Lyt-san is a person with many mysteries," Tanaka said.

Kaiyo glanced at him and was relieved to find at least half of a sardonic smile on his lips.

"They don't feel like family," she admitted, as she and Tanaka slowly moved to catch up with the group ahead.

"You've only just met them. Of course they don't feel like family."

He took a deep breath and let it out slowly.

"But Lyt-san might have a point that thinking of them as people would be the first step towards making them feel like anything other than your enemies."

Kaiyo's eyes widened and her lips pressed together.

"I don't—"

"Of course you do, Kaiyo-san, they *were* your enemies until very recently, and it's normal enough to distance yourself from people you're concerned you might have to kill, but… perhaps we shouldn't do that here. Those women are your sisters, that little girl is your niece. Do you have any other nieces?"

Tanaka's voice was tight with an emotion Kaiyo could not name, but she shook her head.

"None of my sisters have married yet. Though I suppose that now Mother has forced you to marry me, my sisters won't be far behind. The older ones, at any rate."

"I have a niece. You met her at the wedding. She was… pretending to be my little sister. My family are almost all here on the island. Your parents must have learned of my niece and… they asked her guardians to stand as my parents and for her to pretend to be my little sister."

Kaiyo shook her head. How had she not known any of this? Gods, she'd noticed that Tanaka's "parents" had seemed a little awkward at the wedding, but… how had she not asked him about his family?

"You were a bit overwhelmed, if I recall," he said, as if reading her mind.

"Don't you start now! It's bad enough that Lyt-san seems to know my every thought. Not you as well."

Tanaka smiled and offered her his hand. She glanced across the courtyard they were cutting through, the last before they would enter the detainment housing. Their motley crew was all ahead of them: wolves, children, warriors, scribes, and all. She took his hand and was surprised by how right it felt to make that simple contact.

Then Tanaka rubbed the back of her hand with his thumb and a thrill raced through her that reminded her of far less simple contacts.

"I can't read your mind Kaiyo-san," he said, even as they hurried forward to catch up with the others. "But I know you well enough to know what it looks like when you're feeling guilty."

Kaiyo sighed and found herself entranced by the small circle that Tanaka's thumb was tracing on her skin.

Then she took a good look at the door to the detainment housing and dropped Tanaka's hand, reaching for her knives instead.

"Your lack of mind-reading is going to have to wait," she said, starting forward at a run, Tanaka matching her stride for stride.

They were both sprinting by the time they reached the detainment housing, Kaiyo with her weapons drawn and Tanaka with a flicker of energy waiting to be released encircling him. The group they'd arrived with was already moving through the doors, which had been thrown open wide as what appeared to be a full-on battle raged in the entryway.

⇜ *Torako* ⇝

TORAKO TOOK IN the mass of people in the entrance hall to what Saito had called the detainment house, visible through the double sliding doors that had been opened wide sometime before their arrival, and wondered, for perhaps the hundredth time that day, what kind of battle the so-called "guards" stationed in these detention houses were actually trained for.

They were very clearly not trained for people who took their escapes seriously.

The tableau in front of her was so puzzling as to almost be humorous. There were two dozen unarmed people who looked nothing like anyone Torako had seen before—their hair and skin all dazzling shades that Torako had long associated with flowers and frogs—who now held a half-dozen guards hostage with the guards' own weapons. This was clear in a glance to Torako's bat-tle-trained eyes, which counted empty scabbards compared to unsheathed blades and came to the obvious conclusion without any conscious effort on her part. It was no surprise to her to see the guards at such a disadvantage, after her own experiences earlier that evening. The ones that had been protecting Raku had clearly known how to fight, and it was only the element of surprise and her ability to drain kisō that had allowed her to come as close to overcoming them as she had. The ones who had been guarding the detainment house… they had fought like raw recruits. And now half a dozen of them were being held hostage by two dozen prisoners, while another two dozen guards stood awkwardly just outside the entrance of the detainment house. Just beyond the knot of prisoners Torako could see that they'd blockaded the passage leading from the entrance hall to the residence itself with a hastily relocated collection of very large potted plants and long, padded benches. Four of the prisoners had their eyes and newly acquired weapons trained in the direction of the hall and stairs, the rest faced forward, pushed right up to the edge of the entrance from the courtyard, blades at the ready to end a hostage's life at the least provocation.

Torako felt her hand shift towards her sword hilt, grateful that Saito had ordered all of their weapons returned to them before they had set off, but she hesitated.

Don't, Sairō said silently. *Do you even know which side you would fight for?*

Torako's lips quirked up on one side, because they had a point. She had no reason to suspect that Saito's people were in the right here, and quite a bit of evidence to suggest they likely weren't, but still, the people who were taking hostages might be even more unsavory than Saito and his Kaigun. Besides, she had

Itachi wrapped to her back—the girl had fallen asleep almost as soon as they'd started walking—and she didn't feel like putting her down, or fighting with her so close to danger.

She sighed and dropped her hand to her hip instead.

The woman at the front of the prisoners, or newly escaped prisoners, she supposed, had fuchsia hair and skin the color of a warm shallow sea. Her eyes were a bright yellow that reminded Torako a bit of Kitsu's. And she must have been the one the messenger had been speaking of, because even now, with a guard pressed to her chest and a blade held to his neck she was saying the word "Admiral" over and over again.

"That would be me," Saito said, stepping forward, his own weapons still sheathed and his empty hands raised slightly to show that he was unarmed.

"Admiral?" the woman asked, her head tilted to one side.

"Yes. Sansa, where is the on-shift Linguist?" Saito asked over his shoulder, addressing the messenger who had led them all here.

"A runner went to get her a few minutes ago, but these prisoners haven't responded to questions in any language we've tried."

Saito frowned but turned back to the woman with the fiery hair and icy expression.

"Do you speak any other languages?" he asked, half-heartedly.

"Admiral, if I may?" said the tall guard that Torako had heard referred to as Lyt.

Saito raised an eyebrow, but Kaiyo interjected on the guard's behalf.

"Admiral, this is Lyt-san, xe has been very helpful since you released xir into my command at the start of the mission."

Torako had to forcibly keep her hand from going to her sword at the casual reminder of the "mission" Kaiyo referred to, which clearly had been the abduction of Raku.

"I believe I will be able to ease our communications substantially, Admiral, but I will need to approach the prisoners. With your permission?"

Saito frowned for a moment, looking to Kaiyo, who only gave a curt nod.

"Try not to get killed," he said, waving a hand towards the frozen tableau of guards and prisoners.

Lyt nodded and then walked forward, through the throng of uneasy guards, up the three wide low stairs that separated the courtyard from the entryway, and then stood directly in front of the woman with fuchsia hair and teal skin.

"Eredi," xe said, followed by a string of sounds that Torako had never heard before, but which were clearly part of a language as complicated and rich as Gensokan.

Torako was so entranced by the sound of another language being spoken in front of her that she almost didn't notice the slight widening of the fuchsia-haired woman's eyes as Lyt approached. She barely registered the open shock on the face of one of the other prisoners, who stood just behind the woman with fuchsia hair and held no hostage of their own.

But she could never have missed the way that Lyt knelt before the woman with the fuchsia hair and offered up xir wrist to her, or the way xe pulled a dagger from xir belt, cut into xir own vein, and allowed the woman to close her mouth around it, swallowing a mouthful of xir blood.

≈ *Raku* ≈

RAKU STARED IN fascination at the exchange between the guard named Lyt and the woman with the fuchsia hair, trying to keep her mouth closed. Another language! She'd never heard someone speak words that weren't Gensokan. She was almost as shocked by the lack of reaction from the guards and the Admiral when a language from another nation was spoken right in front of them as she had been by the offering of blood.

Everyone around her, however, had reacted a good deal more to the blood offering, which was also interesting. Raku had found it no more off-putting than seeing any other wound inflicted, but she'd watched enough wild animals eat their prey—hard to avoid when one lived in the wilderness and was friends with a talking tree that held court with all the animals in the valley—that she wasn't all that put off by someone swallowing blood. The same could not be said of all the Kaigunka around her.

Their reactions to that exchange, ranging from loud sounds of disgust to a drawing of weapons that Saito had to squelch with a shouted order and an emphatic glare, were almost as interesting as the exchange itself.

But a voice addressing them from the top of the stairs soon captured Raku's full attention again.

"Now then, that's better. Thank you, Lyt-san. I believe there's someone who'd like to speak with you."

That had all come from the woman with the fuchsia hair, who still held her hostage, albeit more loosely than she had a moment before, and who had shifted to the side so that Lyt could step past her and fall into the wide-open arms of the person standing behind her, a similarly tall, narrow-featured person with skin tones that were much closer to what Torako considered normal, but who sported very green hair. The two embraced so enthusiastically that Raku wanted to turn away to give them some privacy.

Instead, she refocused her gaze on the commanding presence of the woman with fuchsia hair, who was now speaking in perfect, unaccented Gensokan.

"I believe there has been some misunderstanding," she said, her eyes bright with confidence and conviction, the likes of which Raku rarely saw in anyone who wasn't selling something. "I'm Eredi Tak, Captain of the Idari Sail, and Ruler of the Idari. Now, you've sunk my ship and killed some of my people, which is generally considered an act of war. However, as we were on our way here to ask for your alliance against a much greater enemy, if you'd be so kind as to lend us your navy, we'd be willing to overlook the whole thing. Which of you wants to take me to this Council of yours and smooth the way? Oh, and who stole that damned sword we brought along? It was meant to be a gift to your people, ancient artifact that it is. I'd like it back."

Raku couldn't help it. It was simply too much for one single day, and… well, what else was she meant to do?

She laughed.

All eyes, including the unsettling yellow ones of the woman with fuchsia hair, turned to Raku, and most of them seemed to be wondering if she'd lost her mind. Perhaps she had. She glanced at Torako, who stood beside her with Itachi wrapped against her back and the enormous wolf beside her. Kitsu stood a few paces away, eyeing the whole scene with his head tilted to one side and half his mouth quirked into a smile.

"Sorry, it's just, apparently you'll have to get in line if you wish to declare war on us," Raku explained. She had just barely wrapped her mind around all that Saito had explained to them about the nations that would immediately declare against them if they made themselves visible to the outside world. It seemed ridiculous that the threat of one more would somehow tip them into an alliance with these strange newcomers.

"Idari," Saito murmured, just ahead of her, and Raku's ears perked up at the reverence with which he said the word. "I'd begun to think your people were a myth," he added, more loudly.

"We're no myth." The woman looked down at the hostage she held and then back at Saito. "Would you be willing to offer a truce while we speak? I believe your guards are rather uncomfortable, and I'd hate for someone to get injured because their legs gave out."

Saito bowed slightly and ordered his people to all stand down. As soon as their weapons were put away, the woman turned and spoke to her own people in their tongue and they all released their captives, though Raku noticed they kept the katanas they'd stolen. She couldn't really blame them for that.

"Admiral," Kaiyo said stepping forward. "Captain Eredi came into Gensokan waters eight days ago at the helm of a hundred-gun vessel. Once the inner patrol spotted her, we lured her ship into Kaigunjima's harbor, but she made her escape and the Wind Serpent pursued. Our raiko sank her between the inner and outer patrol rings, but then we did our best to pull her people from the water."

She stepped back, her report complete.

Saito glanced at her.

"And the sword?"

Kaiyo stepped forward again.

"The blade was registered properly, but before it could be stored, one of the doshigatai liberated for your mission took it from the registry. A few of the doshigatai fought over the blade, but eventually it was claimed by the Night Stalker when she defended herself from their attack."

"The Night Stalker?" Saito asked.

Kaiyo frowned, though Raku wasn't sure why. *She* was thoroughly enjoying hearing her wife described as the hero of legends.

"Torako-san, Admiral," Kaiyo explained, before stepping back once more.

"Torako-san," Saito said, and Raku wondered at how composed he seemed now compared to the man who had been sobbing into his tea and shakily explaining the history of the Kaigun before the messenger had come to retrieve him. "Do you still have the blade?"

Torako did *not* step forward. She barely moved at all, except to run a hand across Itachi's sleeping cheek.

"I do. But you'll pry it from my cold, dead fingers. The blade belongs to Sairō-san, and I won't pass it to anyone unless they ask me to."

Saito blinked for a moment.

"I believe I missed the pertinent introductions earlier. Who is Sairō-san?"

The wolf beside Torako growled, and then, to almost everyone's surprise, spoke.

"That would be me. And while the Idari took fine care of the blade in question for the centuries it stayed with them, it has now been returned to its rightful place."

They said nothing else and Eredi, the Idari captain, stared at the wolf for a moment before speaking again.

"Then all is as it should be on that front. I wonder, Sairō-sama, if you'd be so kind as to offer a word of recommendation to the New Council when I make my case?"

Sairō said nothing, but bowed their head slightly in what could easily be taken as assent.

"Thank you," Eredi continued. "Now, Raku-san," and Raku had to work very hard to hide her surprise that the woman somehow knew her name. She was fairly certain no one had named her since their arrival at this strange hostage situation, but then again, no one had taught this woman Gensokan either, and yet now she spoke it fluently. Perhaps whatever magic had conveyed the language had also conveyed other knowledge. The thought sent a shiver down her spine, but she listened to the woman speak regardless. "You made an excellent point about the sheer number of countries that wish to declare war against you. If they can find you, that is. But I believe we can help with that. We've been in trade with most of the known world for centuries now, but we still keep ourselves hidden from them. Our island nation is rather full of things that other people want, but which we cannot possibly provide enough of to share. At least, not the way they would like us to. So we've become very adept at hiding. However, we could use your particular skills at naval warfare, and we'd be willing to share something with you that no other nation can."

That had Raku's breath hitching, and she found it interesting indeed, that this woman she'd never met, who had been begging to speak with the Admiral until only a few moments ago, now seemed to be negotiating, with, of all people, Raku.

"And what, may I ask, is that?" Raku's own voice was far more even and controlled than she would have believed possible.

"Magic," the fuchsia-haired woman replied.

The silence that greeted that word matched the absolute lack of enthusiasm that Raku felt.

"Magic?" she asked, beginning to wonder if the woman really was some strange traveling salesperson after all.

"Specifically, healing magic," the woman replied.

Raku simply raised a single eyebrow at that.

"We have very competent healers in Gensokai," she said, doing her best to sound neutral, as if the suggestion that they needed healing magic when they had thousands of powerful yukisō throughout the land weren't a bit absurd.

"Ah yes, I don't mean to insult them, it's just that… well, no one quite has the same grasp of medicine that we do. Allow me to demonstrate."

Eredi turned briefly back to where Lyt and xir—friend, sibling, lover?—were standing. Raku had no notion of what the relationship between them might be, only that they were quite close.

The foreign captain said something in her own language.

"Please keep your weapons sheathed," Eredi said, as she turned back to Raku and the other Gensokans while the person behind her stepped forward and raised a single hand. "BriTak has volunteered and xe is well aware of what I'm about to do."

BriTak, the green-haired, brown-skinned person behind Eredi, stepped forward and nodded, though they looked faintly put out.

Eredi, for her part, raised the katana she was still holding and very carefully used it to cut one of BriTak's fingers from xir hand.

Everyone gasped, but Saito's outstretched hand kept them from pulling their weapons on the woman at first, and then sheer fascination and horror mixed together as they watched the finger grow back before their eyes.

"Now, I know that you will all assume that this is some kind of trick, and we are, I promise, willing to prove the entire thing to your healers given a bit more time. However, please don't assume that we can be cut up willy-nilly and simply grow it all back. It does not quite work that way. Nonetheless, it is a service we can provide to others when necessary, on a scale that does not please most of the world, but which we can offer to you and your people for the duration of the war. And regrowing limbs isn't the half of it—it's merely the only part we can't teach others to accomplish. We also have medicines that fight infection and healing practices that cure long illnesses. Most importantly, the majority of our practices can be taught to those who are patient enough to learn and have the resources to supply their own ingredients. Sadly, that doesn't describe the majority of the nations we've encountered, but it might describe Gensokai. Much of that is up to you."

Raku allowed her own frown to show.

"It sounds like a bit of a gamble to agree to an alliance when we don't know if we'll even have the resources to create the medicines that you claim you can teach us to make."

"Ah, no, I have been unclear, it seems. You most definitely have the resources to make the medicines—it's the primary reason we are approaching you instead of some other nation with a sizable navy—it's only a question of whether or not you have the patience to learn what we would teach you."

Raku considered all that had been said. On the one hand, this entire scenario was ridiculous. She had been kidnapped by a secret navy that was meant to keep all foreign contact away from Gensokai at the same time that a prisoner from a foreign nation offered them an alliance in a war that they knew nothing about. It was certainly far beyond her pay grade as historian and scribe. It was also not really up to her. She could promise to make introductions to the New Council and act as a go-between if Eredi decided she trusted her, but she couldn't even promise to get them off of this island without being killed by Saito and his people, who clearly thought this entire scenario was what their navy had been created to stop.

Just as she opened her mouth to say as much, Saito spoke again.

"Captain Eredi, I hope that Raku-san will do her best to convince the New Council of your need, and I, for one, will be happy to put you on the next ship heading for the mainland and use our raiko to speed you on your way."

Well, thought Raku, *I suppose that takes care of that.*

What could she do but bow her head and hope they survived the trip?

11日 6月, 新議 8年

11th Day, 6th Moon, Cycle 8 of the New Council

≈ Torako ≈

TORAKO DIDN'T THINK she was the only person on the deck of the Wind Serpent who was finding the trip back to the mainland awkward. Sairō stood beside her, delightfully hale after the Idari called BriTak gave them a small white pill that had cured them of any trace of nausea. Raku had taken one as well and seemed to be enjoying the trip almost as much as Itachi. But Sairō had still grumbled about being careful not to dismiss them because they couldn't be summoned at sea, so Torako had taken their word and left them in their extra-large wolf form while they walked stiltedly across the deck while pretending *not* to be following Itachi everywhere she went.

Torako was not fooled.

But she *was* distracted. Not by Kitsu, who had taken to playing a wild game of hide and seek with Itachi, though that was so endearing it was hard to focus on much else, and not even by Raku, who she couldn't seem to keep her hands off of after their brief but violent separation days earlier. No, she was distracted by the way the captain of the Idari kept looking at her, and by the glares her *sister* kept directing her way.

She wasn't sure which one she should address first, or whether she should address them at all. After all, she wasn't the one who'd invaded a foreign country looking for help, or who had abducted her own sister-in-law, so she didn't think she should be the one to go around unruffling anyone's feathers. Besides, she was terrible at that kind of thing. She usually let Raku deal with all the problems that required talking while she focused on the ones that required stabbing. Applying the sharp end of a blade was something she knew herself to be competent at, while using words to bridge gaps like "we should probably declare war on you, but we're here to ask for an alliance instead" or "I abducted your wife and tried to kill you a few times, but now it turns out we're siblings" was not.

"You can ask us, you know," said a low, pleasant voice to her right. She looked up, finding the Idari captain beside her.

"Eredi-san," she said, unsure what the other woman was talking about.

"Most people are curious about our skin and hair," Eredi went on. "You can ask. We're used to it."

Torako frowned.

"What is there to ask about? Your hair is bright fuchsia, and your skin is teal. My hair is black and my skin is light brown. These aren't really statements that engender questions."

Eredi beamed, and Torako wondered if there was something she was missing.

"You make an excellent point," the foreign captain said, leaning her elbows against the railing in a move to match Torako's posture.

Torako didn't know what to say to that, so she looked out at the water and took a deep breath of the fresh sea air. She rolled her neck, which had been stiff that morning, along with the rest of her, but which a brief touch from one of the Idari had healed before she could count more than a single heartbeat. Whatever their claims, the Idari had proven to be very adept healers indeed in the few hours she'd known them.

Torako was grateful that they'd waited until the morning tide to head for the mainland. She was glad to be able to make this trip in daylight, and she and her family had definitely needed the sleep. She turned to look over the stern of the ship and took note of the two ships behind them, which carried the remainder of Eredi's crew. They could all have crammed onto the Wind Serpent, Kaiyo had explained that morning, but if they wanted to have room to move about the deck comfortably, it was best to travel in a convoy.

"Perhaps we should talk about your mother, then," Eredi said, startling Torako from her wandering thoughts.

"What do you know of my mother?"

Torako almost growled the words, and she felt her fingers stiffen on the rail in front of her.

"Not much, actually, except that she's recently been taken from you. Would you be interested if I told you that I believe we know who is responsible for that?"

Torako couldn't bring herself to speak. A mixture of rage and sorrow blocked her throat when she tried.

"If you can help us make allies of your New Council, we may find ourselves fighting a common enemy," Eredi continued, yellow eyes glinting in the morning sunlight.

The woman walked away as Torako stared wide-eyed at the sea, and Torako couldn't decide if she wanted to chase her down and demand an explanation or simply cut her down where she stood.

Could Eredi really know who had taken Tenshi away? Could she possibly mean that the threat the Idari faced was somehow tied to her mother's death? That seemed unlikely at best, and some sort of terrible conspiracy at worst, but, then again, if the past few days had taught Torako anything, it was that her world was not what she'd thought it was. After all, there were whole nations she'd never heard of before, people with skin and hair the color of summer birds, and a secret navy that had been in hiding for centuries. After all that, why wouldn't she assume that the threat facing the Idari and whatever had killed her mother were connected? It made as much sense as anything else.

It was cold comfort, thinking that she might gain vengeance against those who had taken Itachi's grandmother away, but, if nothing else, her brief exchange with the Idari captain made one thing perfectly clear.

Eredi knew more than she should, and Torako didn't trust her at all.

Epilogue

14日 6月, 新議 8年

14th Day, 6th Moon, Cycle 8 of the New Council

⚔ *Kaiyo* ⚔

KAIYO TOOK A sip of tea and tried to keep her hand from reaching for any of her knives. In the end, she set down her cup and rested her hands inside her sleeves, with her arms crossed, a motion that both shielded her from the onslaught she expected and allowed her to touch the hilts of her throwing knives. She took a deep breath and tried to remember that she found the scent of green tea and summer tatami comforting. Usually.

"Married life seems to suit you."

Kaiyo flinched. Would anyone really be upset with her if a throwing knife found its way into her mother's arm? Just a flesh wound. Nothing fatal.

Nijiko took a demure sip of tea and smiled.

Kaiyo rolled her eyes and dropped her hands to her obi.

"Sailing through open oceans and fighting sea battles suits me, Mother. Married life has nothing to do with it."

She heard her mother's tsk when her hand found her hanko and began to flip it between her fingers, but she ignored her.

"Love is a thing that can grow, Kaiyo-chan, you don't have to ——"

"Don't lecture me about love, Nijiko-san," Kaiyo snapped, no longer willing to put up with the charade. "Did you know that father had a lover before you? Did you know that they had a child?"

She shouldn't have said it. She hadn't particularly meant to. It's not as if any of this was her mother's fault. But her father had ridden off to New Council City the moment they'd reached land, along with the rest of their strange entourage, and as much as she'd wanted to go with him, her mother had met their ship and insisted that she and Kaiyo travel together instead. Tanaka, curse him, had gone with them on the Admiral's orders.

Kaiyo had been furious with the delay that inherently came with traveling with her mother. Not that the woman couldn't handle a hard day's ride in hakama when needed, she could and did, but she insisted on staying at expensive ryokan, instead of sleeping on the side of the road as Kaiyo knew that her father would be doing. He'd reach New Council City at least a full day ahead of them, if not two, and Kaiyo chafed under the delays brought on by needless luxuries like tea and warm beds.

Her mother was the only outlet for her frustrations, and Kaiyo had lasted a full three days before she'd finally said something awful. She was almost proud of her restraint. Almost. Until she looked up and saw the hurt in her mother's eyes.

"Okaa-san, I'm—"

"No, no. It's something we should have spoken of long ago, I suppose. After all, I've lectured you about marrying for the family, so you deserve to know how your father and I wed."

Nijiko took another sip of her tea as if that would somehow remove the emotion from her voice, and strangely, it worked. When next she spoke, her voice was steady and her eyes barely shone in the flicker of the lamp that lit the small private dining area the owner of the ryokan had ushered them into after they'd finished bathing.

"Your father was very young when his family decided to marry him off. At the time, he was deeply in love with some village girl. He never told me her name or anything about her, but I could tell from… well, you're married now, so you may as well know… from his lack of enthusiasm in our marriage bed, that he'd already been with someone else, and that he found me utterly lacking."

She smiled stiffly, an expression that Kaiyo immediately wished she'd never seen, for all the obvious hurt it was meant to conceal, but before she could think of any comfort to offer her mother, she continued.

"Things didn't improve for almost a decade. For one thing, his parents sent him away almost the moment we were wed. They insisted we consummate the marriage right after the ceremony and then put him on a ship the moment we were done. It was… well, awful. And I was left alone, terrified I'd be with child, and married to a man I barely knew. For two whole cycles, he was simply gone. He sent no word, and now… well, I wonder if he simply wasn't allowed to. But… oh, there's no easy way to explain the rest. Not in a single evening. We made the best of it. He was determined to do his duty to his family. I was determined not to be cast aside like some unwanted dog. Eventually, I learned all the ways of doing things that made me indispensable to him and employed them all. Eventually, he learned to trust me. Now… well, we respect each other. We love each other the way old friends who have been through many trials together love one another, and… I wish I could say otherwise, but it's much more than many of my childhood friends have in their marriages."

Kaiyo realized that somewhere in her mother's story her hand had stilled and she was simply gripping the small owl-topped hanko as if it were a lifeline and she had been taken over the rails of the Wind Serpent and out into the sea.

She'd never heard her mother talk that way, as if anything mattered, as if *she* mattered. It was the first time she'd had any inkling that the woman harbored any ambitions at all besides finding suitable spouses for her daughters.

"But you—" Kaiyo wasn't even certain what she planned to object to, but Nijiko either didn't hear her, or decided to continue before she could be stopped.

"I didn't know about your… half-sister. I am certain that Kuzuri-san didn't know about her either. We would have done something for them. Sent money, offered to send the girl to school, *something.* He would never have ignored an obligation, and even if he had, I would never have let him."

And *that* confused Kaiyo more than anything her mother had said yet.

"But the scandal—you've always said—"

"Scandal be damned, I would never have left a young unwed mother alone with a child and nothing to keep her safe."

Nijiko said the words with such finality that Kaiyo was certain she meant them, for all that they sounded like they came from someone else. What strange reality was this? Had her mother never been honest with her before now? Had the woman she'd *thought* had raised her ever even existed? And then Kaiyo's mind reflected back to what Nijiko had said moments earlier about being terrified that she'd get pregnant after that first unenthusiastic coupling.

Kaiyo found her mind full of a series of questions she had no intention of asking.

"Why…" she let her voice drift off. She wasn't sure what she wanted to ask. But this conversation was like none she'd ever had with her mother. As if Kaiyo's marriage had somehow transformed Nijiko into someone who looked exactly the same but who expressed her own opinion readily, whether others might consider it distasteful or not.

"Why do you seem like a different person?" she finally asked.

Nijiko's eyebrows rose as she lifted her tea to her lips once more.

"Your father has just revealed his family's sworn secret, one they've kept for centuries. I've spent decades trying to keep us safe from scandal, or even undue attention, as best I know how, all in order to help him avoid scrutiny and do his duty. It surprises you to discover that I haven't always meant what I've said?"

Kaiyo felt as if the floor had been taken out from under her, or as if the breath had been taken from her lungs.

"But… you forced me to marry—"

"I forced you to do nothing. I held no weapons. I didn't even threaten you. I explained your options and you chose. Do you regret it?"

Kaiyo was too angry to consider that question logically, but before she could even blurt out the jumble of irate thoughts that clamored for position in her mind, her mother continued.

"Besides, that part was your father's idea. I just organized it."

And with that, Kaiyo found she had no words left. She simply stood up from the low table holding their tea, slid open the thin door that separated them from the main dining area, and silently stalked away from her mother.

Maybe, if she rode fast enough, she could catch up with her father in time to stab him.

21日 6月, 新議 8年

21st Day, 6th Moon, Cycle 8 of the New Council

⇒ Raku ⇐

"RAKU-SAN, SAITO-san, welcome." Tsuku-san sat in the same place Raku had last seen her, in the same gracefully folded position, with the same guards in attendance. If she hadn't been wearing a different kimono, Raku might have believed that the woman with grey hair and perfect poise hadn't moved in the intervening time.

It was strange indeed to see Tsuku-san so unchanged, when it felt like a lifetime had passed for Raku. Nevertheless, she kept her face carefully neutral, as always, while she performed the low bow that marked the start of her usual report—complete with the faint hint of citrus mixed in with the dry-straw scent of the tatami—and tried to ignore the fact that the man responsible for the worst tenday of her life was folded on the floor beside her, performing his own obeisance.

"Raku-san, I believe I'd like to hear your news first, if Saito-san has no objections."

Tsuku's tone suggested that if Saito objected he would be taught a quick and painful lesson about Tsuku's patience, but Raku was relieved to hear him say, "None at all, Tsuku-sama."

And then it was left to Raku to recount everything that had happened to her since she'd last been in New Council City. From the hawk that she'd sent explaining her latest findings, which it seemed Tsuku-san had never received, to her abduction, to her rescue. She did her best to keep her tone neutral, even though it went against her better storytelling instincts, hoping that doing so would help her to keep some of the strongest emotions out of her voice. Her rage at being ripped from Itachi, her sorrow when she thought Torako was lost, even her joy at seeing her wife and daughter again—she had no wish to share those pieces of herself with the man responsible for her pain. When she finally added what little she knew about the Idari captain and her people, she fell silent.

Tsuku-san, without a single outburst, question, or any show of emotion, called for a runner and scribbled out a quick note that the young girl sped away with before the ink had even fully dried.

Then she turned her eyes on the Admiral beside Raku.

"Saito-san," she said, in a tone that made Raku shiver. "I find myself immensely curious as to how you plan to justify your behavior."

Saito bowed again, and when he sat up once more he sighed.

"Tsuku-sama, I can only tell you that I believed I was doing what was best for Gensokai at the time. I… well, I still agree with my choices based on the information I had at the time. Everything I've done I have done in order to prevent bringing war to Gensokai but… the information has changed."

"Has it?" Tsuku looked less than amused, and Raku was so angry that she found herself speaking without meaning to.

"What has changed? You had all the information before. You knew there were dozens of other nations in the world, you knew that some of them wanted to wage war on us, you knew more than any of the rest of us did, because you and your people have worked for centuries to keep us ignorant. What about the past few days has taught you anything that you did not already know?"

Saito looked at Raku but did not argue. Indeed, he bowed slightly before he spoke next, as if in deference to all that she had said.

"There is one more piece of information I have withheld from you," he said, his voice steady. "It concerns the moon Kami, Tsukuyomi-sama. He is—no, he *was*—the Kami the Kaigun most often called on for aid. For decades now, he has helped us to turn away outsiders, even when they had superior weapons, before we learned to make our own improved cannon. It has been largely thanks to his involvement that the Kaigun has been successful, even in the face of advanced enemy technologies."

Saito took a deep breath before continuing.

"However, I fear that he has changed allegiances, and can no longer be trusted. And, if we no longer have Tsukuyomi-sama on our side, then we will need the strongest allies we can get."

Tsuku frowned and Raku couldn't help but mimic the gesture. She didn't know where Tsuku's consternation came from, but Raku's mind raced back to Torako's account of all that had happened as she'd tried to rescue her, and the story of a grandfather she'd never met before suddenly trying to kill her. Then Tenshi's story rose up in her memory as well.

Tsuku was already talking before Raku's mind came back to the room.

"So, the Idari conveniently arrive just as your favored Kami abandons you? And to whom? You said that he changed allegiances, so to whom does he give his allegiance now? What are the sides that are taken by the Kami? How does any of this pertain to your secret naval force and our homeland?"

The questions were perfectly reasonable, but Tsuku's tone was clipped enough for Raku to recognize the anger in it. Before Saito could open his mouth to answer Tsuku's barrage of questions, however, Raku posed her own.

"Saito-san, you knew Tenshi-san when she was younger. Were you aware that Tsukuyomi-sama was her father?"

Until that moment, Saito's features had been surprisingly composed, even in the face of all of Tsuku's angry questions. Raku's final query, however, appeared to completely unbalance him.

"Wh-what?" he asked, his voice low.

"Tsukuyomi-sama was Tenshi-san's father."

Raku tried not to let the satisfaction of having completely destabilized someone who had done the same to her entire nation come through in her voice, but she wasn't certain she managed it.

"I… I didn't know. Though I'm ashamed to say it makes a terrible kind of sense, now that I do know it."

"Why?"

"She…" Saito's voice sounded rough, and he had to clear it twice before he could continue past that one syllable. "When I knew her, she had a habit of talking to the moon when she was worried. I asked her why, once, when I caught her at it. She told me it was a comfort to her, even if the moon never answered."

He paused for a long time then, his gaze somewhat distant, and Raku took a brief moment to wish desperately that Torako were here to witness this revelation of her mother's past.

"After we were forced apart, I was often alone…. I thought of her, more than was wise, and… well, one night I decided that if I talked to the moon, perhaps Tenshi-san might somehow hear me… I know that's ridiculous, but… I was young, and desperately in love with her still. So, I began to tell the moon the story of how we'd met. How much I'd loved her… it was silly of me, certainly, but… one night, the moon answered me. Or Tsukuyomi-sama did, anyway. He didn't ask me about her, or perhaps I would have put the whole thing together much sooner, he simply came to me and answered a question I'd posed to the moon that night in the midst of all my ramblings. He offered to help me, and my people, in exchange for a few favors. I agreed."

If the first part of Saito's tale had been so riddled with emotion that he could barely speak, then the second part had fallen into the same neutral tones that Raku had used when she'd made her own report to Tsuku, in all likelihood for the same reasons.

"And what favors did you grant the moon?"

"Many. Over the cycles, he asked for a number of them, but none of them were particularly grand until…"

"Until?"

"Well, his last request before betraying us was to ask that he be present to bless my daughter's marriage."

"That doesn't seem like much of a request," Tsuku replied, her voice a careful monotone.

"It wouldn't be, had she had *any* intention of getting married."

Tsuku and Raku both simply blinked at the man for a long moment.

"You *forced* your daughter into marriage at the behest of a moon Kami?" Tsuku growled. Raku was impressed at the sound coming from such a graceful, usually poised, older woman.

Saito said nothing, only hanging his head in reply.

Raku fumed silently. How many lives had this man ruined for the sake of what he thought was right?

"You must understand," he said finally, his voice even, if not loud. "Everything I have done has been to prevent war from coming to Gensokai. Tsukuyomi-sama was an invaluable ally. And you must think me the basest hypocrite if you think I would risk Raku and her family but refuse to alter my own daughter's fate."

Raku felt a knot of anger in her stomach but couldn't decide how to untangle the mess that Saito had just put forth.

"Saito-san, you're an ass," Tsuku said from the dais. Raku's head snapped to the older woman, but she no longer looked angry so much as tired. "But, unfortunately, we have bigger problems than your own perverse sense of honor. What does Tsukuyomi-sama want with your daughter's marriage, and what does he want with Gensokai?"

"I don't know," Saito said, deflated. "I asked, of course, but he never revealed his motives. I only know that he's betrayed us because he said as much at his last visit. He appeared to me, just in time to hurry me to my meeting with Raku-san. Which, in turn, had me arrive just in time to prevent my daughter's death. But he also informed me that I should no longer trust him. That he was no longer acting on his own will."

"I assume he didn't take the time to explain any of that?" Tsuku asked, her voice dry as a winter wind.

"Indeed not, Tsuku-sama."

Tsuku looked as though she planned to say more, but just then the sliding door opened again, and the same runner entered to bow before the dais. Then she handed Tsuku another small scroll.

"We'll have to end this here," Tsuku said, standing up.

"What's happening?" Raku asked, not liking the edge to Tsuku's voice.

"The Council is ready to hear our new friends' plea," she replied.

Neither Raku nor Saito could object because she was already gone by the time they had gained their feet. Raku frowned, a shiver coursing down her spine as she considered how quickly things were moving now. Gensokans had thought themselves alone in the world yesterday, and today they would decide whether or not to tie their fate to a nation on the brink of war.

⇒ *Torako* ⇐

TORAKO CLOSED HER eyes and listened to the delighted laughter that Itachi let loose as she chased Raku around the decorative garden. She breathed in air scented with sun-warmed flowers and damp soil, and thought that for all that she hated New Council City, and especially the parts of it that had once housed the most prominent of the Rōjū, as this section with its fine decorative gardens surely had, this moment was a good one, and this garden was a fine place for a child to spend the afternoon with her mothers.

She opened her eyes and couldn't restrain a smile as Itachi was caught mid-run by an extra set of arms, attached to a familiar lopsided grin, swung round and round as she squealed, and then set down to chase her mother again.

"And her father too, I suppose," Torako muttered, to no one in particular.

The wolf at her feet let out a dry huff.

"What?"

"You are allowed to have a whole pack, Torako-san. You don't have to limit yourself to a mating pair."

Torako rubbed her booted foot through the thick fur of Sairō's ruff and then gave them a slight shove with her toes.

"Now you're willing to dole out sage advice?" Her tone was wry, but she was actually pleased that the old wolf Kami was willing to suggest anything that involved accepting Kitsu—the wolf had been oddly opposed to the man from the moment they met.

"You are wounded, you need coddling. As the leader of your pack, I am responsible for your well-being, and more love is better than less."

"Leader of *my* pack?"

"Well, I am the oldest and wisest," Sairō replied, without even lifting their head.

"You are an insuff—"

"Excuse me?"

Torako looked up to see a pair of startlingly grey eyes staring at her from just over a wolf's-length away. She would have been frustrated at being caught unawares by this new arrival, but if there was anyone whose stealth she did not begrudge, it was the young woman standing before her.

"Ryūko-san!" Torako said, jumping to her feet and almost stepping on Sairō's tail in the process. "I'm sorry, I didn't realize the time. Taka-san had said you might wish to speak with me, but I—"

"Please, sit. I didn't mean to disturb you. Is there room on that bench for both of us, do you think?"

Torako nodded and tried to get her thoughts in line. She probably shouldn't be tongue-tied by meeting a woman over a decade her junior, especially when that woman was the dearest friend of her long-time friend and midwife, but... when that woman was also the only reason that this city was no longer the stronghold of the corrupt regime that had been slaughtering infants for centuries, she thought she was allowed a bit of fluster.

"Come, sit. The wolf generally doesn't bite."

"That is a lie," the wolf in question grumbled, without opening their eyes. "I often bite. But I would never bite the woman who saved Gensokai from itself."

Torako heard a long-suffering sigh beside her and looked over to see Ryūko looking at the sky with a bit more interest than the clear morning probably warranted.

"Please call me Mishi," she said after a moment. "I'm still not used to people calling me by the name my parents gave me, and… well, you're basically family, to hear Taka-san tell it."

"Mishi-san? I suppose I can do that, if you like."

Torako frowned for a moment, then smiled when she thought she understood.

"I suppose I've never enjoyed being called Night Stalker much either," she admitted. "At least, not by anyone I actually know."

Ryūko—no, Mishi—smiled in return then, and Torako finally noticed how tall the other woman was. Torako considered herself tall, taller than most women she knew, taller than half the men, too. But Mishi was taller than she was by a good hand's span, and lean as well. Striking, certainly, and all lean muscle and grace, even when she slouched against a stone bench, as she was doing now.

"I've heard some of the stories," Mishi said, her grey eyes sparkling in the morning light. "Your legend may exceed mine in certain circles."

"Ha! Only in Sōryū Valley, and even there, everyone speaks of you with a reverence they usually reserve for the Kami."

Mishi rolled her eyes.

"They speak of you like a Yōkai, but one that only threatens bandits."

Torako laughed.

"Well, I suppose Kuma-sensei would be proud of both of us, then," she said.

Seeing Mishi's eyes darken almost made Torako wish the words unsaid, but she was fairly certain this was why Taka had suggested they meet today, after cycles of sharing so many connections. Torako and Raku had known Taka for cycles. She'd been Torako's healer during her entire pregnancy with Itachi, had played the part of midwife at her birth, and then had insisted that Raku and Torako take up residency in her own mountain cave while Torako had been healing. In all that time, Torako had known that Taka and Mishi were close friends, but Taka had never once suggested they meet. She understood *that* well enough. Torako herself had gone far out of her way to avoid the young woman training in Yanagi-sama's woods, first because she had a connection to the school of midwives, and later *because* of her connection with Mishi, and consequently, with Tenshi. That was before Torako and Tenshi had reconciled. She'd always suspected that Taka had never suggested she meet with Mishi because of Torako's connection with Kuma-sensei.

Now it was those very connections that had them sitting on a stone bench and comparing legends.

"Taka-san mentioned that you had news," Mishi said quietly, after a long pause.

Torako swallowed, trying to drive back the emotion that had been threatening to overwhelm her since she'd stopped needing to play the hero.

"I'm told you and Tenshi-san are close," she said. Damn. She hadn't meant to use the present tense. She just couldn't quite bear to use the past tense yet. It was so… final.

"She's your mother, isn't she?" Mishi's voice was full of curiosity now. "I have to admit, when Taka-san told me that, I didn't believe her at first. I had no idea Tenshi had children of her own. She must have been quite young when she had you."

Torako nodded, happy to have a slightly less emotional topic to discuss for a moment.

"I left that school when I was 18 cycles old. From what I understand, you arrived a few cycles after that."

"Did you…" Mishi's voice trailed off, but Torako could easily guess what was meant to fill that blank. "Know your parents? Yes. Your mother was five cycles my senior, and may as well have been a legend herself. I was terrified to speak with her."

Mishi's eyes widened and Torako wondered what she'd said for a moment before hastily explaining. "She wasn't cruel! In fact, she was invariably kind to me, which is something I can't say for the rest of her sisters. She was just… good at everything. She had powerful kisō, was an excellent archer, and Kuma-sensei doted on her. I didn't know her well, though."

Mishi's eyes resumed a more normal size at this explanation and she sighed. Torako wasn't sure if she'd disappointed her or not. She realized that she was bound to disappoint her soon, though, and it was probably best to get it over with.

"Mishi-san, I don't know any other way to share this news, so I'm just going to say it. My mother, Tenshi-san, she's… I still don't know what happened, exactly—Itachi-chan saw something in a vision or a dream, but she's very young still and the spirit world may not work quite the way our world does—but she's dead, Mishi-san. Tenshi-san is dead."

Torako didn't want to look at the younger woman's eyes, but she made herself do it anyway. She knew that it was *her* mother who had died, and she didn't owe Mishi any more bravery than she owed herself, but… well, she was probably something like a big sister, if they compared enough of their childhoods, and she didn't want to ignore Mishi's suffering, even if she was still trying to ignore her own.

She looked into the grey gaze of the young woman who had been asked to give up far too much to save her people and immediately wished she hadn't. Mishi looked nothing like Torako, but she still could have sworn she was looking into a mirror.

Instantly, and without bidding, tears rose to her eyes. Then sobs. Then she felt long, strong arms wrap around her and could no longer tell where her shaking ended and Mishi's began. And perhaps she'd never mourned properly when she'd learned of Kuma-sensei's death, perhaps she'd been too caught up in all the ways that she'd felt he and Tenshi had failed her. Resentful of the power her mother had stolen from her, and how she'd never managed to be the person Kuma-sensei had hoped she would be, because of it. But she was holding the person Kuma-sensei had been looking for right now, and what did any of it matter? Kuma-sensei had loved her, fiercely, even if she'd struggled to accept his love because she'd felt it only half-earned. And Tenshi… Tenshi had always loved her. It was only once she'd given birth to Itachi that Torako had come to realize the truth of just how deep that love had been. She hadn't truly understood why her mother had chosen to rob her of her kisō while she was still in the womb, even for all the times Tenshi had told her she'd have done anything to protect her, until she'd been looking into Itachi's eyes and imagining the lengths she would go to keep her safe.

Torako could only guess at the problematic ways that Kuma-sensei and Tenshi would have loved the first kisōshi powerful enough to truly challenge the Rōjū. Mishi's relationships with them must have been just as fraught, if in different ways. And that changed nothing, because two of the people who had loved them most fiercely in all the world were gone.

It was a long while before she and Mishi finally broke apart.

"I believe that was long overdue," Mishi muttered, wiping at her face with the sleeve of her uwagi. "Taka-chan is always telling me not to bottle things up. Yanagi-sensei would probably have me setting fires all across his precious forest by now."

Torako laughed. It was a choked, wet sound, but she didn't care. She wiped her nose as best she could with her leathers, but her wrist bracers weren't well designed for absorbing… well, anything.

"Here," said a quiet voice from behind them.

And before Torako could berate herself for being snuck up on by *two* people today, a familiar petite figure shuffled into view with two silk handkerchiefs extended.

"Taka-san requests that you two share happy memories also. But, I, for one, am enjoying the spectacle of seeing two of Gensokai's fiercest warriors cry all over each other."

And with that message and her silk kerchiefs delivered, Kusuko turned on her heel and went to greet a delighted ball of three-cycle-old child, who happily leapt into her arms, heedless of the exquisite kimono she wore, or the perfect makeup and hair that made her look more like a work of art than a person.

"Taka-san is using Kusuko-san to do her dirty work now, do you think that means she's afraid of us?"

Torako asked the question idly, but she saw the smirk that lifted the corner of Mishi's mouth at the suggestion.

"No, but I have every intention of insisting she must be, from now until solstice."

"Won't that just get you rendered unconscious?" Torako asked.

"Yes, but I could do with the extra sleep anyway."

Torako laughed, and decided not to speculate on why Mishi wasn't getting enough sleep.

"I think I'm beginning to be annoyed with Taka-san for not introducing us sooner," Torako said, without a trace of annoyance in her voice.

"Ah yes, we should blame her for that as well. But first, I want to hear an account of—"

But Torako didn't get to hear what Mishi wanted an account of because it was in that moment that a messenger came running into the garden. A choice the young man was likely to regret soon, as five adults and one enormous wolf instantly came alert and moved into protective positions around one small child.

Torako could see the messenger swallow from where she sat on the far side of the garden. Neither she nor Mishi had stood, though they'd both moved their bodies such that launching themselves at the young man would be easy if he were stupid enough to threaten them.

"Um… I have a message for Raku-san?" he hedged.

"That would be me," Raku replied, all smiles despite the firm grip she had on Itachi's shoulders.

"Tsuku-sama and the leaders of the New Council request your presence in the Council chambers."

Message delivered, the young man turned and left. And if he moved like someone who wanted to run but was half-certain an angry predator would chase him if he did, no one chose to comment on it.

"They must have decided," Raku said.

"Already? I thought you just gave testimony this morning."

Torako couldn't help but be disturbed by the idea that the New Council hadn't taken more than a day to deliberate on the question of a new ally in a world they barely understood.

Raku picked up Itachi and headed for the path that led back to the New Council chambers.

Torako, Kitsu, Kusuko, and Mishi all watched her go.

Then she stopped in the path, turning back to them.

"Well, come on," she said. "They're clearly impatient if they've sent a runner for us."

"Raku-chan, they didn't say that we should—"

"Tora-chan, if you think I'm going *anywhere* without my family after the tenday I've just had, you must be out of your damned mind."

Torako laughed, then shook her head and started forward.

When no one else followed her, she turned to Kusuko, Sairō, Kitsu, and Mishi and cocked a single eyebrow.

"Well, you heard her," she chided. "She's not going anywhere without her family, so you'd all better hurry up."

1日 7月, 新議 8年

1st Day, 7th Moon, Cycle 8 of the New Council

⇒ *Raku* ⇐

RAKU WAS STILL stunned by how quickly it had all happened. They'd traveled to New Council City in record time. The Council had convened faster than Raku had thought was possible. That had been part luck, since they were preparing for the mid-cycle session and all the Council members had been in the city already, with the usual session only two days away to begin with. It had also been part curiosity. Raku had given a full report to Tsuku-san and had even introduced Eredi to the unofficial head of the New Council, and from there Tsuku-san had clearly told the convening members enough to pique their curiosity such that starting their session two days early didn't even cause a stir.

But the thing that had Raku most concerned was how quickly the Council had decided that allying themselves with the Idari was not only wise but expedient. They'd decided it at the end of a single session.

And now, here she stood at the bow of the Wind Serpent—because of course the Kaigun had volunteered all of their fastest vessels for the Idari mission—with her wife, a wolf Kami, a smuggler, and a handful of the people who'd abducted her, sailing past the known waters of Gensokai, all on the word of a foreign captain and her crew. She shook her head, leaning against Torako's shoulder., then turned when the sound of a high-pitched giggle came from behind her. Nothing could suppress the grin that bloomed on her face at the sight of Itachi playing chase with Kitsu across the deck behind her.

"Remind me why we've brought the three-cycle-old child on a dangerous mission across the sea?" she asked Torako, even as she leaned against her.

Torako's voice rumbled against Raku's chest as she pulled her close and answered, "Because, for reasons that still make little sense to me, all the people we would have trusted to care for her are either dead, missing, or coming with us."

Raku felt her smile slide away.

"Do you really think these people know where the ones who attacked Tenshi-san are?" she asked, more quietly.

She could feel Torako's sigh as much as hear it.

"I don't know. But even if they don't… Yanagi-sama is still missing, Tsuku-san and Yasuhiko-san are so busy they'll barely have time to sleep in the coming tendays, let alone care for Itachi-chan, and… everyone else I would trust to keep her safe when we face unfamiliar enemies…"

Torako's voice trailed off, but another familiar voice picked up where she'd left off.

"Is here on this ship," Taka said, stepping up beside them and beaming. "Really, Tora-chan, if I'd known you were so desperate for a child-minder that you'd fabricate an entire war, I would have done a better job of visiting the old cave."

Raku felt her smile return in full force as she looked at Gensokai's greatest healer. The younger woman was a bit taller than Raku, but nowhere near as tall as Torako, yet she carried herself with the confidence of someone much more imposing. Her eyes were alight with mischief, though.

"Of course I would start a war just to fill a ship with the short list of people to whom I'd entrust my daughter's safety. Now Raku-san and I will spend the entire journey in our hammock and you, Kusuko-san, and Mishi-san can all keep the child entertained while we play bed games."

Torako started to walk away, with Raku still wrapped in her arms, as if to do just as she'd said, until all three of them dissolved into laughter before she'd gotten even three strides away.

"How is Mishi-san?" Raku asked more solemnly, after they'd all wiped the tears of laughter from their eyes.

Taka's smile dimmed slightly, but it didn't dissolve altogether.

"She's well enough," Taka said. "Mitsu-san is keeping her largely distracted."

The way her eyes twinkled as she said it, Raku had a few guesses as to how he was distracting the young warrior.

"I hadn't realized Mitsu-san would be joining us," Raku said, hoping the statement sounded casual.

"I'm not certain he was invited. I am quite certain, however, that Mishi-chan would gladly slit the throat of anyone who suggested he stay ashore."

And with that, Taka bowed playfully and walked away.

Raku watched her go, then remembered how she had hoped to distract Torako in a similar way from a very similar sorrow.

"Will you be alright, Love?" Raku asked, after a long moment, leaning back against Torako's chest and pulling her arms closer around her.

"I'm sure I will be… eventually. But I won't pretend I'm alright now."

Raku accepted this silently, pulling Torako's arms even tighter around her, enjoying the feel of the muscle underneath the rough leather she always wore, and letting her mind wander to all the ways she might use that muscle for their shared pleasure later.

So it wasn't until the second time that the gruff voice behind them coughed that she finally snapped to attention and stepped away from Torako's embrace.

⫸ Kaiyo ⫷

KAIYO STOOD BEHIND her half-sister and her wife, trying to ignore the fact that they were clearly having a fairly intimate moment, for all that they were both facing out to sea with their arms wrapped around each other. A large part of her wanted to walk away, but she'd already been avoiding them for days, and Tanaka was right. This wasn't going to get any easier if she pretended it didn't need to be done.

She coughed again.

This time the two women stepped apart and turned to look at her. Torako looked about ready to clean her katana with Kaiyo's kidneys and Raku looked flushed, like she'd been caught doing something inappropriate. Kaiyo ignored them both.

Or rather, she ignored their reactions, and looked them both in the eyes, first Torako, then Raku.

Then she bowed at the waist, her back as straight as she could make it, her hands straight at her sides, and she held it for a long moment.

She stood up again, probably sooner than was technically appropriate, but bowing wasn't going to make anything right and if she waited much longer the apology that she'd practiced so many times in the past few days would die in her throat.

"Torako-san, Raku-san, I offer you my sincerest apologies. I know I cannot undo all the harm that I've done to you and that mere words will never make up for all the pain I've caused you. I do not expect you to forgive me, and I won't ask you to, but I hope you know that I deeply regret the circumstances under which we met and the part I played in your abduction. The Admiral… my father… made the wrong choice, and I was wrong to follow his orders. The fact that I was following orders doesn't excuse it, and I shouldn't have had to learn I was related to you to realize that it was wrong."

She took a deep breath, then turned to Raku alone.

"You did not deserve what we did to you, and I regret my involvement in it."

She turned to go but, almost to her own horror, found herself swiveling back to Raku's startled face once more.

"But if you ever stab my husband again, I will kill you myself."

Then she turned and walked away, ignoring the startled exclamation of "husband?" behind her.

She hadn't meant to say that last part—it hadn't been part of the carefully rehearsed apology—but she'd been feeling surly ever since her father had informed her of her orders for this mission. Nothing about it made sense. That the Council had approved the alliance, so quickly and without any evidence from the Idari, was laughably rash on their part, and yet no one else seemed to notice or object. Well, scratch that, Torako had seemed fairly surly about the whole thing too, from what little she'd heard her say, but as far as Kaiyo could tell, Torako was surly about everything, especially if the thing couldn't be made right by putting a sword through it. It was a feeling she empathized with, even if she couldn't afford to act that way most of the time.

Still, something was off about this whole thing, and it had left her on edge. She should probably apologize about threatening Raku at some point, but right now she couldn't make herself turn around and go back to them. Besides, Torako would likely run her through with a katana for her efforts if she didn't let the woman calm down first.

When she had climbed the stern deck once more and was staring out at the line of ships that followed behind them, she felt Tanaka's presence at her shoulder.

"Well, *that* went well," he murmured beside her.

She rolled her eyes and turned to look at him.

"I really did try," she said, flicking her hanko between her fingers. "And I *meant* it. Well, most of it, anyway. I know the whole thing was wrong. Even though I would do it all again if I thought I was preventing a war."

Tanaka leaned his elbows against the railing and turned to face the bow of the ship in a completely uncharacteristic slouch.

"It is difficult to make the right choice when you're starting with a false premise," he conceded. And then, after a moment. "Did you really have to threaten her again for stabbing me?"

Kaiyo frowned.

"You heard that?"

"I was standing next to Suzuki-san." He shrugged, as if there was nothing shady about positioning oneself next to a raiko and asking them to use their wind kisō to eavesdrop. "I *also* heard you publicly refer to me as your husband."

His gaze, when she met his eyes, was alight with a fire she felt all the way in her stomach.

"I liked it," he added.

Then he turned so that he was facing the other ships that trailed behind them again, just as she was, and his left hand casually draped across her right, his fingers tracing small patterns across the back of her hand.

"I've noticed that the Idari crew are sharing rather close quarters, even though we've spread them out across the fleet. Perhaps..." And her stomach did a small betraying flip as he hesitated after that word. "Perhaps it would be polite to offer them my cabin for the remainder of the journey."

"Ah," she said, feeling the warmth in her stomach spread outward. She licked her lips, her eyes following closely the patterns that he drew against her skin. "Perhaps that could be arranged. You are, technically, allowed to bunk with your spouse, if you happen to be assigned to the same ship."

"How convenient," Tanaka said, and the smile he gave her made her rather wish that their watch was already over so that they could go and take their rest.

So, of course, that was when a dozen enormous sea serpents broke the surface of the water surrounding the ship and shrieked in what sounded like purest outrage.

"Kuso," Kaiyo muttered, as she stared at the creatures. She was just about to ask if he thought there was any chance the serpents *weren't* here to kill them when the closest one turned and bared a mouth full of thousands of arm-length razor-sharp teeth, and then dove towards the Wind Serpent.

More from Virginia McClain

Chronicles of Gensokai:
Blade's Edge
Traitor's Hope

Gensokai Kaigai:
Sairō's Claw
Eredi's Gambit (coming soon)

The Victoria Marmot series:
Victoria Marmot and the Meddling Goddess
Victoria Marmot and the Inconvenient Prophecy
Victoria Marmot and the Shadow of Death
Victoria Marmot and the Dragon's Rage
Victoria Marmot and the Road to Hell

Short Story Collections:
Rain on a Summer's Afternoon

Acknowledgements

IT IS KNOWN that I am terrible at remembering things. In order to attempt to remember everyone who I wanted to thank for making this book happen, I started taking notes around six months ago and then adding people when I thought of someone else to add. Now it's finally time to make the list into a nicely worded note and I'm terrified I've forgotten someone. So, let's just start this off with a catch-all: If you get to the end of this list and are sad that your name isn't on it, please add yourself. My memory isn't great at the best of times, and 2020 and 2021 have not been the best of times. So, if you did anything at all to encourage me or help me, or suggest that maybe my writing isn't total shite, I appreciate the hell out of you.

Now then, onto everyone else.

To the DNF This crew: I love you all. You are the best friends anyone could want, but especially an anxiety-ridden author in the middle of a pandemic. You make everything better and you made writing this book way less stressful than it would have been. Thank you for all of the encouragement, crabs, cakes, insults, inside jokes, shenanigans, and general foolishness. Y'all singlehandedly (nine handedly? eighteenhandedly?) saved me in one of the shittiest years of my life (possibly the shittiest but I don't want to tempt fate).

To Corey: Writing it all out would take a whole other book. Thank you for supporting the dream. I love you.

To Cedar: You are a constant inspiration to me both in fiction and in life. I hope you like Itachi, she might have been inspired by you.

To Aurora: In addition to being a stellar editor, you are also a speed demon, a rock star mom, an excellent designer, AND

YOU MAKE GORGEOUS FURNITURE. Thank you for everything you do to make my books shine, and everything you do to save me from both myself and my abuse of commas.

To Claire: Would this book exist without our weekly writing sessions? Would it exist without our NaNoWriMo efforts? Would I exist without you there to cheer me on through the highs and lows of life? These are questions that may not have answers. But YOU are the best friend and writing buddy I could ask for, and I can't wait to see your brilliant ideas in print. So much love to you, dear friend.

To Miracle: For the additional late-night chats, shared anxiety, potential co-writing schemes, and for letting me steal your sword drawings. I totally traced one and made it into Torako's fleuron.

To SFF Book Twitter: There are too many of you to list, but y'all know who you are. Thank you for the late-night shenanigans, the counting of the swears, the waxing philosophical and the supporting of those who are struggling. If 2020 had a bright side, it was learning that SFF book twitter was willing to step up and help out when folks hit hard times. Hugs all around.

To my QuaranCon peeps: Again, I am not going to list you all out, but if you helped make QuaranCon happen in 2020 and/or 2021, this means you! Thank you for all the awesome discord chats, for keeping me going with encouragement. And especially to Pam for holding the fort when I had to step away to finish this book on time.

To my Grief Anthology frens: I'm not listing all of you out since that's basically announcing the anthology before it's ready, but you all know who you are. Thank you for the support, the sharing, the random chatter and the late-night support. Y'all are a great group of folks to bare a soul to.

To my siblings: TJ, PJ, & Jill, 2020 was a repeated hammering in the nuts, but talking to you three every week made a lot of the unbearable bearable. Massive hugs to you all, and may we all have brighter days ahead.

To Artemis: Yes you're a dog. No, you probably can't read this on your own. But you're also one of my best friends and you've been with me through EVERYTHING. I love you and I'm so grateful for every day that we have together.

To anyone who spent time with Cedar between November of 2019 and May of 2021: That's actually a pretty short list, but it's enough people that I'm not entirely sure who to list. Long story short, if you hung out with my kid while I worked on this book, you are the best and I appreciate the hell out of you.

Anna S: Your continued enthusiasm for my books is one of the things that keeps me going anytime the crappy voice in my head tries to tell me I'm not that good at this writing thing. Thank you for all the times you have reached out to tell me you enjoy my work; it really helps me stay motivated when the going gets tough.

To Amy Gerardy: The artwork you did for these characters fills me with joy and was inspirational for me during the rewrite. Thank you for bringing my characters to life!

JC Kang: You, sir, are the glue of the SFF community and talking to you about books and writing is always a pleasure. Thanks for all of your support!

My Patreon Patrons: Small but mighty is my Patreon crew! Paul, Corey, Mishy, ML, Jill, Marie, & Jessica - Thank you for your continued support!

To Paul: For all of the proofreading help! You rock!

To Gavin: For all the Japanese usage consults! (All errors are mine, Gavin does his best to help me, but sometimes I ask him something and then change how I was going to use it months later and forget to ask him if the change was ok.) Also, Gav, did you spot your cameo?

To Andrea Stewart: A shoutout for the line about cats & kids, and for all our random writing, running, and workout chats.

To readers who reach out to say hi, who leave reviews, and who simply continue to buy and read my books. THANK YOU!

To Ursula Vernon: I very much doubt you'll ever read this, but this book probably would not exist if I hadn't followed your ADHD journey on Twitter and then finally gotten myself an adult diagnosis and some meds last year when my world fell apart. It is thanks to your tweets that I was able to recognize where I could find a lifeline when nothing else was working. Thank you for being so open and honest about your own experiences.

To my counselor, and to therapists everywhere: For helping people to gather the pieces of themselves back together after they break.

To my doctor, and other doctors who take ADHD seriously: Thanks for not making a difficult thing worse, and for helping people heal and grow in the ways that they need to.

To literally everyone who said or did something nice to me/for me, in my general direction, or to/for anyone else in 2020, the year from hell: Seriously, everyone who had the capacity to offer kindness to others in 2020 has my thanks. Keep at it, y'all. The world needs more kindness.

 Virginia McClain is an author who masqueraded as a language teacher for a decade or so. When she's not reading or writing she can generally be found playing outside with her four legged adventure buddy and the tiny human she helped to build from scratch. She enjoys climbing to the top of tall rocks, running through deserts, mountains, and woodlands, and carrying a foldable home on her back whenever she gets a chance. She's also fond of word games, and writing descriptions of herself that are needlessly vague.

Find out more about Virginia, and sign up for her newsletter at:

www.virginiamcclain.com

or

www.virginiamcclain.ca

www.ingramcontent.com/pod-product-compliance
Lightning Source LLC
Chambersburg PA
CBHW050602170726
48283CB00001B/75